About the

Carol Marinelli recently [...] her job title. Thrilled to be a [...] she put writer. Then it a[...] relaxation and she put down the truth – writing. The third question asked for her hobbies. Well, not wanting to look obsessed she crossed the fingers on her hand and answered swimming but, given that the chlorine in the pool does terrible things to her highlights – I'm sure you can guess the real answer.

Fiona Hood-Stewart credits her mother with putting her on the path to becoming a writer, who encouraged her to read avidly! Fiona has led a somewhat cosmopolitan life – schooled in Switzerland and fluent in seven languages, she draws on her own experiences in the world of old money, big business and the international jet set for inspiration in creating her books. Fiona lives on a stud ranch in Brazil with her two sons. Readers can visit her at: www.fiona-hood-stewart.com

Kay Thorpe was born in Sheffield in 1935. She tried out a variety of jobs after leaving school. Writing began as a hobby, becoming a way of life only after she had her first completed novel accepted for publication in 1968. Since then, she's written over fifty books and lives with her husband, son, German Shepherd dog and lucky black cat on the outskirts of Chesterfield in Derbyshire. Her interests include reading, hiking and travel.

Latin Lovers

December 2020
**The Billionaire's
Persuasion**

March 2021
**Claiming the
Heiress**

January 2021
Under the Latin Sun

April 2021
Spanish Sunsets

February 2021
Duty and Desire

May 2021
Dusk 'til Dawn

Latin Lovers: Duty and Desire

CAROL MARINELLI

FIONA HOOD-STEWART

KAY THORPE

MILLS & BOON

First Published in Great Britain 2021
by Mills & Boon, an imprint of HarperCollins*Publishers* Ltd,
1 London Bridge Street, London, SE1 9GF

www.harpercollins.co.uk

HarperCollins*Publishers*
1st Floor, Watermarque Building,
Ringsend Road, Dublin 4, Ireland

LATIN LOVERS: DUTY AND DESIRE
© 2021 Harlequin Books S.A.

Playing the Dutiful Wife © 2013 Carol Marinelli
The Brazilian Tycoon's Mistress © 2001 Fiona Hood-Stewart
The Italian Match © 2001 Kay Thorpe

ISBN: 978-0-263-29912-0

MIX
Paper from
responsible sources
FSC™ C007454

This book is produced from independently certified FSC™ paper to ensure responsible forest management.

For more information visit: www.harpercollins.co.uk/green

Printed and bound in Spain
by CPI, Barcelona

PLAYING THE DUTIFUL WIFE

CAROL MARINELLI

CHAPTER ONE

'I'M GOING TO have to go,' Meg said to her mother. 'They've finished boarding, so I'd better turn off my phone.'

'You'll be fine for a while yet.' Ruth Hamilton persisted with their conversation. 'Did you finish up the work for the Evans purchase?'

'Yes.' Meg tried to keep the edge from her voice. She really wanted just to turn off the phone and relax. Meg hated flying. Well, not all of it—just the take-off part. All she wanted to do was close her eyes and listen to music, take some nice calming breaths before the plane prepared for its departure from Sydney Airport— except, as usual, her mother wanted to talk about work. 'Like I said,' Meg said calmly, because if she so much as gave a hint that she was irritated her mum would want to know more, 'everything is up-to-date.'

'Good,' Ruth said, but still she did not leave things there.

Meg coiled a length of her very straight red hair around and around one finger, as she always did when either tense or concentrating.

'You need to make sure that you sleep on the plane, Meg, because you'll be straight into it once you land. You wouldn't believe how many people are here. There are so many opportunities...'

Meg closed her eyes and held on to a sigh of frustration as her mum chatted on about the conference and then moved to travel details. Meg already knew that a car would meet her at Los Angeles airport and take her straight to the hotel where the conference was being held. And, yes, she knew she would have about half an hour to wash and get changed.

Meg's parents were prominent in Sydney's real estate market and were now looking to branch into overseas investments for some of their clients. They had left for Los Angeles on Friday to network, while Meg caught up with the paperwork backlog at the office before joining them.

Meg knew that she should be far more excited at the prospect of a trip to Los Angeles. Usually she loved visiting new places, and deep down Meg knew that really she had nothing to complain about—she was flying business class and would be staying in the sumptuous hotel where the conference was being held. She would play the part of successful professional, as would her parents.

Even though, in truth, the family business wasn't doing particularly well at the moment.

Her parents were always very eager to jump on the latest get-rich-quick scheme. Meg, who could always be relied on for sensible advice, had suggested that rather than all of them flying over maybe just one of them should go, or perhaps they should give it a miss entirely and concentrate on the properties they already had on their books.

Of course her parents hadn't wanted to hear that. This, they had insisted, was the next big thing.

Meg doubted it.

It wasn't that, though, which caused her disquiet.

Really, when she had suggested that only one of them go—given that she dealt with the legal side of things—Meg had rather hoped they might have considered sending only her.

A week away wasn't just a luxury she required—it was fast becoming a necessity. And it wasn't about the nice hotel—she'd stay in a tent if she had to, just for the break, just for a pause so that she could think properly. Meg felt as if she were suffocating—that wherever she turned her parents were there, simply not giving her room to think. It had been like that for as long as she could remember, and sometimes she felt as if her whole life had been planned out in advance by her parents.

In truth, it probably had.

Meg had little to complain about. She had her own nice flat in Bondi—but, given that she worked twelve-hour days, she never really got to enjoy it, and there was always something at work that needed her attention at weekends: a signature to chase up, a contract to read through. It just never seemed to end.

'We're actually going to look at a couple of properties this afternoon…' Her mum carried on talking as there was a flurry of activity in the aisle beside Meg.

'Well, don't go agreeing to anything until I get there,' Meg warned. 'I mean it, Mum.'

She glanced over and saw that two flight attendants were assisting a gentleman. His face was blocked from Meg's vision by the overhead lockers, but certainly from his physique this man didn't look as if he required assistance.

He was clearly tall and extremely fit-looking, and from what Meg could see he appeared more than capable of putting his own laptop into the overhead locker, yet the attendants danced around him, taking his jacket and offering their apologies as he went to take the seat beside Meg.

As his face came into view Meg, who was already struggling, completely lost her place in the conversation with her mother. The man was absolutely stunning, with very thick, beautifully cut black hair worn just a little too long, so that it flopped over his forehead. He had a very straight Roman nose and high cheekbones. Really, he had all the markings of a *very* good-looking man, but it was his mouth that held her attention—perfectly shaped, like a dark bruise of red in the black of his unshaven jaw, and even though it was a scowling mouth, it was quite simply beautiful.

He threw a brief nod in Meg's direction as he took the seat beside her.

Clearly somebody wasn't very happy!

As he sat down Meg caught his scent—a mixture

of expensive cologne and man—and, though she was trying to focus on what her mother was saying, Meg's mind kept wandering to the rather terse conversation that was taking place beside her as the flight attendants did their best to appease a man whom, it would seem, wasn't particularly easy to appease.

'No,' he said to the attendant. 'This will be sorted to my satisfaction as soon as we have taken off.'

He had a deep, low voice that was rich with an accent Meg couldn't quite place. Perhaps Spanish, she thought, but wasn't quite sure.

What she *was* sure of, though, was that he demanded too much of her attention.

Not consciously, of course—she just about carried on talking to her mother, her finger still twirling in her hair—but she could not stop listening to the conversation that was none of her business.

'Once again,' the flight attendant said to him, 'we apologise for any inconvenience, Mr Dos Santos.' Then she turned her attention to Meg, and although friendly and polite, the flight attendant was not quite so gushing as she had so recently been to Meg's fellow passenger. 'You need to turn off your phone, Ms Hamilton. We are about to prepare for take-off.'

'I really do have to go, Mum,' Meg said. 'I'll see you there.' With a sigh of relief she turned off her phone. 'The best part of flying,' she said as she did so—not necessarily to him.

'There is nothing good about flying' came his brusque response as the plane started to taxi towards the runway. Seeing her raised eyebrows, he tempered his words a little. 'At least not today.'

She gave him a small smile and offered a quick 'Sorry,' then looked ahead rather than out of the window. After all he could be in the middle of a family emergency and racing to get somewhere. There could be many reasons for his bad mood and it was none of her business after all.

She was actually quite surprised when he answered her, and when she turned she realised that he was still looking at her. 'Usually I do like flying—I do an awful lot of it—but today there are no seats in first class.'

Niklas Dos Santos watched as she blinked at his explanation. She had very green eyes that were staring right at him. He expected her to give a murmur of sympathy or a small tut tut as to the airline's inefficiency; those were the responses that he was used to, so he was somewhat taken aback at hers.

'Poor you!' She smiled. 'Having to slum it back here in business class.'

'As I said, I fly a lot, and as well as working while flying I need to sleep on the plane—something that is now going to be hard to do. Admittedly I only changed my plans this morning, but even so…' He didn't continue. Niklas thought that was the end of the conversation, that he had explained his dark mood well enough. He hoped that now they could sit in mutual silence, but before he could look away the woman in the seat next to him spoke again.

'Yes, it's *terribly* inconsiderate of them—not to keep

a spare seat for you just in case your plans happen to change.'

She smiled as she said it and he understood that she was joking—sort of. She was nothing like anyone he usually dealt with. Normally people revered him, or in the case of a good-looking woman—which she *possibly* was—they came on to him.

He was used to dark-haired, immaculately groomed women from his home town. Now and then he liked blondes—which she was, sort of. Her hair was a reddish blonde. But, unlike the women he usually went for, there was a complete lack of effort on her part. She was very neatly dressed, in three-quarter-length navy trousers and a cream blouse that was delicate and attractive. Yet the blouse was buttoned rather high and she wore absolutely no make-up. He glanced down to nails that were neat but neither painted nor manicured and, yes, he did check for a ring.

Had the engines not revved then she might have noticed that glance. Had she not looked away at that moment she might have been granted the pleasure of one of his very rare smiles. For she seemed refreshingly unimpressed by him, and Niklas had decided she was not a *possibly* good-looking woman in the least…

But she spoke too much.

He would set the tone now, Niklas decided. Just ignore her if she spoke again. He had a lot of work to get through during this flight and did not want to be interrupted every five minutes with one of her random thoughts.

Niklas was not the most talkative person—at least he did not waste words speaking about nothing—and he certainly wasn't interested in her assumptions. He just wanted to get to Los Angeles with as much work and sleep behind him as possible. He closed his eyes as the plane hurtled down the runway, yawned, and decided that he would doze till he could turn on his laptop.

And then he heard her breathing.

Loudly.

And it only got louder.

He gritted his teeth at her slight moan as the plane lifted off the runway and turned to shoot her an irritated look—but, given that her eyes were closed, instead he stared. She was actually fascinating to look at: her nose was snubbed, her lips were wide and her eyelashes were a reddish blonde too. But she was incredibly tense, and she was taking huge long breaths that made her possibly the most annoying woman in the world. He could not take it for the next twelve hours, and Niklas decided he would be speaking again to the flight attendant— someone would have to move out of first class.

Simply, this would not do.

Meg breathed in through her nose and then out through her mouth as she concentrated on using her stomach muscles to control her breathing as her 'fear of flying' exercises had told her to do. She twisted her hair over and over, and when that wasn't helping she gripped onto the handrests, worried by the terrible rattling noise above her as the plane continued its less than smooth climb. It really was an incredibly bumpy take-off, and she loathed this part more than anything—could not relax until the flight stewards stood up and the seatbelt signs went off.

As the plane tilted a little to the left Meg's eyes screwed more tightly closed. She moaned again and Niklas, who had been watching her strange actions the whole time, noted not just that her skin had turned white but that there was no colour in her lips.

The minute the signs went off he would speak with the flight attendant. He didn't care if it was a royal family they had tucked in first class; someone was going to have to make room for him! Knowing that he always got his way, and that soon he *would* be moving, Niklas decided that for a moment or two he could afford to be nice.

She was clearly terrified after all.

'You do know that this is the safest mode of transport, don't you?'

'Logically, yes,' she answered with her eyes still closed. 'It just doesn't feel very safe right now.'

'Well, it is,' he said.

'You said that you fly a lot?' She wanted him to tell her that he flew every single day, that the noise overhead was completely normal and nothing to worry about, preferably that he was in fact a pilot—then she might possibly believe that everything was okay.

'All the time,' came his relaxed response, and it soothed her.

'And that noise?'

'What noise?' He listened for a second or two. 'That's the wheels coming up.'

'No, that one.'

It all sounded completely normal to him, yet Niklas realised *she* probably wasn't quite normal, so he continued to speak to her. 'Today I am flying to Los Angeles, as are you, and in two days' time I will be heading to New York…'

'Then?' Meg asked, because his voice was certainly preferable to her thoughts right now.

'Then I will be flying home to Brazil, where I am hoping to take a couple of weeks off.'

'You're from Brazil?' Her eyes were open now, and as she turned to face him she met his properly for the first time. He had very black eyes that were, right now, simply heaven to look into. 'So you speak…?' Her mind was all scrambled; she could still hear that noise overhead…

'Portuguese,' he said and, as if he was there for her amusement—which for a moment or two longer he guessed he was—he smiled as he offered her a choice. 'Or I can speak French. Or Spanish too, if you prefer…'

'English is fine.'

There was no need to talk any more. He could see the colour coming back to her cheeks and saw her tongue run over pinkening lips. 'We're up,' Niklas said, and at the same time the bell pinged and the flight attendants stood. Meg's internal panic was thankfully over, and he watched as she let out a long breath.

'Sorry about that.' She gave him a rather embarrassed smile. 'I'm not usually that bad, but that really was bumpy.'

It hadn't been bumpy in the least, but he was not going to argue with her, nor get drawn into further conversation. And yet she offered her name.

'I'm Meg, by the way.'

He didn't really want to know her name.

'Meg Hamilton.'

'Niklas.' He gave up that detail reluctantly.

'I really am sorry about that. I'll be fine now. I don't have a problem with flying—it's just take-off that I absolutely loathe.'

'What about landing?'

'Oh, I'm fine with that.'

'Then you have never flown into São Paulo,' Niklas said.

'Is that where you are from?'

He nodded, and then pulled out the menu and started to read it—before remembering that he was going to be moving seats. He pushed his bell to summon the stewardess.

'Is it a busy airport, then?'

He looked over to where Meg sat as if he had forgotten that she was even there, let alone the conversation they had been having.

'Very.' He nodded, and then saw that the flight attendant was approaching with a bottle of champagne. Clearly she must have thought he had rung for a drink—after all, they knew his preferences—but as he opened his mouth to voice his complaint Niklas conceded that it might be a little rude to ask to be moved in front of Meg.

He would have this drink, Niklas decided, and then he would get up and go and have a quiet word with the attendant. Or an angry one if that did not work. He watched as his champagne was poured and then, perhaps aware that her eyes were trained on him, he turned, irritated.

'Did you want a drink as well?'

'Please.' She smiled.

'That is what your bell is for,' he retorted. She didn't seem to realise that he was being sarcastic, so he gave in and, rolling his eyes, ordered another glass. Meg was soon sipping on her beverage.

It tasted delicious, bubbly and icy-cold, and would hopefully halt her nervous chatter—except it didn't. It seemed that a mixture of nerves about flying and the fact that she had never been around someone so drop-dead gorgeous before resulted in her mouth simply not being able to stop.

'It seems wrong to be drinking at ten a.m.' She heard her own voice again and could happily have kicked herself—except then he would perhaps have her certified. Meg simply didn't know what was wrong with her.

Niklas didn't answer. His mind was already back to thinking about work, or rather thinking about all the things he needed to get finalised so that he could actually take some proper time off.

He *was* going to take some time off. He had not stopped for the last six months at the very least, and he was really looking forward to being back in Brazil, the country he loved, to the food he adored and the woman who adored him and who knew how it was…

He would take two or perhaps three weeks, and he was going to use every minute of them indulging in life's simple but expensively prepared pleasures—beautiful women and amazing food and then more of the same.

He let out a long breath as he thought about it—a long breath that sounded a lot like a sigh. A bored sigh, even—except how could that be? Niklas asked himself. He had everything a man could want and had worked hard to get it—worked hard to ensure he would never go back to where he had come from.

And he *had* ensured it, Niklas told himself; he could stop for a little while now. A decent stretch in Brazil would sort this restless feeling out. He thought of the flight home, of the plane landing in São Paulo, and as he did he surprised himself. His champagne was finished. He could get up now and have that word with the flight attendant. But instead Niklas turned and spoke with *her*.

With Meg.

CHAPTER TWO

'São Paulo is very densely populated.'

They were well over the water now, and she was gazing out at it, but she turned to the sound of his voice and Niklas tried to explain the land that he loved, the mile after mile after mile of never-ending city.

'It is something that is hard to explain unless you have seen it, but as the plane descends you fly over the city for very a long time. Congonhas Airport is located just a couple of miles from downtown…'

He told Meg about the short runway and the difficult approach and the physics of it as she looked at him slightly aghast.

'If the weather is bad I would imagine the captain and crew and most *paulistanos*…' He saw her frown and explained it a little differently. 'If you come from Sao Paulo or know about the airport then you are holding your breath just a little as the plane comes into land.' He smiled at her shocked expression. 'There have been many near-misses—accidents too…'

What a horrible thing to tell her! What a completely

inappropriate thing for him to say at this moment! And she had thought him so nice—well, nice-looking at least. 'You're not helping at all!'

'But I am. I have flown in and out of Congonhas Airport more times than I can remember and I'm still here to tell the tale… You really have nothing to worry about.'

'Except that I'm scared of landing now too.'

'Don't waste time in fear,' Niklas said, and then stood to retrieve his computer. He did not usually indulge in idle chatter, and certainly not while flying, but she had been so visibly nervous during take-off, and it had been quite pleasant talking her around. Now she was sitting quietly, staring out of the window, and perhaps he did not have to think about moving seats after all.

The flight steward started to serve some appetizers, and Meg had an inkling that Mr Dos Santos was being treated with some tasty little selections from the first-class menu—because there were a few little treats that certainly weren't on the business class one—and, given that she was sitting next to him, by default Meg was offered them too.

'Wild Iranian caviar on buckwheat blinis, with sour cream and dill,' the flight attendant purred to him, but Niklas was too busy to notice the selection placed in front of him. Instead he was setting up a workstation, and Meg heard his hiss of frustration as he had to move his computer to the side. Clearly he was missing his first-class desk!

'There is no room—' He stopped himself, realising

that he sounded like someone who complained all the time. He didn't usually—because he didn't have to. His PA, Carla, ensured that everything ran smoothly in his busy life. But Carla simply hadn't been able to work her magic today, and the fact was between here and LA Niklas had a lot to get done. 'I have a lot of work to do.' He didn't have to justify his dark mood, but he did. 'I have a meeting scheduled an hour after landing. I was hoping to use this time to prepare. It really is inconvenient.'

'You'll have to get your own plane!' Meg teased. 'Keep it on standby…'

'I did!' he said. Meg blinked. 'And for two months or so it was great. I really thought it was the best thing I had ever done. And then…' He shrugged and got back to his laptop, one hand crunching numbers, the other picking all the little pieces of dill off the top of the blinis before eating them.

'And then?' Meg asked, because this man really was intriguing. He was sort of aloof and then friendly, busy, yet calm, and very pedantic with his dill, Meg thought with a small smile as she watched him continue to pick the pieces off. When the food was to his satisfaction there was something very decadent about the way he ate, his eyes briefly closing as he savoured the delicious taste entering his mouth.

Everything he revealed about himself had Meg wanting to know more, and she was enthralled when he went on to tell her about the mistake of having his own plane.

'And then,' Niklas responded, while still tapping

away on his computer, 'I got bored. Same pilot, same flight crew, same chef, same scent of soap in the bathroom. You understand?'

'Not really.'

'As annoying as your chatter may be…' he turned from his screen and gave her a very nice smile '…it is actually rather nice to meet you.'

'It's rather nice to meet you too.' Meg smiled back.

'And if I still had my own plane we would not have met.'

'Nor would we if you were lording it in first class.'

He thought for a moment. 'Correct.' He nodded. 'But now, if you will forgive me, I have to get on with some work.' He moved to do just that, but just before he did he explained further, just in case she had missed the point he was making. 'That is the reason I prefer to fly commercially—it is very easy to allow your world to become too small.'

Now, that part she *did* understand. 'Tell me about it.' Meg sighed.

His shoulders tensed. His fingers hesitated over the keyboard as he waited for her to start up again.

When she inevitably did, he would point out *again* that he was trying to work.

Niklas gritted his teeth and braced himself for her voice—was she going to talk all the way to Los Angeles?

Except she said nothing else.

When still she was quiet Niklas realised that he was actually *wanting* the sound of her voice to continue their conversation. It was at that point he gave up working for a while. He would return to the report later.

Closing his laptop, he turned. 'Tell *me* about it.'

She had no idea of the concession he was making—not a clue that a slice of his time was an expensive gift that very few could afford, no idea how many people would give anything for just ten minutes of his undivided attention.

'Oh, it's nothing…' Meg shrugged. 'Just me feeling sorry for myself.'

'Which must be a hard thing to do with a mouthful of wild Iranian caviar…'

He made her laugh—he really did. Niklas really wasn't at all chatty, but when he spoke, when he teased, when she met his eyes, there was a little flip in her stomach that she liked the feeling of. It was a thrill that was new to her, and there was more than just something about him…

It was *everything* about the man.

'Here's to slumming it,' Niklas said. They chinked their glasses and he looked into her eyes, and as he did so somehow—not that she would be aware of it—Niklas let her in.

He was a closed person, an extremely guarded man. He had grown up having to be that way—it had meant survival at the time—yet for the first time in far too long he chose to relax, to take some time, to forget about work, to stop for a moment and just be with her.

As they chatted he let the flight steward put his

laptop away. They were at the back of business class, tucked away and enjoying their own little world.

The food orders were taken and later served, and Meg thought how nice Niklas was to share a meal with. Food was a passion in waiting for Meg. She rarely had time to cook, and though she ate out often it was pretty much always at the same Italian restaurant where they took clients. They'd chosen different mains, and he smiled to himself at the droop of her face when they were served and she found out that steak tartare was in fact raw.

'It's delicious,' he assured her. 'Or you can have my steak?'

At the back of her mind she had known it was raw, if she'd stopped to think about it, but the menu had been incredibly hard to concentrate on with Niklas sitting beside her, and she had made a rather random selection when the flight steward had approached.

'No, it's fine,' Meg said, looking at the strange little piles of food on her plate. There was a big hill of raw minced steak in the middle, with a raw egg yolk in its shell on the top, surrounded by little hills of onions and capers and things. 'I've always wanted to try it. I just tend to stick to safe. It's good to try different things…'

'It is,' Niklas said. 'I like it like this.'

Something caught in her throat, because he'd made it sound like sex. He picked up her knife and fork, and she watched him pour in the egg, pile on the onions and capers, and then chop and chop again before sliding the mixture through Worcestershire sauce. For a fleeting moment she honestly thought that he might load the fork and feed her, but he put the utensils down and returned to his meal, and Meg found herself breathless and blushing at where her mind had just drifted.

'Good?' Niklas asked when she took her first taste.

'Fantastic,' Meg said. It was nice, not amazing, but made by his hands fantastic it was. 'How's *your* steak?'

He sliced a piece off and lifted the loaded fork and held it to her. This from a man who had reluctantly given her a drink, who had on many occasions turned his back. He was now giving her a taste of food from his plate. He was just being friendly, Meg told herself. She was reading far, far too much into this simple gesture. But as she went to take the fork he lifted it slightly. His black eyes met hers and he moved the fork to her mouth and watched as she opened it. Suddenly she began to wonder if she'd been right the first time.

Maybe he *was* talking about sex.

But if he had been flirting, by the time dessert was cleared it had ended. He read for a bit, and Meg gazed out of the window for a while, until the flight attendant came around and closed the shutters. The lights were lowered and the cabin was dimmed and Meg fiddled with her remote to turn the seat into a bed.

Niklas stood and she glanced up at him. 'Are you off to get your gold pyjamas?'

'And a massage,' Niklas teased back.

She was half asleep when he returned, and watched idly as he took off his tie. Of course the flight attendant rushed to hold it, while another readied his bed, and then he took off his shoes and climbed into the flight bed beside her.

His beautiful face was gone now from her vision, but it was there—right there—in her mind's eye. She was terribly aware of his movements and listened to him turn restlessly a few times. She conceded that maybe he did have a point—the flight bed was more than big enough for Meg to stretch out in, but Niklas was easily a foot taller than her and, as he had stated, he really needed this time to sleep, which must be proving difficult. For Niklas the bed was simply too small, and it was almost a sin that he sleep in those immaculate suit trousers.

She lay there trying not to think about him and made herself concentrate instead on work—on the Evans contract she had just completed—which was surely enough to send her to sleep. But just as she was closing her eyes, just as she was starting to think that she might be about to drift off even with Niklas beside her, she heard him move again. Her eyes opened and she blinked as his face appeared over hers. She met those black eyes, heard again his rich accent, and how could a woman not smile?

'You never did tell me...' Niklas said, smiling as he invited her to join him in after hours conversation. 'Why is your world too small?'

CHAPTER THREE

THEY PULLED BACK the divider that separated them and lay on their sides, facing each other. Meg knew that this was probably the only time in her life that she'd ever have a man so divine lying on the pillow next to hers, so she was more than happy to forgo sleep for such a glorious cause.

'I work in the family business,' Meg explained.

'Which is?'

'My parents are into real-estate investments. I'm a lawyer...'

He gave a suitably impressed nod, but then frowned, because she didn't seem like a lawyer to him.

'Though I hardly use my training. I do all the paper-work and contracts.'

He saw her roll her eyes.

'I cannot tell you how boring it is.'

'Then why do you do it?'

'Good question. I think it was decided at conception that I would be a lawyer.'

'You don't want to be one?'

It was actually rather hard to admit it. 'I don't think I do...'

He said nothing, just carried on watching her face, waiting for her to share more, and she did.

'I don't think I'm supposed to be one—I mean, I scraped to get the grades I needed at school, held on by my fingernails at university...' She paused as he interrupted.

'You are *never* to say this at an interview.'

'Of course not.' She smiled. 'We're just talking.'

'Good. I'm guessing you were not a little girl who dreamed of being a lawyer?' he checked. 'You did not play with wigs on?' His lips twitched as she smiled. 'You did not line up your dollies and cross-examine them?'

'No.'

'So how did you end up being one?'

'I really don't know where to start.'

He looked at his watch, realised then that perhaps the report simply wasn't going to get done. 'I've got nine hours.'

Niklas made the decision then—they would be entirely devoted to *her*.

'Okay...' Meg thought how best to explain her family to him and chose to start near the beginning. 'In my family you don't get much time to think—even as a little girl there were piano lessons, violin lessons, ballet lessons, tutors. My parents were constantly checking my homework—basically, everything was geared towards me getting into the best school, so that I could get the best grades and go to the best university. Which I did. Except when I got there it was more push, push, push. I just put my head down and carried on working, but now suddenly I'm twenty-four years old and I'm not really sure that I'm where I want to be...' It was very hard to explain it, because from the outside she had a very nice life.

'They demand too much.'

'You don't know that.'

'They don't listen to you.'

'You don't know that either.'

'But I do.' He said. 'Five or six times on the telephone you said, "Mum, I've got to go." Or, "I really have to go now..."' He saw that she was smiling, but she was smiling not at his imitation of her words but because he had been listening to her conversation. While miserable and scowling and ignoring her, he had still been aware. 'You do this.' He held up an imaginary phone and turned it off.

'I can't.' she admitted. 'Is that what you do?'

'Of course.'

He made it sound so simple.

'You say, *I have to go*, and then you do.'

'It's not just that though,' she admitted. 'They want to know everything about my life...'

'Then tell them you don't want to discuss it,' he said. 'If a conversation moves where you don't want it to, you just say so.'

'How?'

'Say, *I don't want to talk about that*,' he suggested.

He made it sound so easy. 'But I don't want to hurt them either—you know how difficult families can be at times.'

'No.' He shook his head. 'There are some advantages to being an orphan, and that is one of them. I get to make my own mistakes.' He said it in such a way that there was no invitation to sympathy—in fact he even gave a small smile, as if letting her know that she did not need to be uncomfortable at his revelation and he took no offence at her casual remark.

'I'm sorry.'

'You don't have to be.'

'But…'

'I don't want to talk about that.' And, far more easily than she, he told her what he was not prepared to discuss. He simply moved the conversation. 'What would you like to do if you could do anything?'

She thought for a moment. 'You're the first person who has ever asked me that.'

'The second,' Niklas corrected. 'I would imagine you have been asking yourself that question an awful lot.'

'Lately I have been,' Meg admitted.

'So, what would you be?'

'A chef.'

And he didn't laugh, didn't tell her that she should know about steak tartare by now, if that was what she wanted to be, and neither did he roll his eyes.

'Why?'

'Because I love cooking.'

'Why?' he asked—not as if he didn't understand how

it was possible to love cooking so much, more as if he really wanted her tell him why.

She just stared at him as their minds locked in a strange wrestle.

'When someone eats something I've cooked—I mean properly prepared and cooked…' She still stared at him as she spoke. 'When they close their eyes for a second…' She couldn't properly explain it. 'When you ate those blinis, when you first tasted them, there was a moment…' She watched that mouth move into a smile, just a brief smile of understanding. 'They tasted fantastic?'

'Yes.'

'I wanted to have cooked them.' It was perhaps the best way to describe it. 'I love shopping for food, planning a meal, preparing it, presenting it, serving it…'

'For that moment?'

'Yes.' Meg nodded. 'And I know that I'm good at it because, no matter how dissatisfied my parents were with my grades or my decisions, on a Sunday I'd cook a meal from scratch and it was the one thing I excelled at. Yet it was the one thing they discouraged.'

'Why?' This time he asked because he didn't understand.

'"Why would you want to work in a kitchen?"' It was Meg doing the imitating now. '"Why, after all the opportunities we've given you…?"' Her voice faded for a moment. 'Maybe I should have stood up to them, but it's hard at fourteen…' She gave him a smile. 'It's still hard at twenty-four.'

'If cooking is your passion then I'm sure you would be a brilliant chef. You should do it.'

'I don't know.' She knew she sounded weak, knew she should just say to hell with them, but there was one other thing she had perhaps not explained. 'I love them,' Meg said, and she saw his slight frown. 'They are impossible and overbearing but I do love them, and I don't want to hurt them—though I know that I'll probably have to.' She gave him a pale smile. 'I'm going to try and work out if I can just hurt them gently.'

After a second or two he smiled back, a pensive smile she did not want, for perhaps he felt sorry for her being weak—though she didn't think she was.

'Do you cook a lot now?'

'Hardly ever.' She shook her head. 'There just never seems to be enough time. But when I do...' She explained to him that on her next weekend off she would prepare the meal she had just eaten for herself and friends...that she would spend hours trying to get it just right. Even if she generally stuck with safer choices, there was so much about food that she wanted to explore.

They lay there, facing each other and talking about food, which to some might sound boring—but for Meg it was the best conversation she had had in her life.

He told her about a restaurant that he frequented in downtown São Paulo which was famed for its seafood, although he thought it wasn't actually their best dish. When he was there Niklas always ordered their *feijoada*, which was a meat and black bean stew that tasted, he told her, as if angels had prepared it and were feeding it to his soul.

In that moment Meg realised that she had not just one growing passion to contend with, but two, because his gaze was intense and his words were so interesting and she never wanted this journey to end. Didn't want to stop their whispers in the dark.

'How come you speak so many languages?'

'It is good that I do. It means I can take my business to many countries…' He was an international financier, Niklas told her, and then, very unusually for him, he told her a little bit more—which he never, ever did. Not with anyone. Not even, if he could help it, with himself. 'One of the nuns who cared for me when I was a baby spoke only Spanish. By the time I moved from that orphanage…'

'At how old?'

He thought for a moment. 'Three, maybe four. By that time I spoke two languages,' he explained. 'Later I taught myself English, and much later French.'

'How?'

'I had a friend who was English—I asked him to speak only English to me. And I—' He'd been about to say looked for, but he changed it. 'I read English newspapers.'

'What language do you dream in?'

He smiled at her question. 'That depends where I am—where my thoughts are.'

He spent a lot of time in France, he told Meg, especially in the South. Meg asked him where his favourite

place in the world was. He was about to answer São
Paulo—after all, he was looking forward to going back
there, to the fast pace and the stunning women—but
he paused for a moment and then gave an answer that
surprised even him. He told her about the mountains
away from the city, and the rainforests and the rivers
and springs there, and that maybe he should think of
getting a place there—somewhere private.

And then he thanked her.

'For what?'

'For making me think,' Niklas said. 'I have been
thinking of taking some time off just to do more of the
same…' He did not mention the clubs and the women
and the press that were always chasing him for the latest scandal. 'Maybe I should take a proper break.'

She told him that she too preferred the mountains to
the beach, even if she lived in Bondi, and they lay there
together and rewrote a vision of her—no longer a chef
in a busy international hotel, instead she would run a
small bed and breakfast set high in the hills.

And she asked about him too.

Rarely, so rarely did he tell anyone, but for some
reason this false night he did—just a little. For some
reason he didn't hold back. He just said it. Not all of it,
by any means, but he gave more of himself than usual.
After all, he would never see her again.

He told her how he had taught himself to read and
write, how he had educated himself from newspapers,
how the business section had always fascinated him and
how easily he had read the figures that seemed to daunt

others. And he told her how he loved Brazil—for there you could both work hard and play hard too.

'Can I get you anything Mr Dos Santos…?' Worried that their esteemed passenger was being disturbed, the steward checked that he was okay.

'Nothing.' He did not look up. He just looked at Meg as he spoke. 'If you can leave us, please?'

'Dos Santos?' she repeated when the steward had gone, and he told her that it was a surname often given to orphans.

'It means "from the Saints" in Portuguese,' he explained.

'How were you orphaned?'

'I don't actually know,' Niklas admitted. 'Perhaps I was abandoned, just left at the orphanage. I really don't know.'

'Have you ever tried to find out about your family…?'

He opened his mouth to say that he would rather not discuss it, but instead he gave even more of himself. 'I have,' he admitted. 'It would be nice to know, but it proved impossible. I got Miguel, my lawyer, onto it, but he got nowhere.'

She asked him what it had been like, growing up like that, but she was getting too close and it was not something he chose to share.

He told her so. 'I don't want to speak about that.'

So they talked some more about her, and she could have talked to him for ever—except it was Niklas who got too close now, when he asked if she was in a relationship.

'No.'

'Have you ever been serious about anyone?'

'Not really,' she said, but that wasn't quite true. 'I was about to get engaged,' Meg said. 'I called it off.'

'Why?'

She just lay there.

'Why?' Niklas pushed.

'He got on a bit too well with my parents.' She swallowed. 'A colleague.' He could hear her hesitation to discuss it. 'What we said before about worlds being too small…' Meg said. 'I realised I would be making mine smaller still.'

'Was he upset?'

'Not really.' Meg was honest. 'It wasn't exactly a passionate…' She swallowed. She was *so* not going to discuss this with him.

She should have just said so, but instead she told him that she needed to sleep. The dimmed lights and champagne were starting to catch up with both of them, and almost reluctantly their conversation was closed and finally they slept.

For how long Meg wasn't sure. She just knew that when she woke up she regretted it.

Not the conversation, but ending it, falling asleep and wasting the little time that they had.

She'd woken to the scent of coffee and the hum of the engines and now she looked over to him. He was still asleep, and just as beautiful with his eyes closed. It was almost a privilege to examine such a stunning man more intently. His black hair was swept back, his beautiful mouth relaxed and loose. She looked at his dark spiky lashes and thought of the treasure behind them. She wondered what language he was dreaming in, then watched as his eyes were revealed.

For Niklas it was a pleasure to open his eyes to her.

He had felt the caress of her gaze and now he met it and held it.

'English.' He answered the question she had not voiced, but they both understood. He had been dreaming in English, perhaps about her. And then Niklas did what he always did when he woke to a woman he considered beautiful.

It was a touch more difficult to do so—given the gap between them, given that he could not gather her body and slip her towards him—but the result would certainly be worth the brief effort. He pulled himself up on his elbow and moved till his face was right over her, and looking down.

'You never did finish what you were saying.'

She looked back at him.

'When you said it wasn't passionate…'

She could have turned away from him, could have closed the conversation—his question was inappropriate, really—only nothing felt inappropriate with Niklas. There was nothing that couldn't be said with his breath on her cheek and that sulky, beautiful mouth just inches away.

'I was the one who wasn't passionate.'

'I can't imagine that.'

'Well, I wasn't.'

'Because you didn't want him in the way that you want me?'

Meg knew what he was about to do.

And she wanted, absolutely, for him to do it.

So he did.

It did not feel as if she was kissing a stranger as their lips met—all it felt was sublime.

His lips were surprisingly gentle and moved with hers for a moment, giving her a brief glimpse of false security—for his tongue, when it slipped in, was shockingly direct and intent.

This wasn't a kiss to test the water, and now Meg knew what had been wrong with her from the start, the reason she had been rambling. This thing between them was an attraction so instant that he could have kissed her like this the moment he'd sat down beside her. He could have taken his seat, had her turn off her phone and offered his mouth to her and she would have kissed him right back.

And so she kissed him back now.

There was more passion in his kiss than Meg had ever tasted in her life. She discovered that a kiss could be far more than a simple meeting of lips as his tongue told her exactly what else he would like to do, slipping in and out of her parted lips, soft one minute, rougher the next. Then his hand moved beneath the blanket and stroked her breast through her blouse, so expertly that she ached for more.

Meg's hands were in his hair and his jaw scratched at her skin and his tongue probed a little harder. As she concentrated on that, as she fought with her body not to arch into him, he moved his hand inside her top. Now Niklas became less than subtle with his silent instructions and moved his hand to her back, pulling her forward into his embrace. She swallowed the growl that vibrated from his throat as beneath the blanket he rolled her nipple between his fingers—hard at first, and then with his palm he stroked her more softly.

To the outside world they would appear simply as two lovers kissing, their passion indecent, but hidden. Then Niklas moved over her a little more, so all she could breathe was his scent, and his mouth and his hand worked harder, each subtle stroke making her want the next one even more. Suddenly Meg knew she had to stop this, had to pull back, because just her reaction to his kiss had her feeling as though she might come.

'Come.' His mouth was at her ear now, his word voicing her thought.

'Stop,' she told him, even if it was not what she wanted him to do, but she could hardly breathe.

'Why?'

'Because,' she answered with his mouth now back over hers, 'it's wrong.'

'But *so* nice.'

He continued to kiss her. Her mouth was wet from his but she closed her lips, because this feeling was too much and he was taking her to the edge. He parted her lips with his tongue and again she tried to close them, clamped her teeth, but he merely carried on until she gave in and opened again to him. He breathed harder, and his hand still worked at her breast, and she was fighting not to gasp, not to moan, to remember where they were as he suckled her tongue.

Meg forced herself not to push his hand far lower, as her body was begging her to do, not to pull him fully on top of her as Niklas made love to her with his mouth.

She hadn't a hope of winning.

He removed his hand from her breast and prised her knotted fingers from his hair. Then he moved her hand beneath his blanket, his body acting as a shield as he held her small hand over his thick, solid length. Her fingers ached to curl and stroke around him, but he did not allow it. Instead he just flattened her palm against him and held it there. His mouth still worked against hers, and she tried to grumble a protest as her hand fought not to stroke, not to feel, not to explore his arousal.

He won.

He smothered her moan with his mouth and sucked, as if swallowing her cry of pleasure, and then, most cruel of all, he loosened his grip on her hand and accepted the dig of her fingers into him. He lifted his head and watched her, a wicked smile on his face, as she struggled to breathe, watched her bite on her lip as he too fought not to come. And he wished the lights were on so he could watch her in colour, wished that they were in his vast bed so the second she'd finished they could resume.

And they would, he decided.

'That,' Niklas said as he crashed back not to earth but to ten thousand feet in the air, 'was the appetiser.'

She'd been right the first time.

He *had* been talking about sex.

She put on a cardigan and excused herself just as the lights came on.

As she stood in the tiny cubicle and examined her face in the mirror she fastened her bra. Her skin was pink from his prolonged attention, her lips swollen, and her eyes glittered with danger. The face that looked back at her was not a woman she knew.

And she was *so* not the woman Niklas had first met.

Not once in her life had she rebelled; never had she even jumped out of her bedroom window and headed out to parties. At university she had studied and worked part-time, getting the grades her parents had expected before following them into the family business. She had always done the right thing, even when it came to her personal relationships.

Niklas had been right. She hadn't wanted her boyfriend in the way she wanted Niklas, and had strung things out for as long as she could before realising she could not get engaged to someone she cared about but didn't actually fancy. She had told her boyfriend that she wouldn't have sex till she was sure they were serious, but the moment he'd started to talk about rings and a future Meg had known it was time to get out.

And *that* was the part that caused her disquiet.

She wasn't the passionate woman Niklas had just met and kissed—she was a virgin, absolutely clueless with men. A few hours off the leash from her parents and she was lying on her back, with a stranger above her and the throb of illicit pulses below. She closed her eyes in shame, and then opened them again and saw the glitter and the shame burned a little less. There was no going back now to the woman she had been, and even if there were she would not change a minute of the time she had spent with Niklas.

She heard a tap against the door and froze for a second. Then she told herself she was being ridiculous. She brushed her teeth and sorted her hair and washed in the tiny sink, trying to brace herself to head back out there.

As she walked down the aisle she noticed her bed had been put away and the seats were up. She attempted polite conversation with Niklas as breakfast was served. He didn't really return her conversation. It was as if what had passed between them simply hadn't happened. He continued to read his paper, dunking his croissant in strong black coffee as if he *hadn't* just rocked her world.

The dishes were cleared and still he kept reading. And as the plane started its descent Meg decided that she now hated landing too—because she didn't want to arrive back at her old life.

Except you couldn't fly for ever. Meg knew that. And a man like Niklas wasn't going to stick around on landing. She knew what happened with men like him, wasn't naïve enough to think it had been anything more than a nice diversion.

She accepted it was just about sex.

And yet it wasn't just the sex that had her hooked on him.

He stretched out his legs, his suit trousers still some-how unrumpled, and she turned away and stared out of the window, trying not to think about what was beneath the cloth, trying not to think about what she had felt be-neath her fingers, about the taste of his kisses and the passion she had encountered. Maybe life would have been easier had she not sat next to him—because now everything would be a mere comparison, for even with the little she knew still she was aware that there were not many men like Niklas.

Niklas just continued reading his newspaper, or ap-peared to be. His busy mind was already at work, can-celling his day. He knew that she would have plans once they landed. That she probably had a car waiting to take her to her hotel and her parents. But he'd think of something to get around that obstacle.

He had no intention of waiting.

Or maybe he would wait. Maybe he'd arrange to meet up with her tonight.

He thought of her controlling parents and turned a page in the paper. He relished the thought of screwing her right under their nose.

She, Niklas decided, was amazing.

There was no *possibly* about it now.

He thought of her face as she came beneath him and shifted just a little in his seat.

'Ladies and gentlemen…' They both looked up as the captain's voice came over the intercom. 'Due to an incident at LAX all planes are now being re-routed. We will be landing in Las Vegas in just over an hour.'

The captain apologised for the inconvenience and they heard the moans and grumbles from other passengers. They felt the shift as the plane started to climb, and had she been sitting next to anyone else Meg might have been complaining too, or panicking about the prolonged flight, or stressing about the car that was waiting for her, or worried about what was going on…

Instead she was smiling when he turned to her.

'Viva Las Vegas,' Niklas said, and picked up her remote, laid her chair flat again and got back to where he had left off.

CHAPTER FOUR

'IT WAS A false alarm.'

They were still sitting on the plane on the tarmac.
The second they had landed in Vegas Niklas had pulled
out his phone, turned it on and called someone. He was
speaking in Portuguese. He had briefly halted his conversation to inform Meg that whatever had happened
in Los Angeles had been a false alarm and then carried
on talking into his phone.

'Aguarde, por favour!' he said, and then turned again
to Meg. 'I am speaking with my PA, Carla. I can ask
her to reschedule your flight also. She will get it done
quickly, I think.'

And make sure he'd sit next to her too, Niklas decided.

'So?' he asked. 'When do you want to get there?'

Of course the normal response would be as soon
as possible, but there was nothing normal about her
response to him. Niklas was looking right at her, and
there was undoubtedly an invitation in his eyes, but
there was something he needed to know—somehow

she had to tell him that what had happened between them wasn't usual for her.

To put it mildly.

Except Niklas made her stomach fold into herself, and his eyes were waiting, and his mouth was so beautiful, and she did not want this to end with a kiss at an airport gate. She did not want to spend the rest of her life regretting what would surely be a far more exciting choice than the one she should be making.

He made it for her.

'It sounds as if there is a lot of backlog. The airport will be hell with so many people having to re-route. I could tell her to book our flights for tomorrow.' Niklas had already made the decision. He had not had twenty-four hours to himself in months, had not stopped working in weeks, and right now he could think of no one nicer to escape the world with.

'I'm supposed to be…' She thought of her parents, waiting for her at the conference, waiting for her to arrive, to perform, to work twelve-hour days and accept weekends constantly on call. Hers was a family that had every minute, every week, every year of her life accounted for, and for just for a little while Meg wanted to be able to breathe.

Or rather to struggle to breathe under him as he kissed her and took her breath.

He looked at her mouth as he awaited her answer, watched the finger that twirled in her hair finally pause as she reached her decision, saw her tongue moisten her lips just before she delivered her answer.

'Tomorrow,' Meg said. 'Tell her tomorrow.'

He spoke with Carla for a couple more moments, checked he had the right spelling of her surname and date of birth and passport number, and then clicked off his phone.

'Done.'

She didn't know what his life was like—didn't really understand what the word *done* meant in Niklas Dos Santos's world…

Yet.

They waited for their baggage and she got to kiss him for the first time standing up, got to feel his tall length pressed against her. He loaded their bags onto one trolley and then he did a nice thing, a very unexpected thing: he stopped at one of the shops and bought her flowers.

She smiled as he handed them to her.

'Dinner, breakfast, champagne, kisses, foreplay…' God, he didn't even lower his voice as he handed her the flowers. 'Have I covered everything?'

'You haven't taken me to the movies,' Meg said.

'No…' He shook his head. 'There was a movie on. You chose not to watch it. I cannot be held responsible for that…'

Oh, but he had been. She felt the thorns of the roses press in as he moved closer again and crushed the flowers.

'Consider yourself dated.'

There was no waiting in long queues for Niklas. Customs was a very different thing in his world, and as his hand was holding hers, she too was processed quickly. Suddenly they had cleared Customs and were walking out—and it was then she got her first glimpse of what *done* meant in a world like Niklas's.

Carla must have been busy, for there was already a driver waiting, holding a sign with 'Niklas Dos Santos' written on it. He relieved them of their bags and they followed him to a blacked-out limousine. She never got a glimpse of Vegas as they drove to the hotel, just felt the brief hit of hot desert sun.

No, she never saw Vegas at all.

She was sitting on his lap.

'I'm going to be the most terrible let-down...' She peeled her face from his.

'You're not,' he groaned.

'I am...' God, her head was splitting just at the attempt to be rational. 'Because I have to ring my mum...'

Her hands were shaking as she dialled the number, her mind reeling, because she *had* to tell him she was a virgin. Oh, God, she really was going to be a let-down! His fingers were working the buttons on her trousers now, his hand slipping in and cupping her bum. His mouth was sucking her breast through her blouse as she was connected to her mother, and she heard only smatters of her conversation.

'Yes, I know it was a false alarm...' She tried to sound normal as she spoke with a less than impressed Ruth. 'But all the flights are in chaos and tomorrow was the earliest I could get.' No, she insisted for a third time, there was simply nothing she could do that would get her there sooner. 'I'll call you when I've sorted out a hotel and things. I have to go, Mum, my battery's about to go flat.'

She clicked off the phone and he turned her so that she was sitting astride him. Holding her hips, he pushed her down, so she could feel what would soon be inside her, and for the first time she was just a little bit scared.

'Niklas…'

'Come on…' He did her blouse up. 'We are nearly there.'

She made herself decent, slipped her cardigan over her blouse to hide the wet patch his mouth had made, and found out once again what it was like in his world.

They breezed through check-in, and even their luggage beat them to their huge suite—not that she paid any attention to it, for finally they were alone. As soon as the door shut he kissed her, pushing her onto the bed. He removed his jacket and pulled condoms from his pocket, placing them within reach on the bedside table, and then he removed her trousers, taking her panties with them at the same time.

God, he was animal, and he moaned as he buried his face in her most private of places. Meg felt the purr of his moan, and this new experience coupled with her own arousal terrified her.

'Niklas…' she pleaded as his tongue started to probe. 'When I said my relationship wasn't passionate…'

'We've already proved it had nothing to do with you.' His words were muffled, but he felt her tense and as he looked up he met anxious eyes.

'I haven't done this before.' She saw him frown. 'I haven't done anything.'

There was a rather long pause. 'Good. I will look after you…'

'I know that.'

'I *will*.'

And then his mouth resumed, and she felt his breath in places she had never felt someone breathe before, but still the tension and fear remained. Niklas must have sensed it too, as he raised himself up on his elbows and looked down at her beneath him, her face flushed.

Niklas was a very uninhibited lover; it was the only piece of himself that he readily gave. Sex was both his rest and recreation, and with his usual lovers there was no need for long conversation and coaxing, no need for reticence or taking his time. But as he looked down at her flushed cheeks he recalled their long conversations on the plane, and the enjoyment of spending proper time with another person. He thought of all the things he had told her that he never usually shared with anyone, and he realised he liked not just the woman who lay beneath him but the words that had come from her mouth.

He kissed it now, as if doing so for the first time.

Not their first kiss. Just a gentle kiss—albeit with his erection pressing into her as he thought about what to do.

His first intention had been to push her on the bed and take her quickly, just so that they could start over again, but he really liked her, and he wanted to do this well.

Thoroughly.

Properly.

'I know…'

He sounded as if he'd had an idea, and he stopped kissing her, smiling down at her before rolling off and picking up the phone. He told Meg that a bath would relax her, and as they waited for a maid to come and run it he wrapped her in a vast white dressing gown. She lay on the bed, watching him as he went through his case, and then he joined her on the bed and showed her some documents, his fingers pointing to the pertinent lines, which she read, frowning.

'I don't get this.'

'I had to get a check-up when I was in Sydney, for my insurance…' he explained.

'So?'

'I wasn't worried about the results. I always use protection…' He was so completely matter-of-fact.

'I'm not on the pill,' Meg replied as she understood his meaning, and she saw his eyes widen just a little as she dampened his plans.

'But still…' He stopped himself, shook his head as if to clear it. What the hell had he been thinking? For a second a baby had seemed a minor inconvenience compared to what they might miss out on. He was, Niklas decided, starting to adore her, and that always came with strong warnings attached—that was always his signal to leave.

'Niklas…am I making a big mistake?'

He was as honest with Meg as he was with all

women, because his was a heart that would remain closed. 'If you are looking for love, then yes,' Niklas said. 'Because I don't do that.'

'Never?'

'Ever,' Niklas said. He could not bear even the thought of someone depending on him, could not trust himself to provide for another person, just could not envisage sharing, yet alone caring—except already a part of him cared for *her*.

'Then I want as long as we've got,' Meg said.

When the maid left he took her by the hand and led her to the bathroom. The bath was sunken, and as she slid into the water he undressed, and she was looking up at his huge erection, her cheeks paling in colour. Niklas found himself assuring her that nothing would happen between them just yet—not until she was sure she was ready. The need to comfort her and reassure her was a new sensation for him, and as he looked down at her he decided that for the next twenty-four hours he would let himself care.

He climbed into the water with her and washed her slowly, sensually, smoothing the soap over her silky skin. He dunked her head in the water too, just so he could see the red darken.

'Your last boyfriend—did he try...?' Niklas asked as he soaped her arms, curious because he wondered how any man could resist the beautiful woman he held in his arms.

'A bit...' Meg said.

Even her arms blushed, he noted.

'I just…'

'What?' He loved her blushing, and found himself smiling just watching her skin pinken, feeling the warmth beneath his palms as she squirmed.

'I told him I didn't want to do anything like that till we were really serious. You know…'

His eyes widened. 'Married?'

'Engaged,' she corrected.

'Do people really say that?' He sounded incredulous, his soapy hands moving lower, past her breasts and down to her waist. 'How would you know if you wanted to marry someone if you hadn't—?'

'That had nothing to do with it. I wasn't demanding a ring. I realised I was just making up excuses…'

'Because?' He was sliding his soapy hands between her legs now, and she didn't know how to answer. 'Because?' he insisted.

'Because I didn't have any compulsion to sit in a bath with him and let him wash me *there*…' She couldn't believe he expected her to speak as he was doing what he did. 'And then he started talking rings.'

'I bet he did,' Niklas said, because, naked with her like this, what man wouldn't want his ring on her finger?

Suddenly his brain went to a place it should not, and Niklas tried hard to shut it down. This had to stay as just sex between them. He pulled her straight over to him, hooked her legs over his and kissed her shoulder.

'I loved flying with you…' He said it like a caress

as he lifted her hair, and his mouth moved to the back of her neck and sucked hard.

She closed her eyes at the bruise he was making, and then felt his hand move up her thigh. It was his neck she was now kissing, licking away the fragrant water just to get to his skin. As they continued to nip and kiss each other Niklas moved his hand, his finger slipping inside, and when she felt a moment's pain she sucked harder on his neck. He pushed in another finger, stretching her, and again she bit down on his shoulder as pain flashed through her body. She knew he had to stretch her—she had seen that he was huge and this was her first time after all—but he did it with a gentleness that moved her.

He continued to slide his fingers in and out, and then kissed her breast, sucking on her wet nipple. She began to moan and lift herself to his fingers as pleasure washed over her. Niklas realised that things were moving rather faster than he had intended. He wanted her on the bed—or rather they needed to get back to the condoms.

'Come on…' He moved to stand, except her hand found him first and, yes, she deserved a little play too.

He liked being touched by a woman. He had just never expected to enjoy it as much as he did now. Had never expected the naked pleasure in her eyes and the tentative exploration of her hands, just her enjoyment of him, would make him feel as it did.

For enjoy him, Meg did. It was bliss to hold him, huge and slippery and magnificent in her hands, and she was still scared, but rather more excited at the prospect of him being inside her.

'Like this?' she checked, and he closed his eyes and leant his head back on the marble wall behind him.

'Like that,' he said, but then changed his mind. 'Harder.' And he put his hand over hers and showed her—showed her a little too well.

'Come here.' He pulled her up over him. He was seconds away, had to slow down, but he had to have her. He was rubbing himself around her and she was desperate for him to be inside her too.

'We need…' It was him saying it, and he knew he should take her to bed and slip on a condom, but he wanted her this moment, and for once in his life he was conflicted. He knew he could have her now, that he was the only one thinking, and he wanted the pleasure. But as he looked at her, hovering over him, Niklas knew he wouldn't have a hope of pulling out in time.

Her hands were on his shoulders and he was holding her buttocks, almost fighting not to press her down. He wanted to give in, to drive her down and at the same time lift his hips, and he would have—absolutely he would have, in fact—had her phone not rung.

He swore in Portuguese, and then French, and then Spanish at the intrusion.

'Leave it,' he said.

But it rang again, and for a brief moment common sense returned. He stood, taking her wet hand and helping her out as they headed for the bed. He turned off her phone, and checked that his was off too, for he was tired of a world that kept invading his time. Then he looked at the shiny foil packets and realised that the last thing he wanted was to be sheathed when he entered this woman.

'I want to feel you,' he said. 'I want you to feel me.'

And his mind went to a place he never allowed it to go.

He'd been told by plenty of people that he was damaged goods, that a man with his past was not capable of a stable relationship.

Yet he wanted to be stable for a while.

He was tired of the noise and the endless women. Not once had he considered commitment, and he didn't fully now, but surely for a while longer he could carry on caring? He had amassed enough that he could trust himself to take care of another person for a while at least, and if there were consequences to his reckless decision then he could take care of that too.

He could.

In that moment he fully believed that he could.

He would.

No, he did not want others around him today—did not want his thoughts clouded. Usually, to Niklas, rapid thoughts were right, and they were the ones that proved to be the best. He looked at her, pink and warm and a virgin on his bed, and decided he would do this right.

Thoroughly.

Properly.

'Marry me.'

She laughed.

'I'm serious,' he said. 'That's what people do when they come to Vegas.'

'I think they usually know each other first.'

'I know you.'

'You don't.'

'I know enough,' Niklas said. 'You just don't know me. I *want* to do this.'

And what Niklas Dos Santos wanted he usually got.

'I'm not talking about for ever—I could never settle with one person for very long, or stay in one place—but I can help you sort out the stuff with your family. I can step in so you can step back...'

'Why?' She didn't get it. 'Why would you do that?'

He looked at her for a long time before answering, because she was right. Why *would* he do that? Niklas had had many relationships, many less than emotional encounters, and there had been a couple of long high-maintenance ones. Yet not once in his life had he considered marriage before. Not once had he wanted another person close. He had actually feared that another person might depend on a man who had come from nothing, but as he looked at her for the first time he wasn't daunted by the prospect at all.

Around her—again for the first time—he trusted in himself.

'I like you.'

'But what would you get out of it?'

'You,' he replied, and suddenly it seemed imperative that he marry her—that he make her his even if just for a little while. 'I like sorting things out...and I like you. And…' He gestured to the condoms on the bedside table. 'And I don't like them. So,' he said, reaching for the hotel phone, 'will you marry me?'

There was nothing about him she understood, but more than that there was nothing about herself she understood any more, for in that moment his proposal seemed rather logical.

A solution, in fact.

'Yes.'

He spoke on the phone for just a few moments and then turned and smiled at his bride-to-be.

'Done.'

CHAPTER FIVE

IT WAS THE quickest of quick weddings.

Or maybe not.

They were in Vegas, after all.

Niklas rang down to the concierge and informed them of their plans, telling him how they wanted them executed.

'Do you want them to bring up a selection of dresses?' he asked Meg. 'It's your day; you can have whatever you want.'

'No dress.' Meg smiled.

But there were *some* traditional elements.

He ordered lots of flowers, and they arrived in the room along with champagne, and there was even a wedding cake. Meg sat at a table trying on rings as the celebrant went through the paperwork.

He'd arranged music too, but Niklas chose from a selection already on his phone, and Meg found herself walking at his side to music she didn't know and a man she badly wanted to.

The bride and groom wore white bathrobes, and she

stood watching as the titanium ring dotted with diamonds she had chosen was slipped onto her finger. Perhaps bizarrely, there was not a flicker of doubt in her mind as she said yes.

And neither was there a flicker of doubt in Niklas's mind as he kissed his virgin bride and told her that he was happy to be married to a woman he had only met yesterday.

'Today,' Meg corrected and, yes, because of the time difference between Vegas and Australia it *was* still the day they'd first met.

'Sorry to rush you.' He grinned.

There was a mixture of nerves and heady relief when everyone had left.

He undid her robe and took off his, and then he pulled her onto the bed.

'Soon,' Niklas promised as his hands roamed over her, 'you will be wondering how you got through your life without this.'

'I'm wondering now,' Meg admitted, and she wasn't just talking about the sex. She was talking about him too. She had never opened up more fully with another person, had never felt more like herself.

Niklas's kiss was incredibly tender—a kiss she would never have expected from him. He kissed her till she almost relaxed, and then his mouth became more consuming. He needed to shave, but she liked the roughness, liked his naked body wrapped around hers.

She was on her back, and he was on top as he had so badly wanted to be on the plane. He could not wait—

not for a moment longer. His knees nudged hers apart and he slipped his fingers briefly in, checking she was ready for him, finding that she was.

And now there was nothing between them.

And he was no longer patient.

He warned her it would hurt.

He watched her face as she blanched in pain, then kissed her hard on the mouth.

As he drove into her she screamed into his mouth, because that first thrust seemed to go on for ever, and every part of her felt as if it was tearing just to accommodate his long, thick length. He tried to be gentle, but he was too large for that. But once he had ripped off that Band-Aid he kept moving within her, kept on kissing her mouth, her face, giving her no choice but to grow accustomed to the new sensations she was feeling. He moved within her as his tongue had earlier described that he would, moving deep till he had driven her wild. He wasn't kissing her now, and she looked up to see his face etched with concentration, his eyes closed, his body moving rapidly as hers rose to meet him.

Now it was Meg's hands urging him on, digging her fingers into his tight buttocks, whimpering as she sought relief, and then he opened his eyes and let her have it, spilled every last drop deep into her. Her orgasm followed quickly after, and she was frenzied as she came, almost scared at the power of her body's response, at the things he had taught her to do.

And then he collapsed on top of her, his breathing heavy, and although it felt like a dream somehow it was real. Meg realised that he had been right—she had no idea how she'd got through her life without this.

Without him.

'Shouldn't we be regretting this by now?' Meg asked.

They were lying in a very rumpled bed and it was morning. Her body ached with the most delicious hurt, but Niklas had assured her for this morning's lesson she would need only her mouth.

'What's to regret?' He turned on the bed and looked over to her.

He didn't do happiness, but he felt the first rays of it today. He liked waking up to her, and the rest was mere detail that he would soon sort out.

'You live in Brazil and I live in Australia…'

'As we both know, there are planes…' He looked across the pillow. 'Do you worry about everything?'

'No.'

'I think you do.'

'I don't.'

'So how shall we tell your parents?'

He saw her slight grimace.

'They might be pleased for you.'

As the real world invaded so too did confusion. 'I doubt it. It will be a terrible shock.' She thought for a moment. 'I think once they get used to the idea they'll be pleased.' And then she swallowed nervously. 'I *think*.'

He smiled at her worried face. 'First of all *you* need to get used to the idea.'

'I don't know much about you.'

'There isn't much to know,' Niklas said.

She rather doubted that.

'I don't have family, as I said, so you have avoided having a mother-in-law. I hear from friends they can sometimes be a problem, so that's an unexpected bonus for you!'

He could be so flippant about things that were important, Meg thought, and there was so much she wanted to find out about him. She wondered how he had survived without a family, for a start, how he had made such a success of himself from nothing—because clearly he had. But unlike their wedding some things, Meg guessed, had to be taken more slowly—she couldn't just sit up and fire a thousand questions at him. Somehow she knew it wasn't something he would talk about easily, but she tried. 'What was it like, though?' Meg asked. 'Growing up in an orphanage?'

'There were many orphanages,' he said. 'I was moved around a lot.' Perhaps he realised he wasn't answering her question, because he added, 'I don't know, really. I try not to think about it.'

'But…'

He halted her. 'We're married Meg. But that doesn't mean we need every piece of each other. Let's just enjoy what we have, huh?'

So if he didn't want to talk about himself she'd start with the easier stuff instead. 'You live in São Paulo?'

'I have an apartment there,' Niklas said. 'If I am working in Europe I tend to stay at my house in Villefranche-sur-Mer. And now I guess I'll have to look for somewhere in Sydney…' His smile was wicked. 'If your father gets really cross, maybe I can ask if he knows any good houses—if he would be able to help…'

Meg started to laugh, because it sounded as if he did understand where she was coming from. Niklas was right—a nice big commission would certainly go a long way towards appeasing her father. She realised that the shock would wear off eventually, and that her rather shallow parents would be delighted to find somewhere for their rich new son-in-law to live.

As Meg lay there, and the sun started to work its way through the chink in the curtains, she started to realise that this was the happiest she had been in her life. But even with that knowledge there was one part about last night that had been unjustifiably reckless.

'I'll go on the pill…' she said. 'If it isn't already too late.'

He had said this wasn't for ever, and the wedding ring that had seemed a solution yesterday was less than one now.

'If last night brings far-reaching consequences you will both be taken care of.'

'For a while?'

He looked over and knew that, unlike most women, Meg wasn't talking about money. But his bank account was the only thing not tainted by his past.

'For a while,' Niklas said. 'I promise you—we'll be arguing within weeks, we'll be driving each other insane—and not with lust…' He smiled in all the wrong places, but he made her smile back. 'You'll be glad to see the back of me.'

She doubted it.

'I'm hard work,' he warned.

But worth it.

Though she *was* going on the pill.

And then he looked over to her again, and for as long as it was like this she could adore him.

'I am going to write to the airline tomorrow and thank them for not having a first-class seat,' he said.

'I might write and thank them too.'

'It will be okay,' he told her. 'Soon I will ring Carla and I will have her re-schedule things. Then we will meet with your parents and I will tell them.' He grinned at her horrified expression.

'*I'll* speak to my parents.'

'No,' Niklas said. 'Because you will start apologising and doubting and I am a better negotiator.'

'Negotiator?'

'How long do you want off for our honeymoon?' Niklas said. 'Of course you will want to give them notice— you don't want to just walk out—but for now we should have some time together. Maybe I'll take you to the mountains…' There was no gap between them now, so he pulled her across. 'And I will also tell them that we will have a big wedding in a few weeks.'

'I'm happy with the wedding we had.'

'Don't you want a big one?'

Her hand slid down beneath the sheet and she loved it that he laughed, not understanding that laughter was actually rare for him. Then her mouth followed her hands, and he lay there as she inexpertly woke another part of him.

'Don't you want a proper wedding, with family and dancing?'

'I hate dancing…' She kissed all the way down his length and she felt his hand in her hair, gently lifting her to where he wanted more attention.

'I do too.'

'I thought all Brazilians could dance?'

'Stop talking,' Niklas said. 'And I never said I couldn't. I just don't.'

She looked up at the most stunning, complicated man who had ever graced her vision and thought of his prowess and the movement of his body. All of it had been for her, and she shivered at the thought of the days and nights to come, of getting to know more and more of him. Already she knew that she was starting to want for ever, but that wasn't what this was about.

And then she tasted him again.

His hands moved her head as he promised she would not hurt him and told her exactly what to do with her mouth. She was lost in his scent, the feel of him in her mouth, and the shock of his rapid come was a most pleasant surprise. It was a surprise for Niklas too, but this was how she moved him.

He did not want to get out of bed—did not want to get back to the world. Except no doubt it was screaming for him by now—he had never had his phone turned off for so long.

He climbed out of bed and she lay there, just staring at the ceiling, lost in thoughts of him and the time they would take to get to know the other properly.

And Niklas was thinking the same. He had been looking forward to some time off, had been aware that he needed some, now he could not wait to take it.

He showered quickly and considered shaving, and then he picked up his phone, impatient to speak to Carla, to change his plans yet again. He grimaced when he saw how many missed calls he'd had, how many texts, and then he frowned—because there were hundreds. From Carla, from Miguel, from just about everyone he knew...

It was his first inkling that something was wrong.

Niklas had no family, and the only person he had ever really cared about was in bed in the next room, so he didn't have any flare of panic, but there was clearly a problem. Problems he was used to, and was very good at sorting them out.

It just might take a little time, that was all, when really he would far rather be heading back to bed. He dialled Carla's number, wondering if he should tell Meg to order some breakfast. He would just as soon as he made this call.

She could hear him in the lounge, speaking in his own language into his phone. She lay there for ages, twisting her new ring around her finger. Then, as he still spoke on the phone, she realised she wasn't actually terrified at the prospect of telling her parents, and even if this wasn't the most conventional of marriages, even if he had warned her it would end some day, she was completely at peace with what had occurred.

The only thing she was right now, Meg realised, was starving.

'I'm going to ring for breakfast,' she said as he walked back into the room, and then she looked over and frowned, because even though he had been gone ages she was surprised to see that he was dressed.

'I have to return to Brazil.'

'Oh.' She sat up in the bed. 'Now?'

'Now.'

He was not looking at her, Meg realised. What she did not realise was that precisely two seconds from now he was going to break her heart.

'We made a mistake.'

As easily as that he did it.

'Sorry?'

'The party's over.'

'Hold on…' She was completely sideswiped. 'What happened between there and here?' She pointed to the lounge he had come from. 'Who changed your mind?'

'I did.'

'What? Did you suddenly remember you had a fian-cée?' Meg shouted. 'Or a girlfriend…?' She was start-ing to cry. 'Or five kids and a wife…?' It was starting to hit home how little she knew about him.

'There's no wife…' he shrugged '…except you. I will speak with my legal team as soon as I return to Brazil, see if we can get it annulled. But I doubt it…'

He didn't even sit on the bed to tell her it was over,

and she realised what a fool she had been, how easily he had taken her in.

'If it cannot be annulled they will contact you for a divorce. I'll make a one-off settlement,' he said.

'Settlement?'

'My people will sort it. You can fight me for more if you choose, but I strongly suggest that you quickly accept. Of course if you are pregnant…'

He stood there with the sun streaming through the curtains behind him, and all she could see was the dark outline of a man she didn't know.

'It might be a good idea to think about the morning-after pill.'

And then there was a knock on the door and it was a bellboy to take his case.

'I've asked for a late check-out for you, if you want to reschedule your flight. Have breakfast…' he offered, as if this was normal, and then he tipped the bellboy, who left with his luggage.

'I don't understand…' She was turning into some hysterical female, sitting screaming on a bed as her one-night stand walked off.

'This is the type of thing people do in Vegas. We had fun…'

'Fun!' She couldn't believe what she was hearing.

'It's no big deal.'

'But it is for me.'

'It's about time that you grew up, then.'

She had never expected him to be cruel, but she had

no idea what she was dealing with. Niklas could be cruel when necessary, and today it was.

Very necessary.

He could not look at her. She was sitting on the bed in tears, pleading with him, and also, he noted, growing increasingly angry. Her voice rose as she told him that *he* was the one who needed to grow up, that *he* was the one who needed to sort out his life, and her hands were waving. Any minute now he thought she would rise and attack him. He wanted to catch her wrists and kiss the fear away, wanted to feel just for a moment her body writhing in anger and to reassure her—except he had nothing he could reassure her with. He knew how bad things would be shortly, so he had to be cruel to be kind.

'What did you have to marry me for?' she shouted. 'I was clearly already going to sleep with you…'

She was about to lunge at him, Niklas knew. She was kneeling on the bed, still grabbing the sheet around her for now, but in a moment it would be off. Her green eyes were flashing, her teeth bared and with his next words he knew he would end this.

'I told you yesterday.' He went to the bedside and flicked a few foil packets to the floor. 'I don't like condoms.'

He took the clawing to his cheek, stood there as she sprang towards him, then caught and held her naked fury by the arms for a moment. And then he pushed her back on the bed.

And as simply as that he was gone.

* * *

A minute ago the only things on her mind had been breakfast and making love with her new husband.

Now they were talking annulments and settlements.

Or rather they weren't talking.

He was gone.

He had left with cruel words and livid scratches on his cheek and she just lay there, reeling, her anger like a weight that did not propel her, but instead seemed to pin her down to the bed. It was actually an achievement to breathe.

A few minutes later Meg realised she was breathing in through her nose and out through her mouth, as she had done on the plane during take-off. Her own body was rallying to bring her out from the panic she now found herself in. Still she lay there and tried to make sense of something there was no sense to be made of.

He had played her.

Right from the start it had all been just a game to him.

Except this was her life.

Maybe he was right. Maybe she did need to grow up. If a man like Niklas could so easily manipulate her, could have her believing in love at first sight, then maybe she *did* need to sort herself out. She curled into herself for a moment, breathed for a bit, cried for a bit, and then, because she had to, Meg stood.

She didn't have breakfast.

She ordered coffee instead, and gulped on the hot

sweet liquid in the hope that it would warm her, would wean her brain out of its shock. It did not.

She showered, blasting her bruised, tender body with water, for she could not bear to step into the bath where they had kissed and so nearly made love.

Sex, Meg reminded herself. Because as it turned out love at first sight had had nothing to do with it.

She dressed quickly, unable to bear being in a room that smelt of them, and then she looked at the rumpled and bloodstained sheet on the bed where he had taken her and thought she might throw up.

Within an hour she was at the airport.

And just a little while later she was sitting on a plane and trying to work out how to get her life back to where it had been yesterday.

Except her heart felt as bruised and aching as the most intimate parts of her body, and her eyes, swollen from crying, felt the same.

Meg ordered a cool eye mask from the attendant. Before putting it on she slid off her wedding ring and put it on a chain around her neck, trying to fathom what had happened.

She couldn't.

She did her best with make-up in the toilet cubicle just before they came in for landing. She lifted her hair and saw the bruise his mouth had left on her neck and felt a scream building that somehow she had to contain. She covered her eyes with sunglasses and wondered how she would ever get through the next few hours, days, weeks.

'Thank God...' Her mum met her at the baggage carousel. 'The car's waiting. I'll bring you up to speed on the way.' She peered at her daughter. 'Are you okay?'

'Just tired,' Meg answered, and then she looked at her mum and knew she could never, ever tell her, so instead she forced a smile. 'But I'm fine.'

'Good,' said her mum as they grabbed her case and headed for the car. 'How was Vegas?'

CHAPTER SIX

MEG STOOD IN her office, looking out of the window, her fingers, as they so often did, idly turning the ring that still, almost a year later, lived on a chain around her neck.

She wasn't looking forward to tonight, given what she had to tell her parents.

It had nothing to do with Niklas. There had been eleven months of no contact now. Eleven months for Meg to start healing. Yet still she didn't know how to start.

She couldn't bear to think about him, let alone tell anyone what had happened.

And even though she could not bear to think about him, even though it actually hurt to do so, of course all too often Meg did.

It hurt to remember the good bits.

The bad bits almost killed her.

Surprisingly, she couldn't quite work out if she regretted it.

Niklas Dos Santos, for the brief time he had appeared

in it, had actually changed her life. Meeting him had changed her. Hell *did* make you stronger. This was her life and she must live it, and Meg had decided that she was finally going to follow her dreams and study to be a chef. Now she just had to tell her parents. So in a way tonight did in fact have something to do with him.

The strange thing was, she wanted to tell Niklas about her decision too—was fighting with herself not to contact him.

As painful as it was to remember, as brutal as his departure had been, still a part of her was grateful for the biggest mistake of her life and, fiddling with his ring as she so often did, Meg felt tears sting her eyes.

That was the only thing that was different today.

She hadn't cried for him since that morning. Actually, she had, but it had only been the once—the morning a couple of weeks later when she had got her period. Meg had sunk to her knees and wept on the toilet floor, not with relief, but because there was nothing left of them.

Nothing to tell him.

No reason for contact.

Apart from the paperwork it was as over as it could be.

So for the best part of a year she had completely avoided it. Had tried not to think of him while finding it impossible not to.

Every day had her waiting for a thick legal letter with a Brazilian postmark and yet it had never arrived.

Every night was just a fight not to think.

Sometimes Meg was tempted to look him up on the internet and find out more about the man who she could not forget—yet she was scared to, scared that even a glimpse of his face on her computer screen would have her picking up the phone to beg.

That was how much she still missed him.

Sometimes she grew angry, and wanted to contact him so that they could initiate the divorce, but that would be just an excuse to ring him. Meg knew she didn't need to speak with him to divorce him, yet she had not even started the simple process, because once she started down that path it would stop being a dream—which sometimes she thought it must have been...

Then her fingers would move to the cool metal of his ring and she'd find out again it was real.

She looked up at the clock and saw that it was time for lunch. Grateful for the chance of some fresh air while she worked out exactly how to tell her parents she was leaving the family business, Meg was tempted to ignore the ringing phone.

She wished she had when she answered it, because some new clients had arrived and were insisting that they be seen immediately.

'Not without an appointment.' Meg shook her head. She was fed up with pushy clients and the continual access she was expected to provide. 'I'm going to lunch.'

'I've told them that you're about to go for lunch.' Helen sounded flustered. 'But they said that they would wait till you get back. They are adamant that they see you today.'

Meg was sick of that word—everyone was *adamant* these days, and because there wasn't much work around her parents insisted more and more that they must jump to potential clients' unreasonable demands.

'Just tell them that they need to book,' Meg said, but as she went to end the call she froze when she heard a certain name.

A name that had her blood running simultaneously hot and cold.

Cold because she had dreaded this day—dreaded their worlds colliding, dreaded the one mistake in her crafted life coming back to haunt her—but at the same time hot for the memories the name Dos Santos triggered.

'He's here?' Meg croaked. 'Niklas is here?'

'No,' Helen answered, and Meg was frustrated at her own disappointment when she heard that it wasn't him. 'It's *regarding* a Mr Dos Santos, apparently, and these people really are insistent…'

'Tell them to give me a moment.'

She needed that moment. Meg really did.

She sank into her chair and poured a drink of water, willed herself to calm down, and then she checked her appearance in the mirror that she kept in her drawer. Her hair was neatly tied back and though her face was a touch pale she looked fairly composed—except Meg could see her own eyes were darting with fear.

There was nothing to fear, Meg told herself. It wasn't

trouble that had arrived. It had been almost a year after all. No doubt his legal team were here to get her signature on divorce papers. She closed her eyes and tried to calm herself, but it didn't help because all she could see was herself and Niklas, a tangle of legs and arms on a bed, and the man who had taken her heart with him when he left. Now it really was coming to an end.

She stood as Helen brought her visitors in and sorted out chairs for them. Then Helen offered water or coffee, which all three politely declined, and finally, when Helen had left and the door was closed, Meg addressed them.

'You wanted to see me?'

'First we should introduce ourselves.'

A well-spoken gentleman started things off. He introduced himself and his colleague and then Rosa, a woman whom Meg thought might be around forty, took over. It was terribly difficult to tell her age. She was incredibly elegant, her make-up and hair completely immaculate, her voice as richly accented as Niklas's had been, and it hurt to hear the familiar tone—familiar because it played over and over each night in her dreams. But she tried not to think of that, tried to concentrate on Rosa as she told Meg that they worked at the legal firm Mr Dos Santos used. She went through their qualifications and their business structure, and as she did so Meg felt her own qualifications dissolve beneath her—these were high-end lawyers and clearly here to do business. But Meg still didn't understand why Niklas had felt it necessary to fly three of his most powerful lawyers all the way to Australia, simply to oversee their divorce.

A letter would have sufficed.

'First and foremost,' Rosa started, 'before we go any further, we ask for discretion.'

They were possibly the sweetest words that Meg could hope to hear in this situation.

'Of course' was her response, but that wasn't enough for Rosa.

'We *insist* on your absolute discretion,' Rosa reiterated, and for the first time Meg felt her hackles rise.

'I would need to know what you're here in regard to before I can make an assurance like that.'

'You are married to Niklas Dos Santos?'

'I think we all know that,' Meg said carefully.

'And do you know that your husband is facing serious charges of embezzlement and fraud?'

Ice slid down her spine. Her hackles were definitely up now, and Meg thought for a moment before answering, 'I had no idea.'

'If he is found guilty he will probably never be released.'

Meg ran her tongue over her lips and tasted the wax of the lipstick she had applied earlier. She could feel beads of sweat breaking out on her forehead and felt nauseous at the very thought of a man like Niklas confined and constricted. She felt sick, too, at the thought of what he must have done to face serving life behind bars.

'He is innocent.' The man who had first introduced

them spoke then, and Meg couldn't help raising one of her eyebrows, but she made no comment.

Of course his own people would say that he was innocent.

They were his lawyers after all.

She didn't look at Rosa when she spoke. Instead she examined her nails, tried incredibly hard to stop her fingers from reaching for her hair. She did not want to give them any hint that she was nervous.

'We believe that Niklas is being set up.'

What else would they say? Meg thought.

'I really don't see what this has to do with me.' Meg looked in turn at each of the unmoved faces and was impressed by her own voice when she spoke. She possibly sounded like a lawyer, or a woman in control, though of course inside she was not. 'We were married for less than twenty-four hours and then Niklas decided that it was a mistake. Clearly he was right. We hardly knew each other. I had no idea about any of his business affairs. Nothing like that was ever discussed…'

Rosa spoke over her. 'We believe that Niklas is being set up by the head of our firm.'

It was then that Meg started to realise the gravity of the situation. These people were not just defending their client, they were implicating their own principal.

'We have had little access to the case, which in something as big as this is unusual, and without access to the evidence we cannot supply a rigorous defence. For reasons we cannot yet work out, we believe Miguel is intending to misrepresent Niklas. Of course we cannot let our boss know that we suspect him. He is the only one who has access to Niklas while he is being held awaiting a trial date.'

'He's in prison now?'

'He has been for months.'

Meg reached for her water but her glass was empty. Her hands were shaking as she refilled it from the jug. She could not stand the thought of him locked up, could not bear to think of him in prison, did not want those thoughts haunting her. She didn't like the new nightmares these people had brought, and she wanted them gone now.

'It really is appalling, but…' She didn't know how she could help them—didn't know the Brazilian legal system, just didn't know why they were here. 'I don't see how it has anything to do with me. As I said, I'm not involved in his business…' And then she started to panic, because maybe as his wife she had a different involvement with Niklas that they were here to discuss.

'We have made an application of behalf of Niklas for him to exercise his conjugal rights…'

Meg could hear her own pulse pounding in her ears as Rosa continued speaking and she drained her second glass of water. Her throat was still impossibly dry. Her fingers moved to her hair and she twirled the strand around one finger, over and over.

'Niklas is entitled to one phone call a week and a two-hour conjugal visit once every three weeks. He is being brought before the judge in a fortnight for the trial date to be set and we need you to fly there. At your visit with him on Thursday you are to tell him that only when he is in front of the judge he is to fire his lawyer. Before that he is to give no hint. Once he has fired Miguel we will step in for him.'

'No.' Meg shook her head and pulled her finger out of her hair. She was certain of her answer, did not need to think about this for a moment. She just wanted them gone.

'The only way we can get in contact with him is through his wife.'

'I'll phone him.' It was the most she would do. 'You said that he was entitled to a weekly phone call…' And then she shook her head again, because of course the calls would be monitored. 'I can't see him.' She could not. 'We were married for twenty-four hours.'

'Correct me if I am wrong…' Rosa was as tough with the truth as she was direct. 'According to the records we have found you have been married for almost a year.'

'Yes, but we—'

'There has been no divorce?'

'No.'

'And if Niklas was dead and I was here bringing you a cheque would you hand it back and say, *No, we were only married for twenty-four hours? Would you say, No, give this to someone else. He had nothing to do with me…?*'

Meg's face was red as she fought for an answer, but she did not know that truth—not that it stopped Rosa.

'And because you have not screamed annulment I am assuming consensual sex occurred.'

Meg felt her face grow redder, because sex had been the only thing they had had between them.

'If you had found yourself pregnant, would you not have contacted him? Would you have told yourself it did not count as you were only married for twenty-four hours? Would you have told your child the same…?'

'You're not being fair.'

'Neither is the system being fair to my client,' Rosa said. 'Your husband will be convicted of a crime he did not commit if you do not get this message to him.'

'So I'm supposed to fly to Brazil and sit in some trailer or cell and pretend that we're…?'

'There will be no pretending—you *will* have sex with him,' Rosa said. 'I don't think you understand what is at stake here, and I don't think you understand the risks to Niklas and his case if it is discovered that we are trying to get information in. There will be suspicions if the bed and the bin…'

Thankfully she did not go into further detail, but it was enough to have Meg shake her head.

'I've heard enough, thank you. I will start preparing the paperwork for divorce today.' She stood.

They did not.

'Marrying Niklas was the biggest mistake of my life,' Meg stated. 'I have no intention of revisiting it and I'm certainly not…' She shook her head. 'No. We were a mistake.'

'Niklas never makes mistakes,' Rosa countered. 'That is why we know he is innocent. That is why we have been working behind our own principal's back to ensure justice for him.' She looked to Meg. 'You are his only chance, and whether or not it is pleasant, whether or not you feel it is beneath you, this *must* happen.'

She handed her an envelope and Meg opened it to find an itinerary and airline tickets.

'There is a flight booked for you tomorrow night.'

'I have a life,' Meg flared. 'A job, commitments...'

'A visit has been approved for Thursday. It is the only chance to make contact with him before the pre-trial hearing in two weeks' time. After you have seen him you can go to Hawaii—though we might need you to go back for another visit in three weeks, if things don't go well.'

'No.' How else could she say it? 'I won't do it.'

Rosa remained unmoved. 'You may want this all to go away, but it cannot. Niklas deserves this chance and he will get it. You will see, when you check your bank account, that you are being well compensated for your time.'

'Excuse me?' Meg was furious. 'How dare you? How on earth did you...?' But it wasn't about how they had found out her bank details. It wasn't that that was the problem right now. 'It's not about money...'

'So it's the morality of it, then?' Rosa questioned. 'You're too precious to sleep with your own husband even it means he has to spend the rest of his life behind bars?'

Rosa made it sound so simple.

'For the biggest mistake of your life, you chose rather

well, did you not?' Rosa sneered. 'You are being paid to sleep with Niklas—it's hardly a hardship.'

Meg met her eyes and was positive that he and Rosa had slept together. They both stared for a moment, lost in their own private thoughts. Then Rosa stood, a curl on her lip, and another sassy Brazilian gave her opinion of Meg as she upended her life.

'You need to get over yourself.'

CHAPTER SEVEN

WHEN THEY HAD GONE, Meg did what she had spent a year avoiding.

She looked up the man she had married and found out just how powerful he was—or had been before he had been charged. She understood now that the Niklas Dos Santos she was reading about would be less than impressed to find himself in business class. And then she read about the shock his arrest had caused. Niklas might have a reputation in business as being ruthless, but he had always seemed honest—which was apparently why it had made it so easy for him to con some high-flying people into parting with millions. They had believed the lies that had been told to them. His business peers' trust in him had made them gullible, and despite Rosa's and her colleagues' protestations of his innocence, for Meg the articles cast doubt.

She knew, after all, how effortlessly he had read *her*, how easily he had played *her*. Meg had seen another side to Niklas and it wasn't one she liked.

And yet, as Rosa had pointed out, he was her husband, and she was apparently his one hope of receiving a fair trial.

And then Meg clicked on images and wished she had not.

The first one she saw was of him handcuffed and being bundled into a police car.

There were many more of Niklas, but they were not of the man she knew. The suit was on and the tie was beautifully knotted, the hair was as she remembered, but not in one single image did she see him smiling or laughing. Not one single picture captured the Niklas she had so briefly known.

And then she found another image—one that proved the most painful of all to see.

His arrogant face was scowling, there were three scratches on his cheek that her nails had left there, and a deep bruise on his neck that her mouth had made. Meg read the headline: *Dos Santos vira outra mulher!* Meg clicked for a translation. She wanted to know if he had returned that morning and been arrested—wanted to know if that was the reason he had been so cruel to her. Had he known he was about to be arrested and ended it to protect her? She waited for the translation to confirm it, held her breath as it appeared: *Dos Santos upsets another woman!*

And even in prison, even locked up and a world away, somehow he broke her heart again.

There was a knock at the door. Her mother didn't wait for an answer, just opened it and came in. 'Helen said you had visitors?'

'I did.'

'Who were they?'

'Friends.'

She saw her mum purse her lips and knew she would not leave until she found out who her friends were and what they wanted. Even without the arrival of her visitors Meg remembered she had been due for a difficult conversation with her parents today, and now seemed like a good time to get it over with.

'Can you get Dad…?' Meg gave her mum a pale smile. 'I need to speak to you both.'

It didn't go well.

'After all we've done for you' was the running theme, and the words Meg had expected to hear when she told them that she had chosen not to continue working in the family firm.

She didn't mention Niklas. It was enough for them to take in without giving them the added bonus of a son-in-law! And one in prison too.

It should have been a far harder conversation to have, yet she felt as if all her emotions and fears were reserved for the decision that was still to come, and Meg sat through the difficult conversation with her parents pale and upset, but somehow detached.

'Why would you want to be a chef?' Her mother simply didn't get it—didn't get that her daughter could possibly want something that had not been chosen for her. 'You're a lawyer, for God's sake, and you want to go and work in some kitchen—?'

'I don't know exactly what I want to do,' Meg broke in. 'I don't even know if I'll be accepted…'

'Then why would you give it all up?'

And she didn't know how to answer—didn't know how to tell them that she didn't feel as if she was actually giving up *anything*, that she was instead taking back her life.

Just not yet.

She told them she was taking a holiday, though she still wasn't sure that she was, but even without Niklas looming large in her thoughts taking a few weeks off while her parents calmed down seemed sensible.

'And then I'll come back and work for a couple of months,' Meg said. 'I'm not going to just up and leave…'

But according to her parents she already had.

Later, as she sat on the balcony of her small flat and looked at the stunning view, Meg thought about her day. What should have been a difficult conversation with her parents, what should have her sitting at home racked with guilt and wondering if she'd handled things right, barely entered her thoughts now. Instead she focused on the more pressing problem looming ahead.

Quietly she sat and examined the three things she had that proved her relationship with Niklas had actually existed.

She took the ring from the chain around her neck and remembered the certainty she had felt when he had slipped it on—even though he had told her it could never be for ever, somehow she had felt it was right.

And then she picked up the marriage certificate she

had retrieved from her bedside table and examined the dark scrawl of his signature. *Niklas Dos Santos*. She saw the full stop at the end of his name and could even hear the sound his pen had made as he'd dotted the document.

Finalised it.

And then she examined the third thing, the most painful thing—a heart that even eleven months on was still exquisitely tender.

There had been no one since, no thought of another man since that time. She felt dizzy as she peered into her feelings, scared as to what she might find. The truth was there waiting and she hadn't wanted to see it. It hurt too much to admit it.

She loved him.

Or rather she had.

Absolutely she had, or she would never have married him. Meg knew that deep down. And, whether or not he had wanted it, still that love had existed. Her very brief marriage with him had for Meg been the real thing.

And, as Rosa had pointed out, they *were* still married.

It was getting cool, so Meg went inside and read the itinerary Rosa had handed her. Then she looked up the prison he was being held at and could not believe that he was even there, let alone that on Thursday she might be too.

Would be.

Meg slid the ring back on her finger.

A difficult decision, but somehow easily made. Yes, Rosa was right. In legal terms he was still her husband.

But it wasn't in legal terms only that she made her choice. There was a part of herself that she must soon sort out, must work out how to get over, but for now at least, in every sense, Niklas was still her husband.

Though her hotel and flights had been arranged, any problems had to be dealt with by the travel agent, Rosa had told her. Meg must not, under any circumstance, make contact with them. She must not be linked to them in any way—not just to protect them, or even Niklas, they had warned her, but to protect herself.

And she registered the danger but tried not to dwell on it, just tried to deal with a life that had changed all over again.

There was another row with her parents—a huge one this time. They had no comprehension as to why their usually sensible daughter might suddenly up and take off to Brazil.

'Brazil!' Her mother had just gaped. 'Why the hell do you want to go to Brazil?'

They didn't come to the airport to say goodbye. Still, there was one teeny positive to the whole situation: Meg barely noticed the plane taking off. Her thoughts were too taken up with the fact that she was on her way to see Niklas.

And she barely noticed it a second time, when she transferred at Santiago and knew she was on the last leg of her journey to see him. Shortly after take-off the stewards stood, and after a little while she was offered a drink.

'Tonic water...' Meg said, and then changed her mind and added gin.

'Off on holiday?'

She turned to her friendly fellow passenger, an elderly lady who had cousins in São Paulo, she told Meg.

'Yes...' Meg said. 'Sort of.'

'Visiting family?'

'My husband.' How strange it felt to say it, but she was, after all, wearing his ring, and her documents were in her bag, and she might have to say the same thing at Customs, so maybe she'd better start practising.

'Brazil first and then three weeks in Hawaii...'

'Lovely.' The old lady smiled and Meg returned it. Just as Niklas had that first day, she wished her neighbour would just keep quiet.

She could hardly tell her the real purpose for her visit!

Instead she ordered another gin.

It didn't help.

She cried as they descended over São Paulo—she had never seen anything like it. Stretched below her was a sea of city, endless miles of buildings and skyscrapers. The population of this city alone was almost equivalent to the entire population of Australia, and never had Meg felt more small and lost.

The final approach was terrifying—more so because of all he had told her about it, more so now that she could see just how closely the cars and the planes and the city co-existed, more so because she was actually here.

Bizarrely, her eyes searched for him after she'd cleared Customs—a stupid flare of hope that this was a strange joke, that he was testing her, that he might be waiting with flowers and a kiss. Perhaps she might once more feel the thorns press into her skin as he teased her about the lengths she'd go to for just a couple of hours with him.

It wasn't a joke, though. It wasn't a game. There was no one here to greet her.

Meg exited the airport and tried to hire a taxi, but she had never seen a taxi queue like this one. She was exhausted and overwhelmed as once again Niklas pushed her out of her comfort zone.

The driver's music was loud, his windows were down, and he drove her through darkening streets into Jardins. Everything was loud there too. The city pulsed with life. There were food stalls on the streets—unfamiliar scents came in through the windows of the car whenever they stopped at traffic lights—and it was more city than she could deal with. Which made sense, Meg thought with a pale smile. After all it was the city Niklas was from.

All Meg wanted to do was to get to her room.

Dishevelled, confused, *tired*, after they pulled up at a very tall hotel Meg paid the taxi driver. The second she stepped inside she knew she was back in his world.

Modern, cosmopolitan, with staff exquisite and beautiful.

It was a relief to get to her room and look out of the window at the bewildering streets below, to fathom that she was actually here—that tomorrow she would be taking another taxi to visit Niklas in prison.

Meg scanned the confusing horizon, wondered as to his direction, wondered if he had any inkling at all that she was even here.

Wondered all night how she could stand to face him tomorrow.

'Hi, Mum…' She rang not because they had insisted she did—they were hardly talking, after all—she rang because, despite their problems, Meg loved her parents and wanted the sound of normality tonight.

'How's Brazil?' Her mother's voice was terse, but at least she spoke.

'Amazing,' Meg said. 'Though I haven't seen much of it…'

'Have you booked any trips?'

'Not yet,' Meg said, and was quiet for a moment. She didn't like lying, especially to her parents, but she found herself doing it at every turn. Tomorrow she would be ringing her parents again to tell them that she had changed her mind about Brazil and was going to spend the rest of her vacation in Hawaii—how would they react to that?

More than anything Meg just wanted tomorrow over with, so that she could lie on a beach and hopefully heal once and for all. She hadn't dared risk putting her divorce application in her luggage in case it caused questions at Customs, but the second she landed home it would be posted.

Her heart couldn't take any more of him.

'How's Dad?'

'Worried,' her mum said, and Meg felt her heart sink—because she hated that they were worried about her. 'It's going to cost an arm and a leg to hire a new lawyer…'

Meg knew her mum didn't mean to hurt her, but unintentionally she had. The business was always the biggest thing on their minds.

'I've told you that I'll work for a couple of months when I get back. You don't have to rush into anything. And you don't need a full-time lawyer; you can contract out. We'll go through it all properly when I get back.'

'You *are* coming back?'

And Meg gave a small unseen smile, because maybe it wasn't just about the business. As difficult as they could be at times, they did want what they thought was best for her, and they did love her—that much Meg knew.

'Of course I am. I'm just taking a few weeks to sort out my head—I'll be back before you know it.'

It was impossible to sleep. She was dreading tomorrow and seeing him again, dreading the impact of seeing him face to face. It was emotionally draining just thinking about him, let alone seeing him.

Let alone having sex with him.

If Meg slept, she didn't sleep much, and she was up long before her alarm call. She ordered breakfast, but her stomach was doing somersaults and she could hardly manage to hold down a small piece of bread and grilled cheese.

The coffee she was more grateful for.

Had she not loved him, she doubted she could do this.

But had she not loved him she would not have married him in the first place and wouldn't be in this mess.

Except she remembered his cruel words from that morning long ago and knew that love had no place in this.

She gave up on breakfast and lay in the bath, tried to prepare herself for what lay ahead, but had no idea how. As she picked up a razor and shaved her legs she did not know if her actions were for his pleasure or for her pride. It was the same with the body oil she rubbed in. She wore simple flesh-coloured underwear and an olive green shift dress with flat leather sandals. Her hand was shaking too much to bother with make-up so she gave in.

Rosa had given her the name of a good car company to use, rather than getting a taxi, and the desk rang to tell her that her driver was here. As she left the room she glanced around and wondered how she would feel when she returned. This time tomorrow she would be on a plane on her way to Hawaii. This time tomorrow it would be done—for despite what Rosa had said she would not be returning to him.

Once was enough.

Twice might kill her.

So she looked at her room and tried not to think too much about what had to happen before she returned.

They drove through the most diverse of cities, passed the Court of Justice, where in two weeks Niklas would be, and in daylight Meg saw more of this stunning city. There was beauty and wealth, and such poverty too. She thought of Niklas growing up on the streets, and of how much he had made of himself only to fall. She didn't know enough to believe in his innocence. She might be a fool for love, but she wasn't a blind fool. Still, he deserved a fair trial.

Meg had never known such fear in her life as they approached the jail. The sight of the watchtower, the sounds when she entered, the shame of the examination… Her papers were examined and her photograph taken and she was told her rights—or rather her husband's rights. She could return in three weeks; she could ring him once a week at a designated time and speak for ten minutes. And although Meg took the paper with the telephone number on it, she knew that she would never use it.

Then a female guard examined her for contraband and Meg closed her eyes, thinking she would spit at her if she ever faced Rosa again, before being allowed to pull her knickers back up. Maybe she did need to get over herself, but as she was led through to an area where two guards chatted she heard the Dos Santos name said a few times, and even if Meg didn't understand precisely what they were saying she got their lewd drift. As she stood waiting for Niklas to arrive Meg knew that, yes, she might have to get over herself—but right about now she was completely over *him*.

CHAPTER EIGHT

THE SLOT ON the door opened and lunch was delivered. Niklas ate beans and rice. It was tepid and bland and there were no herbs to pick out, but he was hungry and cleared his plate in silence.

His cellmate did the same.

It was how they both survived.

He refused to let the constant noise and shouts from other inmates rile him. He made no comment or complaint about the bland food and the filth. From the first day he had arrived here, apart from the odd necessary word, he had been silent, had conformed to the system though some of the guards had tried to goad him.

As he had entered the jail they had told him of the cellmate they had for him, of the beatings he could expect. They'd told the rich boy just how bad things would be in there for him as he'd removed his suit and shoes and then his watch and jewellry before they searched him and then hosed him.

Niklas had said nothing.

He had been hosed many times before.

There was no mirror to look in, so after his hair was shaved he'd just run a hand over his head. He wore the rough denim without real thought. He had worn harsher clothes and been filthier and hungrier than this on many occasion.

Niklas was streetwise. He had grown up in the toughest place and survived it. He had come from nothing and he'd returned to nothing—as he had always silently feared that he would. This anonymous, brutal world was one that he belonged in, and the one he truly deserved. Perhaps this was actually his home, Niklas had realised—not ten thousand feet in the air, swigging champagne as caviar popped in his mouth; not considering a home in the mountains and a family to take care of. He had been a fool to glimpse it, a fool to let down his guard, for those things were not his to know.

Assets frozen, friends and colleagues doubting him… The eventual snap of cuffs on his wrists had provided temporary relief as Niklas went back to the harsh world he had known one day would reclaim him. He'd returned to another system and navigated it seemingly with ease. But the temporary relief had soon faded and a sense of injustice had started to creep in. His head felt as if it would explode at times, and his body was so wired that he was sure he could rip the bars from the cell window with his bare hands or catch bullets with his teeth—but then, as he had long ago taught himself to, he simply turned those thoughts off.

Not for a second did he show his anger, and rarely did he speak.

His cellmate was one the most feared men in the prison. He ran the place and had contacts both inside and out. The guards had thought it would be like two bulls put in the same paddock. The motto of São Paulo was *I am not led. I lead.* So they had put the rich boy who led the business world in with the man who led the inmates and had waited for sobs from Dos Santos. But Niklas had held Fernando's eyes and nodded when he had been placed in his cell. He had said good evening and got no answer, and from that point on Niklas had said nothing more to him. He had ignored his cellmate—as suited Fernando, as suited him—and over the months the tension had dissipated. The silence between the two inmates was now amicable; both men respected the other's privacy, in a friendship of no words.

Niklas finished his lunch. He would exercise soon.

They had not been let out to the yard in over a week, so in a moment he would use the floor to exercise. He paced himself, sticking to routines to hold onto his mind. For while he slotted in with the system, while he followed the prison rules, more and more he was starting to reject them. Inside a slow anger had long been building and it was one that must not explode, because he wanted to be here when his trial date was set—did not want solitary till then.

He lay on his bunk and tried not to build up too much hope that he might be bailed in a fortnight, when he appeared for the pre-trial hearing. Miguel had told him that he thought bail was unlikely—there were too many high-profile people involved who did not want him to have freedom.

'But there is no one involved,' Niklas had pointed out at their last meeting. 'Because I did not do anything. That is what you are supposed to prove.'

'And we will,' Miguel said.

'Where's Rosa?' Niklas had asked to see Rosa at this visit. He liked her straight talking, wanted to hear her take on things, but yet again it was Miguel who had come to meet with him.

'She…' Miguel looked uncomfortable. 'She wants to see you,' he said. 'I asked her to come in, but…'

'But what?'

'Silvio,' Miguel said. 'He does not want her in here with you.'

And Niklas got that.

Rosa's husband, Silvio, had complained about Rosa working for him. Niklas and Rosa had once been an item for a few weeks, just before she had met Silvio, and though there was nothing between them now, her working for Niklas still caused a few problems.

As he lay there replaying conversations, because that was all he was able to do in this place, Niklas conceded that Silvio was right not to want Rosa to visit him here.

Nothing would happen between them, but it was not just Rosa's sharp insight he wanted. The place stank of testosterone, of confined angry male, and Rosa was open enough to understand that his eyes would roam. She would let them, and he knew that she would dress well for him.

He tried not to think of Meg—did not want even an image of her in this place—but of course it was impossible not to think of her.

As his mind started to drift he turned those thoughts off and hauled them back to his pre-trial hearing. His frustration at the lack of progress was building—his frustration at everything was nearing breaking point.

He climbed down from his bunk and started doing sit-ups, counting in his head. And then he changed to push-ups, and for those he did not bother to count. He would just work till his body ached. But anger was still building. He wanted to be on the outside—not just for freedom but because there he could control things, and he could control nothing here except his small routines. So he kept on doing his sit-ups and as a guard came to the door Niklas carried on, ignoring the jeering, just kept on with his workout.

'Lucky man, Dos Santos.'

He did not miss a beat, just continued his exercise.

'Who did you pay?'

Still Niklas did not answer.

'You have a beautiful wife.'

Only then did he pause, just for a second, mid-push-up, before carrying on. The guard didn't know what he was talking about. No one knew of Meg—they were winding him up, messing with his head, and he chose not to respond.

'She's here waiting to see you.'

And then the slot in the door opened and he was told to get up. There was no choice now but to do as he was told. So Niklas stood, met Fernando's eyes for just a second, which was rare. The change in routine was notable for both of them.

Niklas put his hands through the slot and handcuffs were applied, then he pulled his cuffed wrists back as the cell door was opened. He walked along the corridor and down metal steps, heard the jeers and taunts and crude remarks as he walked past. There were a couple of shoves from the guard but Niklas did not react, just kept on walking while trying to work things out.

Miguel must have arranged a hooker, finally pulled a few strings.

Thank God.

Maybe now his mind would hold till the trial date.

Not that he showed any emotion as they walked. He'd learnt that many years ago.

Show weakness and you lose—he'd learnt that at eight.

He had walked through the new orphanage he'd been sent to—he had been on his third orphanage by then—and this one was by far the worst. Still, there was good news, he had been told—his new family were waiting to meet him. A beautiful family, the worker had told him. They were rich, well fed and well dressed and had everything they wanted in the world except children. More than anything they wanted a son and had chosen Niklas.

His heart had leapt in hope. He'd hated the orphanage, a rough home for boys where the staff were often cruel, and he had been grinning and excited as the door had been pushed open and he had prepared himself to meet his new family.

How the workers waiting for him in there had laughed at his tears—how they had jeered him, enjoying their little joke long into the night. How could he have been so bold as to think that a family might want him?

It was the very last time that Niklas had cried.

His last display of true emotion.

Now he kept it all inside.

He would not give the prison guards the same pleasure. Whatever their plan, he would not give them the satisfaction of reading his face.

But then he saw her.

It had not properly entered his head that it might actually be Meg.

He had not allowed it to.

She did not belong in here. That was his first thought as he saw her dressed in a linin shift dress. Her hair burned gold and copper, the colour of the sun at night through his cell window, and then he saw the anxiety in her eyes turn to horror as she took in the shaved head and the rough clothing. A lash of shame tore through him that he should be seen by her like this, and his expression slipped for just a second. He stared ahead as his cuffs were removed, and though he remained silent his mind raced. To the left was Andros, the guard he trusted the least, and he thought again how Meg did not belong here. He wanted to know who the hell had arranged this, who had approved this visit, for even though he was confined and locked up he still had a system in place, and he had told Miguel that everything was to be run by him.

He could feel Andros watching as she walked towards him, heard the fear and anxiety in her voice as she spoke.

'I've missed you so much.'

She was playing a part. Niklas got that. But as her lips met his cheek it did not matter. Her touch was the first reprieve for his senses in months. Her skin on his cheek was so soft that the contact actually shocked him. He wanted to know the hows and whys of her visit here, wanted to know exactly what was going on, yet his first instinct was not to kiss her, but to protect her— and that meant that he too must play a part, for Andros was watching.

It was a kiss for others, and his mind tried to keep it at that—except her breath tasted of the outside and he drank her in. The feel of her in his arms allowed temporary escape and it was Meg who pulled back.

Meg stood with her cheeks burning red, tears of shame and hurt and anger in her eyes, and her lips pressed closed as one guard said something that made the other laugh. Then a door opened and they walked into a small, simply furnished room. The guard shouted something to them, and whatever language you spoke it was crude, before closing the door behind them. Meg stood and then realised that she couldn't stand for very much longer, so she sat on a chair for a moment, honestly shaken.

It wasn't just shock at the sight of him—seeing Niklas with his hair cropped almost as short as the dark stubble on his chin, dressed in rough prison denim. Even like this he was still the most beautiful man she had ever seen. It was not just the shock that she had again tasted his mouth, felt his skin against hers, relighting all those memories from their one night together. It was everything: the whole journey here, the poverty in the streets she had driven through, the sight of the prison as she had approached, the watchtower and the guns on the guards and the shame of the strip-search. Surely all of those things had severed any feelings she had for him?

But, no, for then she'd had to deal with the impact of seeing him again, of tasting him. For a moment she just sat there and wondered how, after all she had been through, she could still hear her heart hammer in relief to be back at his side. She wanted to be over him—had to be for sanity's sake—so she tried not to look at him, just drank from the glass of water he offered her.

He stood and watched her and saw her shock, saw what just a little while in this place had done to her, and thought again how she did not belong here.

'Why?' He knelt down beside her and spoke in a rough whisper. 'Why would you come here?'

She didn't answer him—Meg couldn't open her mouth to speak.

'Why?' he demanded, and then she looked at him and he was reminded of the last time he had seen her. Because even with the absence of her bared teeth he could feel her anger, could see her green eyes flash with suppressed rage and hear the spit of her words when finally she answered him.

'You're *entitled* to me, apparently.'

Niklas remembered the first time he had met her. She had been anxious, but happy, and he knew that it was he who had reduced her to this. He could see the pain and the disgust in her eyes as she looked at the man she had married, as she saw the nothing he really was.

And he did not want her charity.

'Thanks, but no thanks.'

He moved to the door, preparing to call for the guards. He might regret it later, but he did not want a minute more in this room.

As he moved to go he heard her voice.

'Niklas.' She halted him. This was not about what had happened between them, not about scoring points, she was here for one reason only. 'Your people told me…' He turned to face her. 'I'm to tell you…'

He silenced her by pressing his finger to his lips and nodded to the door. He trusted no one—never had in his life, and wasn't about to start in here. But then he closed his eyes for a second, for that was wrong. Because for a while he had trusted *her*, and did still. He came over to her, knelt down again and moved his head to her mouth, so she could quietly tell him the little she knew.

'Miguel is working against you. You are to ask for a change of representation at your trial…'

His head pulled back and she watched as he took in the news. Quietly she told him the little she knew. His face was grey and his eyes shone black. He swallowed as if tasting bile and she heard his rapid angry breathing. His whisper was harsh when it came.

'*No.*'

It had to be a lie, because if his own lawyer was working against him he was here for life.

She *had* to be lying.

'How?' he demanded. 'Why?'

'I don't know anything more than that,' Meg said. 'It's all I've been told.'

'When?' he insisted, his voice an angry whisper. 'When were you told?'

And she told him about the visit—how on Monday morning Rosa and her colleagues had arrived at her place of work. He thought of her momentarily in Sydney, getting on with her life without him, and now here she was in Brazil.

'They should never have sent you...' He was livid. 'It's too dangerous...'

'It's fine...'

It was so *not* fine.

'Niklas...' She told him *all* they had told her—that they had to have sex, about the bed and the bin, and that the guards could not know she was here for any other reason.

He saw her face burn in shame, and she saw his disgust at what he had put her through.

'It's fine, Niklas,' she whispered. 'I know what I'm doing...' She could feel his fury; it was there in the room with them.

'You should not be here.'

'It's my decision.'

'Then it's the wrong one.'

'I'm very good at making those around you, it would seem. Anyway,' she whispered harshly, 'you don't have to worry—you're paying me well…'

'How much?'

She told him.

And he knew then the gravity of his situation, understood just how serious this was—because he had no money any more. Everything had been frozen. He thought of his legal team paying her with money of their own and it tempered the bitterness that sometimes consumed him a little. Then he looked at the woman he might even have loved and tasted bitterness one again, for he hated what the world had done to him.

'So you're not here out of the goodness of your heart?'

'You've already had that part,' Meg said. 'So can we just get it over with?'

She looked over to the bed and he saw the swallowing in her throat, knew that she was drenched in fear. He looked to the door again, knowing there was a guard outside, one he did not trust, who must never get so much as a hint as to the real reason she was here.

Paid to be here, Niklas reminded himself.

He trusted no one again.

He stood and ripped the sheet from the bed, and she sat there as he twisted it in his hands before throwing it back. She heard his anger as he took the bedhead in angry hands and rocked the bed against the wall. He felt his anger building as he slammed the bed faster and faster. He had never paid for sex in his life. Yes, he'd have been grateful for a hooker, but he'd never taken Meg as one and his head was pounding as the bed hit the wall again and again. He did not know who to believe any more, and as the bed slammed faster he shouted out.

Meg sobbed as he shouted, but it did nothing to dissipate the fury still building, and then he picked up the condoms by the bedside and went to the small wash area and got to work to make sure evidence of their coupling was in place. Meg sat there, listening and crying. She understood his anger but she did not understand her own self, for even here, amidst this filth and shame, she wanted him. So badly she wanted to be with the man she had so sorely missed. Not just the sex, but the comfort he somehow gave.

'Niklas…' She walked into the washroom and ignored him when he told her, less than politely, to go away. His back was to her. She moved to his side and saw his fury, saw his hand working fast. He repeated his demand for her to leave him, and when it was clear that she didn't understand just how much he meant the words he told her in French and then Spanish.

'How many ways do you need to hear it…?'

How deep was his shame to be seen like this, to be reduced to this? His back had been to Meg, for he could not face her, yet she'd slipped into the space between him and the wall and her mouth was on his. One of her hands joined his now.

'Leave me.'

'No.' She stroked him too.

'Leave me,' he said as her other hand slipped off her panties.

'No.'

And she put her hands around his neck and pressed herself against him, tried to kiss him. He spat her out.

'You don't know the fire you are playing with.'

'I want to, though.'

She wanted every piece of him—wanted a little more of what she could never fully have. Because a man like Niklas could only ever be on loan to her. She had flown to him not because she had to, not for the money, and not for the morality of doing the right thing by her husband. Purely because of him, and not once did his anger scare her.

Not once, as rough hands pulled her dress up, did she fear him.

He lifted her up and onto him and positioned her, pulling her roughly down to him. The most basic sex was their only release and she wrapped her legs tight around him, locked her arms around his neck. His kiss was violent now, and she felt the clash of their teeth and tongues and the rapid angry stabs of him. The rough feel of denim on her thighs was nothing compared to the roughness deep inside, and her back was hard against the wall. Meg could feel his anger, it blasted deep inside her, and it let Meg be angry too—angry at so many things: that she was here, that she still wanted him, even that this man still moved her so.

Her moans and shouts that he blocked with his mouth

shocked Meg even more—scared her, almost—but she was not scared of him as he pulled her down on him, as she felt the bruise of his fingers in her hips. She could feel her orgasm building rapidly, as if she had waited eleven months just to come to him, as if her body had been waiting for him to set it free.

There was a flash of confusion for Niklas too, for her cries and the grip of intimate muscles, the arch of her back and the spasm of her thighs, could never be faked. He had thought this was charity, a paid act at best, a sympathy screw at worst, but she was craving him again, the way she once had, and as he shot into her he remembered all the good again—the way they had been. He never cried, but he was as close to it now as he had ever been. They were both drenched in brief release and escape and his kisses turned softer now, to bring her back to him. Then he heard the drizzle of the tap and his eyes opened to his surroundings, to the reality they faced. There were no more kisses to be had and he lifted her off.

Stood her down.

But she would not lose him to his pride and she carried on kissing him, opened his shirt and put her palms to his chest. He felt as if her hands seared him, for there had been no contact, no touch of another on his skin for many months, and he loathed the exposure, the prying of her hands. It was just sex he wanted, not her, but her hands were still moving, exploring the defined muscles. Her fingers were a pleasure and he did not want her to be here—yet he wanted her for every second that they had.

There would be hours later for thinking, for working out what to do about Miguel. For now he wanted every minute he had left with her.

He took her to the bed and undressed her, took his clothes off too, and she looked at all the changes to his body. He was thinner, but more muscled, and his face wasn't the one she had turned to on the plane—it was closed and angry, and yet she had felt his pain back there, felt him slip into affection, and for a small moment had glimpsed the man she had once met.

'Is that why you ended things?' She looked over to him as he joined her on the bed, but he just lay and looked up at the ceiling. 'Did you find out the trouble you were in?'

'I didn't know then.' It would be easier for her if he lied.

'So what happened that morning to change things?'

'I spoke to my people at work, realised how much I had on...'

'I don't believe you.'

'Believe in your fairytale if you want.' Niklas shrugged.

'Are you going to tell me to grow up again?' she asked. 'Because I grew up a long time ago—long before you met me. I've realised that I wasn't being weak staying in my job—I simply won't ride roughshod over the people I care about. And I don't believe that you would either and,' she finished, 'I *do* believe that you cared about me.'

'Believe what you want to.'

'I will,' Meg said. 'And I care about you.'

'It makes no difference to me.'

She had been paid plenty to be here with him so he should turn and start things. She had told him what she had came to say and the clock was counting down. He should use every minute wisely. They should not bother with talking—there were more basic things to be getting on with. Except this was Meg, and she didn't know how to separate the two.

'How are you dealing with being in here? How—?' she started, but he soon interrupted.

'I was right the first time.' He turned to look at her face—the face he had first seen on a plane. 'You talk too much. And I don't want to talk about me.' But before he moved to kiss her he allowed himself the luxury of just one question. 'Are you still working for your parents?'

'I resigned…' Meg said. 'I'm trying to choose my course at the moment…'

'Good,' Niklas said. He should push her hand down to where he was hardening again, but first there was something else he wanted to know. 'Are you okay?'

'Of course.'

'Are you happy?'

'Working on it.'

'Do your parents know you are here?'

'They know that I am in Brazil…' he saw tears pool

in her eyes '…they don't know I have a husband that I'm visiting in prison.'

'You need to get away from here,' Niklas said. 'As soon as this visit is over.'

'I fly to Hawaii tomorrow.'

'Okay.' Tomorrow should be okay, he told himself, but he wasn't sure. 'Maybe change it to tonight…'

'I fly out at six a.m.'

He saw her grimace at the thought, remembered the first time they had met and the conversation they had had.

'How was your landing?' And for the first time he smiled. He didn't care how much they'd paid her, that she'd flown into Congonhas was enough for him to know that this had nothing to do with money.

'It wasn't so bad…' she attempted, and then told him the truth. 'I was petrified. I thought I was going to throw up. Although,' she added, 'that might have been the gin!'

He laughed, and so did she. He hadn't laughed for almost a year, but this afternoon he did. She kicked him and they fought for a bit—a nice fight, a friendly fight—and he took her back to when they'd been lovers so easily, far, far too easily. But, given this was the last time she would be here, she let him. No one could kiss like he did. It was quite simply perfect, and the feel of him hard in her hands was perfect too.

This time he would be gentle, Niklas decided, worried that he had been too rough before. He didn't just kiss her mouth, he kissed her everywhere—her hair and her ears and down to her neck, breathing in her scent. He kissed down to her waist and then further, to where he wanted to be. He had been too rough, for she was hot and swollen, but Meg lay there and felt his soft kiss and was lost to it.

When he couldn't hold on any more he reached for the condom that was a requirement in here. Her hands reached for it too, and he let her put it on, but before she did she kissed him there, and he closed his eyes as she did so. Two hours could never be enough for all they wanted to do. She slid it on. He should roll her over and take her, but he let her climb on top of him, because if he looked up to her hair and her body for a little while he could forget where he was.

And she looked down as she moved on him and knew exactly why she was here. She loved him. Still. Her real fear at coming here had nothing to do with the flight or the prison or the danger, it was *him*—because she'd known all along that this was the only way she would ever be over him.

She should be grilling him about his involvement in the charges, insisting she find out, or just lying on her back martyred as he took her, ready to get the hell out once he'd finished. Instead she'd told him she cared about him. Instead she was riding him, and his hands were busy elsewhere, roaming her body. He was watching her. She was moaning, and he told her to hush, for he would not give the guards the turn-on of the sounds that she made. He put his hand over her mouth and she licked it, bit it, and he pushed his fingers into her mouth.

He was coming, and so was she, and when the moment finally came she folded on top of him, buried his face with her hair, and he felt the silent scream inside her as she clutched him tightly over and over till it ended.

That was when she told him she loved him.

'You don't know me,' he said.

'I want to, though.'

'Divorce me,' he said, still inside her, and pulled her close. 'Send the papers to Rosa and I'll sign them.'

'I don't want to.'

'You do.'

She didn't.

'I can see you again in three weeks…' She was drunk on him. 'I can come to the trial.'

'You are to *leave*!'

'I can ring you on Wednesday each week…'

He was scared now as to what he'd unleashed. Scared not of her passion, but that she might stay.

'No.'

'I can. I'm allowed one phone call a week.'

He looked up at her and all he knew was that she was not coming back here. With his own lawyer working against him he was probably done. Here was where he would always be and he would not do this to her. Even with new lawyers, trials took for ever in Brazil. Even with the best legal team he would be here for years at best. He lifted her off him and swore in three languages when he saw the condom was shredded. 'Get the morning-after pill and when I speak with my new lawyers I will have them file for divorce…'

'No…'

'You are to go to Hawaii.'

'Niklas—'

The guards were knocking at the door. Their time was up. He stood and threw her clothes at her, telling her to dress quickly for he did not want them getting one single glimpse of her. She continued to argue with him as he picked up her bra and clipped it on her, before lifting each leg into her panties, followed by her dress, and even as he zipped it up still she argued.

'We're finished,' he told her.

And he wasted time telling her that they *had* to be over when he should have told her how dangerous this was, just how little he knew about what was going on, and that he was scared for her life. But the guards were here now and he could not say.

He gave her a brief kiss, his eyes urging her. 'Have a safe flight.'

CHAPTER NINE

SHE DIDN'T WANT to lie on a beach in Hawaii.

There could be no healing from him.

She wanted to be close to him, wanted to be there for his trial hearing at least. She hoped for a miracle.

He would not want her there. Meg knew that.

But he was her husband, and she could at least be here in the city for him. Could watch it on the news, could be close even if he didn't know it.

And then she could visit him again before she left. She did not want a divorce from him now, and she wanted one more visit to argue her case.

She was probably going insane, Meg realised as she cancelled Hawaii and stayed on in Brazil, but that was how he made her feel.

She ventured out onto the busy streets and toured the amazing city. The sights, the smells, the food, the noise—there was everything to meet her moods.

And without Niklas she might never have seen any of this—might never have visited the Pinacoteca, a stunning art museum, nor seen the sculptured garden beside it.

At first Meg did guided tours with lots of other tourists around her, but gradually she tuned in to the energy of the place, to the smiles and the thumbs-up from the locals and ventured out more alone. She was glad to be here—glad for everything she got to see, to hear, to feel. Every little thing. She could have lived her whole life and never tasted *pamonah*, and there were vendors selling them everywhere—from the streets, from cars, ringing triangles to alert they were here. The first time Meg had bought one and had sunk her teeth into the new taste of mashed and boiled corn she had been unable to finish it. But the next day she had been back, drawn by the strange sweet taste—inadvertently she'd bought savoury, and found that was the one she liked best.

There were so many things to learn.

So badly she wanted to visit the mountains, to take a trip to the rainforests Niklas had told her about, yet it felt too painful to visit the mountains without him.

She didn't dare ring him that first week. Instead when six p.m. on Wednesday neared she sat in a restaurant the concierge had told her was famed for its seafood and ordered *feijoada*. Maybe it wasn't the same restaurant Niklas had told her about, but she felt as if angels were feeding her soul and that she was right to be there.

As the days passed she fell more and more in love with the city—the contrasts of it, the feel of it and the sound of it. The people were the most beautiful and elegant she had seen, yet the poverty was confrontational. It was a world that changed at every turn and she loved the anonymity of being somewhere so huge, loved being lost in it, and for two weeks she was.

As instructed, she did not contact Rosa. The only people she spoke to were her parents, and she gave Niklas no indication that she was there until the night before his trial date.

His face was on the TV screen, a reporter was already outside the court, and Meg had worked out that *amanhã* meant tomorrow. Until *amanhã* she simply could not wait. She just had to hear his voice. She had fallen in love with a man who was in prison and she should be signing paperwork, should be happily divorced, should be grateful for the chance to resume her life—but instead she sat in her hotel room, staring at the phone...

Confused was all she was without him. The passion and love she felt for him only made real sense when he was near her and she had an overwhelming desire to talk to him. She counted down the moments until she could make that call.

He knew that she would call.

Niklas could feel it.

Andros came and got him from his cell and he sat by the phone at the allotted time. The need for her to be safe overrode any desire to hear her voice.

His teeth gritted when he heard the phone ring, and he wondered if he should let it remain unanswered, but he needed her to get the message—to get out of his life and leave him the hell alone.

And then he heard her voice and realised just how much he craved it, closed his eyes in unexpected relief just to hear the sound of her.

'I told you not to ring.'

'I just wanted to wish you good luck for tomorrow.'

'It is just to arrange a trial date…' He did not trust the phones. He did not trust himself. For now he wanted her to visit him again. He wanted her living in a house in the mountains right behind the prison and wanted her to ring him every Wednesday, to come in to see him every three weeks. What scared him the most was that she might do it. 'You did not need to ring for that. It will all be over in ten minutes.'

She understood the need to be careful. 'Even so, I hope they give you a date soon.'

'What are you doing now?'

'Talking to you.'

'Is everything okay?'

She knew what he was referring to—had seen his face when he'd removed the condom.

'It's fine.'

'Did you go to a *pharmacia*?'

He closed his eyes when she didn't answer, thought again of her in a home in the mountains, but this time he pictured her with his baby at her side and selfish hope glimmered.

'How's Hawaii?'

He heard her pause, heard that her voice was a little too high as she answered him. 'You know…' She attempted. 'Nice.'

'I *don't* know,' Niklas said, and it was not about what he wanted, it was not about him, it was about keeping her safe. His words were harsh now. 'I've never been and I want a postcard,' he said. 'I want you, *tonight*, to write me a postcard from Hawaii.'

He was telling her what to do and she knew it.

'Niklas,' she attempted, 'I still have some holidays left. I thought maybe next week…'

'You want to be paid again?'

'Niklas, please—' She hated that he'd mentioned money. 'I just want to see you.'

'You've already earned your keep…go spend your money on holiday.'

'Niklas…I know you don't mean that.'

'*What* do you know?' His voice was black. 'We were married for one day; we screwed an awful lot. You know nothing about me.'

'I know that you care. I know when you saw me—'

'Care?' he sneered down the phone. 'The only way I can get sex in here is if they bring in my wife—that's it. I am sick of conversations, and you seem to want just as many of those as you give of the other.'

'Niklas, please…'

But he would not let her speak. He had to get her away from here. Did she not get that she could be in danger? He had no idea what was happening on the outside, had no idea what was going on, and he wanted her safely away—had to make sure she was safe.

So again he drowned her with words.

'Meg, if you want to come back and suck me, then do. But just so long as you know you mean nothing to me.'

He slammed down the phone—not in fury but in fear. He put his hands through the door and felt the cool of the cuffs. His mind was racing. Since her visit, since getting the information that Miguel was working against him, his mind had been spinning, trying to work out what the hell was going on, trying to figure things out. But now he had a head full of *her*, and he had more to be concerned with than that she was still here in Brazil.

He needed to speak with Rosa—had to work out what the hell was going on.

As he was walked back to his cell his face was expressionless, but his mind was pounding like a jackhammer and he cursed under his breath in Portuguese as Andros made some reference to his wife, about his nice little family, and asked how scum from the streets had managed that. Then Andros pushed him up the stairs and Niklas cursed again, but in French this time.

'Watch it, Dos Santos…' Andros told him, sensing his prisoner's rising anger and slamming him up against the wall.

The move was not meant to overpower him, Niklas realised, simply to provoke him, because Dos Santos was an orphan's name. Niklas went to swear again, in Spanish, but his brain was working quickly, far more quickly than his mouth, and in that second he knew what was happening.

Dos Santos meant something different in Spanish.

And it was a Spanish nun who had named him.

Dos Santos in Spanish meant two saints.

He had a twin.

In that very second it was as if a bomb had exploded in his brain and he worked it all out. He knew instantly how he had got to be here. Knew that his double was out there and had been working with Miguel against him. And with a lurch of fear that was violent to his soul he knew that Meg was in serious danger.

Niklas said nothing when Andros jeered again, just stood silent against the wall as Andros spoke filth about his wife. He stood still and refused to react as another guard came over. A decent guard this time, because there were plenty of them around.

'Trouble?' the guard asked.

'No trouble,' Niklas said, because he did not want to go to solitary tonight. He really needed to get to his cell.

He stood compliant as his cuffs were removed and went quietly into his cell. There he met the eyes of Fernando, and for the first time since his arrival he spoke with the other man.

'I need your help,' Niklas said, for he had worked out what was happening and urgent help was required. 'I need you to make contact on the outside.'

CHAPTER TEN

ANOTHER NIGHT CRYING over Niklas Dos Santos and Meg swore it would be the last.

Part of her could almost convince herself that he was just trying to get her to leave, that that was the reason behind his cruel words, but the more sensible part of Meg soon talked herself round. Her sensible side reminded her that this was a man she knew nothing about—a man who had caused her nothing but heartache and trouble since the day that they had met.

Hawaii sounded pretty good to Meg right now.

A week lying on the beach concentrating on nothing but how best to forget him.

It was well after lunchtime now, and Meg was *still* waiting for the travel agent to return her call. When she did, Meg would ask to be booked onto the earliest flight that could be arranged, and she packed her suitcase in preparation. Very deliberately she did not turn on the vast television to see how his trial was going, or to catch a glimpse of him on the news, because one glimpse of Niklas and she was lost to him—that much she knew.

She wanted her divorce now, wanted to be the hell away from him, would not waste even one more single minute on him.

But as she packed up her toiletries Meg threw tampons into her make-up bag and suddenly realised that it might be rather more complicated than that.

She looked at the unopened packet, an Australian brand because she hadn't bought any since she had arrived here, and tried to remember when she'd last had a period.

She tried to remember the days in Australia before her life had been changed so dramatically by the visit from Niklas's lawyers. No, she hadn't had her period for a while.

There should be the reassurance that they'd used condoms, but the last one hadn't held.

Could she be pregnant?

Would she tell him if she was?

Meg looked in the mirror and decided that, no, she could not deny him that. Even if his life was to be spent on the inside, he would have to know the truth, and it wasn't the kind of news she could reveal in a letter— maybe she would have to visit him again.

Maybe not.

A letter was probably more than he deserved.

But first she had to know for sure.

She was probably overreacting, Meg told herself as she headed out of her hotel room and to the elevators. Worrying too much, she tried to convince herself as she headed onto the street. With all that she'd been through these past weeks it was no wonder that her period was late.

The streets were busy, as always—the cars jammed together, horns blaring, and sirens blazing as police tried to thread their way through the impossible madness that was downtown São Paulo. She found a *pharmacia* and inside it was the same as the world over, with numerous pregnancy testing kits sitting on the shelves. Meg didn't need to speak the language to know she was making the right purchase.

What was different from Australia, though, was that instead of being pounced on by an assistant the second she entered the store, here Meg was pretty much ignored. Even when she tried to pay the pharmacist and his checkout assistants were all taking an impromptu break and watching the television, and Meg could feel mounting impatience. She really had to know now if she was pregnant. Had to make the decision of facing Niklas and telling him while she was still here.

Finally someone came over to serve her, still talking to her colleagues, and Meg froze when she heard one of them shout the name Dos Santos. She felt sweat bead on her forehead as she paid, because despite herself—despite all this—she wanted to turn the television on, wanted to know how he was.

She almost ran back to the hotel, terrified of her feelings for him, that even a mention of his name could reduce her to this petrified state.

It was blissfully cool and quiet in her room—such a contrast to the chaos down below. She fought not to turn on the television, picked up the remote and hurled it, tried not to look where it landed. The light on the phone said she had a new message. She hoped it was the travel agent and played it back, but heard her mum's voice instead. Meg honestly didn't know how she could ever begin tell her parents all that had happened. She had always hoped she would never have to, but if this test proved positive...

She could feel the tears starting again but refused to give in to them—just bit them back and headed to the bathroom, put her purchase in its bag on the bench, ready to find out. Then there was a knock on the door and Meg assumed it was the cleaner. She didn't want her coming in now. She wanted privacy for this at least.

So she went to tell them. She didn't even look through the peephole, just opened the door, and what was left of the sensible part of her mind struggled to remain calm because standing at her door was Niklas. She froze for a moment, unable to respond to seeing him in such an ordinary setting. She wanted to sob at him, to rage at him, to ask him how on earth he was here—except she just stood there.

'It's okay...' He stepped in. 'I know it must be a shock to see me here.'

'I don't understand...'

'The judge understood,' he said. 'Didn't you see it all on the news?'

'I haven't been watching it.'

'That is good.' He gave her a smile. 'I get to tell you the good news myself.'

'I don't want to hear it.' She was so very angry with him, and now finally she could tell him. 'I haven't been watching it because I'm sick of this, Niklas. I'm sick of how you make me feel at times. I can't do this any more.'

'You're upset.'

'Do you blame me?' She looked at him. She could smell his cologne—the same cologne he had worn the day they had met. He was dressed in a stunning suit now, just as beautiful as the day they had met, just as cruel as the day he had ended things between them, but she wanted to know. 'You've been let off?'

'I've been bailed while they take some time to review new evidence.'

'Well, after the way you spoke to me last night I need some time for a review too,' Meg answered. She refused just to go back to loving him. He had hurt her too much. And she could not find out if she was pregnant while he was near. She needed to do that part alone.

'Come here...' He moved to pull her into his arms.

'Just leave.' It took everything she had to shake her head. 'Just go, Niklas. I'm doing as you told me. I'm going to Hawaii...'

'You're upset.'

'Why do you keep saying that? Of *course* I'm upset!' she flared. 'Did you think I wouldn't be? How the hell do you justify speaking to me like that?'

'Meg...'

He walked over and she did *not* want him to take her in his arms, did not want him to melt her all over again.

'I say stupid things at times. You know that…'

'Stupid things?' There were so many other ways she could describe his words. 'It was more than stupid, it was foul…' She would not be fobbed off. 'Why?' she demanded. 'Why did you speak to me like that?'

'I've said I'm sorry.'

'No, you haven't, and you're clearly not as sorry as I was to hear it.' She went to open the door, to tell him to get out of here, but he stopped her and wrapped his arms around her shoulders. Meg just stood there, tears rising, remembering the love they had made and all the ways he made her feel. But she could not go back there. 'Get out!' She pushed him off her. 'I mean it, Niklas…'

'Meg…' His mouth was on her cheek and she pulled her head away. His hands were in her hair but she brushed them off.

'Please,' she said, 'can you just leave me? I'll call you later. I'll—'

His phone rang then, and it annoyed her that he took the call. Yes, of course he was busy, she knew that, and maybe she should be flattered that he had come straight to her, but it annoyed her that in the middle of a row he could just stop and take a call. It made her even more angry, and she was tired of making excuses for him. She wanted him gone and she told him so when he ended his call.

'You are cross…' He smiled at her. 'You look beautiful when you are cross…'

He aimed his phone at her and she blinked at the flash. 'What the hell are you doing?'

'I've missed things like this. I want to capture everything…'

'I just you want you to leave.'

But he simply refused to listen. 'Let's go for a walk.'

'A walk?'

The last thing she wanted was a walk. She wanted him to leave. She looked at his lips and not even his beautiful mouth could silence her doubts now. She just wanted him gone.

'A walk to clear the air…' Niklas said.

'No.' She shook her head. 'I'm waiting for the travel agent to ring me back.'

'She'll call back if you're not here.' He shrugged. 'Come,' he said. 'I want to taste the fresh air. I want to feel the rain…'

She looked out of the window. Yes, it was raining, and she realised that he wouldn't have felt the rain in a long time. She was relieved that he wasn't all over her, trying to kiss her back to confusion as he so often did, but she didn't feel she knew him at all.

'Meg, after all we have been through will you at least come for a walk with me?'

'You hurt me last night.'

'I apologise.' His black eyes met hers. 'Meg, I truly apologise. We can start again, without all this hanging over us…'

But she was stronger than she'd thought she could be.

She looked into his eyes and quite simply no longer wanted him—didn't want to get back on the rollercoaster ride beside him. It was then that she made a decision that was surprisingly easy; she looked at the man who had broken her heart and knew that he would break it all over again. She simply refused to let him.

It was over.

Whatever the pregnancy test told her, Meg knew it was far better that she find out well away from him. She would fly to Hawaii today, search for the clarity he so easily clouded and make better decisions alone.

'Come…' he said. 'I want to taste my freedom.'

Maybe it would be easier to tell him that they were finished while they were walking. Maybe it would prove easier out there. Because she knew his kisses made her weak. So she nodded and she went to get her jacket, to comb her hair.

'Don't worry about that…' he said. 'Your hair is fine…'

Niklas was right. Her hair really didn't matter right now—it was her heart Meg had to worry about. They rode down in the lift together and Meg looked at him more closely. She hated her swollen eyes. Even more she hated that she had let him cause them.

They headed out through the foyer and into the street and she felt the warm rain that was so regular here. His hand reached for her, but she pulled hers back, refusing to give this man any more chances. He'd already used his last one with his filthy words to her the previous night and now his pathetic attempt at an apology.

'I'm ending it, Niklas.' He kept on walking. 'I'm going to file for divorce.'

'We'll go to a bar and talk about it.'

'There's nothing to discuss.' Meg stopped—which wasn't the most sensible thing to do on such a busy street.

There were moans from a few pedestrians and he took her hand and they kept walking. She really was sure that she was making the right choice, because she did not know him, and he did not know her, and a walk would not clear the air. Only his kiss could possibly have given them a chance, because sex was the only thing they had going for them. Maybe she was mad for thinking it, but shouldn't that be the way a man celebrated his freedom? If he loved her, if he wanted her, wouldn't the first thing he wanted be taking her to bed, not out for a walk?

'There's a bar up here that I know,' Niklas said. 'It's not far—just a couple of blocks away…'

'I don't want to go to a bar…'

'The street is too noisy. Come on, we can talk properly there.'

'I don't want to talk.'

Meg was starting to panic now, and she didn't really know why. His hand was too tight on her wrist, and he was walking her faster, and she had the most appalling thought then that he hadn't been bailed at all. There was an urgency in the steps he was taking. She looked over to him and his head was down, and it dawned on Meg that maybe he had escaped from jail. She recalled the screams of the police cars and bikes. They were screaming in the streets even louder now. She remembered too the pharmacy staff all huddled around the television, saying his name. Maybe it was because Niklas Dos Santos had escaped. Still he walked her ever faster.

'Niklas…'

She could hear the thud of music as they turned into a side street, could hear the clang of triangles and the smell of *pamonah*. There were so many people around; surely she was safe. She pulled her hand from his and stopped walking, but he turned and put a hand to her cheek. She shivered, but not with pleasure. There was something dark and menacing in his eyes. She was a fool to have got involved with this man, a fool to follow her heart, for look where it had led her—to a dingy side street in Brazil with a man she was now terrified of.

'Come,' he said. 'We will talk about where our relationship is going later. Right now I want to celebrate my freedom and I want you to celebrate it with me.' His hand was tight on her arm. 'You wouldn't deny me that?'

'I do,' she said. 'And I want you to let me go.'

'Don't spoil this day for me, Meg—it's been a hell of a long year for both of us. Now we can drink *cachaca*, unwind, dance. Later we can talk, but first…'

He lowered his head to kiss her, but it was too late for that and she moved her head back from his, suddenly confused. Because Niklas didn't dance. It was one of the few things that she *did* know about him—or had that been just another of his lies? Suddenly she was scared, and with real reason now.

Meg turned to go but he pulled her roughly back and

pushed her against the wall. Then he opened his jacket and she saw that he had a gun.

'Try to run and it will be the last thing you do…'

'Niklas…' she begged, and when Meg heard her own voice she heard the way she sounded when she pleaded for her life. She was trying to show him that she wasn't panicked, trying to reason with a man she absolutely didn't know, trying to get away. 'Why do you need me?' she said. 'If you've escaped…'

People were turning to look at them, maybe alerted by the panic in her voice even though she wasn't screaming. Or perhaps it was that if he had just escaped then his picture would be everywhere, being flashed over the news. Perhaps that was why he lowered his face to her.

'Why do you need me with you?'

'Because you're my last chance.'

And his mouth came down on hers.

She could hear a car pulling up beside them and Meg knew this was *her* last chance to get away. She knew instinctively that when the car doors opened she would be shoved in, that that was why he had taken the call—to arrange all this. Terrified, Meg did the only thing she could think of to survive. She bit hard on his lip with all she had—took that beautiful mouth and bit it as hard as she could. In the second when he recoiled, as he cursed her in Portuguese and reached for his gun, Meg ran—ran as she never had—ran and ran faster as she heard gunshots.

She kept running till rough arms grabbed her and pulled her down, slamming her to the ground. She felt her cheek hit the pavement and the skin leave her leg as she rose to run again, heard another volley of gunshots and looked behind her. She saw police cars screeching up. Whoever had shielded her from him had gone. Then she stared at the body on the ground and it was the only thing she could see.

'Niklas!' she screamed, and tried to run back to him, for she hated the man but it was agony to see him lying dead and riddled with bullets.

She could not stop screaming. Not even when other arms wrapped around her and her face was buried in rough prison denim and she smelt him again—not his cologne, but the scent of Niklas, her drug of choice, a scent that till now had been missing. She heard him saying over and over that she was safe, that he was here, that now it would all be okay, but she still did not believe it was him—until he lifted her face and she met his eyes, saw that the beautiful mouth had not been bitten and knew that somehow it was him.

That she was safe.

It was just her heart that was in danger again.

CHAPTER ELEVEN

MEG DID NOT get to see him again. Instead she was taken to a police station. There were press clamouring outside as she was taken in to give a statement, and while she was waiting for a translator Rosa arrived.

Meg gave her statement as best she could. They kept talking about twins, and although she had already worked that out when she was being held in Niklas's arms, her brain was so scrambled and confused that even with a translator she could hardly understand the questions, let alone answer them.

Every time she closed her eyes she saw Niklas—or rather the man she had thought was Niklas—lying there dead. The raw grief and panic, the *knowing* in that moment that she would never see him again, that the man she had fallen so heavily in love with was now dead, was not a memory or a feeling she could simply erase.

Fortunately Rosa had told the police she would return with Meg tomorrow, but that for now she needed peace, and thankfully they accepted that.

'We will return at ten tomorrow,' Rosa told her.

They stepped out into the foyer and she saw him standing there, still dressed in prison denim. He took her in his arms and she knew then that she had to be careful, because the one thing she had worked out before this embrace was that she wasn't strong around him—that she'd only been able to break up with Niklas when it hadn't actually been him.

'I'm still angry with you.'

'I thought you might be.' He kissed her bruised cheek and didn't let her go as he spoke. 'We can row in bed.'

Which sounded a lot more like the Niklas she knew. He held her tight and pressed his face into her hair and she could feel his ragged breathing. For a moment she thought he was crying, but he just held her a moment longer and spoke into her hair.

'The press are outside so we have to go out the back. I am taking you far away from here. I need to stay in the city, but—'

'*Não,*' Rosa said.

Meg heard the word *amanhã* again, and realised Rosa was telling him that Meg must return to the police tomorrow.

'I'll ring Carla, then.'

With his arm still around Meg he took Rosa's phone and started to dial the number. Whilst he was occupied Meg stepped out of his embrace, and a little later, when they climbed into a waiting car, she sat on the back seat far away from him, needing some time alone.

Even though they went out the back way the press still got some photos and it was horrible. They scrambled over to the car and blocked their exit, but the driver shook them off. Niklas told her it might be like this for a while, and that he was taking her to a hotel. He saw the start in her eyes.

'We're not going back *there*—I've asked Carla to book us into a different one.'

Us.

So easily he assumed.

They entered the new hotel the back way too, and were ushered straight to a waiting lift where Niklas pressed a high number. They stood in silence till Meg broke it.

'Did you get off?'

'I've been released on bail.'

'So why are you still wearing...?' And then she shook her head, because she was simply too tired for explanations right now.

They stepped out of the lift and there was hotel security in the corridor—'For the press,' Niklas said, but it felt a lot like prison to her, and no doubt to him too, but he said nothing, just swiped open a door, leading her into a plush suite.

Meg stood there for a moment, only knowing for certain the city she was in and that Niklas was alive. She remembered her feeling at seeing him dead, and the fear that had gripped her in the moments before, and started shaking.

'I wanted to take you away from the city tonight, but because we need to go back to the police station tomorrow it is better that we stay here. I've had your stuff packed up, but it is in the other place…you'll have to make do for now…'

It was hardly 'make do'; there was food and soon she would take a bath, and then she sat and had a strong coffee. Niklas offered her *cachaca*—the same drink she had been offered a little while ago—and she shuddered as she remembered. He opened the fridge and opened a bottle of champagne instead.

Which seemed a strange choice and was a drink she hadn't had it in almost a year.

Not since their wedding.

It was the drink they had shared on the day they had met, and he poured her a glass now, kissing her forehead as they chinked glasses and celebrated that somehow they were both here. It was a muted celebration, and there was still so much to be said, but Niklas dealt with the essentials first.

'You need to ring your parents.'

'I don't know what to say to them,' Meg admitted. She felt like crying just at the thought of them, was dreading the conversation that had to be had—and how much worse it was going to be now, after not telling them anything.

'Tell them the truth,' Niklas said. 'A bit diluted.' He nudged her. 'You need to speak to them now in case they hear anything on the news, or the consulate might contact them. Have they tried to ring *you*?'

'I didn't even bring my phone with me,' Meg said.

'It will be at the other hotel,' Niklas said. 'For now

they just need to know you are safe. I will speak to them if it gets too much.'

'No.' She shook her head—not at phoning them, but at the thought of him talking to them. She knew how badly things were going to go. 'I'll do it…'

'Now.'

'I still don't really know what happened.' But she took the phone, because he was right. They needed to know she was safe. 'Leave me,' she said, and was glad that he didn't argue.

Niklas headed into the bedroom and she dialled the number, then looked out of the window to a very beautiful, but very complicated city. She held her breath when she heard the very normal sound of her mum.

'How's Brazil?' Ruth asked. 'Or is it Hawaii this week?'

'Still Brazil,' Meg said, and because Ruth was her mum straight away she knew.

'What's wrong?'

It was the most difficult of conversations. First she had to tell her how Vegas had been and how she had married a man she had only just met. She diluted the story a lot, of course—an awful lot—but she still had to tell them how, the morning after their wedding, Niklas had upset her, how she had been trying to psyche herself up to divorce him.

And her mum kept interrupting her with questions that her father was shouting—questions that weren't really relevant because they still didn't know half of the story. So she told them she was here to visit him, that he had been arrested a while ago, but was innocent of all charges. Her mother was shouting and sobbing now, and her dad was demanding the phone, and they were simply getting nowhere, and then Niklas was back and she was so glad to hand the phone over to him.

She found out for certain then just how brilliant he was, how clever he was with people, for somehow he calmed her father down.

'My intention when I married your daughter was to take proper care of her. I was on my way to tell you the same when I found out that I was being investigated.'

He said a few more things, and she could hear the shouts receding as he calmly spoke his truth.

'I was deliberately nasty to her in the hope she would divorce me—of course she was confused, of course she was ashamed and did not feel that she could tell you. I wanted to keep her away from the trouble that was coming—in that I failed, and I apologise.'

They didn't need to know all the details, but he told them some pertinent ones, because as soon as they hung up they would be racing to find out the news for themselves. So he told them about the shooting, but he was brief and matter-of-fact and reiterated that Meg was safe. He told them that they could ring any time with more questions, no matter the time of day or night, and that he would do his best to answer them. Then he handed the phone back to Meg.

'You're safe,' her mum said.

'I am.'

'We need to talk…'

'We will.'

When she hung up the phone she looked at him. 'You could have told me the truth that day.' She was angry that he hadn't.

'What? Walk back in and tell you that I am being investigated for fraud and embezzlement? That the man you met twenty-four hours ago is facing thirty-five years to life in jail…?' He looked at her. 'What would you have said?'

'I might have suggested you didn't go back till you found out the case against you…' she flared. 'I might not be the best one in the world, but I *am* a lawyer…'

'My own lawyer was telling me to get straight back.' He kicked himself then, because had he confided in her—had he been able to tell her—he might not have raced back, might have found out some more information before taking a first-class flight to hell.

'I had to return to face it,' Niklas said. 'Would you have stood by me?'

'You never gave me that chance.'

'Because that was what I was most afraid of.' He was kneeling beside her and she could hear him breathing. 'You never asked if I did it.'

'No.'

'Even when you visited…even when you rang…'

'No, I didn't.'

'Did you believe I was innocent?'

'I hoped that you were.'

'There was too much love for common sense,' Niklas said.

She sat there for ages and was glad when he left her alone and headed to the bathroom. She heard his sigh of relief as he slipped into the bath water and thought about his words—because while she had hoped he was innocent, it hadn't changed her feelings towards him and that scared her. After a little while she wandered in to him.

'I am so sorry.' He looked at her. 'For everything I have put you and your family through.'

'It wasn't your fault.'

'No,' he said. 'But still, I have scared you, and nearly cost you your life…'

And then he looked at her and asked the question the police had asked her earlier.

'Did he do anything to you?'

'Apart from hold a gun at me…' she knew what he meant '…no.'

She watched him close his eyes in relief and knew then that he *had* cried.

'He wanted to walk,' Meg said. 'That was when I started to worry.' She gave him a pale smile. 'Not quite the Niklas I know.' And then there wasn't a pale smile. 'I'm still cross about what you said on the phone.'

'I wanted you to leave,' he said. 'I wanted you to be so angry, so upset, that you got on the next plane you could…'

'I nearly did.'

'Do you want me tell you what happened?'

She wanted to hear it now, and he held his hand out to her. Yes, he assumed she would join him—and for now he was right. Her clothes and her body were filthy, and she wanted to feel clean again, to hear what had happened, and she wanted to hear it as she lay beside him. So she took off her clothes and slid into the water, with her back to his chest, resting on him, and he held her close and washed all her bruises and slowly he told her.

'There was bedlam in court,' Niklas said as he washed her gently. 'The place erupted when I asked for a new lawyer, and then Rosa presented the evidence implicating Miguel. He was arrested immediately, but of course I had to go back to prison...I knew they were never going to release me just like that. I told them that you were in danger, but they would not listen, and then, as they were taking me back, *he* made contact with Carla, asking for money. He said that he had my wife and texted a photo. The police only believed me then that I had a twin.'

She frowned and looked up to him. 'You *knew* you had a twin?'

'I guessed that I did last night, after I spoke to you.'

'How?'

'It made sense. I knew I was innocent.'

'But how did you work it out?'

'I swear in several languages...' She smiled, because that *was* what he did. 'I was angry after speaking to you—worried that you would not leave—and I swore in Portuguese. The guard warned me to be careful, he called me Dos Santos and I heard the derision in his voice, in his tone. I thought he was referring to me having no one, and I swore again, and then he said something about you. I went to curse again, but in Spanish…'

He was soaping her arms and his mouth was at her neck—not kissing, just breathing.

'The first nun who looked after me, till I was three, she taught me Spanish…'

Still Meg frowned.

'Dos Santos means something different in Spanish,' Niklas explained. 'In Portuguese it means "from the saints", in Spanish it means…'

'Two.' She turned and looked to him. '"Two saints".'

'There were two of us… That is why the Spanish nun chose our surname. It made sense. Apparently in the month before I was arrested I was having meals and meetings with very powerful people, persuading them to invest….'

'My God!'

'He and Miguel were rorting every contact I have made. A couple of months before it happened I thought I had lost my phone, but of course they had it and were diverting numbers. Both of them knew that they didn't have long before I found out, or the banks or the police did, so they were busy getting a lot of money based on my reputation. My lawyer had every reason to want me to be convicted and spend life in jail—every reason not to tell me about the evidence that would convict me. Because as soon as I saw it, I would know the truth. It was not me.'

She felt him breathe in deeply.

'I can see how people were fooled. When I saw him

lying there I felt as if I was looking at me.' He elaborated on his feelings no more than that, and told her the little he knew. 'His name was Emilios Dos Santos. The police said he had lived on the streets all his life but had no criminal record—just a few warnings for begging. I guess he was tired of having nothing. When he found out Miguel had been arrested he must have seen you as his last chance to get money from me…'

'How did he know I was here? How did he know what hotel…?'

'The prison guards, maybe.' He shrugged. 'Miguel would have been paying someone to keep an eye on me. You would have had to give your address for the prison visitors' list.'

She knew then how dangerous it had been not to listen to him, not to leave when he had told her to.

'I should have gone to Hawaii.'

'Yes,' he said, 'you should have.' But then he thought for a moment. Because without her here, without his fear that she was in danger, he might not have worked things out.

'It doesn't matter anyway,' Meg said. 'It's over now.' He didn't answer, and she turned and saw the exhaustion and agony still in his face. She could have kicked herself, for at the end of the day he had lost his twin, and Meg knew that despite all that had happened it had to hurt.

'Maybe he did want to talk to you when he found out he had a twin—perhaps Miguel dissuaded him, saw the chance to make some serious money and told him it was the only way.'

'I don't want to speak about that.'

So quickly he locked her out.

And then the phone rang—trust the hotel bathroom to have one.

Niklas answered it.

'It's your father.' He handed it to Meg, and she spoke with her parents. Neither shouted this time, just asked more questions—and, more than that, they told her how much they loved her, and how badly they wanted her to come home as quickly as possible.

She was glad she was facing away from him, but glad to be leaning on him as they spoke and he held her. Later her father asked to speak with him, and he held out his wet hand for the phone and listened to what her father was saying.

'We have to give some more statements to the police, so Meg needs to be here for a few more days,' he said, 'but I will take her somewhere quiet.' He listened for a moment and then spoke again. 'She's tired now, but I will see what she wants to do in the morning, once she has spoken to the police.'

And then he said goodbye, and she frowned because they almost sounded a little bit friendly.

'He's coming around to me.'

It was, as Meg knew only too well, terribly easy to do so.

'They want you home, Meg.'

'I know that, but I want to be here with you.'

'Well, they need to see you,' Niklas said. 'They need to see for themselves that you are not hurt.'

'I know that…' She wanted him to say he'd come with her, wanted him to say he would never let her go, but he didn't. She wanted more from him, wanted to be fully in his life, but still he would not let her in.

She turned her head and looked at him—looked at this man who'd told her from the start that they'd never last.

'This doesn't change things, does it?'

He didn't answer.

She surprised herself by not crying.

'You'll never find another love like this.' She meant it—and not in an arrogant way—because even if he didn't accept it, even if he refused to believe it, whether he wanted it or not, this really *was* love.

'I told you on the first day that it would not be for ever.'

'We didn't love each other as much then.'

'I have never said that I love you.'

'You did earlier.'

'I said there was too much love for common sense,' Niklas said. 'Too much love for you to think straight…'

'I don't believe you.'

'Believe in fairytales if you want to.' He said it much more nicely than last time, but the message was the same. 'Meg, I told you I could never settle in one place, that I could not commit to one person for ever. I *told* you that.'

He had.

'And I told you that I don't do love.'

He had.

'You said you wanted this for as long as it lasted.'

His voice was the gentlest and kindest she had heard it.

'In a few days, once all the questioning is over, you need to go home to your family.'

And even if she'd promised herself not to cry she did a bit, and he caught her tear with his thumb before lowering his head and tasting it. She could hear the clock ticking, knew that every kiss they shared now might be their last, that soon it would be a kiss goodbye.

'It could last…' She pulled her head away and opened her mouth to argue, but he spoke over her.

'I don't want to wait for the rows and the disenchantment to kick in. I don't want to do that to us because what we have now is so good. But, no, it cannot last…'

Which was why she'd accept his kisses—which was why, tonight, she would shut out the fact that this was temporary. Because tonight maybe she just needed to escape, and maybe he did too.

And even if he wouldn't admit it, even if he chose not to share his feelings, Niklas felt as if he'd just stepped out of hell's inferno into heaven as his mouth met hers.

Her mouth was bruised, but very gently he kissed it. Her cheek was hurting and her legs were grazed where she'd fallen. She knew she could never keep him, that for now guilt and fear would drive his kisses, and that later this man she didn't really know would return to a life she had never really been in. This wasn't love they were making. It was *now*.

Over and over she told herself that.

She thought he'd make love to her in the water, but he took her wet to the bed and dried her with a towel, every inch of her, and then he kissed her bruises, up her legs, and he kissed her *there* till she was crying and moaning in frustration. His hand was over her mouth again, because there were still guards outside, but she wanted him—wanted all of him. Then he slipped inside her, and it was incredibly slow, a savour in each thrust, but the words she needed were not in her ears. She bit down as she came, and gave him her body while trying to claim back a heart this man didn't want but already had.

CHAPTER TWELVE

MEG WOKE IN the night, crying and scared, and Niklas held her tightly before he made love to her again.

And he would have had her again in the morning—was pulling her across the mattress when the phone rang to tell them that Rosa was on her way up.

'Later!' he said, and kissed her. 'Or just really, really quickly now?'

She looked into black eyes that smiled down at her and simply could not read him—couldn't be his sex toy any more.

'Later,' Meg said, and climbed out of bed.

She let Rosa in. She had brought fresh clothes for both of them. Surprisingly, she gave Meg a hug and told her that she would accompany them to the police station.

'I am very sorry for the way I spoke to you,' Rosa said.

'What way?' Niklas checked.

She looked at Niklas. 'I gave her a hard time.'

'You weren't the only one,' Meg said, and then went purple when Rosa laughed. God, was that the only place minds went in Brazil? 'What I meant,' she said in her best cross voice, 'was that I do understand why you said what you did.'

'I am grateful,' Niklas said to Rosa. 'To all three of you, but especially to you. I will repay you just as soon as I get my assets back.'

'Hopefully it won't be long now,' Rosa said, and then smiled as she scolded, 'But did you *have* to drink the most expensive champagne in the fridge? I just paid your room bill.'

'*You* paid?' Meg blinked. She wasn't talking about the champagne. 'That was your money?' Meg had assumed it came from Niklas's funds, but of course she now realised that while he was being investigated they would all be frozen.

'I put up my home,' Rosa said. 'I believed in him.'

'You're the richest one of us in the room,' Niklas said to Meg, and even Rosa laughed.

'I'll buy you all a coffee on the way to the station.' Meg smiled, but it was strained. She headed to the bathroom to get changed and thought about Rosa's belief in Niklas. It was clear to Meg that in the past Rosa and Niklas had slept together, but it wasn't that fact that riled her. It was the friendship they had that ate at her—a friendship that would not waver, one that would always last.

It was the longevity that riled her.

Meg opened the bag of fresh clothes and noticed that Rosa had chosen well for her. There was a skirt that was soft and long and would cover the grazes on her legs, a thin blouse and some gorgeous, albeit completely see-through, underwear. Meg inspected the underwear more closely and saw that there wasn't an awful lot of it, and when she pulled the knickers on she was silently mortified to realise that there was a hole in the middle—which was intentional. They were the most outrageous things she'd ever worn, but she could hardly complain to Rosa.

There were sandals too, because hers had broken yesterday.

She dressed and brushed her teeth, and combed her hair, and looked in the mirror and examined her solemn face. She should be happy and celebrating, except she couldn't quite rise to it. Memories of yesterday were still too raw, and she didn't understand how Niklas and Rosa could be smiling and chatting.

Didn't understand how Niklas could just turn his pain off.

But she had to learn how to, because soon she had to go home.

Had to.

She could not hang around and watch as his guilt for what he had put her through and the attraction he clearly had for her faded. She couldn't bear the thought of his boredom setting in as she waited for the news that she was to be dismissed from his life.

If Niklas didn't want for ever, then she couldn't carry on with it being just for now.

'Ready?' Niklas checked, looking over as she walked out of the bathroom.

'I guess so.' There was nothing to pack, after all.

'Do you want me to take your clothes and have them cleaned?' Rosa offered.

'I'll bin them.' Meg headed back to the bathroom to do so. 'I never want to see them again.'

'Okay.' Rosa hitched up her bag and headed off. 'I'll go and make sure the car is ready.'

When she'd left Meg picked up all the clothes from the wet bathroom floor and took them through to the bin in the lounge, but as she went to throw them in he stopped her.

'Not those.'

She looked at the denims he was retrieving and he turned and smiled.

'You might want me to shave my head again one day...'

She wasn't smiling back.

'It's all a game to you, isn't it?'

'No, Meg.' He shook his head, and he wasn't smiling now. 'It's not.'

But as they took the lift down she noted that he was holding a bag. He hadn't binned the denim clothes he'd worn in prison.

He pulled her into him and shielded her from the press as they left the hotel, did it again when they got to the police station, but she was actually shielding herself from him. He gave her a thorough kiss before she headed in to give her statement, but all it did was make her want to cry, because she wanted more than just sex from him.

'You'll be fine.' He wiped a tear with his thumb. 'Just tell them what happened. Rosa will be there…'

'I know.'

'It's nothing to be scared of,' he said. 'And then I'm going to get you right away from here—just us…' He smiled as he said it, gave her another kiss to reassure her.

She returned neither.

The statement was long and detailed, and she felt as if she were going over and over the same thing.

No, she had never met Miguel, and nor had Emilios mentioned him.

She didn't know who had called Emilios, but it had been after that call that he had suggested they go for a walk.

'They ask,' Rosa said, 'when did you realise it was not Niklas?'

'I never realised,' she said again.

'But you said you started to panic long before you saw the gun?'

She nodded, but Rosa told her she had to answer. 'Yes.'

They made her go over and over it, and she tried to explain things but it was so hard. It was hard to understand herself. She didn't want to say in the police station that she was surprised he hadn't taken her to bed, that perhaps that had been the biggest clue that it wasn't Niklas—which for Meg just rammed home how empty their relationship really was.

'So what made you panic?' Rosa checked again.

'I realised what a mistake I'd made marrying him,' Meg said, in a voice that was flat as she relived it. 'That there was no real basis for a relationship, that he'd always said it wouldn't last. All I wanted was to be away from him.'

'From Emilios?'

She shook her head. She remembered her swollen eyes and flinging things in a suitcase, the pleasure and pain of the last year, mainly the pain, and still, *still* he delivered it.

'From Niklas.' As she said it she saw Rosa's slight frown.

And then they took her further back, to her first meeting with Niklas on the plane and their late-night conversation.

'I asked how he'd been orphaned and he said he wasn't sure.'

'You asked if he had ever tried to look for his family?'

'Yes.'

'And what was his response?'

'He said that he had got Miguel, his lawyer, onto it, but he had got nowhere.'

'He said that?' the police officer checked via Rosa. 'He definitely said that?'

'Yes.'

The officer looked long and hard at her, and then Rosa asked if Meg was sure, as this was from a conversation a year ago. 'He asks if you are sure this is not the conversation you had with Niklas last night.'

Meg blinked.

'I told the police.'

'You remember this conversation exactly?' the officer checked, and she said yes, because she had been replaying every second of their time over and over for close to a year now.

'Exactly.' She nodded. 'And then I asked what it had been like, growing up in an orphanage, but he didn't respond,' Meg said. 'He told me he didn't want to speak about that sort of thing.'

But the police weren't interested in that part.

Only Meg was.

She went over and over everything again. She said that, no, she hadn't been aware she was being followed at the time, and looked to Rosa for explanation, but she gave a brief shake of her head. Then her statement was read back to her. She listened and heard that basically they had had an awful lot of sex and just a few conversations, but he had definitely mentioned that he had asked Miguel to look for his family. She signed her name to it.

'That is good,' Rosa said as they walked out. 'You have a good memory. They will jump on that part in court if Miguel denies that he was asked to find Niklas's family,' she warned. 'Just stay with that.'

'Am I free to fly home?' Meg asked. She saw the brief purse of Rosa's lips. 'My family's worried about me.'

'It might be better for Niklas's case if you were here.'

'What case?' Meg asked. 'It's clear he's innocent.'

'To you,' Rosa said. 'And it is to me. But dead men can't speak.' She gave a thin smile. 'I correct myself.

When I said that Niklas never makes mistakes, he has made one—he hired Miguel, and he is a brilliant lawyer. He might say it was both of them that were conning people. He might insist he believed it was Niklas giving him instructions, or that the directions came from both of them...'

'No!'

'Yes,' Rosa said. 'I will fight it, but it might look better for Niklas if his wife was here beside him—not back home, counting the money his legal team has placed in her account.'

'You know it isn't like that.'

'Tell the judge,' Rosa said, and she was back to being mean. 'I get that your family is worried about you, but if you can pretend for a little while longer that Niklas is a part of your family...'

'Niklas doesn't want me to,' Meg retorted. 'Niklas doesn't want a family...'

'He doesn't even know what one is!' Rosa shouted. 'Yet he has done everything right by you.'

'Everything *right* by me?' It was Meg who was shouting now. 'Are we talking about the same man?'

It wasn't the best choice of words, given the circumstances—especially as Niklas appeared then.

'My mother had triplets, maybe?' he quipped.

It was her poor choice of words, perhaps, but his response was just in bad taste. She did not understand how he could be so laid-back about it. How could he have his arm around her and be walking out of the police station as if the nightmare of the last year hadn't even happened?

It was the same circus of cameras as before, and then they left Rosa to give the press a statement. A car was waiting for them. It's driver handed the keys over to Niklas, who sat behind the wheel as Meg sat in the passenger seat. The moment she was seated Niklas accelerated away at speed—away from the crowds of press. After a while the car slowed, and the drive was a long one, taking them out of the city and through the hills. There was little conversation, just an angry silence from Meg, whereas with every mile the car ate up Niklas seemed more relaxed.

'You're quiet,' he commented.

'Isn't that what you want me to be?'

Sulking didn't work with Niklas. It didn't bother him a bit. He just carried on driving, one hand on the wheel, the other out of the window. Any minute now he'd start whistling, just to annoy her further. She was still bristling from Rosa's words. The first thing she would do when she got back to Sydney was send back all the money that she had been paid.

He looked over at her tense profile. 'We'll be there soon.'

She didn't answer him.

Nothing made sense: the policeman's questions had confused her, Rosa had angered her, and as for him... She turned and could not fathom how calm he was after all that had happened. He was fiddling with the sound system now, flicking through channels. She did not need background music, and her hand snapped it off.

'The police said I was being followed. That it wasn't the police who shot him…'

'It was a bodyguard.'

'Bodyguard?'

'Just leave it.'

'No,' Meg snapped. 'I will not.'

'He will not do any prison time. I have my lawyers working for him. I had a couple of people following you when I realised you were still here—when I guessed I had a twin. I did not know exactly what was happening, but I knew you would not be safe, so I arranged to have people protect you.'

'How?'

'I owe a favour to a very powerful man,' Niklas said. 'He got a message to the outside after you rang me.'

And then he stopped talking about it, and she felt his hand come to rest on her leg, and she could not understand how easily he dismissed the fact that it was a bodyguard *he* had arranged who had shot his twin.

Did nothing get to him?

He gave her thigh a squeeze, which she guessed meant they were nearly at their destination and would be off to look at another bedroom any time soon.

'We're here.'

It was the most stunning house she had ever seen, with dark wood, white furniture and screens on the windows so the sun and the sounds of the mountains could stream in. It was gorgeous and, Niklas said, the place he had dreamt of when he was on the inside.

'You like it?'

'It's gorgeous.'

'Look…'

He took her by the hand and led her to the bedroom, then walked and opened huge glass doors, revealing lush grass that rolled towards another mountain. The sound of birds was all that could be heard. In a place like this, Meg thought, you could start to heal.

'There are servants, but I have told them not to come till I call them. They've left us lots of food…'

And there were her things, hanging in the wardrobe, and there were his arms around her, and again he was holding her close.

She started crying and he didn't seem surprised at all.

'You're exhausted,' he said.

She was.

From nearly a year of loving him.

'Are you about to suggest we go to bed?'

'Meg…' He saw her anger and he didn't blame her. 'I don't care how cross you are. You deserve to be. If you want to shout, go ahead. I have put you through hell and I am just trying to make you feel better, to say the right thing. I'm probably getting it wrong, but for now you are here, and safe.'

It was the 'for now' part that was killing her, but she wasn't going to go there again. 'I don't know what's wrong,' she said. 'I'm so angry! I'm so confused…'

'It's shock,' he said. 'You were nearly kidnapped. You saw a man shot.'

'I saw your *twin* shot!' she shouted. 'I thought it was you.'

He did not react—he just held her.

'Shouldn't it be the other way round?' She pulled away from him, so angry. 'Shouldn't *you* be the one crying? He was your brother.'

'That's for me to deal with,' Niklas said.

'Can't you deal with it with me?'

'I prefer to do things like that alone.' He was nothing if not honest. 'I don't want to talk about me. Right now I want to be here for you.'

He said all the right things, but they were the wrong things too. He took all of her, but didn't give himself back, and maybe she had better just accept it. He felt nothing for anyone, and as she looked out to the mountains she hoped here she might find a little peace before she left him.

'I hope the press don't find us here.'

'Not a chance,' Niklas said. 'I told you that.'

'If they know that you own it they soon will.' She looked down the mountain and hoped there were no cars loaded with press following them up, because she was beyond tired now, could not face moving again. She just wanted a moment to gather her thoughts. 'They'll be going through all your assets...'

'I don't own it,' Niklas said. 'It's not listed in my assets. This is in your name...' He lifted up her face and kissed her frowning forehead. 'I bought this for you before I got arrested. I wanted the divorce, I knew I might be going away for a very long time, and this was to be part of your settlement. The sale went through the day before my finances were frozen…' He gave her a smile. 'They could not seize this because it is yours…'

'You bought this for me?'

'It is big enough for a bed and breakfast…' He shrugged. 'If that is what you want to do with it. I knew you would probably sell it…'

He had known he was about to be arrested and go to prison and yet he had still looked after her—had come to this place and chosen it. It was more than she could take in.

'Why are you crying?'

'Because of this.'

'I said I would take care of you.'

'And you have…'

He had kept every promise he had made, had listened to all her dreams.

They walked through the house and he showed her every room before he took her into the kitchen, with its massive ovens and benches, and huge glass doors that opened to let in the sound and the breeze of the mountains. He had chosen the perfect home—except he hadn't factored that he might live in it.

'I might have to stay here a while,' Niklas said. 'You can be my landlady.'

He came over for a kiss, because that was what he always did.

'I'll send you the rent I owe when I get it.'

'Send it?' Meg said.

'You need to go back.'

He did care about her. She knew it then—knew why he was sending her away. 'And you can't come with me.' It wasn't a question, she was telling him that she knew why.

He tried to hush her with a kiss.

'You can't come to Sydney even for a little while because you're still on bail.'

'Meg…'

When that didn't work, she was more specific. 'And you won't let me stay because you think you might go back to jail.'

'More than might,' Niklas said. 'Miguel is the best legal mind I have met…' He smiled. 'No offence meant.'

Always he made her smile, and always, Meg knew then, he had loved her—even if he didn't know it, even if he refused to see it. Rosa was right. He had always been taking care of her and he was trying to take care of her now.

'I'm on bail,' he said, 'and I doubt the charges will be dropped. Miguel will not simply admit his guilt. There will be a trial, there could be years of doubt, and then I might be put away again. You need to go back to your family.'

'*You're* my family.'

'No…' He just would not accept it. 'Because as much as I might want you here, as much as I thought of you here in this home while I was in that place, as much as a three-weekly visit might keep me sane, I will *not* do that to you.'

'Yes.'

'No,' Niklas said. 'We will have a couple of nights here and then, as I promised your father, I will make sure you get home. By the time you are there I will have divorced you.'

He was adamant.

And she both loved and loathed that word now. She wanted to kiss the man she was certain now loved her, yet she wanted to know the man she loved. He kissed her as if he would never let her go, yet he had told her that she must.

'You're so bloody selfish…' She could have slapped him. She pulled her head back, would not be hushed with sex. 'Why don't I get a say?' She was furious now, and shouting. 'You're as bad as my parents—telling me what I want and how I should live my life…'

'What?' he demanded. 'You *want* to be up here, living in the mountains, coming to prison for a screw every three weeks?'

'Your mouth can be foul.'

'Your life could be,' Niklas retorted. 'Barefoot and pregnant, with your husband—'

She didn't hear the next bit. It was then that Meg remembered—only then that she remembered what she had been preparing to find out before Emilios had come to her door. He watched her anger change to panic, and in turn she watched the fear that darted in his eyes when she told him that she might already be.

It was not how it should be. Meg knew that.

He just stood there as she walked off, as she walked into the bedroom and went through her things. Yes, there was her toiletry bag and, yes, Rosa had packed everything. The pregnancy testing kit was there.

She kicked off her shoes when she returned to the kitchen, because barefoot and pregnant she *was*.

'You need to go home to your family.'

'That's all you have to say?'

'That's it.'

She couldn't believe his detachment, that he could simply turn away.

'You'd let us both go, wouldn't you?'

'You'll have a far better life…'

'I probably would,' Meg said. 'Because I am sick of being married to a man who can't even talk to me, who sorts everything out with sex. Who, even if he won't admit it, *does* actually love me. I'm tired of trying to prise it out of you.'

'Go, then.'

'Is that what you want?' Meg persisted. 'Or are you telling me again what I *should* want?'

'I could come out of this with nothing!'

And if Meg thought she had glimpsed fear before, then she had no idea—because now that gorgeous mouth was strung by taut tendons. His black eyes flashed in terror as he saw himself searching bins for food—not just for himself but for the family she was asking him to provide for. Meg knew then that she had never known real fear…would never know the depth of his terror.

She would not die hungry.

She would not leave the earth unnoticed.

She would be missed.

'I might not be able to give you anything…'

She glimpsed the magnitude of his words.

'We might have nothing.'

'We wouldn't have nothing,' Meg argued, with this man who had no comprehension of family. 'We'd have each other.'

'You don't know what nothing is.'

'So tell me.'

'I don't want to discuss it.'

'Then I *will* leave, Niklas, and I *will* divorce you. And don't you dare come looking for me when the charges are dropped. Don't you dare try to get back in my life when you think the going can only be good.'

He just stood there.

'And don't bother writing to find out what I have, because if I walk out now I will do everything I can to make sure you can't find out. I will write "father unknown" on the birth certificate and you really will be nothing to your child.'

And she was fighting for the baby she had only just found out about, and the family she knew they could be, and as she turned to go Niklas fought for them too.

'Stay.'

'For what?' Meg asked. 'Shall we go to bed?' she demanded. 'Or shall we just do it here? Or…' she looked at him as if she'd had a sudden idea '…or we could talk.'

'You talk too much.'

He pulled her to him and kissed her mouth, running his hands over her, down her waist to her stomach. He pressed his hands into it for a second and then, as if it killed him to touch her there, he slid his hands between her thighs and moved to lift her skirt. He tried desperately to kiss her back to him, but she halted him and pulled her head away.

'And you don't talk enough.'

She would not let him go this time, and he knew he could not kiss her back into his life. And she *would* walk—he knew it. She was a thousand times stronger than she thought, and so must he be—for without her and his baby he was back to nothing.

'Don't waste time in fear, Niklas,' Meg said. 'You told me that.'

So he stood there and slowly and quietly told her what it had been like to be completely alone, to be moved on to yet another boys' home when he caused too much trouble, to boys' homes that had made living on the streets preferable.

And she *was* stronger than she'd thought she was, because she didn't cry or comment—just stood in his arms and listened. She'd asked for this, she reminded herself a few times at some of the harder parts.

'You would make a friend and then you would move on. Or he would steal from you and you would decide to go it alone. Then you might make another friend, and the same would happen again, or you would wake up and he would be lying dead beside you. But you keep on living, and you get a job, and it turns out you are clever—more clever than most—so you start to make money and you start to forget. Except you never do. But you make a good life for yourself, make new friends, and you would not change it, this new life, but still you taste the bitterness of your past. You make more money than you can spend because you're scared of having nothing again and, yes, you're happy—but it still tastes bitter.'

He didn't know how to explain it neatly, but he tried. He looked at her and could not fathom why she wanted to get inside his messed-up head.

'You never forget—not for one minute. You remember eating from bins and beatings, and running away, and the smell of sleeping on the streets, and you trust no one. You remember how people will take from you the second your back is turned—would steal from a beggar who sleeps on the streets. So you relish each mouthful you take and you swear you will never go back to being nothing. But always you fear that you will.'

And then he stopped.

'You want to hear the rest?'

'Yes.'

He paused, took a deep breath before continuing. 'Then you meet a woman on a plane, and this woman feels worried because in living her own life and following her dreams she might hurt her family, and you know then that there are people who do worry about others, who do care. And this woman changes your life.'

'I didn't.'

'More than that—you saved my life. Because when

I did go back to having nothing I survived. More than I should have, I thought of you. Every night I saw the sun, and it was the colour of your hair. Then last night I got to hold you, and look back, and I realised that it is a good world. There are people you cannot trust, but there are also people you can—people who help you even if you don't know it at the time.'

She didn't understand.

'That a woman you only dated for a while would put up her house...' He hesitated. 'Rosa and I...'

'I worked that out.'

'It was before she was married, and there has been nothing since, but her husband is still not pleased that she works for me. That she should go to him, that Silvio should trust her and me enough—that is real friendship,' he said. 'That does not let you taste bitterness.'

And that part she understood.

'Then you look back further and realise that the nun who taught you Spanish, the woman who named you, was the one good thing you can properly remember from your childhood and will end up saving the life of the woman you love—how can you not be grateful for that?'

'You can't not be.'

'And that woman you met on the plane—who your gut told you was right—who you married and then hurt so badly—would fly into Congonhas Airport to come and have paid sex with me...'

She thought of his anger in the prison, and the roughness of the sex, and then his tenderness afterwards, and she was so glad that he'd known he was loved, that she'd told him.

'I'd have done it for nothing.'

'I know,' he said, and he was honest. 'You loved me when I had nothing, and you will never properly appreciate what that means. But I might again have nothing, and I thought that was my worst nightmare, but to have nothing to give you or my child…'

'We've got a home that you chose for us,' Meg said. 'And I can work, and I have parents who will help me. Your child—our child—will never have nothing, and neither will you, so long as we have each other.'

He still could not really fathom it, but maybe he was starting to believe it.

'It might not mean prison…the charges could be dropped…' he said. 'Rosa thinks they have enough already to prove I was not involved. They are going through the evidence now.'

'And, unlike your wife, Rosa's got a good legal brain!' Meg said.

He didn't smile, but he gave a half-smirk.

'Rosa thinks it was Miguel who suggested the plan to my brother.' He tested this new thing called love. 'I want him to have a proper funeral. I want to find out more about him. I want to know about his life. Do you understand that?'

'Yes.'

'I might not talk about it without you.'

And still he said all the wrong things, but they were the right things for them.

'Whatever feels right for you.' And now she understood him a little better. She didn't have to know everything, didn't have to have all of him—just the parts that he chose to give. They were more than enough. And when he did choose to share, she could be there for him.

'Can you accept now that, even though I don't tell you everything, there are no secrets that might hurt you between us?'

'Yes.'

And then he did what Niklas did when he had to: he simply turned the pain of his past off. He smiled at her, held her, and then for the longest time he kissed her—a kiss that tasted deeper now, a kiss that had her burning.

But, unusually for Niklas, he stopped.

'And just to prove how much I love you,' he said, 'there will be no more sex for a while, so we can talk some more.'

'I didn't mean that.'

'No.' He was insistent. 'I can see what you were saying. We can go for a walk in the mountains.' He smiled and it was wicked. 'We can get some fresh air and we can talk some more…'

'Stop it.' His mouth had left her wanting.

She tried to kiss him, tried to resume, but Niklas shrugged her off and found a basket, started loading it from the fridge.

'We're going to have a picnic,' Niklas said. 'Is that romantic?'

He was the sexiest guy she had ever met, Meg realised, and she'd been complaining because they were having too much sex…

'Niklas, please.' She didn't want a picnic in the mountains, didn't want a sex strike from her Brazilian lover, and she told him so.

'Husband,' he corrected. 'I married you, remember?'

'Yes.'

'How can you say it was all about sex? I was nothing but a gentleman that day…I could have had you on the plane, but I married you first!'

'Hardly a gentleman,' she said. 'But, yes, you *did* marry me, and I get it all now. So can you put the basket down and…?'

'And what?' Niklas said.

Seemingly shallow, but impossibly deep, he was gorgeous and insatiable, and he was hers for ever.

His sex strike lasted all of two minutes, because now he was lifting her onto the kitchen bench even as he kissed her. His hands were everywhere and his mouth was too, but so were her hands before he slapped them away. '*I'm* doing this.'

He was the most horrible tease.

He whistled when he lifted up her skirt. 'What are you wearing?'

She writhed in embarrassment at his scrutiny. 'They're new.'

'You didn't buy these, though.' He smiled, because he couldn't really imagine his seemingly uptight girl buying knickers you didn't even have to take off.

'I might have.'

'Meg…' He was very matter-of-fact as he pulled down his zipper. 'You wore sensible knickers the day I met you. You even wore sensible knickers when you came to visit me in prison.' And then carefully he positioned her. 'Watch.'

And when he slipped straight into her the outrageous knickers she was wearing seemed like a sensible choice now.

'Never think I don't love you.' He would say it a hundred times a day if he had to. 'Never think that this is not love.'

And she knew then that he *did* love her, and that what they shared was much more than just sex. He was very slow and deliberate, and it was Meg who couldn't stop. He kept going as the scream built within her, and she waited for his hand to cover her mouth, waited for him to hush her—except they were home now, as he told her, and he pushed harder into her.

'We're home,' he said again, and moved faster, and for the first time she could scream, could sob and scream as much as she wanted, could be whoever and however she pleased.

And so too could he.

He told her how much he loved her as he came, and over and over he told her that he would work something out, he would sort this out.

And as he looked over her shoulder to the mountains he knew how lucky he was—how easily it could have been him lying dead on the pavement instead of his brother. His twin who must have tasted so much bitterness in his life too and been unable to escape as Niklas had done. When still he held her, when he buried his face in her hair and she heard his ragged breathing, for a moment she said nothing.

And then, because it was Niklas, he switched off his pain and came to her, smiling. 'Do you know what day it is today?'

'The day we found out we—' She stopped then, and blinked in realisation as her husband moved in to kiss her.

'Happy anniversary.'

CHAPTER THIRTEEN

SHE LOVED BRAZIL more and more every day she spent there, but it was the evenings she loved the most.

Meg lay half dozing by the pool, then stretched and smelt the air, damp from the rain that often came in the afternoon, washing the mountains till they were gleaming, and thought about how happy she was.

The charges had been dropped, but it had taken a couple of months for them to get back on their feet. They had paid Rosa back her money and lived off Meg's savings, but only when the nightmare of his returning to prison had stopped looming over them and Meg's pregnancy had started showing had Niklas really begun to think this was real.

There were now regular trips into São Paulo, and Niklas came to each pre-natal visit, and she loved that her family adored Brazil as much as Niklas did Australia when they were there.

She saw her parents often—they had only just left that day—and, thanks to a few suggestions and more than a little help from their new son-in-law, business was going well in Sydney.

They had surprised her—after the shock of finding out had worn off, they'd been wonderful. Niklas had flown them over to Brazil and the first day he'd met them he'd begun to work out why sometimes you couldn't just hang up the phone or shut someone out. He'd started to get used to both the complications and the rewards of family.

They hadn't shared their good news about Meg's pregnancy on that visit—it had seemed all too new and too soon to give them another thing to deal with, and there had also been a funeral to prepare for.

She had thought Niklas would do that on his own, except he hadn't.

Only a few other people had been invited. Meg had met Carla for the first time, and she was, of course, stunning, and there had been Rosa and her colleagues, and Rosa's husband Silvio too. And, even if they hadn't wanted to attend at first, her parents had come too, because they loved Meg and Niklas, and Niklas had told them how much it was appreciated. There had been flowers sent from Fernando—a fellow *paulistano* who knew only too well how tough it was on the streets, who knew that sometimes it was just about surviving.

Meg had been a bit teary, saying goodbye to her parents that morning, but they'd reassured her that they'd be returning in a month's time, so that they could be there for the birth of their grandchild.

If she lasted another month, Meg thought as she felt a tightening again and picked up her baby guidebook.

No, it wasn't painful, and they were ages apart. So she read about Braxton Hicks for a while. But then another one came, and this time she noted the time on her phone, because though it didn't quite hurt she found herself holding her breath till it passed. Maybe she should ring someone to check—or just wait because Niklas would be home soon? It probably was just Braxton Hicks…

Her pregnancy book said so…

Meg loved being pregnant. She loved her ripening belly, and so too did Niklas. And she loved *him* more than she had thought she was capable of.

No, she'd never fully know him. But she had the rest of her life to try and work out the most complicated man in the world.

The nightmares had stopped for both of them and life had moved on, and more and more she realised how much he loved her.

There was plenty of happiness—they had friends over often, and many evenings she got to do what she adored: trying out new recipes.

Meg looked at her phone. It had been ages since the last pain, so she should be getting started with dinner really. They had Rosa and her husband and a few other guests coming over tonight, to cheer Meg up after saying goodbye to her parents.

They had such good friends. She could even laugh at things now, and she and Rosa had become firm allies. Rosa would sometimes tease Meg about the earlier conversations they had shared—not to mention the outrageous knickers.

God, she'd been such an uptight thing then.

She lay blushing in her bikini at the thought of the lovely things they did, and then she felt another tightening. She looked at her phone again, noting the time. They were still ages apart, but as she heard the hum of the helicopter bringing Niklas home she was suddenly glad he was here. She walked across the lush grounds to meet him and picked a few ripe avocados from the tree to make a guacamole. As she did so she felt something gush.

It would seem the book was wrong. These weren't practice contractions, because there was real pain gripping her now—a tightening that had her blowing her breath out and feeling the strangest pressure.

Niklas saw her double over as he walked towards her. He could hear the chopper lifting into the sky and was torn between whether to ring and have the pilot return or just to get to her. He walked quickly, cursing himself because they had been going to move to his city apartment at the weekend, so that they could be closer to the hospital.

'It's fine...' He was very calm and practical when he found her kneeling on the grass. 'I'll get the chopper sent back and we will fly you to the hospital. Let's get you into the house...' He tried to help her stand but she kept moaning. 'Okay...' he said. 'I will carry you inside...'

'No…' She was kneeling down and desperate to push—though part of her told her not to, told her it couldn't be happening, that she still had ages, must keep the baby in. And yet another part of her told her that if she pushed hard enough, if she just gave in and went with it, the pain would be gone.

'It's coming!'

She was vaguely aware of him ringing someone, and frowned when she heard who it was.

'Carla?'

She wasn't thinking straight, the pain was far too much, but why the *hell* was he calling Carla?

'Done,' he said.

'Done?'

'Help is on the way…'

She could see him sweating, which Niklas never did, but his voice was very calm and he was very re-assuring.

'She will be ringing for the helicopter to come back and for an ambulance…'

He saw her start to cry because she knew they would be too late—that the baby was almost here.

'It's fine…' He took off his jacket and she watched him take out his cufflinks and very neatly start to fold up his sleeves. 'Everything will be okay.'

'You've delivered a lot of babies, have you?' She was shouting and she didn't mean to.

'No,' he said, and then he looked up and straight into her eyes, and he turned her pain and fear off, because that was what he did best. 'But I did do a life-skills course in prison...'

And that he made her smile, even if she was petrified, and then she started shouting again when he had the gall to answer his ringing phone.

'It's the obstetrician.'

She must remember to thank Carla, Meg thought as he pulled down her bikini bottoms. From what she could make out with her limited Portuguese he was telling the doctor on speakerphone that, yes, he could see the head.

She could have told the doctor that!

But she was sort of glad not to know what was being said—sort of glad just to push and then be told to stop and then to push some more. She was *very* annoyed when he said something that made the obstetrician laugh, and she was about to tell him so when suddenly their baby was out.

'*Sim,*' he told the doctor. '*Ela é rosa e respiração.*'

Yes, her baby was pink and breathing. They were the best words in the world and, given he had said *ela*, it would seem they had a baby girl.

The doctor didn't need to ask if the baby was crying for it sang across the mountains—and Meg cried too.

Not Niklas—he never cried. Just on the day he'd found out she was safe she had seen a glimpse, and then the next day she had guessed he might have been, but he was in midwife mode now!

He did what the doctor said and kept them both warm. He took his shirt off and wrapped his daughter in it, and there was his jacket around Meg, and then he got a rug from beside the pool and covered them both with it. He thanked the doctor and said he could hear help arriving, and then he turned off his phone.

'She needs to feed,' he told her, and he must have seen her wide eyes. He was an expert in breastfeeding now, was he? 'The doctor said it will help with the next bit...'

'Oh...'

'Well done,' he said.

'Well done to you too.' She smiled at her lovely midwife. 'Were you scared?'

'Of course not.' He shook his head. 'It's a natural process. Normally quick deliveries are easy ones...'

He said a few other things that had her guessing he'd been reading her book—the bit about babies that come quickly and early.

'She's early...' Meg sighed, because she had really been hoping that this would be a very late baby, that somehow they could fudge the dates a little and she would never know she'd been made in prison.

'It will be fine,' he said. 'She was made with love. That's all she needs to know.'

They had a name for a boy and one for a girl, and he nodded when she checked that he still wanted it. She tasted his kiss. Then she saw him look down to his daughter and thought maybe she glimpsed a tear, but she did not go there—she just loved that moment alone, the three of them, just a few minutes before the helicopter arrived—alone on their mountain with their new baby, Emilia Dos Santos.

The Portuguese meaning, though.

From the saints.

* * * * *

THE BRAZILIAN
TYCOON'S MISTRESS

FIONA HOOD-STEWART

CHAPTER ONE

IT WAS a grey Tuesday afternoon in October when Araminta Dampierre, abstractedly parking her old Land Rover in front of the village shop, felt a jolt and heard a thud. With a sinking heart she twisted her head. Close behind her stood a four-wheel drive that she'd just hit.

With a sigh Araminta climbed out of her vehicle and took stock of the gleaming silver Range Rover's squished bumper. Her own Land Rover was not in a great state anyway, but this Range Rover had been in pristine condition—obviously the latest model, and brand-new. Wishing she'd paid more attention to her surroundings, Araminta looked up and down the empty village street, searching for a possible owner. But there was no one to be seen.

Taking a last reluctant look at the damage she'd done, Araminta decided to proceed with her shopping and wait and see if the owner of the Range Rover appeared. Maybe the proprietor of the glistening vehicle that she was fast beginning to loathe would have returned by then, no doubt filled with much righteous indignation.

As she turned to head towards the grocer's she visualised a dreadfully chic corporate wife—with whom Sussex seemed to be teeming lately—complaining furiously about her careless behaviour.

At the grocer's Araminta handed her shopping list to dear old Mr Thompson and waited patiently while he shuffled about the shelves in search of several items.

'And how is Her Ladyship?' the white-haired bespectacled grocer asked solicitously.

'My mother is fine, thank you,' Araminta responded, smiling. 'She's recovered after that bout of bronchitis.'

'Well, thank goodness for that. A bad spell it was. My wife had it too.'

'I'm so sorry,' Araminta murmured, glancing out of the window back towards the cars, hoping she wouldn't have to hear all the details of Mrs Thompson's illness.

'Will that be all?' Mr Thompson smiled benignly from across the counter at Araminta, whom he had known since she was a small child, when she'd come in after going to the Pony Club to buy sweets.

'Thanks, I think that's everything. Just pop it onto the account as usual, will you? And do send my best to Mrs Thompson. I hope she makes a quick recovery.'

'Thank you, miss, I will.'

Araminta stepped back onto the pavement, brown paper bag held under her arm, thinking how quaint it was that the villagers still called her 'miss', even though she was twenty-eight and had been married and widowed.

She made her way back to the car, deposited her bag of shopping on the passenger seat, and wondered what to do, since there was still no sign of the driver of the Range Rover. For all she knew, she or he might not appear for ages. She could hardly stand around waiting all afternoon.

With a reluctant sigh Araminta took out a pad and pen from her well-worn Hermès bag and scribbled what she hoped was a legible note, which she slipped behind the windscreen wiper of the Range Rover. There was little else she could do. The driver could get in touch with her and they could exchange information about their respective insurance companies over the phone.

'I'm back!' Araminta called round the drawing room door of Taverstock Hall to where her mother sat reading by the fire.

'Ah. Good. I've just told Olive to bring in tea.'

'Okay, I'll be down in a minute. Just popping the groceries into the pantry. Mr Thompson sends his best, by the way.'

'Ah. Thank you.' Lady Drusilla inclined her head graciously. 'I really must do something about the Christmas bazaar. Perhaps you could help, Araminta? Instead of scribbling away at those wretched children's books of yours. It's time you pulled yourself together and did something useful. After all, when your father died I didn't spend *my* time drifting. I took charge.'

'Mother, please don't let's get into this again.'

'Oh, very well.' Lady Drusilla cast her eyes heavenwards and Araminta made good her escape.

She really must set about finding a place of her own again, she reflected as she descended the back stairs and popped the bag on the pantry table. It was her own fault that she was subjecting herself to her mother's endless comments. But she just hadn't been able to face—or afford—staying in the house she'd lived in with Peter. It had taken all her will-power to get the strength together to clear it up and put it on the market, and be able to unload the mortgage. Still, it was time, she knew, to move on.

The first thing Victor Santander saw as he walked towards his new Range Rover was the gaping dent in the right bumper. With a muffled exclamation he moved forward and inspected it closely. Some idiot had backed into him and hadn't had the courtesy to wait and own up. He crouched, studied the dent, and realised that the whole bumper would need replacing.

He rose with an annoyed sigh, and then noticed the note flapping behind the windscreen wiper. At least the perpetrator had had the decency to leave a phone number, he noted, slightly mollified by the apology. It was signed 'A. Dampierre'. No Mr or Miss or Mrs. Just the initial.

Oh, well, he supposed he'd better give A. Dampierre a call once he got home to Chippenham Manor, which he'd moved into the day before. An accident on his first day in this quaint English village didn't bode too well for the future.

Usually when he drove down the country lane Victor enjoyed the sight of the rolling hills, the trimmed hedges and the horses grazing in the fields. But not after the car incident. And the weather was foul. Yet it suited his mood, he reflected sombrely. So much better than the blaring sun of his homeland, which, for now, he could do without.

At least here he could lick his wounds in peace and quiet, without having to undergo the social scandal that would inevitably be his lot in Rio de Janeiro once Isabella's latest affair became known. At least here he would be left alone.

Back at the Manor he entered the hall and was greeted by loud barks. He smiled as Lolo, his golden retriever, came frolicking across the oriental carpet, thrilled at her master's return.

'*Calma, linda,*' he said stroking the dog's head and heading towards the study. 'You'll get used to living in a large English country house. Surely you'll like it better than the penthouse in Rio?' he murmured, suddenly remembering his vast, white-marbled modern apartment in Ipanema, glad he was far away from it and all the horror of his soon-to-be ex-wife's unwelcome surprises. This was about as far removed as he could get from Isabella, both physically and mentally, he reflected, entering the study.

In fact, nowhere could be far enough, he added to himself, pulling out the crumpled note from his pocket and glancing briefly at it. He realised he'd better give A. Dampierre a call right away and sort the mess out.

Stifling his irritation, he sat down at the large partner's desk, covered with files and photographs of racehorses, and dialled the number, noting that A. Dampierre must be a local, since he had the same area code. Probably some careless local farmer.

The number rang several times.

'Hello, Taverstock Hall,' an aristocratic female voice answered.

'Good afternoon. Could I speak to…' He hesitated. 'A. Dampierre?'

'A Dampierre?' the haughty female voice replied.

'Yes, I was referring to the initial A,' he replied, in arctic tones.

'The initial— Oh, I suppose you must be referring to— Hold on a moment, would you?' He heard a muffled sound in the distance.

'Hello?' Another, much softer female voice came on the line, and for some reason he could not define Victor was surprised to find that 'A' was a woman. He really had imagined a burly red-faced farmer. This voice certainly did not match that image! But neither did it diminish his annoyance.

'Excuse me, madam, I had a note left on my windscreen by A. Dampierre. Is that you?'

'Oh, yes. The bumper. Look, I'm really sorry about what happened. I backed into your car by mistake, you see.'

'In no uncertain terms,' he muttered dryly.

'I wasn't paying proper attention, I'm afraid,' the female voice murmured apologetically.

'That,' he remarked wryly, 'has become abundantly clear.'

'Well, I'm sure my insurance company will deal with it,' replied the woman's voice, now slightly less apologetic.

'Of course,' he said dismissively.

'I'm sorry to have put you to all this inconvenience,' she continued, her tone definitely chillier. 'If there is anything I can do to be of assistance…' Her voice trailed off.

'I don't think there is.'

'Perhaps I could give my insurance company a call immediately and explain?'

Victor's eyes narrowed and he hesitated a moment. Then curiosity got the better of him and his lips curved. 'Perhaps it would be preferable if we met, and then I could give you my insurance information.'

A hesitation followed. 'All right. When would suit you?'

Victor thought. He really had nothing to do now that he'd moved in and his horses were safely ensconced at the training farm a few miles down the road. And for some inexplicable reason this voice intrigued him.

'How about tomorrow morning?'

'Fine. Would ten o'clock do?'

'Okay. But not in front of the grocer's, if you don't mind,' he added with a touch of humour.

A delicious tinkling laugh echoed down the line. 'No, I think better not. Where are you exactly?'

'I'm at Chippenham Manor.'

'At Chip— Oh! I see. So in fact you're our new neighbour.'

'Neighbour?'

'Yes. I live at Taverstock Hall. Our property shares a boundary with yours.'

'Ah. I see. Then it is high time we introduced ourselves,' Victor said, wondering if someone with such a charming voice might turn out to be sixty-five, fat and have a double chin. Serve him right if she did. 'Victor Santander, at your service.'

'Uh, Araminta Dampierre.'

'A pleasure. Shall I come over to the Hall at ten o'clock, then?'

'Um…if you don't mind I'll pop over to the Manor. I have to go out around that time anyway,' she said hurriedly.

'As you wish. I shall expect you at ten.'

'And again, I'm very sorry about your bumper.'

'Don't be. The damage is done, so there is little use in being sorry. Until tomorrow.'

He hung up and glanced at the picture of Copacabana Baby, his favourite filly, wondering why the woman had so definitely not wanted him to go over to Taverstock Hall. Maybe she had a difficult husband who would give her hell because she'd had an accident.

Then he let out a sigh and got up to pour himself a whisky before settling down to study the future of two of his horses which he kept at his stud near Deauville.

'Who on earth was that odd-sounding man on the phone?' Lady Drusilla demanded, gazing in a speculative manner at the platter of fresh scones baked earlier in the day by Olive.

'Oh, he's our new neighbour at the Manor. He sounds rather autocratic.'

'Hmm. Very odd indeed. Foreign, if you ask me. A. Dampierre, indeed. What a strange way to ask for you.'

'It wasn't his fault. I left a note for him on his windscreen and I must have signed it A. Dampierre.'

'A note on a strange man's windscreen?' Lady Drusilla raised horrified brows. 'Really, Araminta, whatever were you thinking of?'

'I bumped into his car by mistake,' Araminta explained

patiently, sweeping her long ash-blonde mane off her shoulders and leaning over to pour the tea.

'How extremely careless of you.'

'I'm very well aware of that,' she said tightly. 'Actually, he was very nice about it.'

'So he should be. It's not every day he'll have the privilege of being bumped into by a Taverstock, as it were.'

'Mother, why must you be so pompous?' Araminta exclaimed, her dark blue eyes flashing at her mother's ridiculous statement.

'I shall have to find out from Marion Nethersmith who he is, exactly, and what is going on at the Manor,' Lady Drusilla continued as though her daughter hadn't spoken. 'It's been quite a mystery. Nobody knew who was moving in. I think it's too bad that one doesn't know anything about one's neighbours any more. They might be anybody.'

'Well, I'll know soon enough,' Araminta said shortly. 'I'm due over there with my car insurance information to settle this matter tomorrow at ten.'

'Really, Araminta, I find it hard to believe that you, a married woman—a widow, rather—who should know better, are belittling yourself in this manner. Why didn't you tell him to come here?'

'Because—' Araminta had been about to say, *I wouldn't subject anyone, let alone a stranger, to your intolerable manners.* But instead she shut up and shrugged. 'I have to go into the village anyway.

'Oh, very well. Pass me a scone, would you, dear? I know I shouldn't, but I don't suppose one can do much harm.'

CHAPTER TWO

AT TEN o'clock precisely, Araminta, clad in a pair of worn jeans, an Arran sweater, a Barbour rain jacket and Wellington boots, pulled up on the gravel in front of Chippenham Manor, noting that the gardens which for ages had run wild were carefully weeded, the hedges neatly trimmed and the gravel raked. Whoever Mr Santander was, he obviously liked things in good order.

For some reason this left her feeling less daunted. It was reassuring to see the Manor—abandoned and forlorn for so long after Sir Edward's death, ignored by the distant cousin who'd inherited and whose only interest in the property had been to sell it—being properly looked after by the new owner.

Jumping out of the old Land Rover, Araminta winced at the sight of the crushed bumper on the smart new Range Rover parked next to a shining Bentley. With a sigh she walked up the steps and rang the bell. It was answered several moments later by a tanned man in uniform.

'Mr Santander is expecting me,' she said, surprised at the man's elegance. Chippenham Manor was a large, comfortable English home, but one didn't quite expect uniformed staff answering the door.

'Mrs Dampierre?' the man asked respectfully.

'Yes, that's right.'

'Please follow me.' The manservant stood back, holding the door wide, and bowed her in.

Araminta stood and stared for a full minute, barely recognizing her surroundings. The hall had been completely redecorated. She'd heard there was work going on at the Manor, but nobody knew much about it as all the firms employed had come from London.

She looked about her, impressed, enchanted by the attractive wall covering, the contemporary sconces, the bright flashes of unusual art. A particularly attractive flower arrangement stood on a drum table in the centre of the dazzling white marble floor which in Sir Edward's day had looked worn and somewhat grubby, and which his housekeeper had complained bitterly about.

'This way, madam,' the servant said, leading her down the passage towards the drawing room.

When she reached the threshold Araminta gasped in sheer amazement. Gone were the drab, musty Adam green brocade wall coverings, the drooping fringed curtains and the gloomy portraits of Sir Edward's none too prepossessing ancestors. Instead she was greeted by soft eggshell paint, white curtains that broke on the gleaming parquet floor, wide contemporary sofas piled with subtly toned cushions, and the walls—the walls were a positive feast of the most extraordinarily luminous paintings she'd ever set eyes on.

'You seem surprised at the way this room looks.'

Araminta spun round, nearly tripping on the edge of the Arraiolo rug, then swallowed in amazement as her eyes met a pair of dark, slightly amused ones. The man who had come in through the door that linked the drawing room to the study next door stood six feet tall. His jet-black hair was streaked with grey at the temples, and his features— well, his features were positively patrician.

'I hope it is admiration and not disgust that has you eyeing this room so critically,' he said, raising a quizzical brow and giving her the once-over. Then he moved forward and reached out his hand. 'I am Victor Santander.'

'Araminta Dampierre,' she murmured, pulling herself together with a jolt. 'And, no, I wasn't being critical at all—simply marvelling that Sir Edward's dull drawing room could be transformed into something as wonderful as this.'

'It pleases you?'

His hand held hers a second longer than necessary. Surprised at the tingling sensation coursing up her arm, Araminta withdrew her hand quickly.

'Yes. It's—well, it's so unexpected, and bright, and so—well, so un-English. Yet it doesn't look out of place,' she ended lamely, hoping she hadn't sounded rude. It was bad enough that she'd bashed the man's car without insulting him as well.

'Thank you. I'll take that as a compliment. I think it brightens the old place up. I hope I haven't gone overboard with the Latin American art, though,' he said, tilting his head and studying her.

'Oh, no,' she reassured him, eyeing the amazing pictures once more. 'That's what makes it utterly unique.'

Then, remembering why she was here, she drew herself up, wishing now that she'd worn something more flattering than her old jeans and sweater. Not that it mattered a damn, of course. But seeing him standing there looking so sure of himself, so irritatingly cool and suave in perfectly cut beige corduroy trousers, his shirt and cravat topped by a pale yellow cashmere jersey, did leave her wishing she had been more selective.

'I must apologise again for my careless behaviour yesterday. I'm really very sorry to have caused your car damage.'

'It is not important.' He waved his hand dismissively. 'Please, won't you take off your jacket and sit down? Manuel will bring us coffee.' He turned to the manservant hovering in the doorway and murmured something in a language she didn't understand. The man responded by stepping forward and taking her jacket, before disappearing once more.

'Please. Sit down.' He indicated one of the large couches. 'You say that we are neighbours? I remember seeing a reference on the land map to Taverstock Hall. Does it belong to you and your husband?' Victor asked, taking in the gracefully tall woman standing before him, with her huge blue eyes, perfect complexion and long blonde hair cascading over the shoulders of an oversized sweater that did not allow for much appreciation of her figure. Quite a beauty, his new neighbour, even if she was careless.

'Uh, no. It belongs to my mother.' He watched her sink among the cushions, elegant despite the casualness of her attire, and sat opposite. 'As I said, I feel dreadful about yesterday. Still, I brought my insurance papers so that we can get it cleared up as soon as possible. Oh!' she exclaimed, her expression suddenly stricken. 'I put them in the pocket of my jacket.'

'Manuel will bring them. Never mind the papers,' he dismissed.

'Thank you.'

He eyed her up and down speculatively, and drawled, 'Frankly, I'm rather glad you banged into my bumper. I might otherwise never have had the opportunity of meeting my neighbour.'

He smiled at her, an amused, lazy smile, and again Araminta felt taken aback at how impressively good-looking he was. She also got the impression that she was being slowly and carefully undressed.

'Well, that's very gracious of you,' she countered, sitting up straighter and shifting her gaze as Manuel reappeared, with a large tray holding a steaming glass and silver coffee pot, cups, and a dish with tiny biscuits.

'Ah, here comes Manuel with the *cafèzinho*.' He smiled again, showing a row of perfect white teeth. 'In my country we drink this all day.'

'Your country?' She had detected a slight accent but couldn't identify it.

'I'm Brazilian. In Brazil we drink tiny cups of extremely strong coffee all day. This coffee you are about to drink was brought from my own plantation,' he added with a touch of pride. 'If you like it I shall give you some to take home with you.'

'That's very kind,' Araminta murmured, slightly over-whelmed by her handsome host's authoritative manner.

She watched as he poured the thick black coffee into two cups before handing her one. Then, as she reached for the saucer, their fingers touched again, and that same tingling sensation—something akin to an electrical charge—coursed through her. Araminta drew quickly back, almost spilling the coffee.

'I hope you are not a decaf drinker,' he said, his voice smooth but his eyes letting her know he was aware of what she'd just experienced.

'Oh, no. I love coffee. It's delicious,' she assured him, taking a sip of the strong brew, its rich scent filling her nostrils.

'Good. Then Manuel will send you home with a packet of Santander coffee.'

'That's most generous. Now, about the insurance,' she said, laying her cup carefully in the saucer, determined to keep on track and not be distracted by this man's powerful aura. 'Perhaps we should go ahead and—'

'I don't mean to be impolite,' he replied, looking at her, his expression amused, 'but do we have to keep talking about a dented bumper? It is, after all, a matter of little importance in the bigger scheme of things. Tell me rather about yourself—who you are and what you do.'

Araminta, unused to being talked to in such a direct manner, felt suddenly uncomfortable. His gaze seemed to penetrate her being, divesting her of the shroud of self-protection that she'd erected after Peter's death. It seemed suddenly to have disappeared, leaving her open and vulnerable to this man's predatory gaze.

'There's nothing much to tell,' she said quickly. 'I live at the Hall and I write children's books.'

'You're a writer? How fascinating.'

'Not at all,' she responded coolly. 'It's a job, that's all, and I enjoy it. Now, I really feel, Mr Santander, that we should get on with the car insurance. I need to get to the village; I have a lot to do this morning,' she insisted, glancing at her watch, feeling it was high time to put a stop to this strange, disconcerting conversation.

He looked at her intensely for a moment, then he relaxed, smiled, and shrugged. 'Very well. I shall ask Manuel to bring your jacket.'

'Uh, yes—thanks. It was silly of me to leave the papers in the pocket.'

'Not at all,' he replied smoothly. 'You are a writer. Creative people are naturally distracted because they live a large part of their existence in their stories.'

Araminta looked up, surprised at his perception, and smiled despite herself. 'How do you know that?'

'I know because I have a lot to do with artists.' He waved towards the walls. 'Most of these paintings are painted by artists who are my friends. I am a lover of the arts, and therefore have a lot to do with such people. They are brilliant, but none of them can be expected ever to know where their keys are to be found. I am never surprised when I arrive at one of their homes and the electricity has been cut off because someone forgot to pay the bill!'

He laughed, a rich, deep laugh that left her swallowing. And to her embarrassment, when their eyes met once more Araminta felt a jolt at the implicit understanding she read there.

Unable to contain the growing bubble inside her—a mixture of amusement at his perception and embarrassed complicity—she broke into a peal of tinkling laughter. And as she did so she realised, shocked, that she hadn't laughed like this for several years. Not since the last time she and Peter—

She must stop thinking like that—not associate everything in her life with her marriage.

'You obviously have a clear vision of what artists are like,' she responded, smiling at Manuel as he handed her the jacket.

She removed the papers from her capacious pocket, careful not to spill her worldly belongings: keys, wallet, dog leash, a carrot for Rania, her mare, and a couple of sugar lumps. She caught him eyeing the wilting insurance documents and blushed. 'I'm afraid they're a bit crushed, I've had them in my pocket a while.'

'As long as they're valid, it's of no importance.'

'Right.' Araminta pretended to concentrate on the contents of the documents, but found it hard to do so when he got up and came over to the couch, then sat casually on the arm and peered over her shoulder as though he'd known her a while. Araminta caught a whiff of musky male cologne. 'Here, Mr Santander,' she said, shifting hastily to the next cushion. 'Take a look at them. Perhaps we should phone the company?'

'Why don't you leave these with me?' he said, taking the documents from her and glancing over them briefly.

'I'll deal with this matter. And, by the way, since we're neighbours and not in our dotage, perhaps we could call each other by our Christian names?' He raised a thick, dark autocratic brow.

'Yes, I suppose so,' she replied nonchalantly, trying hard to look as if meetings of this nature happened to her every day. Then quickly she got up. 'I think I'd better be going. Thanks for the coffee, and for being so understanding about the accident.'

'*De nada,*' he answered, rising. 'Allow me to help you with your jacket.'

Another unprecedented shudder caught her unawares as his hands grazed her shoulders when he slipped the jacket over them.

'It has been a pleasure to meet you, Araminta.' He bowed, and to her utter surprise raised her hand to his lips. 'I shall phone you once I know more regarding the insurance.'

'Yes, please do.' She smiled nervously and began moving towards the door. The sooner she escaped the better.

Victor followed her into the hall, then after a brief goodbye Araminta hurried down the front steps, a sigh of relief escaping her as she finally slipped onto the worn seat of the Land Rover and set off down the drive.

What on earth was the matter with her? she wondered. And what was it about this man that had left her feeling so bothered, yet so unequivocally attracted?

Which was ridiculous, she chided herself. She wasn't interested in men any more, knew perfectly well that she would never meet another man like Peter as long as she lived. Dear, gentle Peter, with his floppy blond hair, his gentle eyes and charming English manners. Even her mother had liked Peter, which was saying a lot.

Of course he hadn't been terribly capable, or prudent

with their money, and had made some rather unwise investments in companies that his friends had convinced him were a really good idea and that had turned out to be quite the opposite. But that didn't matter any more—after all, it was only money.

The fact that because of his carelessness she was now obliged to live with her mother at Taverstock Hall she chose to ignore. Death had a funny way of expunging the errors and accentuating the broader emotional elements of the past.

Victor Santander walked back into the drawing room of Chippenham Manor and stared at the place on the couch where Araminta had sat. She had come as a complete surprise. An agreeable one, he had to admit. He couldn't remember a time when he'd taken any pleasure in talking to a woman he barely knew.

Oh, there were the occasional dinners in Rio, Paris and New York, that ended in the suite of his hotel, with high-flyers who knew the name of the game. But ever since Isabella had taken him for the ride of his life he'd lost all trust in the opposite sex. So why, he wondered, when he, a cynic, knew perfectly well that all women were wily, unscrupulous creatures, only out for what they could get, had he found Araminta's company strangely refreshing? He'd even taken her insurance papers as an excuse to get in touch with her again. And she'd seemed oddly reticent—something else he was unused to—as though she wasn't comfortable being close to a man.

The whole thing was intriguing. Not that he was here to be intrigued, or to waste his time flirting with rural neighbours. He'd come to the English countryside to seek peace of mind, make sure his horses were properly trained and take the necessary time to study his latest business ventures without interruption.

Still, Araminta, with her deep blue eyes, her silky blonde hair and—despite the shapeless sweater—he'd be willing to swear her very attractive figure, had brightened his day.

With a sigh and a shake of the head Victor returned to the study, and, banishing Araminta from his mind, concentrated on matters at hand.

CHAPTER THREE

'Two hundred thousand copies!' Araminta exclaimed, disbelieving. 'Surely that can't be right? You mean they like my new book that much?'

'Yes,' her agent, Pearce Huntingdon, replied excitedly down the line. 'They're talking about television interviews and the works. It's going to be a raving success. Get ready for the big time!'

'But I don't know that I want the big time. I mean, of course I do want my books to be a success, for children to enjoy them and all that, and perhaps make some money too. But not all the hype the—'

'Rubbish. You'll love it.'

'No, I won't,' she replied firmly. 'And I don't want you making any publicity arrangements on my behalf without consulting me first, Pearce. I'm just not up to that sort of thing yet.'

There was a short silence. 'Araminta, when are you going to let go the past and face the fact that you have a brilliant future ahead of you? I know you started writing as a hobby, as something to get your mind off all that had happened. But it's time you took yourself and your career seriously. *Phoebe Milk and the Magician's Promise* is a wonderful, captivating book that every child in this country is going to adore if it's marketed right. For goodness' sake, woman, wake up and smell the coffee.'

The reference to coffee caused Araminta to remember Victor Santander's flashing black eyes, and then to glance over at the gold and black packet of freshly ground coffee sitting on the kitchen counter. He'd had it delivered later in the day.

'Look, let's talk about this once we know it's real,' she countered, not wanting to argue with Pearce, who could be terribly persuasive when he wanted. 'I'll think about it and be in touch.'

'All right, but don't think too long. I'm not letting you miss the chance of a lifetime because you're determined to wallow in the past.'

'Pearce, that's a cruel thing to say,' Araminta exclaimed crossly.

'No, it's not. It's the truth. And the sooner you face it the better.'

'Oh, shut up,' she muttered, smiling, knowing he meant well.

But as she hung up the kitchen phone Araminta noted that for the first time in months she felt extraordinarily exhilarated. Her book looked as if it might take off, and, despite her desire to banish him from her brain, she could not help but recall her new neighbour's captivating smile, and the musky scent of his aftershave as he'd leaned over her shoulder to look at her car insurance papers.

How absurd. She was reacting like a teenager to a handsome face. She must stop, she admonished herself, glancing at her watch and realising it was nearly time for tea. There was no room in her life for anything except her writing and getting out from under her mother's roof. The rest—a social life, friends, a man and all that—would just have to wait for a time in some remote future that she tried not to think too much about.

'Was he perfectly dreadful?' Lady Drusilla enquired as soon as Araminta brought in the tea tray.

'Who? The new neighbour?'

'Well, of course the new neighbour. I would hardly want to know about the new milkman,' Lady Drusilla muttered disparagingly. 'I wish you would be less dreadfully vague, Araminta, it's a most annoying trait. I would have thought you'd have grown out of it by now.'

Counting to twenty, Araminta placed the tray down on the ottoman and reminded herself that if all went well, if the book really did take off, she might not have to stand her mother's jibes for too much longer.

'Well?' Lady Drusilla prodded. 'What was he like?'

'Oh, all right,' Araminta replied evasively.

'What do you mean, all right? Is he young? Old? Handsome? Rich? Or just dreadfully common? One of these *nouveau* yuppie types?'

'Frankly, Mother, he was very nice. He was most gracious about the fact that I mucked up his car and that it'll have to go into the repair shop, and, no, he was not common in the least. Quite the opposite, in fact. I thought he was very much the gentleman. He gave me a packet of his coffee.'

'Coffee?' Lady Drusilla raised an astonished brow. 'You mean he's a food merchant?'

'Not at all. He is—among, I would imagine, a number of other things—the owner of a coffee plantation in Brazil.'

'Oh, well, that's rather different, of course.'

'I don't see why,' Araminta answered crossly. 'Frankly, I couldn't give a damn what the man does. The main thing is he seems to be quite pleasant and will hopefully be a good neighbour. He's Brazilian, by the way.'

'Well! I never thought to see a Brazilian coffee-planter at the Hall. Poor Sir Edward must be turning in his grave. Why that dreadful cousin of his didn't keep the place, I can't imagine.'

'Thank goodness he didn't. One look at him was enough

to let me know he would be the kind of neighbour we could do without.'

'Mmm. You're right, I suppose. He wasn't very prepossessing, was he?'

'No, Mother, he wasn't. And I can assure you that Victor Santander is far removed from Henry Bathwaite. Plus he speaks perfect English. I should think he was probably brought up here.'

'Perhaps he had an English mother—or maybe a nanny,' Lady Drusilla mused. 'Do be careful pouring, Araminta, I've told you a hundred times to use the strainer properly.' Lady Drusilla let out a long-suffering sigh. 'You are aware that I have to chair the committee for the Hunt Ball this evening, and that I shall require your help, aren't you?'

'Mother, I'm sorry, but I simply don't have the time. I have to finish the proofs of my book.'

Lady Drusilla pursed her lips. 'I find it quite incredible that you should abandon your true responsibilities because of some ridiculous children's story. I thought I'd brought you up better than that.'

Araminta was about to tell her mother about the two hundred thousand copies her publisher was putting on the market, and the launch party being planned, but thought better of it. The less her mother knew about her burgeoning career the better. At least she wouldn't be able to put a spoke in the wheel. So she contained herself with difficulty and remained silent. Perhaps it would even be worth doing some of the public appearances, however hateful, if it meant she could buy her freedom and finally be her own person.

Three days later, Lady Drusilla had just picked up her basket to go and collect some vegetables from the garden when the phone rang.

'Hello?' she said, glancing out of the window, annoyed at being interrupted when she was sure it was about to rain.

'Good morning. Could I speak to Miss Dampierre, please?'

'*Mrs* Dampierre. I'm afraid she's out. Who would like to speak to her?'

'This is Victor Santander.'

'Ah. The new neighbour. I am Lady Drusilla Taverstock, Araminta's mother.'

'How do you do, Lady Drusilla? I haven't yet had the pleasure of your acquaintance, but I'm hoping that may be remedied in the very near future.'

Lady Drusilla unbent. At least the man had good manners. 'How do you do? Perhaps you'd better come over to dinner some time?'

'That would be very kind.'

Lady Drusilla thought quickly. She simply must get him over here before Marion Nethersmith caught him first. Then she could tell the others all about him. 'What about tomorrow night?'

'It would be my pleasure.'

'Good. I'll expect you at seven-thirty for drinks.'

'Thank you. Perhaps you could tell your daughter that I shall bring her car insurance papers back to her then?'

'Certainly.'

'I look forward to tomorrow.'

Well, Lady Drusilla, thought as she picked up the basket once more and headed for the backstairs and the kitchen, where she removed her secateurs from the top drawer, at least she'd steal a march on the other neighbours. Marion would be writhing with curiosity and envy.

The thought brought her a considerable measure of satisfaction.

*   *   *

'You did what?' Araminta exclaimed, horrified, hands on the hips of her other pair of worn jeans.

'I invited him over to dinner. Araminta, are you becoming hard of hearing?'

'But, Mother, how could you? We don't even know the man properly. It's embarrassing—' She threw her hands up in despair.

'I really can't see why you're making such a dreadful fuss. I merely invited our new neighbour—whom you say is perfectly respectable—to dinner. It's the courteous thing to do.'

'I can't believe it. You didn't even ask me if I wanted—' Eyes flashing, Araminta flopped into the nearest armchair, trying to understand why the thought of Victor Santander coming to dinner should be so absolutely disturbing.

After being told by Araminta that Victor Santander had uniformed servants at the Manor, Lady Drusilla decided to call in the local caterer, Jane Cavendish, and have dinner properly prepared, rather than count on Olive's rather dull repertoire of dishes. That would do for old Colonel and Mrs Rathbone, but would certainly not impress someone grand enough to hire a professional cook.

By seven-fifteen the following evening Araminta's bed was piled with discarded clothing as she wavered between a black Armani sheath that she'd bought shortly before Peter died and had never worn, or grey silk trousers and a top.

Perhaps the sheath was too dressy for a simple dinner.

Perhaps the grey silk was too dull.

After changing for the third time, she finally settled on the silk trousers and top, and after a last glance in the mirror—she'd actually gone to the trouble of putting on some make-up tonight, for some unfathomable reason—she walked down the wide staircase, feeling more confident than she had in months.

Perhaps it was time to bother more about her appearance, she decided, reaching the bottom step, particularly if she was going to have to promote herself. The thought made her shudder as she made her way to the drawing room, where her mother was giving last-minute instructions to the hired help. With a sigh, she went to join her.

Even in the dark, and illuminated only by the car lamps and outdoor lights, Taverstock Hall was an imposing old pile, Victor reflected as the Bentley purred to a halt. He alighted thoughtfully, straightened the jacket of his double-breasted dark grey suit, and walked smartly up the front steps and rang the bell. It was opened by a cheery-looking woman in what could be taken for a uniform, and he was ushered through the high-ceilinged hall and on towards the drawing room, from which voices and the clink of crystal drifted.

On the threshold he stopped a moment and took in the scene. Then he saw Araminta. For thirty seconds he enjoyed the view. His intuition had been right, and her figure was as sensational as he'd imagined it. She was stunning—and deliciously sexy, he realised, watching her as she stood sideways, talking to an old gentleman near the open fireplace. Long and lithe, the curve of her breast subtly etched under the sleeveless silk top— His thoughts were abruptly interrupted.

'Ah, Mr Santander, I believe?' A very distinguished, rake-thin woman in her mid-sixties, dressed in a smart black cocktail dress with a large diamond leaf pinned on her left breast, moved towards him. He raised her hand to his lips.

'Good evening, Lady Drusilla, it is most good of you to have me.'

'Not at all. Thank you so much for the lovely flowers. Quite unnecessary, I assure you,' she murmured, taking in every detail of his person. 'Now, do come in and meet the others. You've met Araminta, of course, and this is Colonel Rathbone and Mrs Rathbone—they live not far down the road, at the old vicarage—and this is Miss Blackworth.' He shook hands politely with an elderly lady in a nondescript purple dress and a three-tier string of pearls before turning to meet what must be the vicar. 'Vicar, may I introduce Mr Santander? Our new neighbour at the Manor.'

Her tone of satisfaction was not lost on Victor and he glanced at her, amused. So Lady Drusilla was enjoying in-troducing him into local society, was she? At that moment he raised his eyes and met Araminta's. They held a mo-ment, and he read amusement laced with discomfort and a touch of embarrassment. After exchanging a few words with the balding vicar, he edged his way towards her.

'Good evening.'

'Good evening,' she replied, smiling politely, disguising her racing pulse, the slight film of perspiration that had formed on her brow the minute she'd sensed he'd entered the room. 'I hope you won't be too bored. The country doesn't provide much in the line of entertainment, I'm afraid.'

'I did not come to the country to seek entertainment,' he replied, his presence and the scent of that same cologne leaving Araminta deliciously dizzy. 'In fact, I came here specifically to find peace and quiet. I did not expect to be invited out so soon,' he added. 'Still, it is, of course, a great pleasure to meet one's neighbours. Particularly when they are so…agreeable.' He gave her an appraising look that left her feeling strangely feminine and desirable, something she hadn't felt in ages.

'What can I get you to drink?' she said quickly.

'A Scotch and water, please.'

Glad for the excuse to conceal her perturbed feelings, Araminta busied herself with the drink. What on earth was wrong with her? He wasn't anything special. Just a neighbour.

Victor watched as she fixed his drink. A beautiful woman with tons of sex appeal. She probably had a husband. He wondered where that husband was. Odd that she seemed so shy for a married woman. Or maybe she was recently divorced. That might explain the reticence.

The thought was strangely appealing. Then with an inner shrug he accepted the drink and prepared to amuse himself for an evening.

From the opposite end of the table Araminta watched her mother grilling Victor Santander and admired his polite, concise answers that gave little away. But, oh, what she would have given for this evening not to have taken place! By the time coffee had been drunk, after-dinner drinks consumed and the better part of the guests had taken their leave, she was only too ready to usher him out through the door and send him off to his car.

'This has been a most pleasant evening,' he remarked, eyeing her again in that same assessing manner that left her slightly breathless. 'Could I persuade you to join me for dinner tomorrow at the Manor? After all, we haven't had a moment to go over the insurance papers.'

'No, we haven't,' Araminta admitted, fumbling for words. It was very unlike her to be so—so what? Aware of herself? Of him, standing so close that it left her feeling tingly all over? What on earth was wrong with her?

'Well? Would you like that? Or would you prefer to dine at the Bells in Sheringdon? I hear they serve a very decent meal.'

'I don't think I can,' she said hurriedly, seeing her mother hovering in the hall. 'Why don't we speak tomorrow and set up a convenient time to do the papers?'

'As you wish.' He pressed his lips to her hand. Then, to her amazement, he brushed his lips on the inside of her wrist.

Araminta withheld a gasp as a shaft of molten heat coursed from her head to her abdomen. With a gulp she snatched her hand away, caught the devilish gleam in his eyes and the amused smile hovering at his lips, and seethed inwardly at her silly reaction. Then he moved, lean and predatory, towards the car.

Heart thudding, Araminta watched the Bentley purr smoothly off down the drive, then turned with a sigh of relief and stepped inside. This was ridiculous. How could she be put in a state because a man touched her hand? Thank God she'd refused Victor Santander's offer of dinner if this was the way he affected her.

She never felt stirrings for any of the men she knew, yet for some inexplicable reason this Brazilian—who was almost a stranger—had touched something deep within her that she'd believed gone for ever. It both frightened and excited her. Her instinct warned her that the less she saw of the man the better. She knew very little of him, but sensed there was something sophisticated and dangerous about him. He was, she told herself firmly, the last person she would want to get involved with. That was if she was thinking of getting involved with anyone—which, of course, she wasn't.

'Araminta?'

'Yes, Mother, I'm coming.' Araminta closed the large

front door, then made her way back through the hall to the drawing room, where her mother was seated complacently by the fire, twiddling a final glass of champagne.

'Well, I must say that I was most favourably surprised by our new neighbour. Did you know that he went to Eton?'

'No, I didn't. Mother, if you don't mind, I think I'll go up to bed,' she said, passing a hand over her brow. 'I've a bit of a headache.'

Lady Drusilla, dying to assess the evening further, pursed her lips in annoyance. 'Oh, very well,' she muttered.

And Araminta made good her escape.

CHAPTER FOUR

A COUPLE of days later Araminta told herself that any passing attraction she might have felt for her new neighbour was nothing more than that. She'd kept busy, going over and over the proofs of her book, making sure any last-minute errors did not escape her before she sent back the final version to her editor who was having it published at record speed. But today she was taking a break, and going riding.

As she gave Rania her head and galloped across the Downs, Araminta enjoyed the cool wind in her hair and the sense of freedom that was so far removed from being cooped up in the house, bent over her laptop, as she had been for the past days. But at least the proofs were ready and she could post them off tomorrow.

Slowing her pace, Araminta became aware of another horse and rider coming out of the copse. She glanced in their direction, noting the equestrian's good seat and the fine proportions of the horse. Then all at once her heart stood still and she gulped. Surely it couldn't be Victor Santander?

She'd been so involved in her work for the past few days that she'd forgotten the phone message he'd left and the insurance that still needed to be dealt with. Now, as the horses approached one another, she braced herself. He would probably be cross that she hadn't phoned back. And he'd be entitled.

Victor reined in the fine chestnut and watched appreciatively as Araminta brought her mount to a stop. She looked

quite lovely astride the skittish mare. A flash of amusement
gripped him as he approached, realising that her expression
was that of a guilty child. Amused rather than annoyed that
she had obviously forgotten all about his call, he reined in
next to her. The truth was, it intrigued him to meet a
woman who was so outwardly unresponsive to him, yet
who he was certain held hidden depths of sexual response.

Suddenly the idea of setting out to seduce Araminta and
find out if that response truly existed became vastly appealing. He'd discovered now that she was a widow. Good.
No jealous husband to contend with. Plus, he'd never se-
duced a widow. This could be a first.

'Hello,' he said casually, riding alongside her now, noting how lovely she looked, her cheeks pink and her golden
hair a windblown mass that he wished he could drag his
fingers through.

'Hello.'

'You didn't get my message?' he asked, looking her
straight in the eye, allowing her no escape, amused as the
colour in her cheeks heightened. He smiled inwardly. It
would definitely be amusing to see the fair Araminta
Dampierre writhing to his touch. And writhe she would, he
assured himself, with all the arrogant confidence of one
used to getting his own way.

'I'm afraid I forgot to phone back,' she apologised. 'I've
been very busy with my book the past few days.'

'I see,' he responded coolly. 'Well, I got in touch with
the insurance company and they'll be sending you some
forms to complete.'

'I'm sorry. I should have remembered.'

'Yes, you should.'

'Look, I don't know what to say.' She bit her lip and
reined in the horse. 'I really am sorry. I get a bit carried
away when I'm working.'

'Hmm.' He eyed her carefully, wondering if she was ready. Like the mare she was restraining, she would need careful handling, this one, he reflected, taking her measure. It surprised him, but she obviously had little experience of handling men. Or being handled.

'Is there anything I can do to make up for having put you to all this trouble?' she asked doubtfully.

'Actually, there is,' he said, a smile hovering now he knew he'd got her where he wanted.

'Tell me—what?'

'Have dinner with me tonight.'

'Oh, I don't think—'

'You said you wanted to make up for having put me to so much trouble,' he reasoned, a sardonic gleam in his flashing golden-flecked dark eyes.

'Yes, but—'

'But?' He raised a quizzical brow. 'Is having dinner with me such a penance?'

'Of course not. All right,' she conceded, smiling and giving in. 'What time?'

'Eight o'clock at the Manor. Though I can pick you up, if you'd prefer?'

'Oh, no. I can pop over.'

'Then, *à toute à l'heure*,' he said in French before glancing at the sky. 'You'd better get home before it pours. I'll race you to the road.' He turned his horse and set off across the Downs.

Never able to refuse a challenge, Araminta raced after him. Soon they were riding neck and neck in an exhilarating dash across the Sussex countryside and arrived simultaneously at the roadside.

'We seem to be pretty well matched,' he said, eyeing her admiringly as they pulled up at the crossroads.

'That was fun!' Araminta exclaimed, laughing engagingly.

'We must make sure we repeat the exercise,' he agreed, leaning over and taking her gloved hand in his, seeking her eyes. 'I shall await you at eight.'

Then he wheeled the horse around and cantered off in the direction of the Manor, leaving Araminta wondering why on earth she had accepted what she knew to be a dangerous invitation that must surely spell trouble. She would do well to keep their conversation on neutral ground, she realised, grimacing as the first drops of rain fell. This man was by far too smooth, too knowing, and the increasing attraction she was experiencing was ridiculous, to put it mildly. Instinctively she sensed that she was out of her league. But surely she could control this silly attraction? Surely that couldn't be too hard?

Turning her horse, she headed for home, telling herself that all it took was self-discipline. Nothing more.

He was standing far too close for comfort, and his whole being was far too overpowering, Araminta realised as she listened to his knowledgeable analysis of several paintings gracing the drawing room walls. Araminta showed suitable interest, wondering all the while how it was possible that a man she barely knew could have such a powerful effect on her.

It was as if she'd changed, as if something within her yearned for him in a visceral, primitive way that was not only unladylike, but which she'd also always despised in other women. The truth was she'd never experienced such longing first-hand. In fact, now that she thought about it, she'd rarely been just physically attracted to anyone. Even when she'd met Peter it had taken quite a while before she'd realised she was fond of him. And that had been because of his character, his charm, his fun, not because he oozed charisma and sex appeal.

But this man was different. Even as they chatted he exuded a tense, dangerous quality that should repel but that instead acted upon her like a magnet.

Dinner was delicious—lobster bisque followed by roast pheasant. Victor had gone to great trouble to make her feel at ease. To her astonishment Araminta confided in him, told him about her next book, and some of her future hopes and fears in that domain. And he listened, obviously interested and admiring.

She sighed now, feeling warm and at ease. Perhaps it was a combination of the pleasant conversation, the softly candlelit room, the wine and the after-dinner drink that she held loosely in her left hand that were responsible for her being so aware of him. She smiled when he looked down at her, those dark eyes flecked with gold so penetrating that she wondered suddenly if he could read her soul. She shivered and hoped he hadn't a clue what was on her mind. Wished she didn't know herself.

'Are you cold?' he asked, slipping a firm arm around her shoulder and turning her slowly towards him.

'No, I'm fine,' she murmured, aware that her pulse was beating wildly, willing herself to move away from him. But her body didn't follow her head.

'Let me take your glass.' Victor laid it down on the small table next to him, his eyes mesmerising hers. Jazz played softly in the background, and for a moment Araminta wondered if this was real or merely a dream from which she would suddenly wake.

Then Victor took a step closer, and she could feel the warmth of his body, breathe the scent of his aftershave. For a moment a flash of logic penetrated the delicious haze surrounding her, telling her this was asking for trouble. But his hypnotic gaze was upon her, she could feel his body heat, could not resist the draw as his arms slipped possessively around her. And all at once Araminta knew that, defying all reason, she wanted his kiss more than anything.

And it came. Surprisingly soft at first, then harder, his tongue exploring her mouth in a manner so new and so unknown, so different from anything she'd experienced with Peter that she almost drew back. For this was no quick, purposeful kiss designed to prepare the way for what was to follow, but rather a slow, lazy, languorous, delicious, yet taunting discovery.

Even as the kiss deepened, Araminta knew that she had never experienced anything similar before, and slowly she gave way to the myriad of sensations coursing through her being, felt her body yield, soft and melting in his arms, felt his hardness against her and knew that she had never desired a man as she desired Victor Santander.

His hands were wandering now, travelling up and down her spine, along her ribcage, cupping her bottom, bringing her even closer, caressing, pressing her to him, until, oblivious to reality, she let out a sigh of utter longing.

The next thing she knew they were lying on one of the wide couches and Victor was deftly unbuttoning her silk blouse. Even as her brain told her she should put a stop to this immediately, her body craved his touch and she could do nothing to halt the onslaught. When his thumb grazed her nipple through the thin texture of her bra she gasped, and a shaft of heat, a white hot arrow like none she'd ever known, left her arching, yearning for the touch of his fingers, travelling south, deftly removing all barriers, seeking until he encountered the soft mound of throbbing desire between her thighs. When he cupped her she let out a moan of delight and threw her head back, unable to do more than succumb to the delicious torture, give way to the turmoil of sensation that exploded in a pent-up rush when his fingers finally reached her core.

'You are beautiful,' he whispered, 'gorgeous, and I want you.'

As Araminta lay in his arms, recovering from the most unexpected, mind-shattering orgasm of her life, a tiny voice spoke in the back of her mind. This couldn't be happening, shouldn't be happening. Was she really lying wantonly with Victor Santander—a man she barely knew—allowing him to touch her intimately? What must he think of her?

In fact, at that very instant he was determinedly trying to strip her of the rest of her garments.

With a jerk Araminta pulled herself up and out of his arms.

Victor fell back and looked at her, brows creased. 'Is something the matter, *querida*?' he asked, dragging his fingers through his thick black hair, eyes bright with undisguised desire.

'No—yes—look, I don't know what happened just now,' she mumbled hoarsely, aware of her mussed hair as she fumbled around for her bra and shirt. 'I—I know this will sound absurd, but I honestly don't know how it happened.'

She began fiddling with the hook of her bra, then the buttons of her blouse, wishing she were a thousand miles away, feeling her cheeks burning as all at once she realised just how far this whole episode had gone. And so quickly. It was unthinkable, shaming, even ludicrous that she could have behaved in such a manner with a total stranger.

Victor rose from the couch and, picking up his brandy snifter, stood a few feet away, watching her thoughtfully. He made no attempt to hold her back, merely contemplated her feeble attempts to tidy herself as though he were a spectator at a show. What had happened to make her react thus? he wondered. For, despite his initial spark of anger at her sudden rejection, his interest was piqued.

He considered himself a pretty good judge of character, and her sudden willingness to succumb to his caresses had surprised him. Now, as he stood there in the aftermath of their tryst, he reflected that his first opinion of her—that she was relatively inexperienced and unaware of just how attractive and sexy she was—was probably the correct one. Well, then, perhaps it was better that things hadn't gone any further.

He walked to the window, letting himself cool down while Araminta sorted herself out. Better, he repeated silently. Still, he could not pretend that what had just happened between them hadn't been incredibly seductive and to his utter surprise, incredibly unique. Okay, it was just a kiss and a few caresses but— Victor cut off the thoughts that followed and turned.

'Why don't you stay the night?' he asked, suddenly but smoothly, unwilling to let her go.

'I—look, this never should have happened—never has happened before. I don't know how it did,' Araminta mumbled, embarrassed.

'It happened because we both wanted it to happen,' he said harshly, viewing her through narrowed eyes. 'Because we are two consenting adults who feel desire for one another.'

'Perhaps,' she conceded grudgingly, retrieving her shoe from beneath a cushion. 'But that isn't a reason to—well, to—' She threw up her hands.

'To go to bed together?' he finished. 'Why on earth not? I can't think of any better reason.'

'Can't you?' she exclaimed, suddenly cross. 'Well, I can. Tons of them.'

'It took you rather a long time to remember them, *querida*,' he murmured dryly.

Araminta steadied her gaze and he read anger there. 'Perhaps it did. I don't know where my head was at. I'm sorry if I misled you. I had no intention of giving you the wrong impression. I—look, I need to go home.'

'Why of course,' he murmured with a sardonic twist of his lips. He watched her pick up her purse, ignoring a sudden twinge of disappointment. Though why he should feel disappointment when he barely knew this woman was ridiculous!

Perhaps it was proof that, despite all he'd been through with Isabella, he still hadn't tamed that irrationally romantic nature of his. Or was Araminta Dampierre less innocent than she seemed? He of all people knew what women were capable of. Why, for a single moment, should he imagine that this one might be any different from all the others?

As she drove down the dark country road and headed back to Taverstock Hall Araminta took herself seriously to task, asking over and over how she could possibly have behaved in such a wanton manner. Never had anything remotely similar occurred before in her life, not even when she was a teenager. That Victor was a man whom she'd met only a few times didn't make it any better. And thank goodness for that sudden flash of common sense that had intervened just in time, or right now she might very well be rolling between Victor Santander's wretched sheets!

It was appalling, shocking, and so unlike her that she had difficulty recognizing herself in the writhing woman of minutes earlier. For a moment she thought of Peter, and a new wave of guilt swept over her. She hadn't thought of him once all evening, hadn't remembered the gentle, quiet nights spent in each other's arms after tender but, she had to admit, guiltily comparing the sensations of earlier in the evening, not very exciting sex.

Araminta changed gears crossly as she swerved into the gates of Taverstock Hall. That she should suddenly be denigrating her marriage was as absurd as all the rest. She'd been happy, hadn't she? Had never felt that what they'd had was less than enough, had she? So why this? Why now? Why had she soared to unknown heights at the touch of a near-stranger, and never during the entire course of her sedate marriage to a man she knew—was one hundred per cent certain—that she had loved? Surely there must be something seriously wrong with her?

Too troubled to go straight into the house, and possibly have to face her mother, Araminta dropped her car keys into her pocket and wandered into the rose garden, where she sat down on one of the stone benches. With a sigh she stared up at the half moon flickering through fast-travelling cloud and tried to make sense of the evening. But whichever way she viewed it she still couldn't come up with any justification for her strange behaviour. She must, she concluded, have lost her mind. And she'd better make damn sure it never happened again. Not paying attention while parking, she reflected grimly, could carry a high price.

Victor was also too wound up to go to bed, and he stood for a long time by the window, wondering why she'd allowed him to go that far. Was she innocent, or a hypocrite? he pondered, wishing to banish the niggling feeling of frustration that still hovered. Whatever, it was probably a lot better that she had upped and left when she had, for otherwise it might have proved embarrassing to have her wake up next to him when he'd had no intention of anything more than a night of good, satisfying sex.

In fact, all round it was definitely preferable this way, he persuaded himself, wandering back to the drawing room and absently pouring another cognac, before retiring to the study to do some work before going up to bed.

But half an hour later he found it impossible to concentrate on the project at hand. He must be tired, he concluded, folding up the plans of a new factory in Brazil.

'Damn Araminta,' he exclaimed, banishing the image of her lovely face as she'd reached orgasm in his arms, and the strangely satisfying sensation he'd experienced when he'd heard that little gasp of surprised shock that told him quite clearly she'd never reached those heights before.

With a sigh and a short harsh laugh directed at himself, Victor downed the last of his brandy. Then, switching off the lights, he headed upstairs to bed, determined to rid his mind of his fair neighbour.

CHAPTER FIVE

THERE was no use pretending it hadn't happened, Araminta realised the next day. She just had to face the fact that for a few inexplicable minutes she must have gone mad.

As it happened she was given little opportunity to stew over the events of the night before, for early in the day the telephone rang.

'Araminta, it's Pearce. Look, they're advancing the book-launch date and there's a huge party planned at the Ritz. I can't believe it—they're going to have it published in record time,' he said excitedly.

'Oh. Will I be expected to be there?'

'Well, of course you will, silly girl. You're the one person who has to be there, come hell or high water.'

'But I don't think I—'

'One more word and I'll scream,' Pearce roared down the phone. 'Araminta, get with the programme! This is *your* book, *your* success. Don't you feel the least bit excited about it all? Girl, you're about to make millions if it flies!'

'Really? Yes, I suppose I might,' she muttered vaguely. The thought of being exposed to all those strangers, having to smile and chit-chat, sound intelligent and answer questions about her book was thoroughly daunting.

'Araminta, it's not the end of the world,' Pearce continued patiently. 'You used to be so social before you married Peter. What's the matter with you?'

'Oh, I don't know. I've changed, I suppose.'

'Not really. You're just hiding.'

'Peter didn't like going out much, so we rarely did.'

45

'Araminta, Peter is no longer with us,' Pearce said carefully. 'And you are. You have to make a life for yourself. Thanks to your own efforts you're going to be a great success. Enjoy it, girl, instead of running away.'

'I'll think about,' she murmured, twisting the cord of the telephone. 'When is the party going to be?'

'In three weeks.' He gave her the date.

'So soon?' Araminta squeaked.

'Yes. Goodness knows how they're getting the books done in time. And you'd better get yourself to London and buy a decent dress for the occasion. Don't think you can come in those worn jeans of yours. I won't have it. I want you to look stunning. In fact I'll go shopping with you if need be.'

'That won't be necessary,' Araminta responded in a dignified tone. This was all happening far too fast. First last night, now this. It was as if she couldn't stem the flow of events sweeping her along, despite her desire to stay cushioned from the world at Taverstock Hall.

But as she hung up she heard her mother calling from the stairs and winced, closing her eyes. Perhaps this really was her chance to move on. Of course if she moved it would mean more change. But at least she'd have a choice, which at present she didn't. Plus, it would mean she wouldn't be stuck next door to Victor Santander.

This last did more to get her moving than any other element of the equation. The mere thought of coming across him in the village or elsewhere was enough to cause a rush of hot embarrassment. What would she do? How would she face him if it happened?

'Araminta, I really must have your help for the Hunt Ball,' Lady Drusilla said, walking into the hall and bringing her crashing back to earth.

'I'm sorry, Mother, but I'm afraid I'll be away at that time,' she responded absently.

'Away?'

'I'm going to London. I have to do some stuff for my book. There's going to be some sort of launch party on the same day as the Ball.'

'Goodness. How very tiresome.' Lady Drusilla pulled her cardigan closer and sniffed. 'Couldn't you have got your publishers to arrange it another day? It can't be *that* important, surely?'

'Actually, it is,' Araminta replied, drawing herself up suddenly aware for the first time just what she was about to achieve. 'They're publishing two hundred thousand copies.'

'Goodness. That seems rather excessive, doesn't it?' Lady Drusilla's brows rose in disapproval. 'I hope they won't sit on the shelves. It could be a terrible waste of good paper.'

Furious at her mother's response, Araminta turned on her heel and decided that Pearce was right. She needed out, needed to get on with her life and not tolerate her mother's impossible behaviour any longer. In fact, she decided, running up the stairs and dashing the tears from her cheeks, the sooner she went to London and began looking for something decent to wear for the party the better. After all, if she was going to be the centre of attention then she might as well do it right.

Three weeks later Araminta stood in the ballroom of the Ritz surrounded by Pearce, her publishers, and a number of journalists, critics and miscellaneous celebrities brought in for the occasion. There were stands with copies of *Phoebe Milk and the Magician's Promise* tastefully placed about the room, waiters circulated with trays of champagne and elegant finger food, and a jazz quartet played at the far end of the room.

For a moment Araminta blinked, and wondered if the blend of soft music, the clink of fine crystal, laughter, extravagant compliments and conversation was real. She caught a glimpse of herself in one of the mirrors and felt an adrenaline rush, knowing she looked really good in the Dolce & Gabbana cocktail dress, with her hair beautifully washed and blow-dried by one of London's top hairdressers. It made her feel confident, more able to deal with the hype surrounding the launch and her own role in all this.

Then all at once, as she turned to answer a question put to her by a trendy-looking journalist with spiky hair and little round glasses, she froze. Surely that couldn't be Victor Santander standing across the room by the double doors, in a dark navy blue jacket and grey trousers, looking her over appreciatively?

Glancing quickly away, she tried desperately to calm her racing heart and concentrate on what the young journalist was saying. But her eyes kept wandering. Her tummy lurched and she swallowed nervously, gripping the stem of her champagne flute for dear life. How had he known? What on earth could he possibly be doing here?

Victor Santander watched her from his position near the door and smiled to himself. So he'd been right to come after all. When his old friend Pearce Huntingdon had commented over lunch at White's, their club, that tonight he had the launch of a big book that was going to hit the top of the lists, Victor had asked who the author was. When Pearce had mentioned Araminta's name Victor had pricked up his ears and directed the conversation so that the unsuspecting Pearce had ended up inviting him to come along.

Now, as he watched her from across the ballroom, Victor

felt that same smouldering rush of attraction. She looked very different from the way he'd seen her in the country, deliciously chic and sophisticated in a dress that subtly accentuated each curve of her slim, sensuous figure. He wasn't quite sure why he had come. Perhaps the memory of that same lithe body writhing in his arms had stuck in his mind, despite his determination not to let it linger there.

Realising that she'd seen him, he made a beeline across the room to where she stood, allowing her no room for escape.

'Good evening—and congratulations,' he said, coming smoothly alongside, so that she was sandwiched between him and the keen-looking journalist.

'Good evening.'

'Quite a do, this. Your book looks as if it's going to be a big hit.'

'Hmm. Thanks.'

'Hmm? Is that all you have to say?' He quirked an amused brow.

'Well, what do you expect me to say? "Yes, I'm going to be a number one bestseller"?' she asked crossly.

'Now, now, *querida*, don't get upset,' he murmured, reading the confusion in her eyes and deciding to put her at ease. Perhaps the other night had been an aberration after all. 'I'm sure you've heard all sorts of exaggerated compliments all evening and have had about enough.'

Slightly mollified, Araminta met his eyes and read the humour there. 'As a matter of fact you're right,' she replied ruefully. 'Plus, I'm not used to wearing high heels and my feet are killing me.'

Victor grinned, took quick stock of the room, saw that guests were beginning to trickle out, and made a quick decision. 'You know, we could probably slip away without being noticed and go somewhere for dinner. You could kick your shoes off under the table.'

'I can't leave my own party,' she said, tempted by his offer. The strain of having to smile and be bright all evening was beginning to weigh on her. 'And, by the way, tell me, what are you doing here?'

'I was invited,' he said, with the devastating smile that, Araminta noticed with irritation, already had several women peering in their direction.

'By whom?' she asked coolly.

'By Pearce.'

'Pearce?' she exclaimed. 'How on earth do you know Pearce?'

'We were at Eton together. We happened to lunch today at White's, and he mentioned your name and the launch. I then made it my business to cadge an invite.' His eyes were filled with bold, arrogant laughter, and despite the lingering embarrassment Araminta smiled.

'Come on,' he encouraged, his voice cajoling, 'be a devil. You've done your bit for the book. You don't have to stay till the last guest leaves.'

'Pearce will kill me.'

'Don't worry about Pearce. He'll do as he's told. I was his prefect.'

She looked at him and laughed again. 'You can be very bossy, can't you?'

'So I'm told. But it serves its purpose.'

'And what might that be?' she asked, realising with shock that she was flirting with him.

'That remains to be seen.' He looped his arm through hers and glided discreetly towards the side door to their left. 'Don't look too obvious about it. We'll just slip into the hall as though we were going for a breath of air.'

'I need to fetch my coat.'

'You can get it from the cloakroom tomorrow.'

'But I'll freeze to death. It's—'

'I'll keep you warm, don't worry.'

'I really think—'

'Araminta, just shut up and do as you're told,' he ordered, grabbing her hand as they crossed the lobby of the hotel. 'My car is waiting.'

As they stepped outside Araminta saw the Bentley drawn up on the kerb. A chauffeur jumped out and quickly opened the door. Next thing she knew they were driving down Piccadilly, and Victor had his arm around her and was rubbing her shoulders, not in a seductive way, but in a warm, practical manner.

Several minutes later they drew up in front of Annabel's, a nightclub in Berkeley Square.

As she was freshening up in the Ladies' Araminta thought about the strange course the evening had taken. Surely she must be mad to be here with Victor Santander, the one man she'd been determined to avoid for the past few weeks, had cringed from every time she turned a corner in the village in case she came across him.

But tonight she felt strangely exhilarated. The enthusiasm about her book was real, the press was talking about it, and tomorrow it would be on the shelves. She hoped it would sell as they believed it was going to. It would be too awful if after all this hype it was a flop. She felt a sudden rush of anxiety, then banished it. She might as well enjoy the evening. Whatever else he was, Victor was intelligent, amusing and good company. But tonight she would make sure that she made it back to Pont Street and her friend Sara's flat in one piece, and not allow herself to be sidetracked along the way.

With a determined nod she closed her evening purse and, smiling to the attendant, entered the club.

*   *   *

She was truly lovely, Victor realised as the head waiter settled them at their table and he ordered champagne. Lovely, intelligent and successful. An interesting combination, he mused. He had taken time to observe her as she'd circulated among the guests at the party, observing her poised elegance, her gracious smile—very different from the slightly shy, retiring person she'd given the impression of being before. Intriguing. He wondered now how she was feeling after the excitement of the evening.

As Victor rarely thought about women's feelings at all— or certainly hadn't since the disastrous events in Rio that had burned him more than he liked to remember—he was surprised at his own reaction.

'Shall we dance?' he asked, after they'd finished dinner and their coffee, and were sipping champagne again.

He noted a wary gleam enter Araminta's eyes. 'A truce, Araminta. I am not going to try and seduce you. It's only a dance.'

'Okay.'

They rose and joined the other couples on the dance floor, swaying to the soft Latin rhythm. As his strong arms encircled her, Araminta experienced a frisson—that same dangerously delicious sensation she'd known when he'd touched her before—reminding of just where and how that touch had ended. A tiny sigh escaped her and damp heat melted inside. But she ignored it, determined to enjoy the moment, the music, and the delightful atmosphere, not to hanker after the impossible.

It was ages since she'd been to a club—not since before her marriage, she realised wistfully, for Peter had hated nightclubs and would never come. Tonight took her back to the days when she'd been a girl about town, spending long, amusing evenings with her friends, visiting different fashionable hot spots. But all of that had come to an abrupt end when she'd married and moved to the country.

Victor proved to be an excellent dancer, moving her smoothly about the floor, and she let herself go with the rhythm, enjoying it as she never would have believed possible. He was amusing and friendly all evening, never mentioning their previous encounter, obviously determined to put it behind them and her at ease. But, as though to thwart all logic, she experienced an irritating stab of disappointment.

Perhaps all he'd wanted that night at the Manor was a not-too-bad-looking, conveniently available female. Then another thought occurred and she wondered suddenly if his seemingly bland attitude wasn't a ruse, a way of making her feel comfortable so that he could pounce again when she least expected him to.

This last thought made her laugh inwardly. She wasn't a mouse, was she? She was quite capable of making up her own mind about what she wanted and didn't want to do. It was just a matter of being firm.

The music ended and they returned to their table to sip more of the deliciously crisp champagne. Victor seemed suddenly thoughtful, and she took a sidelong look at his handsome tanned profile, wondering what he was thinking about.

'I have a proposition to put to you,' he said at last, turning on the banquette and looking directly at her through those golden-flecked eyes that, despite her decision to remain indifferent, left her feeling deliciously vulnerable.

'Oh?' A slight flutter of her heart made her swallow. What was he about to suggest?

'I am leaving the day after tomorrow for Normandy. I have a place there, and horses that are being trained. I'd like you to come with me.'

Araminta took a long sip of champagne. 'I don't think that will be possible.'

'And why not? I'm not asking you to sleep with me, but to come as a friend. No ties, just a few days' R&R. My plane is ready.'

'I don't think I should go,' she responded. 'I don't think it would be suitable. Plus, I have don't have enough clothes here, and anyway I need to get back home.'

'To what? To your mother and the aftermath of the Hunt Ball, *querida*?' He quirked a mocking brow at her that told her he knew exactly what was going on back home. 'I would have thought you could use a break from all that.'

The truth of this could not be denied. Still, she knew she was on dangerous ground. Victor Santander was too smooth an operator to be taken at his word.

'It's very kind of you to ask me,' she replied, sounding prissy to her own ears. 'It's just—'

'It's not kind in the least,' he interrupted. 'I like your company. This is not a ploy to seduce you,' he added, his lips twisting in a cynical curve. 'After all, I think you'll agree that what occurred the other night occurred by mutual consent.'

'I—'

'Stop being embarrassed about something perfectly natural that we both enjoyed. What happened happened. It's in the past. Forget it. We can start over as friends. Truly, I'd enjoy your company,' he said in a softer voice, slipping his hand over hers.

'What about my coat at the Ritz?' she said lamely, trying to think of an excuse, and wondering what her mother would say if she knew her daughter was thinking of flying off to France in a private jet with a man of whom she knew very little.

This last thought decided her. She'd had enough of following Lady Drusilla's dictates. And, although she hated to admit it, Victor was right. She needed a break. So why not take the opportunity and go?

'All right. I'll do it,' she said suddenly, flashing him a big smile, astounded at her own daring. 'I can use tomorrow to shop for a few more clothes and things.'

'Good. Then we'd better get moving,' he replied with a satisfied smile, and signalled the waiter.

CHAPTER SIX

THE Gulfstream landed at Deauville airport, and soon Araminta and Victor were whizzing through the Normandy countryside in a shiny Aston Martin, headed towards Falaise, the historic town still dominated by the centuries-old castle where that William was born who later set out in 1066 to conquer England.

It was raining fairly hard by the time they drew up at a delightful eighteenth-century millhouse, just below the castle walls.

'How lovely!' she exclaimed, as Victor drew into the courtyard.

'I'm glad you approve,' he remarked, bringing the car to a standstill. 'I've had this place for a couple of years now, but I don't come here very frequently.' He didn't add that he'd bought the property just before Isabella had performed her stunt, and that coming here somehow reminded him of the whole disastrous affair.

But today it seemed different.

Araminta's presence, her obvious delight at the place and her straightforward manner, made it possible to relegate the negative thoughts that he associated with Isabella to the nether regions of his brain and concentrate on the present.

As they approached the front door it opened and a middle-aged woman in a skirt and twinset appeared with a broad smile.

'*Bonjour, Monsieur Victor,*' she exclaimed, smiling at Araminta while taking the bags from him. '*Bienvenue.* It is so good to see you back here.'

'Hello, Madame Blanc, it's good to see you too.'

'How long does *monsieur* plan to stay?' she asked, leading the way up a wide stone staircase of shallow steps above which hung a delightful chandelier—an old-fashioned bronze balloon with candleholders.

'A few days,' he replied, his tone non-committal. 'You can put Madame Dampierre's things in the turret room,' he added, standing aside for Araminta to enter the large drawing room.

It was very English and different in style from the Manor, with pink walls and classical paintings, and wide velvet armchairs and comfortable sofas before the huge open fireplace where a fire crackled merrily.

'It's delightful!' Araminta exclaimed, moving towards the hearth, stretching her hands out towards the flames. 'I'm surprised you don't spend more time here.'

'Are you?' He looked at her hard, then joined her by the fire. 'I suppose I could. I have my horses at another property of mine, not far from here.'

'So you keep horses here and in Sussex?' she probed.

'Yes. I used to—'

He cut off, staring into the flames, and for a minute she wondered where he was. He seemed far away, as though remembering another time, another place. But she didn't push him.

'What about a drink?' Victor asked, snapping back to the present, then stepping towards a large silver tray weighed down with crystal tumblers and decanters.

'I'd love one.'

'Then I'll open a bottle of champagne. Just wait here and I'll be back in a second.' With that he disappeared down a small flight of stairs that must lead to the dining room and kitchen.

With a sigh of contentment Araminta sank into one of

the enveloping armchairs, glad she'd taken the bull by the horns and come. It was relaxing to be somewhere so quiet and welcoming. Not that Taverstock Hall wasn't quiet, she reflected, but the thought that at any moment her mother might pop into the room and make some unexpected and usually negative comment always left her tense.

Now that she was away, in a place far removed from her family home, she was able to put into perspective just how negative her mother's continuing criticism actually was. She sighed and looked out at the rain pattering on the windowpanes, thinking how good it felt to be ensconced in this lovely warm room, with no stress, no obligations, and no one to accuse her of making mistakes.

'There was a bottle of Cristal on ice,' Victor remarked, coming back up the steps holding it.

He looked so good, in faded jeans and a black polo neck sweater, the sleeves of which he had pulled up so that she could observe the way the muscles of his tanned forearms tensed as he worked on uncorking the bottle. Araminta swallowed and looked away, reminding herself that she had consented to come here just as a friend, and hastily turned her thoughts to the champagne.

It was only a quarter to twelve, but somehow it seemed appropriate. As he handed her a flute she smiled at him. In fact, ever since the plane had left the ground she'd felt an inner smile bubbling inside her.

'To your success,' he said, raising his glass, his eyes firmly upon her. 'May *Phoebe Milk and the Magician's Promise* be at the top of the bestseller list. I love the title, by the way.'

'Thank you,' she responded sincerely. For it was true that now that she'd faced the possibility of success it tasted sweeter than she'd anticipated. And meant that she'd finally be able to escape Taverstock Hall, possibly find a home of her own again. Not that she knew where that home would be.

'A penny for your thoughts?' he said, sitting on the sofa opposite and stretching his long legs out towards the fire.

'Oh, nothing much.'

'Come on, tell me. I don't bite.'

No, Araminta thought wryly, you kiss. And rather well. But she was determined not to allow thoughts like that to penetrate.

'I was thinking that if everything goes according to plan I might be able to buy myself a home,' she remarked taking a long, delicious sip of champagne.

'Are you planning to move away from Sussex?'

'I have no idea yet.' She shrugged. 'It's just a thought.'

'What would your mother have to say?' he asked, his tone deliberately bland, his eyes focused on the contents of his glass.

'I have no idea. But probably quite a lot.'

'She appreciates your company,' he observed shrewdly.

'No, not really. She likes having someone she knows is dependent upon her whom she can boss around.'

'And whom she can bully,' he supplied dryly.

Araminta looked up quickly. 'How do you know that?'

It was his turn to shrug. 'I'm a good judge of character, that's all. Your mother seems to have quite a strong nature, *querida*.'

'Domineering, you mean,' Araminta said with feeling. 'I suppose it's my own fault, for letting her have her way, but sometimes it's just easier than getting into an argument.'

'You don't like arguments?'

'I loathe and detest them. I like living in a harmonious atmosphere.'

'And was your marriage harmonious?' he asked quietly,

shifting his position on the sofa to get a better look into her eyes.

'Yes—yes, it was. Very.'

'I see.'

The tone of his voice made it seem as though 'harmonious' and 'quiet' were uninteresting.

'It wasn't dull,' she added quickly.

'I never said it was.'

'It was— Well, it was…' She tried desperately to think of a word that would define her marriage to Peter without sounding negative.

'Boring?' he supplied, his gaze direct.

'Not all,' she answered, a little too quickly. 'Of course it wasn't boring. It was nice and pleasant and—'

'Predictable?' he pressed.

'Yes. And I don't see what's wrong with that,' she replied defensively.

'Nobody said anything was,' he countered reasonably. 'Now, why don't you take that champagne upstairs with you and see if you approve of your room? It's in the turret.'

'Good idea,' she responded, relieved to bring this uncomfortable conversation to an end.

'I'll see you back down here in half an hour for a refill, as they say in America, and then we'll have some lunch.'

'Lovely.' Araminta smiled brightly and followed him down the tiny flight of stairs to the dining room, then through to the turret and its spiral staircase.

'Why, it's delightful!' she exclaimed, enchanted, gazing at the four-poster bed and the toile de Jouy curtains and hangings.

'I'm glad you approve.' Before she could move into the room he raised her hand to his lips, turned it over, and kissed the inside of her wrist. 'May you be happy here, *querida*.'

Before she could answer he was gone.

Araminta looked about her, delighted by the charm of the place, the peace, and the intoxicatingly heady feeling of being alone and away from the world, with this devastatingly attractive man, and in such a magical spot.

Now, Araminta, she admonished herself. *You mustn't lose your focus. You came for a few days' relaxation, nothing more.*

On that philosophical note, and despite the fact that she knew she might very well be trying to deceive herself, Araminta opened her bag and began unpacking, glad that she'd bought a couple of warm garments in London, as it looked as if it might get quite chilly. She sighed and smiled and began hanging things in the wonderful lavender-scented oak armoire. She really didn't want to think any more than necessary right now. Soaking up the atmosphere and letting go of tension was all that really mattered.

After a delicious lunch of *boeuf à la bourguignonne* and a bottle of Château Haut Brion, an exceptional cheese platter and some amusing conversation, Araminta and Victor sat once more in the drawing room, where Madame Blanc brought in a tray piled with steaming coffee and chocolates.

'I hope you don't plan to have meals like this for the whole length of our stay,' Araminta exclaimed.

'Why not? Didn't you like it?' Victor frowned.

'Quite the contrary.' Araminta laughed. 'Everything was simply delicious, but I dread to think of the weight I'll put on.'

His face softened and he smiled. 'I doubt you need to worry about your weight. In fact it might not do you any harm to fill out a bit. You're very slim.'

'And plan to remain so,' she said meaningfully.

'Why is it women are obsessed about being thin when

we men actually prefer you with a bit of quantity as well as quality?'

'That sounds dangerously familiar,' Araminta mused.

'It was what Spencer Tracy used to say regarding Katharine Hepburn—that quality was all fine and dandy, but what about some quantity?'

Araminta's shoulders shook with laughter.

'Don't laugh,' he continued, handing her a cup of coffee, eyes sparking wickedly. 'It's nice to have something to feel.'

'Hmm. I'm sure,' Araminta responded and, knowing they were getting onto dangerous ground, hastily changed the subject. 'Are your horses far from here?'

'Not very. About twenty minutes. Would you like to see them?'

'I'd love to.'

'Very well, then we shall go and take a look at them tomorrow morning. I thought this afternoon we might drive into Deauville. There's not much going on at this time of year, but still, some of the shops are open.'

'That would be lovely,' she responded, quite happy to fall in with any plan. 'I think it's stopped raining.'

'Perhaps for a little while, but Normandy is like England—renowned for the rain. So take a raincoat and an umbrella.'

'Okay, I will. What time would you like to leave?'

'In about half an hour?' His eyes rested on her for a moment.

'Fine.' Araminta jumped up, his intense gaze making that familiar tingling sensation return. 'I'd better go upstairs, then.'

'I'll see you in the hall when you're ready.'

He stood up as she left the room and watched as she disappeared down the short flight of stairs.

It was strange to have a female guest in this house. He hadn't brought anyone since his marriage to Isabella had collapsed. In fact the thought that he'd actually bought the house for Isabella, when all the while she was two-timing him with another man, still had the power to arouse his anger. But not like it used to. Those days were over. Gone, thank God. He would always despise her, but he didn't hate her any longer. She simply wasn't worth it. What he could never forgive her for was the child she'd been carrying, that she'd aborted so as not to have any further attachment to him. That he would never forgive.

Ever.

Victor stared out of the long French window at the lush green grass and the lawn beyond. He wasn't a man who craved a child, but the thought that any woman could cold-bloodedly kill his offspring was horrifying to him.

Turning slowly, he gazed once more into the flames and thought of Araminta. What had driven him to go to her party and then bring her here? She was a lovely woman—one who, in the few moments she'd spent in his arms, had touched some long-forgotten chord deep within him. But it would be ridiculous, of course, to let anything reach beyond the well-erected walls that for the past couple of years he'd made sure were in place around his emotions.

For a moment he continued to stare into the flames, and wondered if Araminta really believed that they were only here as friends or if she recognised the deep magnetic attraction pulling between them. He sighed, and turning again, looked up through the other window at the castle.

Women were strange creatures; they seemed to take pleasure in deluding themselves. Why couldn't she just take this trip for what it would inevitably turn out to be? A few delightful days consummating their burning desire for one another. Once that was over they could both return to their everyday lives, none the worse for wear. But neither did he plan to rush things. Araminta was not an experienced woman of the world. She'd been married, but he had a good idea what kind of a marriage it had been.

An enigmatic smile touched his lips as he turned back and faced the room. He wasn't in any hurry. In fact, taking his own lazy time would make it all the more amusing.

Two hours later they were walking along the windswept seafront at Deauville, past the restaurants that in summer were packed with tourists and habitués, past the famous hotels and the casino, and along the deserted windblown beach. There was no one else about, except a man with a dog and two elderly ladies.

As they faced the wind Araminta experienced a rush of exhilarating well-being. Victor slipped an arm through hers and they walked for a while in companionable silence, enjoying the bracing fresh air, the fast-traveling cloud.

Then Victor put a friendly arm around her shoulders, and Araminta knew she could not resist the tug, the insatiable desire that had consumed her ever since that first evening at the Manor. Was it not absurd to resist it? she asked herself suddenly, slowing their pace and looking out to sea.

As though sensing her change of mood, Victor turned her towards him and gazed down into her eyes.

'Why deny ourselves when we both want the exact same thing?' he queried, his voice carried on the wind.

A smile touched her lips. 'Why, indeed? Kiss me, Victor. I've decided I want to be kissed.'

'Your wishes are my commands,' he answered promptly. And his mouth closed on hers, strong and demanding, making her gasp with delight as once more her being melted, molten gold pouring into a mould of his making.

After several minutes locked in each other's arms he looked up. 'Let's go home,' he murmured roughly.

'Let's,' she agreed, taking his outstretched hand and running with him along the seafront in carefree delight.

All at once she felt light, liberated, as though all the cares of the world had been lifted and at last she could breathe. For an instant she wondered what the consequences of it all would be. Then, shunning logic, she laughed up at him, determined to enjoy the journey, wherever it led.

An hour later they were back at Le Moulin. There was no time for niceties, no time to do more than make it up the winding turret stairs before Victor ripped off her shirt and, throwing her on the four-poster, proceeded to devour her.

Never in her wildest dreams had Araminta imagined that lovemaking could be like this—hot, wanting, tempestuous and wild. Her hair splayed over the pillows, the sheets; she writhed in his arms, unable to control the shafts of searing heat and need crashing through her. The feel of his skin on hers and the sound of his husky voice whispering words in a tongue she did not understand left her dizzy as never before.

Next morning she woke from a delicious sleep to the feel of something soft gently caressing her hair. She kept her eyes closed and enjoyed the sensation, still half asleep and not quite conscious yet of where she was. Then all at once she opened her eyes and gazed, amazed, into Victor's handsome face looking down at her.

'Good morning,' he murmured. 'I brought you a cup of coffee.'

'Oh, thanks.' Araminta struggled to sit up, but he slid a hand onto her shoulder and she recalled the events of the previous afternoon and evening.

They had only left the bedroom to concoct Victor's su-

perb omelettes and share a bottle of *premier cru* Château
Latour, before returning to their nest in the turret. Now, in
the harsh daylight, Araminta blushed at the things she herself had initiated, had felt uninhibited enough to do with a
man she barely knew.

'No. Stay like that,' he ordered, his hand slipping to her
cheek and down her throat as she reached for her dressing
gown.

His eyes were intense and Araminta drew in her breath.
Was she going to allow this man to dictate the time and
place by a mere look? Be at his beck and call whenever he
decided he wanted her?

There was no use denying that the intense attraction existed—no use pretending they both didn't want to consum-
mate their relationship again, in the light of day now peek-
ing through the toile de Jouy curtains.

But before she could think further Victor had slipped his
hand below the duvet. His eyes dark with desire, he grazed
her taut nipple, making her gasp. Then, before she could
protest, his mouth was on hers, his lips prying hers open.

For a moment she tried to draw back, but he merely
laughed. Then the firm, unyielding insistence of his tongue
working its way cunningly into her mouth left her clutching
his hard shoulders once more as he drew her into his arms,
pressing his hand into the small of her back, moulding her
bottom. Her taut breasts pressed hard against his chest as
he moved onto the bed. His tongue probed further now,
thrusting, leading her to a wild, untamed response. She
could feel his renewed desire to possess her, knew she was
ready for more—knew that once he'd decided she could
not, would not, resist.

Victor took it slowly this time around, sensing her wan-
ing resistance, determined to make her follow her instinct
and her soul. Then, smoothly and firmly, he moved on top

of her until she could feel the length of him, until her tongue sought his as passionately as his sought hers. And, just as it had the previous night, there came a point when Victor knew that he too had lost control.

All at once he heard her moan, and the sound made him groan. In one swift movement he pulled back, leaving her naked before him. She was beautiful, sensual, all woman, he reflected, before kissing her throat, her breasts—those wonderful pink-tipped breasts that betrayed her every feeling as his tongue flicked and taunted them—and she arched, crying, begging him to satisfy her deepest desires.

There was no use resisting, Araminta realised. She could do no more than throw her head back and moan, giving herself up entirely to his expert caresses. He kissed further down, down, until his tongue finally reached her core, laving, taunting, causing such excruciating pleasure that she let out a gasp of sheer delight and surprise.

No man had ever done that.

All at once she relished in the joy, the spiralling tension rising within as she dragged her fingers through his thick black hair, pleading with him to bring her to completion.

But still he lingered.

It was only when she thought she could bear it no longer that he slipped his other hand from behind her and, fondling her breast, worked on her with his tongue, bringing her to a peak in a searing wet rush of heat so intense that she cried out, begging for fulfilment and release. Then, just as she could bear it no longer, as her nails dug into his broad shoulders and she was ready to beg for mercy, the hot intensity that had built up crashed, let loose, and she floated into an incredible ecstatic joyride that prolonged itself on and on, until she fell back among the crumpled sheets limp and weak, yet knowing she wanted what she knew was to follow.

'Minha linda,' Victor whispered, gazing at her before he sat up and slipped off his robe, and joined her again in the bed. Araminta extended a hand and touched his thigh.

'Victor, what is happening between us?' she whispered, dazed. 'Why is this so wonderful?'

'You've never felt like this before, have you?' he murmured, an edge of pride to his voice.

'No.' She shook her head. 'I haven't. I—I never knew it could be like this. Or reacted like this, for that matter,' she added, a faint blush tinting her cheeks.

He smiled down at her, his bronzed features etched in the morning light. 'We have only just begun, Araminta,' he said, leaning on his elbow and observing her.

'I know,' she whispered, with a little smile that curved her lips.

She was beautiful lying there, all woman, her long blonde hair splayed across the pillow, her body so sensual, so feminine and lovely, already well satisfied, yet ready, he sensed, to arch once more to his touch.

Slowly he let his fingers roam over her again, smiling as she shuddered. Her eyes sought his, read the question in them.

Then, knowing he could wait no longer, Victor moved on top of her, waited a second to read her reaction and, seeing her eyes dilate with expectation, thrust deep within her, needing to know her warmth, to feel himself sheathed in her soft, yielding being, to bring his arms around her, kiss her neck and delight in the feel of her legs wrapping around his waist as together they found a hard, fast, all-encompassing rhythm that sought and demanded, each drawing all they could from the other.

Somewhere through the haze that was his mind he heard her gasp, knew she was once more close to completion, and he plunged deeper, determined to reach the inner core of this woman he knew so little of but who, in a strange way, had given him something he'd believed lost for ever.

Then together they came in a rush of ecstasy, Victor throwing his head back and Araminta crying with joy as they exploded, then fell entwined among the sheets, unable to do more than bask in the aftermath of their lovemaking.

'Are you okay?' he whispered several minutes later, when he'd got back his breath and his pulse was beating at a normal pace once more.

'Yes,' she replied, turning her head on his deliciously damp shoulder and nuzzling closer. He pulled her to him, his arm possessively flung around her shoulders.

'This is all so strange—so unexpected. So…so…' She couldn't finish her sentence.

'I know, *querida*,' he answered carefully. Then, 'Does it matter? Why not just enjoy it?'

'Yes,' she answered, knowing that for now all she wanted was the feel of his body close to her, the grip of his arm around her shoulders and the knowledge that they were here, in this magical little world of their own, and could set the rules. For a time.

'We're supposed to go and see the horses this morning,' he said after several moments.

'Then why don't we?' Araminta shifted onto her elbows and grinned at him.

He was incredibly gorgeous lying there bronzed and taut against the white sheets, his hair ruffled, his face softer than she'd ever seen it before. His dark eyes held a new light. Gone was the slightly bored, cynical air, replaced by something intense that she couldn't define and that left her swallowing.

'Okay. Don't just lie there.' She laughed. 'Let's get up and go and see these famous horses of yours.'

She felt full of a new vital energy now—a desire to walk,

to run, to get up and get out. She felt alive. It was intoxicating and wonderful, something she'd never experienced—and the sudden realisation that it was years since she'd felt so energised left her shocked. Hadn't she ever felt like this with Peter?

As though guessing her sudden guilt, Victor rose and slipped his arms around her. 'No memories, okay, *linda*? We are here, now, and that is all that matters. The past and the future can take care of themselves. All that matters is what we're experiencing together at this time. Don't spoil it.'

She looked up, feeling she understood exactly what he meant, and nodded, allowing him to slip his arms loosely around her waist. 'You're right,' she agreed. 'Here and now. I think I'll get into the shower.'

'I'll do the same, and see you downstairs in half an hour.'

Dropping a kiss on her mouth, he turned, picked up his dressing gown and slipped it on, then, patting her bottom, he turned her in the direction of the bathroom. 'Off you go, beautiful.'

Half an hour later Araminta was in the hall. She wore jeans and a pair of Wellington boots that Madame Blanc had produced from the cloakroom, which fitted her perfectly. Mercifully she'd brought her new Barbour jacket, and had shoved a scarf into the pocket in case it rained.

'You look wonderfully English,' Victor remarked as he came down the stairs smiling, hair still sleek and wet from the shower, his dark corduroys and sweater giving him a dangerous look as he reached the flagstoned hall and dropped a kiss on the tip of her nose. 'I'll get a jacket and we'll go. I thought we'd grab some lunch at one of the country inns I know.'

'It sounds great.'

In fact everything sounded great, Araminta realised, as though she were living in a dream from which she hoped she wouldn't wake up. At least not for a while.

As they got in the car she realised she hadn't phoned her mother. Then she banished the thought. She would ring the Hall at a time she knew her mother would be out and leave a message on the machine. That way nothing she said could spoil this perfect moment.

Soon they were driving down charming country roads, complete with hedgerows and green fields that reminded Araminta of southern England.

'It looks rather like Sussex, doesn't it?'

'Yes, it does.'

'Is that why you bought the Manor?' she asked, suddenly curious.

'In part,' he replied stiffly, seemingly unwilling to elaborate.

'I see.'

'No, you don't, but never mind.' He gave her a hard sidelong look. 'If I told you why I bought the Manor it would involve travelling down that memory lane where we decided not to go, *querida*.'

'Okay.' Araminta shrugged and agreed. He was probably right. They were, after all, living a fantasy. A fantasy with no past and no future. Why sully it? Something in his tone told her that whatever it was that had driven him to abandon this spot and buy the Manor was not pleasant. She wondered all at once if he was married, or had been married, and if so where his wife was and if he had any children. But there again she forced herself to keep quiet. They were here together, living this specific moment, weren't they?

And that was all that mattered.

Soon they were drawing up into the courtyard of a beautiful château. Several charming brick buildings surrounded the yard, the grass was beautifully kept and the gravel raked. In the distance she could see a small lake and an exquisite little château.

'It's delightful!' she exclaimed.

'You think so?'

'Of course it is. What an amazing place to keep your horses. I can't think why you don't stay here all the time instead of at the Manor.'

Victor made no response. His expression was dark for a moment, then he smiled and waved to a small bow-legged man hurrying towards them.

'*Bonjour*, Gaston. How are the horses doing?'

'Very well, Monsieur Victor. Very well indeed.'

'Good. Then perhaps we'll take a look at some of them.'

'Certainly. Shall I meet you at the stables?'

'Yes. We'll walk over there.'

Victor slipped Araminta's arm through his and they took a path leading through the trees towards the château. The gardens were beautifully laid out, swans glided gracefully on the lake, and the scent of autumn filled the air.

'Is this property yours?' she asked, suddenly frowning.

'It belonged to my mother. She died three years ago.'

'I'm sorry.'

'I inherited it, and I keep most of my horses here.'

'But the house looks so beautiful,' she exclaimed, gazing across the lake at the château, exquisite in design and size, not too big.

'It is a lovely place. I spent time here as a child. Maybe some day I'll redo the house and—' He cut himself off abruptly, then turned down another path. 'Let's get to the stables before it rains again. It certainly looks as if there will be another downpour, *querida*.'

Since he obviously didn't want to talk about it, Araminta decided not to ask him more. But she concluded there must have been some strong motive for Victor first to have acquired Le Moulin and then the Manor in Sussex. She reminded herself that it was none of her business. Yet, despite her determination to live only in the present moment, she couldn't help but feel curious about him and the rest of his life.

But when they reached the stables all thoughts and conjectures were forgotten as she became engrossed by the fine creatures being presented to them. Some of the horses were champions, or would probably become champions in the next few years. She loved the foals and spent some time stroking their silky coats.

An hour later they were driving into a village. Araminta exclaimed as they entered, for it was exactly what she'd imagined a Normandy settlement would look like: timbered cottages, with tiny windows and crooked roofs, and narrow cobbled streets.

Soon they were seated at a corner table in a delightful low-beamed restaurant, facing an open fireplace. Victor ordered a bottle of excellent red wine, but as they settled in, and Araminta studied the menu, she wondered suddenly what subjects, apart from general ones, they could talk about if the past and future were not to be mentioned.

It was strange how full, yet how empty, a single moment in time could be without those two elements. It left just them and their feelings. Nothing more. Like two ships that cross in the night, she reflected. And although that was enthralling, and made her recall this morning's delicious lovemaking, she could not stop wishing that the man beside her would reveal more about himself, what drove him, and what lay beneath that suave outer shell.

CHAPTER SEVEN

THE weather that evening turned colder, and after dinner Araminta and Victor sat together in each other's arms on the large sofa next to the fire. It seemed strangely natural to be curled up with him among the cushions, Araminta's head resting on the shoulder of Victor's soft cashmere sweater, sipping a cognac and reading her book while he flipped through the paper.

For a moment she experienced a sudden rush of longing for something more than the barren life she lived at present, for something involving warmth and affection and domesticity. She stopped herself with a sharp jolt at the word love, for it was simply too dangerous, too unreal to think of anything like that. Particularly when the man next to whom she was sitting had made it abundantly clear that they were merely living a few moments in time, that in a few days or hours they would come to an abrupt end.

A tiny sigh escaped her as she tried to concentrate on the subject matter of her book.

'What's the matter, *linda*?' Victor asked, bringing his arm closer around her shoulders and looking down at her. Araminta tilted her chin up and smiled. 'Nothing. I'm fine. Really enjoying myself. How about you?'

'I'm fine too,' he said, then turned to stare with a hooded gaze at the flames crackling in the grate. At that moment the telephone rang and, laying the paper on the huge ottoman before the fire, he rose to answer it in the hall.

Araminta heard him reply and tried to continue reading.

But a sudden change in his tone made her look up and take heed.

'What do you mean, she's in trouble?' he demanded. There was a moment's silence, then, 'I see. I suppose you want me to come and deal with it, as usual? I thought by this stage I'd be through having to cope with more of her bloody nonsense.' Another pause. 'Okay. I'll fly out tomorrow.'

Araminta's heart gave a sharp lurch of disappointment. Whatever it was it wasn't good, and 'she', whoever she was, required his presence. This meant an immediate end to their magical time together. And despite her attempt not to let it trouble her she felt let down.

'I'm afraid I have some bad news,' Victor announced tersely as he returned to the fireplace, then stood drumming his fingers on the mantelpiece. 'I shall have to fly to Rio tomorrow, which means we'll have to curtail our visit here. I'm sorry.' His voice had become businesslike and harsh, and his expression was forbidding.

'I'm sorry too,' she replied, trying to keep the disappointment out of her voice. 'I hope it's nothing serious.'

He looked up then, as though seeing her for the first time. 'Serious? I don't know, exactly. Isabella has smashed her car into a bus and she's in hospital. Or so she says. Why they think I should have to go and deal with her is beyond me, but—'

'Isabella?'

'My wife,' he replied shortly.

The words hit Araminta like a ball of lead. She felt lightheaded and swallowed, trying to regain her equilibrium and determined to suppress the knot forming in her throat. So he was married! She should have guessed. It had all been too good to be true.

'Are—are your children in Rio too?' she asked in a small voice.

'My children?' Victor frowned, a dark forbidding frown, and stared at her blankly.

'Yes. I presume that—'

'I don't have children,' he responded harshly, his features almost haggard now as he stared angrily into the flames.

Victor flexed his fingers, mastering his anger. Once again Isabella had imposed her unwelcome presence on him. And he resented her for it more than he could express. Isabella— the bane of his life. Why didn't her damn boyfriend see that she was properly taken care of? Maybe he was too busy sniffing cocaine.

'I need to make a couple of calls,' he said brusquely, 'then I suppose we'd better get to bed early. We'll leave here at seven sharp tomorrow morning.'

Turning abruptly on his heel, he left the room without so much as a sorry, or Would it be convenient?, or any of the things that any civilised normal person would have said.

Araminta's chest heaved with indignation. *He'd* omitted to mention he had a wife, so what right did he have to treat her in this dismissive manner now?

She let out some trapped air from her lungs, wrestling with her hurt feelings. Admittedly, it was partly her own fault. She'd come here by choice, without bothering to find out whether the man was married or not! And this was the result. That would teach her to be bowled over by a handsome face.

She was glad, she convinced herself, that they were to leave so early, for the sooner she got back to England and to reality the better it would be.

With an angry toss of her head, she picked up her book

and, before Victor had a chance to return, headed upstairs to the turret, where, still seething, she prepared for bed.

After an hour of tossing and turning she fell into a troubled sleep, from which she was woken by a peremptory knock at five-thirty a.m.

'Breakfast in half an hour,' Victor's voice announced through the heavy oak door.

'Thank you,' she muttered, making a face at it.

Damn Victor Santander, his lies and his autocratic behaviour. Let him go back to his wretched wife. She just hoped that Isabella Santander was a complete pain in the neck. He deserved it!

Two hours later they were flying over the English Channel. Araminta sat in stony silence staring out of the window as the White Cliffs of Dover came into sight, unwilling to be drawn into conversation. Not that there was much conversation to be had, since Victor had spent the better part of the flight with his ear glued to his cellphone.

Soon the plane landed on the rainy tarmac, and Araminta experienced a wave of relief. Right now all she wanted was to get as far away from Victor Santander as possible—and preferably forget he existed.

Victor concentrated on two long telephone conversations that he could very well have made later in the day. Araminta was part of his life that he was putting on hold until he'd dealt with business back in Brazil.

'We can disembark now, Mr Santander,' the steward said politely.

'Very well. After you.' Victor nodded to Araminta, who picked up her large bag and marched ahead of him, head high, determined not to allow her inner turmoil to show.

In the airport, she was about to say she would rather take a cab when the same chauffeur who had driven them on

the night of the party came forward and took her overnight
bag. It would look silly and impolite to refuse the ride, so
she walked smartly along next to a silent Victor and entered
the vehicle, wondering why he was in such a foul mood.
After all, it was he who had a wife, and it was Isabella
who'd caused the trouble—not her!

By the time they reached Pont Street Araminta was only
too thankful to be leaving his company.

Victor looked out of the window, then at her. 'Will you
be all right?' he asked, making no move towards her.

'I'll be fine,' she answered in a chilly, haughty tone that
left him in no doubt of her feelings.

'I'm sorry it worked out like this.'

'Never mind. It's probably for the best.' She sent him a
bright, brittle smile that didn't reach her eyes and moved
towards the door that the chauffeur was holding for her.
'Have a good trip.'

'I doubt I will. I'll call you when I return,' he added
briefly.

The nerve of him! Araminta seethed, not bothering to
answer as she alighted from the vehicle and made her way
into the apartment block. The sheer nerve of the man! As
she turned the key in the lock of the entrance door she
watched the Bentley purr off into the traffic and let out an
angry sigh. This would teach her to be more selective in
the future.

Upstairs, she flung her bag next to the door and went to
make herself a cup of coffee. Decaf espresso, she noted
with satisfaction. She would throw that damn Santander
coffee he'd given her into the bin the moment she got back
to Taverstock Hall. She wanted no reminders of her stupid
impulsive behaviour and its inevitable consequences.

Married, indeed. She should have guessed he was the
kind of man who would be married and was just fooling

around—should have sensed from the first day that he was the sort who probably kept his wife at home while he roamed the world and had affairs with different women. Only someone as pathetically naïve and stupid as herself would have fallen for his undeniable charm. It was shameful that she hadn't known any better.

As the kettle purred she drummed her foot nervously against a cupboard and glanced at the pile of forwarded letters Sara had left for her on the kitchen table. She noticed a list of urgent telephone calls to respond to as well. With a sigh, she picked it up. There was a message from her mother, and another from Pearce that read *'Very Urgent'*.

She sighed, peered at her watch, then waited for the kettle to boil before taking her mug of coffee and the biscuit tin through to the room with the telephone, aware that in her abstraction she hadn't even remembered to phone Pearce and find out how the first day of the book's sales had gone.

After a couple of sips she lifted the receiver, punched out his office number and was immediately put through.

'Araminta, where the hell have you been?' Pearce exploded righteously.

'Oh, just away,' she answered vaguely. The last person she wanted knowing her whereabouts was Pearce.

'How could you leave the party like that without telling me? There were tons of people who wanted to meet you.'

'Oh, cool down, Pearce, it's not the end of the world. So, how have things been here?' she asked, nibbling at a ginger-snap.

'How have things been?' the irate Pearce squeaked down the phone. 'Things are fantastic, that's how things are. Record sales in the first two days. Of course the author wasn't available for comment,' he added, his voice laced with sarcasm. 'We could quite honestly say that we didn't know where she could be located.'

Araminta put down the biscuit. 'Did you say *record* sales?'

'Sold out lock, stock and barrel. They're printing another three hundred thousand copies as we speak. The kids are crazy about it—clamouring for books, lining the pavements in front of the bookstores, not to mention—'

'You're kidding,' she mumbled, flabbergasted.

'No, Araminta, I kid you not. I even had a telephone call from your wretched mother, who'd actually heard something on the news and wanted to know more, believe it or not.'

'Oh, God.'

'Is that all you have to say? *Oh, God?* Surely after disappearing off the face of the planet for the past few days the least you could do is come up with something a little more imaginative—like, *Wow, Pearce, it's marvellous. You've done a great job*?'

'Pearce, don't be cross. I'm sorry,' she apologised, trying to assimilate all that was going on. 'It's just that— Look, I went away and something happened and I hadn't a clue about any of this. Are you free for lunch?'

'Of course,' he replied, mollified by her appeasing tone. 'I'll take you to Harry's Bar. Probably won't be left in peace anywhere else. By the way, are there any reporters outside Sara's flat?'

'I didn't see any.'

'Good. They were parked on the doorstep yesterday, but they've obviously realised you're not there. Perhaps it wasn't a bad thing you were away after all.'

'Pearce, do you really mean that *Phoebe Milk and the Magician's Promise* is a complete success? Not just us imagining it?'

'I'm telling you, girl, it's the real thing. You'll be looking to install yourself in a tax haven, you're going to make so much money. See you at one at Harry's.'

Araminta laid down the phone and tried to assimilate the twists her life had taken in the past few days. While she'd been away, acting like a starry-eyed teenager, she'd suddenly become famous. It seemed incredible, and she shook her head in bewilderment, kicking off her shoes and wishing Victor knew. It would serve him right. Though why she should care if he knew of her success or not when he was probably already boarding a flight to South America was beyond her.

Realising she'd have to get around to it some time, she lifted the phone again and called Taverstock Hall.

'Hello?' Lady Drusilla's imperious voice answered immediately. 'Ah, Araminta. Where on earth have you been? I've been besieged by the press, who seem to want to know all about you and this wretched book you've written. I've been feeling very off-colour lately. You really should have had some consideration for *me* when you decided to get into this profession. I've had who knows what kind of people ringing the front doorbell and asking all sorts of impertinent questions.'

'I'm sorry, Mother,' Araminta gritted, restraining her anger. Not even now that she'd succeeded, now that she was a success, had achieved what any other parent would have been proud of, could her mother think of anything but herself.

'When are you coming home?'

'I don't know,' she answered curtly.

'Well, what am I supposed to tell these creatures?'

'Oh, tell them whatever you like,' Araminta threw bitterly. 'How about, you have an ungrateful daughter who has no consideration for you or your comfort, and that frankly you'll be glad if she never steps foot over the threshold again?'

With tears running down her face Araminta slammed the phone down and threw herself among the sofa cushions, leaving Lady Drusilla holding the receiver in shocked astonishment.

Victor walked down the corridor of the private clinic in Leblon and knocked on the door of the room that had been indicated.

'Come in,' a soft feminine voice that he knew only too well responded.

'Hello, Isabella. I hope you're better,' he said without warmth, standing in the doorway observing her, his eyes narrowed. There seemed very little wrong with the woman lying there, beautifully attired in a sexy fuchsia lace negligee, her face perfectly made up.

'Victor, *querido*.' She extended a long, exquisitely manicured hand towards him. 'I've been so ill. Simply dreadful.'

'You don't look ill in the least,' he said dismissively, still not moving into the room.

'That's because I'm better now.' She made a moue with her mouth. 'Why are you standing there? Come on in and sit down on the bed. I want to talk to you.' She patted the covers invitingly.

'Isabella, you and I have nothing left to say to each other. I know very well that this accident was a story you and your sister made up to get me to come back here. You've made a big mistake.'

'But, Victor, darling, I had to see you to tell you that I've changed my mind. I thought I didn't love you any more, but—'

'Really?' His mouth took on a cynical twist and he threw

his jacket down on the chair and closed the door sharply. 'Perhaps you should have thought of that before you killed my child.'

'Oh, but that's all in the past.' She waved her tapered fingers dismissively. 'I've decided that I don't want a divorce, that I love you after all. We can have another baby.' She flapped her long dark lashes in his direction, her beautiful eyes swimming with unshed tears.

She was good; Victor had to give it to her. But she'd have to find another fool to seduce with her wiles and tricks. 'Isabella, you're wasting your time. What happened to the boyfriend, by the way?'

'What boyfriend?' she responded innocently. 'You just made all that up to—'

'Shut up,' he hissed, coming into the middle of the room and staring down coldly at her. 'How dare you take me for a fool? Wasn't it enough that you aborted my child and went off with another man? Do you really think that for one minute I would consider taking you back? It's over, Isabella. Find someone else to provide you with all this.' He waved around the room at the vases of cut flowers and palms. 'I'm not impressed by your antics. Not one little bit. The show is over, and unless you get out of that damn bed and over to my lawyer's office first thing tomorrow morning, I'll refuse to pay the alimony I agreed upon.'

'You wouldn't.' She looked at him in astonished anger.

'Don't push me,' he muttered through clenched teeth. 'Just be glad that I happen to have other business to deal with in Rio, apart from your lies. I would recommend you be at my lawyer's office at nine o'clock tomorrow morning. I'll be there, and I plan to bring this whole business to a very fast close. It's over, Isabella. We're through.'

Then, picking up his jacket, he marched into the corridor, slamming the door hard behind him.

CHAPTER EIGHT

ARAMINTA soon discovered that becoming famous overnight had its pros and cons. On the one hand she was welcomed everywhere; her publishers had offered a huge advance for her following book and life was looking rosy. On the flipside she had little or no privacy—couldn't even ride on the Downs without some photographer popping out of the undergrowth to snap her picture.

Finally, realising that she could stand it no longer and would never get her next book written unless she took serious measures, Araminta decided to accept the offer of her friends, Ana and Tim Strathmuir, to stay in a cottage on their Scottish estate and disappear for a while.

There had been no sign of Victor, not a word since he had disappeared from her life so abruptly. And that was almost a month ago. Not that she spent her days thinking about him, but much against her will she found herself dreaming of him at night, recalling those exquisite moments shared in the turret room, the feel of his hands caressing her body. She would wake up feeling soft and yielding, filled with desire for this man who had flitted so quickly through her life, and, she knew, would never appear there again.

Now, as she arrived at Strathmuir Castle, and her new Land Rover headed through the gates to the estate, she experienced a sense of relief at having flown the coop, at being here in the wilds of Scotland, completely on her own, without any press pestering her and without the possibility, however remote, of running into Victor at some unsuspecting moment in Sussex.

Her mother, having finally realised that Araminta had become a star, was now basking in the reflected glory of her daughter's fame. Araminta smiled to herself cynically. All at once she'd become a paragon in Lady Drusilla's eyes, and could do no wrong. Thank goodness she'd decided to take the plunge and come up here by herself, even if it had meant facing driving on icy December roads.

Now, as she travelled slowly up the drive of the Scottish estate, she could tell that a snowstorm was brewing. Thank heavens she'd made it here just in time. The keys were at Home Farm with the factor, she'd been told.

Araminta peered through the looming mist at a building to her left. That must be it, she deduced, seeing a smoking chimney and lights in the windows even though it was only half past three in the afternoon. Turning up the bumpy lane, she parked in front of the door, then pulled on her thick anorak, jumped out of the Land Rover and stretched her legs, stiff from many hours of driving.

She stepped onto the front step and rang the bell. A dog barked from somewhere deep inside the house and she heard the sound of footsteps approaching. Soon the door opened and a cheery-faced woman with grey curls, a tweed skirt and thick Shetland jersey greeted her.

'Och, you must be Mrs Dampierre,' the woman exclaimed. 'I'm Rhona MacTavish. Now, come along in and dinna catch yer death out there, dearie.' She tutted, stepping aside for Araminta to enter.

'Thank you. That's most kind.' Indeed, the inside of the farmhouse was a sharp contrast to the dark, damp, misty weather outside. 'I believe you have the keys of Heather Cottage?' she said, smiling.

'Indeed I do, dearie. Now, you sit yersel' doon by the

fire while I fetch them. And what about a cup of tea and a wee dram to keep out the cold?' Mrs MacTavish added with a broad smile.

'That would be lovely,' Araminta agreed gratefully.

'Then I'll put on the kettle while ye warm up.' She bustled off into the kitchen while Araminta rubbed her cold hands by the fire and looked about her at the walls, covered in pictures of men in kilts playing bagpipes, certificates and prizes won at the Highland Games, and a few paintings of scenes on Scottish moors dotted with shaggy Highland cattle.

With a sigh Araminta let go some of the tension that had weighed on her for the past few weeks. It felt wonderful to be miles away from the hype, in such a simple warm environment, where no one knew who she was. Mrs MacTavish, bless her heart, hadn't even recognised her or asked for an autograph.

With a contented smile she leaned back against the overbright plush orange velvet sofa and gazed into the low-burning coal fire. A few weeks spent here in Scotland would afford her a measure of peace, and the tranquillity she desperately needed to work on her next book, and would leave her no room for any thoughts of Victor. In fact the sooner she got cracking on it the better. Knowing that she already had the book outlined in her mind was a relief. It would help her get through the Christmas season with no regrets. And would prevent her spending it wondering where and how Victor and his wife were celebrating the occasion.

'Here's the tea, and a wee dram.' Mrs MacTavish came scurrying back into the room with a large tray piled high with fruit cake and scones, cream and butter, tea and a glass of whisky.

'You shouldn't have gone to all this trouble,' Araminta exclaimed, touched by her hostess's generosity.

'Well, ye look as if ye need a wee something to fatten ye up,' Mrs MacTavish answered, her face breaking once more into a cheerful smile.

Araminta swallowed, for the older woman's words reminded her of what Victor had said about quality and quantity, and for a moment she experienced a twinge of longing. But she banished it immediately. It was ridiculous to be hankering after the impossible. And Victor was exactly that: imperious, spoiled and impossible. The sooner she accepted that, the sooner she could forget about him and get on with her life and her success.

After finishing the tea, sipping the whisky, and being given the low-down on all the relations in Mrs MacTavish's photographs, Araminta finally got up.

'You've been far too kind, Mrs MacTavish, and I mustn't impose on you any longer.'

'Och, dinna you worry. I like a bit of company now and then. I'll just pop ma coat on and I'll be up to the cottage with ye. Hamish was supposed to put the lights on fer ye earlier, but ye ken what men are like.' She rolled her eyes, and before Araminta could stop her put on a heavy coat.

'Very well, but I'll drive you back down again.'

'Och, no, I'm used to the wee walk. It's not far—just across the field over there. Ye willna be too lonely, will ye?' she asked curiously as they closed the door and headed for the car.

'Not at all. In fact quite the opposite, Mrs MacTavish. I've come here to find some peace and quiet and to write.'

'Aye, that's right. Her Ladyship said ye were a writer. That explains it. Ye artisty types like to be alone. Creativity, that's what it is,' she said with a knowing nod as she climbed into the Land Rover.

Minutes later they drew up in front of a delightful stone cottage, just visible through the veil of heavy mist. Araminta jumped out, excited, and Mrs MacTavish followed with the keys.

'Looks as if Hamish has been here after all,' she remarked with a sniff, noting the gleaming light hanging above the front porch.

And, sure enough, when they opened it up the cottage was bright and welcoming. A fire crackled merrily in the grate of the charming, beamed living room, and Araminta wandered around enchanted. The place was delightful, small and old with gnarled beams and crooked walls covered in pretty fabric. The cottage had been most tastefully refurbished by Ana and Tim, she reflected, smiling, knowing at once that she would feel at home here.

'It's perfectly gorgeous, Mrs MacTavish. Lady Strathmuir's done a wonderful job,' she said after touring the upstairs rooms, delighted with the four-poster in the master bedroom.

'Aye, that she has. It took her a while, though, what with one thing and another.'

'I know I'll be happy here,' Araminta murmured, as though she needed to reassure herself.

'Well, that's good,' Mrs MacTavish answered, satisfied. 'Now, I'll be on ma way, or Hamish'll be hankering after his supper.'

'Please, you must let me drive you home.' Araminta moved towards the door.

'Och, lassie, you settle in now and dinna worry about me. The walk'll give me an appetite fer ma supper.'

Realising there was little use arguing, since Mrs MacTavish was obviously determined she should stay, Araminta thanked her once more, accompanied her to the door and stood for a few minutes watching the older woman disappear into the thickening mist at a strapping pace. She lingered a moment, assimilating her surroundings and breathing in the raw, damp evening air, then closed the door and locked it carefully.

Turning, she leaned against it and looked about her once more. Finally she was on her own, in a place that, for the moment at least, she could call home. With no rules, no regulations, no harping sound of her mother's voice, no criticisms or rebukes, and no pestering journalists to fob off.

Letting out a tired but happy sigh, she moved into the cosy living room and flopped onto one of the wide, plump chintz sofas next to the fire, determined to be as contented as she'd convinced herself she should be. But as she dropped her head back against the cushions and stared into the flames it was impossible not to conjecture, not to speculate, not to wonder about Victor's whereabouts and what he was doing at this very moment.

It was the twenty-second of December by the time Victor finally walked into his apartment in Eaton Place, tired but satisfied with the result of his unexpected journey. He'd only been away a month, but somehow it felt a lot longer. At least he'd achieved his objective and, thanks to some serious manoeuvring on the legal front, had finally managed to get the divorce decree.

At last he was rid of Isabella.

Whatever she got up to now and in the future was no more his affair—just as he would no more be responsible for her actions or her conniving.

He looked about him and sighed. It was almost Christmas, a time of year he usually found depressing. Christmas was only good if you had kids, or still had a family alive to go to. But for a bachelor in a city it was a time of reckoning, a time to rehash all the mistakes he'd made over the past few years and brood over them.

With another sigh Victor sat down in the large living room. He glanced at the mail on the coffee table but there was nothing of importance. Then he caught sight of a magazine next to the letters, and his eyes narrowed as he peered at the front cover in amazement.

He hadn't been mistaken! It *was* Araminta—holding a copy of her book.

He stared at the magazine for a moment, then dropped it back on the table. She'd never been far from his mind these past weeks. He'd decided it was better not to call her, to let sleeping dogs lie, and had tried resolutely to banish her from his thoughts. He'd become determined not to give the episode any importance, but without success. So she'd become famous overnight, had she? Well, he was pleased for her, of course. Perhaps now, with all this going on in her life, she would have forgotten him. So much the better.

Or was it?

All at once Victor regretted that he hadn't phoned or kept in touch. The past weeks had been filled with tying up and making a clean break with the past, ridding himself of the obnoxious problem of Isabella and making sure that it was done right. That had required his complete attention. Now that was done and he was back, maybe things could be different. Perhaps he should phone Araminta after all and explain? When he came to think of it, he had left her in rather an abrupt manner.

Victor got up. To his surprise he realised that he didn't want to let another hour go by without hearing the sound of that soft, husky voice—a voice that, if truth be told, had haunted his every free moment.

Picking up the phone, he dialled the number of Taverstock Hall, surprised when there was no reply. He let it ring for a while. Surely Araminta would be down in Sussex with her mother for Christmas? After several more tries he gave up. Maybe she was here in London, he reasoned, wondering if he had the number of the flat she'd been staying at and realising that in his hurry to depart he hadn't asked her for it.

Damn. This wasn't very promising.

Then he remembered Pearce and new hope flashed. Flipping through his organizer, he called his friend's mobile.

'Hello?'

'Pearce?'

'Yes, who is it?'

'Victor.'

'Aha, the return of the wanderer,' Pearce exclaimed. 'Where do you hail from?'

'I'm just back in London. I went to Brazil for a month.'

'I know. I heard through the grapevine.'

'You mean Araminta told you?'

'Yep. That's right. Didn't sound too pleased either.'

'Was she mad at me?'

'Well, that depends how you interpret mad. Was she about to throw a fit because you'd gone to Brazil? No, I wouldn't say *that*, exactly. Should she have?' Pearce asked, suddenly interested.

'No, no, of course not. Don't be ridiculous.' Victor forced himself to sound uninterested and casual. 'I just happened to mention to her that I might be going to Brazil, that's all.'

'I see. That explains it. Staying in town for Christmas, are you?'

'I haven't really thought about it yet,' Victor remarked, and looked about the room, which was devoid of any festive decorations. 'What about you?'

'Oh, I'm off to Wiltshire, as usual.'

'I see. By the way, I tried to ring Araminta at Taverstock Hall but there was no reply.'

'Not surprising. She's not there, and Lady Drusilla was probably hobnobbing at some Christmas do with the natives. By the by, you may not be aware, but there's been quite a bit going on since you upped and left for the southern hemisphere, old chap.'

'Really? What?'

'Well, thanks to my great management of her career, Araminta has become an overnight sensation. Not a child in this country can think of anything except *Phoebe Milk*. Bestseller on the Christmas lists.'

'That explains why I saw her picture on the cover of a magazine,' Victor responded gloomily.

'Just one?' Pearce laughed. 'The woman's a sensation—the latest phenomenon. And that's just the beginning. Wait till the film rights are negotiated, and the—'

'Yes, yes, I'm sure. But where is she?' Victor interrupted impatiently.

'Away.'

'I gathered that,' he responded, trying not to lose his calm. 'Where?'

'I'm not allowed to disclose her whereabouts.'

'Not allowed to— Why, that's perfectly ridiculous, Pearce. This is me, not some stranger,' he said arrogantly. 'I need to speak to her urgently.'

'What about? I'm her agent. If it's important I can deal with it,' Pearce said cautiously. 'Not trying to get your hands on the South American rights to her novel or anything like that, are you?'

'For God's sake, man, it's none of your business what I want to talk to her about. Damn the rights,' Victor growled. 'Now, come on, Huntingdon, give me her number.'

'Sorry, no go, old chap. But if you give me yours I suppose I could pass it on to her. That way, if she really wants to get in touch she will,' Pearce said, tongue in cheek, knowing exactly how annoyed Victor would be at not getting his own way.

'Oh, very well,' Victor conceded grudgingly. It wasn't satisfactory, but it was better than nothing. All he could do was hope that she might decide to call. But, despite his usual self-confidence, he didn't have any great hopes.

CHAPTER NINE

'ARAMINTA, I spoke to Victor Santander. He wants to talk to you,' Pearce announced during a call the next morning.

Sitting up in bed, Araminta blinked. Her heart leaped and she swallowed. 'When did he phone?' she said stupidly, fingering the duvet.

'Last night. I didn't want to disturb you.'

'Oh.'

'You sound disappointed.'

'Of course I'm not disappointed,' she snapped, irritated. The mere mention of Victor's name was conjuring up images she'd rather forget.

'Well, as I mentioned, he phoned last night, said he was back in town and wanted your number since he couldn't locate you either at Taverstock Hall or on your mobile. Of course I wasn't about to give him the number of Heather Cottage.'

'Oh. No, of course not.'

'Should I have? You said not to give it to anyone.'

'Of course. You were quite right.'

'I had no idea if you wanted to speak to him or not.'

'I don't,' she lied, trying to convince herself that the words were indeed true.

'Well, anyway, I've got his number. I can give it to you if you want, and then you can call him or not—as you wish,' Pearce said, dying to know more.

'Okay,' she replied, trying to sound bored. 'Just let me grab a pen.' She made a fuss of picking up the pad and pen that she kept on her bedside table while trying to calm her racing pulse. 'All right, go ahead.'

Pearce gave her the number and she jotted it down. So he was in London. She was dying to ask Pearce if Victor had said what he was doing for Christmas, then in a rush she remembered. He'd probably brought his wife with him. They'd be spending Christmas together.

His wife.

But as she hung up she realised with a measure of relief that this didn't make sense. If his wife was in London, surely he wouldn't be calling and leaving his number for her?

Araminta sank back among the pillows and stayed staring at the figures in front of her. So he'd returned. He'd disappeared for a whole month, hadn't shown any sign of life, and now he expected her to phone him.

The man really had a nerve.

Placing the number on the bedside table, she climbed out of bed and stretched, before heading downstairs to make herself a cup of coffee. As she boiled the kettle, added milk and sugar and popped a slice of bread in the toaster Araminta mulled over the idea of phoning him, weighing up all the options.

One minute she thought she would. The next she decided that no way would she lower herself to telephoning him after the way he'd behaved. She should banish the whole idea completely since he was married; what was the use of calling a married man and getting involved in a situation she knew could only end in tears?

By the time she'd sat down at the kitchen table and spread a thin layer of butter and jam on her toast she'd come full circle and still could not decide what to do. Perhaps she'd go for a walk, in the hope that the raw, bracing

Scottish air would help blow away the cobwebs and clear her brain.

An hour later she was tramping in her shooting boots across the moors, trying not to give in to weakness. She would not phone him—would not expose herself to Victor Santander who, as far as she was concerned, could stew in his own juice. Talking to him would only revive those tumultuous feelings she'd tried so hard and so diligently to suppress.

In other words it was counter-productive.

Pleased with herself, and her strength of mind, Araminta took a deep breath of fresh air and headed purposefully back towards Heather Cottage, determined to get on with what she'd come here for in the first place: her writing.

From now on she would simply forget that the man existed and dedicate herself to writing only.

Having worked laboriously nearly all day on the synopsis of her new book, Araminta got up from her laptop tired but satisfied with the first results. Keeping busy was helping her forget that in two days it would be Christmas and she would be almost entirely alone.

Her eye wandered once more to the notepad with Victor's number, which sat glaring on her desk top. She had risen several times from her work, arguing that it might be better just to call him and get it over with, only to hang up before punching in the last digit, knowing she had no business encouraging him. He was married, and he'd hurt her enough already with his callous attitude and abrupt departure.

'Blast it,' she muttered, turning her back on the number, which by now she knew by heart. She sighed. What she could use right now was a drink and some supper. Stretching her stiff limbs, Araminta headed towards the kitchen, All at once the doorbell rang.

Surprised, she stopped in the hall and glanced at her watch. It was almost eight o'clock. Not a time when any-body would normally drop by. Plus, she didn't know any-one who'd call unannounced. Then she remembered. It must be Hamish, with the mince pies Mrs MacTavish had so kindly promised.

Heading to the front door she opened it with a smile.

'Do you always open your door to strangers so easily?'

Araminta quite literally froze at the sight of Victor Santander, leaning casually against the doorjamb and smil-ing a wickedly seductive smile that left her pulse leaping and her limbs weak.

'Wh-what are you doing here?' she muttered, backing into the hall as if she'd been stung.

'Isn't that fairly obvious? I came to see you.'

'But how—'

'Aren't you going to ask me in, *querida*?' he continued, not giving her the chance to speak. 'It's rather chilly out here.'

'Who gave you my address and why did you come?' she spluttered, trying desperately to quiet her heart and her lurching stomach and make some sense of the situation.

'If you'll allow me in, I'll endeavour to answer all your questions,' he responded, his tanned features breaking into another smile and his dark eyes flashing gold as he looked her over appreciatively.

'Oh, for goodness' sake, come in,' she muttered crossly. 'And close the door, please. I've had enough surprises for one evening.'

Entering the flagstoned hall, Victor removed his Barbour jacket and hung it on the newel post. Underneath he wore a high-neck, heavy-knit off-white sweater that accentuated his tanned skin and glistening chestnut eyes. If anything he was more devastatingly good-looking than she'd remembered him, Araminta realised, with a hastily suppressed shiver of longing.

'Since you're here, you'd better come and have a drink,' she threw at him grudgingly.

'Thanks. I could do with one. It's very cold out there.' He rubbed his hands together.

'How did you get here?'

'I flew to Edinburgh in my plane and then hired a car.'

'I see,' she said, looking at him coldly. 'I suppose I have Pearce to thank for this.'

'Don't blame him. I didn't let him off the hook until he finally spilled the beans. He didn't give me the phone number, though. Said he'd promised he wouldn't.'

'I'm impressed. I must be sure to enquire from him exactly what part of my whereabouts Pearce feels he should or should not reveal,' she murmured sarcastically. 'I thought I'd made it plain that I came here to be by myself, to get my book written and have some peace and quiet.'

'I know you did.' Victor's voice softened as he joined her next to a silver tray where various decanters and crystal tumblers stood. 'But I didn't come here to disturb you. I—'

'No? Then why exactly did you come?' She whirled around and faced him, her colour heightened by surprise and anger, and the knowledge that her emotions were as out of control as ever they had been causing her eyes to flash.

'Merely to say sorry for the rude way I left you last time we met,' he replied quietly.

Her hand faltered as she poured whisky into a tumbler. 'How very gracious of you. You could have done it just as well by phone.'

'Hardly, since I didn't have your number.'

'You could have waited until I phoned you,' she reasoned, wishing he wouldn't stand so close, that the scent of his aftershave didn't conjure up delicious erotic memories, that the mere sight of him wouldn't leave her weak at the knees.

'Would you have phoned me?' he challenged, raising a thick black brow, his flashing eyes boring into hers and his hand dropping onto her shoulder.

'I have no idea,' she replied crossly, annoyed at being caught in a trap of her own making, and a shiver running down her spine at his touch. 'It's of no consequence, since we have nothing to say to one another anyway.'

'Don't you think you're being a little hasty?' he queried, in a low, tantalising voice. He gave her shoulder a brief caress that sent heat soaring through her, as though determined to remind her of just how exciting his touch could be. Then taking the whisky from her limp grasp, he nursed it carefully, eyeing her while he assessed the situation. 'After all, we—'

'After all, nothing,' she interrupted angrily, moving next to the fire to create as much distance between them as the small room allowed. 'You are a married man, Victor Santander. You have commitments and obligations. It is none of my business how you run your life, but I can assure you I have no intention of being any part of it.'

'I see.' Victor said slowly, sending her a speculative look. So she thought he was still married. He was about to correct this delusion, when all at once he decided against it. Better to let things mature somewhat. This wasn't the moment for confessions.

'Look, I'm sorry if I've insulted you in some way,' he continued smoothly. 'I didn't come here to quarrel. Can't we call a truce? After all, it's Christmas,' he said, with a rueful smile that crinkled the corners of his eyes. 'Even enemies call a truce at Christmas.'

She looked at him a moment, and despite every instinct shouting at her not to listen to him her heart softened. 'What had you in mind?' she asked, suddenly thinking how nice it would be not to be by herself at Christmas after all.

'Well,' he said slowly, 'I'm alone for Christmas, and apparently so are you.' He raised a questioning brow. 'I thought perhaps we might join forces and share the holiday together, *querida*.'

'Did you, now? And where were you planning on staying?' she asked sweetly, still taken aback by his sheer nerve, but unable to suppress her sense of humour.

'I *could* go to a local hotel,' he said, with a smile and a look that would have melted the hardest woman's heart.

Araminta thought for a few seconds, then, despite her reluctance, gave in. 'You might as well stay here,' she muttered grudgingly. 'The only hotel is ten miles away, and there are two bedrooms in this cottage after all.'

'Good. Then I'll bring my stuff in from the car,' he said matter-of-factly.

'Now, wait a minute—'

'Yes? You did just invite me to stay didn't you?'

'Oh… Yes, I did.' Araminta threw up her arms in despair, too confused to understand her own actions.

'*Querida*, don't get upset,' Victor purred, moving closer and putting his hands on her upper arms. 'Nothing is going to happen that you don't want to happen. I promise.'

'I'm very well aware of that,' she bit back, pulling away, omitting to add what was uppermost in her mind. She could hardly tell him that it wasn't him she was worried about but herself, could she?

Just seeing him here in the cottage, feeling his presence in the same room, was enough to send off a myriad of inner signals that she'd much rather had stayed safely locked away. Oh, well. It was too late now to renege, so she'd better make the best of it.

'So, what's on the menu for Christmas lunch?' Victor asked, once he'd brought in his stuff and they were comfortably settled in front of the fire.

'I haven't a clue. I wasn't planning on having one.'

'Not planning Christmas lunch?' he said with mock severity. 'Oh, but I insist.' He looked across at her, eyes sparkling with a mixture of amusement and something more. 'I tell you what, we'll go to Edinburgh tomorrow and do some Christmas shopping.'

'I can't see the point of it.' Araminta replied huffily, still doggedly trying to fight Victor's contagious enthusiasm, trying not to recognise that his commanding presence had filled the small cottage with a new, warm and empowering energy that she was finding very hard to resist.

'Come on, Araminta, give me a break,' Victor replied, taking a long sip of whisky and watching her carefully over the rim of the crystal tumbler. He reached out his hand and touched her knee, sending shudders through her. 'Let's have fun—enjoy this time together.'

'Look, I don't want to start that *let's live the moment* thing again, okay? It may work for you, but it doesn't for me.'

'You mean you need all sorts of justifications?'

'I never said that.' She pulled her knee out of reach and turned towards the fire.

'Then what do you suggest? That we spend the holiday with you telling me all about your failed marriage and me recounting mine?'

'I never said that. And who says my marriage was a failure?' She slammed down her glass on the coffee table and let out a huff.

'Well, that's exactly what it sounded like. Any other suggestions?'

'No, I haven't. I think you're perfectly odious, and I wish I hadn't said you could stay,' she threw crossly, eyes filling all at once with unshed tears.

Victor watched her, concerned. Maybe he'd been too brusque, too brash. He felt suddenly annoyed with himself, wondering why he'd pushed her. What was it about this woman that made him react so unusually? Was he taking his anger at Isabella out on Araminta?

Rising, he moved to where she'd taken refuge by the fire. 'I'm sorry, *minha linda*. I didn't mean to hurt your feelings, *querida*.' He slipped his arm around her shoulders and drew her close. 'I suppose I've become a bit too pragmatic over the years.' He reached out and his finger etched her cheek, a strange sensation akin to nothing he'd felt in many years holding him in its grip. Then, realising that she was about to shy away once more, he placed his arms firmly around her and drew her close. 'Don't send me away, Araminta. I behaved badly with you before and I'm sorry. Please, give me another chance.'

'Why?' she responded, jerking her head up. 'Why, when all you want is pleasure in the moment? You said so.'

He drew in a sharp breath and stared down at her. 'I'm not sure that I'm ready for anything more than sharing a moment, *querida*. It wouldn't be fair to you if I pretended otherwise. But can't we enjoy whatever time we've got?' He drew back, looked deep into her eyes, seeking her response.

'Well?' He smiled at her now, a very different smile, a commanding yet tender smile that demanded an answer. And before she could resist he drew her head gently onto his shoulder and cradled it there.

'For whatever reason, Araminta, we need each other

right now,' he murmured softly into her golden mane. 'Please don't fight it, *querida*. Rather accept it. And let the future take care of itself.'

At first she stood stiffly in his arms. Then slowly, knowing she wanted this more than anything in the world, knowing she could not resist the warmth and the scent of him, the aura of his presence, she allowed herself to relax in his embrace. This was crazy, absolutely mad. Surely she had more personality, more spirit, than to let herself be persuaded into another whirlwind encounter that would very likely end in the same abrupt manner as the last, however sorry he pretended to be?

Then, aware that she couldn't fight it, she let out a long sigh. This time she would have no excuse to fall back on. She knew exactly where she was treading. But, whatever the result, at least this time she would be prepared.

And he was right.

They could enjoy their time together without necessarily letting matters go any further. For that, she knew, would be entirely up to her. And *that*, she reflected with a sinking heart, feeling the hard wall of his chest rubbing against her, far too close for comfort, was exactly where the danger lay.

That night Araminta bade Victor a cheerful, friendly goodnight and closed the master bedroom door firmly behind her. She was not allowing herself any opportunities to give way to temptation. As an afterthought she even turned the key in the lock, remembering the morning at Le Moulin, determined not to let herself in for a repetition of that.

But no nocturnal visits disturbed her rest. Silence reigned and soon she fell asleep, content in the knowledge that he was next door, even if it left her wishing he was filling the bed beside her.

Victor did not get to sleep quite so easily. Having picked

up a copy of *Phoebe Milk and the Magician's Promise* from her table, he read for a while, delighted by how magical the book was but unable to fully concentrate. For a moment he thought of getting up and knocking on her door, but knew he would be jumping the gun. She was still reticent, still afraid of being hurt.

And she was right to be.

He'd hurt many women over the past couple of years, had let the anger of his failed marriage out on others instead of channelling it into other directions. And he had no intention of doing it again. Tomorrow he would explain the situation to her and take it from there.

Still, the thought of her lying curled up in the big four-poster, wearing that deliciously virginal flannel nightdress he'd seen her in earlier, made him long to remove it and rediscover the delights of what he knew lay below.

Next morning was Christmas Eve and, despite trying to minimise its importance, Araminta, who loved the enchantment of the holiday and was dreaming up a delightful Christmas scene for her new volume, tripped downstairs in a much happier mood—which she tried not to attribute to Victor's presence. She was actually quite proud of herself. After all, she had not given in to any longings, and was fast coming to believe that she had the whole situation under control. Which was great, since it would allow her to enjoy the next few days with Victor with no regrets.

She found him in the kitchen, preparing breakfast.

'Good morning, *querida*.' He grinned at her from the stove. 'Do you like your eggs fried or scrambled?'

'Uh, scrambled, please,' she answered, utterly surprised to see the pine table attractively laid with a pretty Provençal tablecloth, mugs, plates and cutlery all set in place, and smell the delicious aroma of toast, eggs and fresh coffee—

which she immediately recognised as Santander Gold—
brewing.

'Sit down, and don't lift a finger,' he ordered authoritatively, dark brows reaching across the bridge of his nose
as he concentrated on stirring the eggs. 'This will be ready
in just a minute. The best eggs you've ever had,' he added
modestly.

'Humble, as usual,' she commented, following his in-
struction and sitting down, unable to contain the gurgle of
laughter that the sight of him expertly wielding a wooden
spoon was causing.

'Now, don't distract me, *linda*,' he muttered, frowning,
'this is the *moment critique*. Ah! Perfect. *Voila!*' He
swooped the eggs out of the pan, onto the plate and placed
them before her. 'What else can I get for you, *madame*?
Some salmon? A little caviar to add to these?'

'Sit down, or your eggs will get cold.' She giggled,
watching his comical stance as he stood there in a silk
dressing gown, still holding the wooden spoon at an angle.

'Very well, *querida*. Your wishes are my commands.'

'Well, in that case my wish is that you sit down and eat
your eggs, and that later we do what you said and go into
Edinburgh. If we're going to do this thing right we'd better
get on with it. And soon,' she added, glancing at her watch,
'or all the shops will close.'

'That's the spirit, *querida*. And the first thing we need
is a Christmas tree.'

'But we'll never find a Christmas tree now. It's too late,'
she exclaimed between mouthfuls.

'Of course it's not.' Victor waved a dismissive hand. 'I'll
ring Harrods and tell them to deliver one immediately.'

'Victor, that's absurd. How can Harrods possibly deliver
a Christmas tree here at such short notice?'.

'I see no reason why not,' he remarked with arrogant surprise. 'After all, I'm a very good customer.'

'I'm sure,' she muttered dryly. 'But why don't we go a simpler route and ask Mrs MacTavish if there is one to be had either on the estate or perhaps in the village?'

He looked at her, impressed. 'Good thinking. I see that fame hasn't yet corrupted you. You're still of a practical mind-set.'

'Fame?' For a minute Araminta had forgotten all about *Phoebe Milk* and the amazing success she was experiencing.

'Don't pretend. I know all about the book. In fact I read part of it last night and it's damn good. You deserve all the kudos—despite Pearce's conviction that he's entirely responsible for your career taking off.' He laughed.

'Well, I suppose in part he is. I never would have known how to go about it.'

'Congratulations.' He lifted his coffee cup. 'I should have said something sooner.'

'Oh, forget all that,' she dismissed. 'I'm glad to be away from the hype. At least the MacTavishes don't know about the book, which is a relief.'

'I wouldn't count on it. Their grandchildren are coming for Christmas. Wait till they hear that the author of *Phoebe Milk* is right on their doorstep,' he teased.

'How do you know about Mrs Mac T's grandchildren?' she asked, putting down her toast, surprised.

'I stopped by there on my way here. Otherwise I wouldn't have known how to get to the cottage.' He grinned and wiggled his eyebrows, enjoying her reaction.

'You mean you wheedled your way into her good graces, I'll bet. You don't miss a beat, do you?' she remarked tartly. 'Now, let's get this washed up and get going—or we won't find a piece of tinsel left in the shops, let alone a Christmas pudding. I dread to think what Princes Street must be like today.'

Later, as they sat in the Café Royal enjoying a late lunch, surrounded by packages filled with Christmas decorations and a number of gifts—Victor had insisted they split up for an hour to buy the other a surprise present—and mellowed by a bottle of Château Lafitte, Araminta recognised that she was awfully glad Victor had stayed, even if it was only a temporary state of affairs. She also recognised all the reasons why she should have sent him packing, but decided to ignore them for now and simply enjoy feeling warmed by his presence.

After coffee they decided it was time to return to Heather Cottage, before the traffic got too bad.

Araminta looked through the window and grimaced. 'Better be on our way,' she remarked. For outside the weather loomed grey and dreary, evening was fast closing in and sleet was beginning to fall. But as they were paying the bill and preparing to leave, three little girls in brightly coloured anoraks sidled shyly up to the table.

'Excuse me,' the tallest one with carrot pigtails asked, 'are you Araminta Hamlin?'

'Yes. I am.' Araminta wrote under her grandmother's name of Hamlin.

'Please will you sign my copy of *Phoebe Milk*?' the little girl asked hopefully extending the book towards her.

'Of course. What's your name?'

'Lizzy.'

With a smile and a suppressed sigh Araminta signed the book and watched the three children scuttle proudly back to their parents' sides. 'I suppose I'd better get used to it,' she remarked to Victor. 'But it's all happened so fast that I can't quite believe it's true.'

'You will.'

'I guess.' She saw the occupants of another table eyeing her and hastily got up. 'Let's go, before somebody has the bright idea of phoning the press. Then we'll have no peace whatsoever.'

'You're right.' Taking quick stock of the situation, Victor rose and, picking up their several packages, they left the restaurant.

Victor watched her, amused at how anxious Araminta was to escape. He found it intriguing that she should spurn the fame and kudos that so many in her position would have welcomed. For a moment Isabella flashed to mind. If she'd had a third of Araminta's success she would have been crowing from the rooftops of Ipanema and finding every opportunity to get herself noticed...

Back at Heather Cottage they were thrilled to see that Mr MacTavish had left a lovely Scotch Pine tree on the doorstep.

'It's perfect,' Araminta exclaimed, now thoroughly caught up in the Christmas spirit. 'Let's trim it immediately.'

Together they mounted the tree in a corner of the living room, and Araminta climbed up a small stepladder while Victor passed her the trimmings that she'd so carefully selected from the Christmas display in Jenner's department store.

Looking up at her, he experienced a sudden tug of desire. It wasn't going to be easy to stay close to her and not touch, he reflected, smothering a sigh and swallowing as she stretched to a far-reaching branch, revealing a delicious strip of midriff.

Had he only known it, he was not alone in experiencing

that desire. Every time their fingers met Araminta had to suppress the thrill searing through her. But she dismissed it summarily, attempting desperately to ignore the sensation, persuading herself that things were just fine like this: amicable, friendly, and not too personal.

She had just placed the angel on the top of the tree, and convinced herself that no intimacy was much the best way to go, when she lost her balance on the stepladder.

'Oh!' she squealed, tottering and falling straight into Victor's strong arms, her top riding up.

He held her there, gazing into her deep blue translucent eyes, reading all the doubts and fears. 'Just let it happen,' he whispered. Then, before she could react, before she could do more than stare into those devastatingly handsome dark features and flashing golden-flecked eyes, he brought his lips down on hers and, holding her tight, lowered them both onto the sofa and concentrated on the kiss.

Araminta lay tense in his arms, willing herself to break free. No, no, no. This couldn't be happening. Surely she had more will-power than this?

But as the kiss deepened, as his purposeful tongue explored the moist contours of her mouth, she recalled Le Moulin, and the delicious moments spent in his arms, the indescribable pleasure she'd experienced. A flaring arrow of white heat speared through her pelvis, leaving her shamefully wet and wanting, able only to cleave to him, her nipples strained taut against the hard wall of his chest, her senses delighted into silent expectant submission.

But Victor was in no hurry to move. For he too was remembering, recalling all too well the time she'd spent in his arms. Before that moment warmth had been lacking for so long in his life, then all at once it had surged out of nowhere when he'd least expected it. Slowly, lazily, he fought down any last barriers of resistance, a flash of male satisfaction transfixing him when he heard her sigh of sur-render.

His hands roamed below the surface of her soft pink cashmere jersey, unhooked the front of her bra, leaving her distended breasts free to enjoy the full extent of his ca-resses. He brushed his fingertips lightly over the swollen peaks, sending shockwaves right down to her core. Araminta gasped, then arched as he raised her sweater and his gaze fell upon her swollen breast.

'Beautiful—you are simply beautiful, *querida*,' he whis-pered hoarsely, before lowering his lips and suckling the tip of each breast, tongue gently teasing, teeth taunting, until a tiny whimper escaped her and the coiling darts of desire spiralling between her thighs suddenly gave way.

Then Victor was tearing their clothes off, dropping them in a careless pile before the fire, his fingers seeking, ca-ressing, delighting in the molten damp heat that welcomed him.

Araminta wanted him—wanted him more than she could describe. But how could she feel this way for a man who was tied to another woman, a man she didn't…love?

The word flashed as he entered her, hard and fast, and she knew that last was not entirely true. Bringing her legs up around him, she suddenly realised that her feelings for this man were far stronger than anything she'd cared to admit. But even as he penetrated deep within her, even as she felt that delicious build-up, that rush, followed by an explosion so violent as to leave her limp, she knew that she must not allow her growing feelings to show.

For even if for her this meant much more than just a pastime, for him it was nothing but that: a way of not spending Christmas alone.

As she came back to earth after the shattering experience Araminta forced herself to look the truth in the face. Once

Christmas and their interlude were over then she must bring this adventure—she could hardly call it a relationship—to a complete end, or she'd get burned.

Badly burned.

'Araminta, *linda*—that is such a lovely, unusual name,' Victor whispered, his voice husky, relaxing in the aftermath of their lovemaking, playing with the golden strands of her hair shimmering in the firelight.

Logs crackled, the decorations on the tree sparkled and the CD they'd bought—a collection of classical Christmas melodies—was playing softly in the background. Suddenly he wondered at himself: what was he doing here? Why exactly had he come?

He wanted to reassure himself, to be convinced it had been just a spur-of-the-moment thing, a decision not taken upon sober reflection but out of a desire to be with some-one—anyone—during a season that for some reason always left him sad. Yet was it only that? As he pulled a soft fur throw over them and brought his arms about her delicious pliable body, Victor reminded himself severely that that was all it could be.

He knew the score. And just because it was Christmas that didn't mean he should become sentimental. He'd been determined to stay shielded in a world where no feelings or emotions could reach him, but something about Araminta had snuck past his guard. However, he knew very well what women were like, how at first they appeared to be one thing then turned out to be another. He had suffered too often and too long from Isabella's hypocritical behav-iour, and that of others, to allow himself to be deceived ever again by emotional tugs that ended up dangling a very high price tag.

Letting out a long wistful sigh, he suddenly wished it were otherwise.

But it wasn't, and experience told him it never would be. As soon as Christmas was over he would leave, before this entanglement became another mess, another embarrassment in his already complicated life. He'd vowed that Isabella would be the last woman to corner him, hadn't he?

And he planned to keep it that way.

That night they slept together, in the large four-poster of the master bedroom, cuddling close under the goosedown duvet.

It seemed so natural to feel his body contouring hers, his arms encircling her, moulding her, Araminta reflected with a little sigh of longing. Dangerously natural, she realised as sleep descended at last and she closed her eyes. So what if it was only a passing fling? At least she felt happier than she had in a long while. Happier, she realised unexpectedly, than she could remember.

Feeling her body pressed to his, Victor experienced another rush of warmth and pulled her closer into his arms, nuzzling the back of her neck.

'Goodnight,' he whispered, ignoring the tug of desire that the feel of her delicious bottom curved into him provoked. That, he reflected sleepily, would have to wait until tomorrow.

CHAPTER TEN

THEY spent Christmas Day as planned, cooking a turkey in the Aga oven, drinking chilled champagne, laughing at each other's jokes between kisses and cuddles.

It was the most delightful Christmas she'd ever spent, Araminta realised, as she stood before the stove and dipped a spoon into the gravy she'd prepared. So natural and cosy and fun. 'Hmm. I think that's about right.'

'Is it, *querida*? Let me try.' Victor sidled up behind her and slipped his arms around her waist.

'You don't trust my cooking?' she queried, handing him the spoon and thinking how wonderful and intimate it felt to be here in this cottage, away from the world, living a romantic idyll.

Even if that was all it was, it was worth every minute, she concluded, eyes sparkling with laughter as he tasted the gravy and nodded approvingly.

'Just a pinch more salt and it'll be perfect,' he teased, dropping a kiss on her head then turning to top up their champagne glasses. 'By the way, aren't you going to wish your mother a happy Christmas?'

'I suppose I'd better,' Araminta answered reluctantly. Frankly, the thought of anything spoiling this perfect moment went against the grain, but she realised, it had to be done. 'What about you?' she asked in an off-hand voice that she hoped didn't expose her true feelings. 'Are you going to phone your—family?'

Her hesitation on the last word did not go unnoticed and Victor looked up. 'No. Not now.'

'Of course. I'd forgotten the time change,' Araminta replied quickly, chiding herself for having asked. It was none of her business after all.

Picking up her glass, she wandered into the living room and picked up the phone with a sigh. Better get on with it. She dialled Taverstock Hall and listened to the ring at the other end.

'Happy Christmas, Mother.'

'Well, at last,' Lady Drusilla's querulous voice replied. 'I expected your call earlier, Araminta. I would have thought that even now you're famous you'd at least remember to call your poor mother on Christmas morning. I haven't been feeling too well.'

'Mother, it's only twelve o'clock. I didn't phone earlier because I knew you'd be at church, attending the morning service.'

'If you remembered at all,' Lady Drusilla countered unreasonably.

Victor stood in the doorway, glass in hand, watching Araminta perched tense and stiff on the arm of the sofa. Lady Drusilla seemed to make her life hell, as far as he could gather. A rush of hot, unexpected resentment surfaced against the older woman for causing Araminta pain on Christmas Day, when she'd been so joyful and carefree only moments earlier. What right had the old witch to make her daughter feel guilty just when she was experiencing so much success and happiness?

Araminta put down the receiver and let out a sigh.

'Everything okay?' he asked, entering the room, his eyes never leaving her pale face, his resentment gathering.

'Fine.' Araminta gave a despondent little shrug. 'My mother never seems to be satisfied with me, whatever I do. Well, no point in dwelling on it, is there?' she said a little too brightly, and got up.

'I think maybe there is,' Victor answered carefully, handing her the champagne, then standing over her and studying her closely. 'No one should be allowed to get to you as your mother seems to.'

'I know. You're right,' she agreed, sinking among the cushions of the sofa and staring into the fire before taking a long sip of champagne.

'Then why do you let her?'

'I don't know.' She shrugged. 'Habit, I suppose. Guilt and all that.'

'Guilt for what?'

'Oh, I don't know. For not being the perfect daughter I suppose. I tried for ages, but I never seemed to get the drift of it. I thought after I married Peter that maybe—' She suddenly realised what tricky territory she was stepping into and closed her mouth.

'What did you think after marrying Peter?' he asked softly.

Araminta hesitated. She had not intended to talk about the past, or her marriage. 'Nothing, really.'

'That seems unlikely,' he answered dryly.

'Okay, then,' she said, flinging her glass down on the coffee table, suddenly cross at his insistence. 'I married Peter in part because Mother thought he was the ideal husband—the perfect English gentleman and all that.'

'And was he?'

'On the surface, I suppose. Look, I don't really know, okay?' She got up quickly, colour slashing her high cheekbones. 'It really doesn't matter any more, since the man's dead anyway.'

'And are you guilty of that too?' he asked, quirking a thick black brow.

'What on earth do you mean?' she asked, spinning around and facing him full-on.

'Just that. Do you feel in some way responsible for his death?'

'No. Of course I don't. Why should I? I had nothing to do with it. It wasn't my fault that his brakes failed. I didn't order there to be ice that night. I didn't have the lorry skid across the road,' she hurled, eyes bright with unshed tears.

'No, but you feel as if you did,' Victor said quietly, standing up and gripping her stiff shoulders. 'Araminta, you're caught in a web of guilt that dominates your whole existence.'

'Really? Do you know me so well that you can stand there doling out advice like a psychologist? You know nothing about me or my life,' she flung angrily. 'Why don't you just leave me alone? I don't even understand why you turned up here out of the blue anyway. I suppose you had nothing better to do for Christmas?'

'That's ridiculous,' he returned fiercely, dropping his hands, offended.

'Oh, really? Then why exactly did you come?' she threw, her flashing blue eyes blazing like two molten pools of fire. 'You don't seem very clear about your own motives for doing things, Victor Santander. Perhaps you should take a look in your own backyard before handing out gratuitous advice to others.'

Grabbing her glass, she flounced out of the room and returned to the kitchen. The man was presumptuous, full of himself and unbearable! The fact that he'd hit the nail on the head, touched a sore spot, made it far worse. It was true that she felt guilty for having quarrelled with Peter on the evening of his death, for perhaps having been the un-witting cause of his going out unnecessarily that night. But that didn't make her responsible.

Angrily, Araminta shoved some Brussels sprouts into a saucepan, which she plonked crossly onto the Aga with a thud. Damn Victor and his cheap psychology. She didn't need that. Least of all on Christmas Day, thank you very much. Instead of doling out high-handed opinions on matters he knew nothing about, he should be thinking of phoning his wife.

Araminta dug her nails into her palms and gritted her teeth. She damn well hoped he had a cellphone available, for she had no intention of letting him call on her landline.

For a moment she stared at the plum pudding, which had been steaming away for the past two and a half hours, and asked herself why she'd allowed him to stay. This was all her own fault, she realised with a ragged sigh, all her own doing. She should have told him to get lost the other night and then none of this would be happening. Had she but banished him on the spot she would not now be standing here making a ridiculous Christmas lunch that she didn't want to eat. Nor would she have spent time choosing a gift for him, a pale green cashmere sweater she'd thought he'd like. Or— Suddenly a rush of tears poured down her cheeks and her shoulders shook.

Victor stood near the sitting room fire, foot on the brass fender, and battled the unwelcome thoughts racing through his mind. She had every right to be angry, every right to be upset. And every right to ask the question of why he had come. The fact that he couldn't answer it himself didn't improve matters.

Suddenly he didn't care what his reason for coming here was. He'd wanted to, and that was good enough.

With masterly steps he crossed the hall and entered the kitchen, only to see Araminta standing with her back turned and her shoulders shaking. A rush of compassion and anger at his own insensitive behaviour made him take a step forward.

'*Querida*, don't cry,' he said, standing close behind her,

reaching his fingers into the mass of blonde hair falling about her shoulders.

'Don't.' She whirled round and pulled away. 'Don't touch me. I wish you'd just leave.'

'Araminta, *linda*, I'm not going anywhere.'

Before she could protest, Victor swept her into his arms and held her pressed to him, gazing down into her tormented face, her eyes so troubled and angered, such a total mass of confusion that all he could do was hold her close.

'You have no right,' she threw. 'No right to judge me.'

'I know,' he replied. Then before she could continue he planted a kiss firmly on her resistant lips, prying them open while his hands travelled up and down her spine, traced the curve of her bottom, pressed her hard against the firm muscles of his chest.

Araminta gasped, tried to pull back but to no avail. And just as her anger had soared so it diminished now, at the feel of his hands soothing her back in that possessive male manner that left her yearning for so much more, when she should actually have the stamina to reject him, send him away.

And mean it.

She could feel his hand travelling upwards underneath her top, knew that whatever she said, however much she remonstrated, the taut swell of her nipples told him better than words how she felt. When his thumb finally grazed the tightly swollen tip of her breast her head fell back and she let out a sigh of delight, unable to contain the ever-increasing spiral coiling within her. Why was it that all this man had to do was to touch her and she melted?

He was working on her other breast now, showing no mercy, titillating, taunting, until she throbbed low down between her thighs, felt herself go liquid and warm, could do no more than submit when he pulled up her kaftan and she felt his hard maleness seek her.

As Victor pushed her against the fridge door Araminta gasped, a rush of delight overwhelming her as, in one swift thrust, he entered her and together they reached new heights. She clung, arms clenched around his neck, while he thrust deep within her, as though trying to expunge some memory, possess her in a way she'd never been taken before.

Then the spiral rose, and all at once she could bear it no longer. She dug her nails into his shoulders and came with an unrestrained cry of release. She could feel him joining her on this exquisite wave of emotion, rising with her on the crest. Together they crashed into the surf, gasping, dizzy with sheer, unadulterated satisfaction.

In the aftermath Araminta felt too weak to do more than lean against Victor's hard male body, her head drooping onto his muscled shoulder, listening to the beat of his heart match hers.

'That was incredible,' he whispered, lifting her in his arms and carrying her through to the living room, where he laid her down carefully on the sofa, kissing her all the while and drawing her head into his lap.

Araminta was too limp, too sated and deliciously saturated to do more than close her eyes and enjoy the incredible peace and fulfilment. How could she live without this now that she'd been given a taste of it? she asked herself suddenly.

Then all at once consciousness returned, and she sniffed warily.

'Oh, my God!' She sat up with a horrified start, realising that something was burning. 'The turkey!'

CHAPTER ELEVEN

'I HAVE to get back to London,' she told Victor the next day over breakfast. It was a decision taken on the spur of the moment. But once she'd decided Araminta knew she had to go through with it. Prolonging the interlude would only make it more difficult to depart if she became more involved with this man.

It was bad enough as it was.

Victor laid his cup carefully down in the saucer and, dark eyes piercing, looked straight at her. 'Why?' he asked peremptorily.

'Because I have some interviews to give for the book,' she lied glibly.

'On Boxing Day?' he enquired smoothly, raising a brow.

'No, not today. But in the next couple of days.'

'Ah! I see. So when you came up here it was only to spend a few days?' He nodded sagely, his eyes never leaving her face.

'Look, what I do is my own business, okay?'

Araminta's flustered behaviour only confirmed what he already sensed: that she was running away before she got in too deep. Well, maybe she was right, he reflected after an initial flash of pain. Methodically he spread some butter on a piece of wholewheat toast, forcing himself to think with his head and not his feelings, which seemed increasingly haywire. Maybe it was better this way. He certainly didn't want to have a serious affair with anyone...did he?

The sudden realisation that neither did he want the interlude to come to an end shocked him. Hadn't he sworn blind that he would never allow that to happen ever again? That no woman was worth the trouble?

Yet there was something about her, something that drew him in a way hitherto unknown, that was slowly eating at him.

'Okay,' he said suddenly, pushing the plate away and smiling blandly. 'When do you want to leave?'

Disguising her disappointment at his quick acquiescence to a plan she was fast beginning to regret, Araminta lifted her chin and pretended to be pleased.

'I think I'll probably set out this afternoon, if that's okay with you?' she asked sweetly, burying her pain and hurt pride behind a neutral smile.

He didn't care about her. That much was plain. The wonderful times spent in bed and out were just part of his ritual, the way he interacted with every woman. And she'd be a fool to take it for anything else.

'I think that might just be possible,' Victor concurred, in much the same half-serious, half-bantering tone that masked his urge to get up, whip her into his arms and forcefully make her forget any desire to go to London or anywhere else for that matter. 'Any specific time in mind?'

'Whatever suits you,' she responded, painfully polite. 'I think I'll pop upstairs, make a couple of calls and start getting my stuff ready.'

'I didn't realise that you needed a whole morning to pack,' he murmured, watching her rise, eyes following her slim, curvaceous figure as she walked to the dishwasher and placed her cup and plate in it. 'Tell me, how do you plan to live, now that you're famous and making tons of money?'

'In the same way I've always lived. Oh, you mean do I plan to find a place of my own?' she queried, turning round and leaning against the counter.

'Yes.'

'Well, of course I do.'

'In Sussex?' he asked casually.

'I—I don't really know yet. I might get a small pad in London and then see.'

The thought of buying a house anywhere in the vicinity of Victor was not in the realm of possibilities. Just looking at him, seeing him sitting so casually unaware of his effect on her, his devastating good looks and his lean muscular body, the jeans and grey T-shirt emphasising each well-etched muscle, left her swallowing and recalling each instance of their lovemaking over the past few days. She looked away. They were only a kitchen floor apart, but it felt like an ocean. All the intimacy of the past days had suddenly disappeared, and in its place loomed a vacant void.

With a tiny sigh Araminta put the milk in the fridge and wondered if her life was really going to change that much now that she was famous. Perhaps. Perhaps not. It all depended on so many outside factors over which she didn't have full control. At least having a place of her own would be a wonderful relief, and would allow her time to write the several books that were being proposed to her. Pearce was even talking of a movie contract.

'You know, I don't think you've quite grasped just what's happening to your life,' Victor said, as though reading her mind. 'Like it or not, your existence is taking a three-hundred-and-sixty-degree spin. There will be just so far you can run to escape.'

'Well, that'll be my problem, won't it?' she said, flashing a brittle, bright smile.

'I guess. If that's how you want it to be.'

For a second she looked at him. What did he mean by that? Probably nothing, she concluded, sweeping the crumbs from the table and almost colliding with him as he rose to put his cup and saucer in the dishwasher. Probably nothing at all.

The emptiness she felt as she dragged up the stairs left Araminta feeling sick and tired, as though all the wondrous energy of the past days had simply dwindled, like a spectre, into the shadows. With a sigh she flopped onto her bed in a lethargic heap, too enervated to fight the black cloud of depression forming over her. Why had she encountered a man who was a dangerous flirt and a playboy? Why couldn't she have come across somebody normal—somebody like Peter?

All at once she sat up, aware of what a coward she was. She had married Peter for all the wrong reasons: because he'd seemed safe, because her mother had approved, because—well, because it had been the easy way out. And what had been the result? A colourless relationship with little sexual satisfaction and her pretending to herself that everything was rosy so as not to upset the apple cart. Yet the apple cart had been upset despite all her attempts to maintain the status quo. Was that what she wanted? A repetition of the same? Surely she had more gumption than that?

But this man she had feelings for—knew that she would have a hard time living without—was not interested in anything but a casual affair consisting of occasional encounters here and there—a weekend in Normandy, a couple of stolen days in Paris or Rome. Was that what she wanted? Did she care for him sufficiently to accept the crumbs, knowing that she would never be offered the whole loaf? Because of course she would be expected to disappear discreetly the minute his wife appeared, which at some point she was bound to do.

Araminta dangled her feet glumly over the edge of the

bed. There was no way out, no solution, and the sooner she recognised this fact and faced it the sooner she'd get over this man who was fast becoming an obsession.

Downstairs, Victor stirred the fire thoughtfully. He still had several days before the New Year, he justified, so he might as well make good use of them. He wondered what Araminta was doing upstairs. For a moment he almost broke the resolution he'd made that morning not to insist. Should he go up and see for himself what she was up to? But he couldn't. Mustn't. It wasn't fair on either of them. After all, he had nothing to offer her.

Or did he?

Suddenly Victor stood up straighter, and for the very first time registered that he actually *had* a divorce decree. The damn thing had come through, hadn't it. Was sitting safely placed in the right-hand upper drawer of his desk in Eaton Place. But that didn't mean he had anything to offer, he reminded himself quickly. He was finally free of the bonds which had tied him for too long. The last thing he planned was to enter into another relationship that would inevitably flounder.

With a sigh, his dark features set in rigid lines, he sat down in the nearest armchair. What was it about Araminta, about this whole time spent together, that had touched a part of him he'd been so sure was numbed for ever? Was it that sweet smile on those luscious lips? Or the haunting look that sometimes flitted through those huge deep blue eyes? Surely he was not dupe enough to fall for something as simple and superficial as that?

Yet, hard as he tried, he found it impossible to convince himself that her attributes were mere wiles. And the only thing that stopped him taking the stairs in several masterful strides, throwing her on the bed and making passionate love to her once again, was the knowledge that he'd be breaking the silent bargain struck between them.

They parted company several hours later, and many hours after that, having made the long journey back down from Scotland, Araminta stood alone in front of the building in Pont Street where Sara's flat was situated, wondering what Victor was doing. It was an all-too-familiar feeling, Araminta reflected sadly as she let herself into the building.

And it would be this way for as long as she allowed it to continue.

Victor was not a man to be tied down. She almost felt sorry for his wife. What kind of a life must she have, with a man who was never there, never faithful, never a part of her own life?

As the elevator ascended Araminta convinced herself that she was very lucky not to be in that position herself. A man like Victor could only bring unhappiness into a woman's life.

As she entered the dark apartment she forced herself to remember the words they'd exchanged on parting.

'I'll call you later this evening,' Victor had pronounced abruptly. And she'd nodded, knowing perfectly well that he didn't mean it, that there was probably a pile of invitations waiting for him at Eaton Place.

Christmas might be a family time for most people, and inspire loneliness for some, but the end of the year was always awash with parties and activities. And an attractive single man was always a plus.

Switching on the light, she noticed the heap of mail on the dining room table that Sara had kindly stacked for her and, laying down her bags, she flipped through it. Her eyes narrowed as they fell on a handwritten envelope with a foreign stamp. The postmark was illegible so she turned it over.

Strange. No sender.

Curious, Araminta split the top of the envelope and pulled out a single sheet of white paper inside which were enclosed several photographs. Unfolding it, she caught a glimpse of the first snapshot and froze. It was of Victor, his arm loosely thrown over the shoulders of a very beautiful brunette with long glossy hair. They were gazing into each other's eyes.

Hands trembling, Araminta studied the other three pictures. More of the same—the woman with her arms linked about his neck and Victor smiling into her eyes, another of the pair embracing in what might have been a nightclub.

Feeling slightly faint, Araminta sat down with a thud on a dining room chair and, hand still shaking, read the sheet of paper. All it said was:

He is not what he seems. Be warned.

A friend

Whoever it was had not identified themselves.

Araminta experienced a moment's disgust at the low nature of the gesture. But as she glanced again at the pictures she realised she must be looking at Victor and his wife—that mysterious woman whose name she suddenly recalled was Isabella. Sudden rage gripped her. How could he be so callous? How could he simply play with women, tinker with their affections, then discard them like old shoes?

He was despicable.

Araminta took another long look at the pictures, determined to overcome the turmoil of pain and anger—and something else, something she'd never experienced before but that she suspected might very well be jealousy. How could she be jealous of a woman she didn't know? A woman who had every right to him? It was ridiculous.

Furious, she rose and marched into the kitchen, tore the pictures up deliberately into tiny shreds and threw them and the letter into the bin.

Good riddance. She had no need for any soap opera episodes in her life—anonymous letters from hurt wives or anything else. She was a woman in her own right, a writer who'd just become famous. What did she need this aggro for?

Then, still livid, she rushed to the bedroom and tore open her address book, damned if she would sit here waiting for a possible phone call that probably wouldn't come and that she didn't want even if it did. No. Although she hated the idea, she would call up friends and make sure she was invited out night after night. She'd even allow the press to photograph her, if that was what it took to keep Victor Santander at arm's length.

Picking up the phone, she punched in a number and waited as it rang, aware that from now on, as far as she was concerned, Victor Santander could rot in hell.

And enjoy it!

The phone rang and rang, but no one picked up.

It was three days since they'd left Scotland, and for three days he'd endeavoured to contact her—had tried everything from ringing her mobile to leaving notes in the letterbox at the flat. He'd even sent a telegram. But to no avail. Either Araminta had left London without a word, or she was simply refusing to take his calls.

But why? Why would she suddenly become incommunicado? Their parting had been somewhat formal, particularly when compared to the intimacy of their days spent together in the cosy warmth of Heather Cottage, but still nothing to merit complete silence.

Plus, to his discomfort, Victor didn't quite know how he felt any more. On the one hand he was annoyed with her, on the other strangely hurt. Not to mention his pride. That had taken a serious jolt. For, after all, no one in their right mind rejected Victor Santander out of hand. That simply didn't happen.

But he was unable to rally the energy to counter the onslaught of—surely it couldn't be depression? He'd never had anything like that! Unease, that was it—unease that Araminta was inconsiderately causing him. She was thoughtless, he argued, and selfishly thinking only of herself and her feelings. What about him? Didn't she realise that he'd become attached to her in the few times they'd shared a bed? So attached, he realised, wary of his own admission, that he missed her dreadfully.

New Year's Eve came and went, with Victor in front of the fire at Eaton Place, nursing a very strong whisky and listening with a jaded ear to the merrymaking in the streets.

Where was she at this very moment? he wondered, gazing at his glass, furious that he was wallowing in discontent because of a woman. It had never happened before, and he vowed he would never let it happen again. Forget Araminta Dampierre. She was probably drunk on her new fame, enjoying being courted by every Tom, Dick and Harry, lapping up the glory of it all. She probably didn't remember he existed.

The thought made him so furious that he brought his fist down with a bang onto the mantelpiece where he'd been leaning thoughtfully. Damn Araminta, and damn his ex-wife. Damn women in general!

But even as he determined to change his lifestyle, to get out on the town and forget the whole affair, even as he marched to his room and undressed, the unwanted image of her stuck. Like Professor Higgins, he reflected bitterly, he'd grown accustomed to her face. And all he could think about as he tossed in bed that night was the way she'd gasped when he'd entered her, the way she moved, the warmth of her, and how he missed each curve of her sensual body moulded to his.

CHAPTER TWELVE

IT WAS fun, of course—had to be fun—being flown off to a Caribbean island for New Year's Eve in a private jet. But even as she threw herself into the spirit of things Araminta found it hard to derive any enjoyment from dancing on the beach till dawn, drinking exotic cocktails and sleeping until the early hours of the afternoon. In fact she was very glad when her return flight finally touched the tarmac in London and she could make a hasty retreat to the flat.

Ignoring the numerous, increasingly angry phone messages on the answering machine, and the notes in the letterbox, Araminta concentrated on planning the next few days. She knew it was time to go down to Sussex. She had to see her mother, even if it was only for a little while. Plus, she needed to organise her things. Once life picked up next week she'd start flat-hunting in London.

Pearce, who'd gone with her to Barbados, had asked her several pointed questions regarding Victor, but she'd answered them guardedly, careful not to show any emotion, warily hiding all the roiling feelings churning inside which wouldn't subside however hard she tried or however far she ran.

With a deep sigh Araminta flopped into an armchair and, after fiddling with Victor's written notes for several minutes, finally opened one.

It was as arrogant and demanding as she'd anticipated. So Victor Santander didn't like being the one rejected, did he? Well, serve him right. Give him a taste of his own medicine.

All at once Araminta leaned forward, suppressing the nausea which rose suddenly in her throat. It had happened several times now, leaving her in no doubt that too much alcohol and partying definitely didn't suit her. She could live without seeing another glass of champagne for a while.

She grimaced. Perhaps the best thing to do *was* to go down to Taverstock Hall right away and take a much-needed break. Not that being with Lady Drusilla would be much of a rest. But, still, she could ride and be quiet, and think about where her life was headed, without the fear of Victor haranguing her. For the last place he'd be at this time of year was at the Manor. Hadn't he mentioned he was off to Central America early in the New Year? Something to do with acquiring coffee for a special blend he was planning to launch on the market?

Later in the day, feeling considerably revived and determined not to think about him any more than she could help, Araminta relegated Victor's many missives to the rubbish bin and, locking up Sara's flat carefully behind her, left for Taverstock Hall.

'I thought perhaps you might have seen her over the past few days,' Victor said casually, eyeing Pearce carefully across the table, looking for any give-away signs the other man might unwittingly put out.

'I have, actually. We spent New Year's together.'

'You what?' Victor laid down his knife next to his lamb chop, eyes glittering.

'Mmm. It was quite a party, actually. We danced all night on some damn beach at Rollo Bolton's; you remember Rollo, don't you? He was in your house at school,' Pearce continued chattily, oblivious of the mounting anger opposite him.

'Do you mean to tell me that while I—?' Victor cut

himself off and took a deep breath. 'Are you saying that you and Araminta are having an affair?' he asked, his voice dangerously quiet.

'What? An affair with Araminta?' Pearce looked up and burst out laughing. 'Good Lord, no, old chap. She just didn't want to stick around town for the festivities, so as I was going to Rollo's I asked if she could join us. Old chap was delighted—of course—thrilled to be able to rake in the latest celeb. Great hit, of course. Not that she seemed on cracking form, now I come to think of it—seemed a bit quiet. But that's writers for you. I *know*. I deal with them all the time.' Pearce rolled his eyes expressively. 'They're up one minute and down the next, like yoyos. How about ordering some trifle for pudding?' he added helpfully. 'Bingo Bingham told me it's jolly good here.'

Victor scorned the trifle with a dismissive wave. 'What I want to know, Pearce, is where Araminta can be found.'

'You seem awfully keen on her all of a sudden,' Pearce said thoughtfully, a canny look entering his amused grey eyes. 'Say, what's happened to the voluptuous Isabella? Sure you don't want to try this trifle? Don't mind if I have some, do you?'

'Damn the trifle. I want to know where I can find Araminta,' Victor insisted, leaning forward. 'And as for Isabella, she's history. I finally got a divorce.'

'Good Lord, you don't say?' Pearce held his trifle spoon in mid-air.

'It came through in December, when I was over in Brazil.'

Pearce let out a long, low whistle and laid down his spoon. 'Well. I must say, old chap, I never thought she'd let you off the hook.'

'I didn't give her a choice,' Victor muttered tightly. 'Now, will you please tell me where Araminta is? I've been trying to reach her for days, and all I get is her damned voicemail, both at that flat she was staying at and on her mobile. I even left notes in her letterbox,' he confessed, dragging his fingers through his hair.

'I see.' Pearce wiped his mouth on a large linen napkin. 'If I didn't know any better I'd say you'd fallen hard, old chap. Sorry I can't help you.'

'Pearce, you are not leaving this table until you tell me,' Victor said, his tone quiet and dangerous.

'Now, now, no South American antics, old boy. This is England, you know. Plus, I'm her agent. I can't go round telling everyone where she is. Wouldn't be right when she's asked me not to. Professional ethics and all that.'

'I am not everyone,' Victor retorted haughtily.

'No. But I'd be willing to bet that you're one of the reasons she's skipped town,' Pearce answered shrewdly, peering at Victor across the empty trifle dish, eyes narrowed.

It was now obvious to him why Araminta had seemed under the weather all the time they were away. He'd even wondered if she was sickening for something. Perhaps there was more going on than met the eye. He took another glance at Victor, staring thunderously at him across the table. Surely it couldn't do any harm if he gave the man a hint. He might even be doing them both a favour.

'Well?' Victor flexed his tense fingers and looked his friend in the eye.

'Let's just say,' Pearce murmured carefully, 'that she's visiting a close family member in the country. Now, don't ask me any more,' he said, raising his hands firmly, 'because you won't get another word out of me. Forget I said that, okay?'

'Thank you.' For the first time in his thirty-five-year existence, Victor felt true gratitude to another human being.

* * *

Araminta was shocked when she arrived at Taverstock Hall to find her mother in a much diminished state. She immediately felt an attack of guilt at having abandoned her during the holidays.

'Mother, I think you should see Dr Collins at once,' she said, looking worriedly at her mother, seated by the fire, her face hollow, her legs wrapped in a cashmere rug.

'I have, darling,' Lady Drusilla said weakly. She seemed so frail and different from the determined power-wielding woman Araminta was used to that she found it hard to equate the two.

'And what did he say?' she asked anxiously.

'I'm afraid it's not good news.'

'Wh-what?' Araminta sat on the edge of her chair her hands clasped tensely in her lap.

'I'm afraid I have cancer.'

'Oh, no.' Araminta rushed across the room and for the first time in memory clasped her mother's bony hands in hers. 'Is it—?' She left the end of the sentence unfinished, unable to say more.

'They don't really know. It's been bothering me for some time. I didn't want to tell you—spoil your success with the book. I know I've not always been very enthusiastic about your ventures, Araminta, but I'm so proud of you.' Lady Drusilla's eyes filled with tears and she squeezed her daughter's hand. 'It hasn't always been easy bringing you up on my own, you know. As a widow one has to be so careful, and I—' Her voice wobbled and Araminta closed her arms about her.

'Oh, Mother, I'm so sorry. Have you seen a specialist?'

'Yes. But I'm afraid he isn't very hopeful. I'm sorry to be such a nuisance to you.'

'Oh, Mother, how can you say that?' Araminta asked,

distressed, horrified that for all these years they might have been close, yet a wall of misunderstanding had kept them apart.

Lady Drusilla Taverstock died in Araminta's arms two days later—on the morning that Victor Santander arrived at the Manor. Mother and daughter had exchanged so many confidences in those past few hours that Araminta could hardly believe life had given them this last, final opportunity to make up the rift of years. What if she hadn't decided to escape London and come home? What then?

She felt increasingly nauseous and ill, but knew it was nerves. She would be better once all this was over—once she'd had time to grieve for the woman she'd only recently learned to know before it was too late.

'*Senhor* Victor?' Manuel knocked on the door of the study and brought in a tray of coffee.

'Thank you, Manuel. Any news to report?' Victor glanced at his watch, wondering what time would be most suitable to catch Araminta at the Hall. He wanted to catch her unawares.

'Yes, *senhor*, actually there is. I just heard from the cleaner that Lady Drusilla, over at Taverstock Hall, died last night.'

'Lady Drusilla? Dead?' Victor exclaimed, horrified.

'Yes. Apparently she had cancer, but no one knew. Her daughter was with her at the end, though, which was a mercy, poor woman.' He crossed himself.

'Thank you, Manuel, that will be all,' Victor murmured, turning towards the window in shocked disbelief. He must get to her—go to her at once.

Without a second thought Victor rushed through the hall

and, grabbing his shooting jacket, ran down the front steps and into the Range Rover.

Minutes later he was pulling up in front of the Hall, where several vehicles were parked. Perhaps this was not a good moment, but he really didn't care—just wanted to be near her, give her the solace she needed at this time.

Olive opened the door and showed him into the study. 'I'll just get Miss Araminta,' she murmured, her tear-stained cheeks telling him more than words how distressed the household was.

Olive left him in the study and crossed the hall to the drawing room, where Araminta was seated with the vicar, planning the funeral service.

'There's a gentleman for you in the study,' Olive murmured, before retreating, hanky in hand, towards the kitchen.

'If you'll excuse me a moment, Vicar?' Araminta said with a sigh. There was so much to cope with, so much to do, and so little time to grieve properly for the woman she'd just learned to know.

'Araminta, I think that about wraps up the arrangements for the funeral. Now, you get some rest and we'll go over this again tomorrow. Don't bother to show me out,' the vicar said kindly.

'Thanks. You've been wonderful.' She shook his hand gratefully.

Then she moved across the hall to the study, wondering if it was the man she was expecting from the undertaker's.

The sight of Victor standing in the middle of the room was so unexpected that she drew in her breath.

'Araminta, darling. I came as soon as I knew.'

Before she could breathe, before she could respond, Victor folded his arms about her, holding her close so that all she could do was lean against him and let out some of the pain and tension she'd been holding for the past days. All at once she sobbed uncontrollably as he held her, soothing her, gently stroking her back, her hair, before moving towards the big leather wing chair by the fire and placing her carefully in his lap.

It felt good, so wonderful, to be safe in his arms. For the moment she forgot all the doubts and fears of the past weeks, knew only that this was the one place she could find solace in her hour of need.

'It's all right, *querida*, I won't leave you,' he whispered, sensing her insecurity, her need to be cherished and taken care of.

Once she was able to speak, Araminta sat up on his knee and poured out all the pain of the stilted relationship with her mother during all these years, and the sudden unexpected reconciliation only days before her death. It had all happened so fast she could barely comprehend or make sense of it.

'The main thing is that it happened,' he told her, wiping her cheeks with his thumb before producing a large white handkerchief. 'Think of it as a gift that you were both given before it was too late. She left you with the knowledge that she did indeed love you, despite everything.'

Araminta nodded, laid her head on his shoulder and absorbed the warmth of him, the scent of him, the wonderful knowledge that he was here, next to her, when she most needed him.

Gently Victor kissed her lips, and Araminta felt her heart melt. For it was not a sensual kiss, but a deep, endearing gesture of—love. The knowledge shocked her into a sitting position. She was already so confused, the last thing she could deal with now was the realisation that she'd fallen madly in love with a married man. She would have to deal with it in the future, but right now all she could do was take what he offered.

Then suddenly she felt another surge of the nausea that had been bothering her for the past few days.

'Are you all right?' Victor asked, looking at her ashen face, worried. You don't look very well.'

'I don't feel very well,' she murmured, rushing from his knee and heading out of the room to the bathroom, where she retched. After several moments the feeling passed, and she took a sip of water before returning to the study where Victor was pacing the floor, his expression deeply worried.

'Araminta, *querida*, you're not well. You'd better see a doctor. I'll drive you immediately.'

'No, it's nothing—just nerves. I'll be fine.'

'Why don't you come and stay at the Manor?' he insisted. 'The press will be here as soon as this leaks out. I'll take you for a long ride on the Downs. The fresh air will do you good.'

'All right.' Araminta smiled up at him, knowing she couldn't leave him right now even if she tried. He took her hand in his, dark eyes gazing possessively down at her.

It was all she had right now, she realised, and Pearce had already warned her that journalists would soon be camping in front of Taverstock Hall. It would be much better to leave and feel protected by Victor's strong presence than stay here, fighting her battles alone.

CHAPTER THIRTEEN

THE next three days passed in a haze for Araminta. All she knew, during the funeral and afterwards, was that she never would have got through it if Victor had not been staunchly yet unobtrusively by her side, attentive to her every need, obstructing the path of obnoxious journalists and photographers who, with no respect for her grief, tried to corner her on the steps of the church, despite the cordoned-off area that the local police had carefully erected.

When she felt sick he held her over the basin; when she was tired he soothed her; when she needed to sleep he provided her with a soft pillow, then tucked her up in one of the guest bedrooms at the Manor, and stayed close to her until she fell fast asleep.

The night after the funeral Victor watched Araminta's exhausted eyelids close and sighed with relief. She'd been through so much during the past few days that he wondered how she'd held up. Especially as she'd hardly eaten a thing, saying that food made her feel sick. Now, as he sat on the edge of the wide guest bed, he reached over and touched her golden hair with his fingertips.

She looked so frail, so young, almost like a child, lying there alone among the pillows. Gently, careful not to wake her, he eased himself onto the bed and lay quietly next to her. He would stay a little longer and make sure she didn't wake up screaming, as she had the previous night, woken by a nightmare. Leaning back, he rested his head against the pillows, realising that the strain of the past few days had rubbed off on him. And despite his efforts to stay awake soon his eyes too were closing, and he fell asleep, one hand reaching across Araminta's sleeping body.

Araminta dreamed now, her pain and exhaustion set aside for a few liberating hours. She dreamed of his arms coming around her, of his body close to hers. Stirring, she turned in her sleep and threw off the covers. Victor stirred too, and unconsciously drew her into his arms. Still half-asleep, Araminta snuggled closer, felt his hand close over her tummy. And somewhere, deep in her subconscious mind a new, mysterious and wonderful knowledge took root.

It was early when he woke and felt the warmth of her wrapped against him, provoking an immediate reaction. He tried to shift, but Araminta was closely cuddled up and it would have been impossible without waking her. When he felt her stir Victor let his hands glide down her body in a soothing, caressing gesture.

'Mmm. That feels so nice,' she murmured, shifting her head on the pillow and slipping her arms around his neck.

Unable to resist her tender, warm, sleepy gesture, Victor kissed her gently, let his mouth roam over her cheek, past her chin and down her throat. He felt her arch like a satisfied cat, and continued on down until his mouth reached the tip of her rose-nippled breast, where he stopped, hesitating for a moment lest she wake completely. But all she did was sigh, eyes still closed.

Unable to stop himself, Victor took the tip of her breast between his lips and taunted it slowly, lazily, while his hands wandered over her legs, edged up the silky texture of her nightgown and allowed his fingers to reach between her thighs to the mass of soft curls between them. She felt so warm, so liquid and pliable, that he reached further, his fingers seeking a pathway to the spot he knew rendered her senseless.

Araminta delighted in the feel of Victor's fingers, caressing her in places that sent incredible sensations rocketing through her, arrows of heat and desire into parts of her being that she'd never thought existed before he'd touched her Then all at once her eyes opened and she came to, realising that this was no dream, but very real.

But it was too late to stop, too late to do more than submit to his expert caresses. When he entered her, gently, with a care hitherto unknown, she felt tears knotting her throat. There was something new, something deep and tender in this loving that hadn't existed previously, and which gave their coming together a new and profound dimension. He moved inside her as though wanting to reach the depths of her, to know each tiny part of her being until he reached her soul. And likewise Araminta opened up, seeking to take him deep within her, to feel this man as she had never felt any other.

She felt something stir in her tummy, knew a desire to cherish and protect, and wondered for a moment why she was feeling so tender. The fact that he was being so gentle, so caring and loving, made her want to cry as they came— not crashing, as they had before, or in a rush, but in a long, lingering flow, like gentle waves lapping the shore, over and over, until finally they lay in each other's arms with no need for words, no need for anything but the wonderful closeness they experienced in this most special of moments.

Dawn was breaking when they fell asleep again in each other's arms, only to wake at ten o'clock to rain pelting the window panes.

'Looks like a rotten day,' Victor murmured, smoothing her hair back before rising and parting the curtains.

'What day is it?' Araminta asked sleepily. She'd lost track of time and knew that however hard it was to focus she must get grip of reality.

'January the eighth,' he answered.

Araminta watched Victor dragging his fingers through his mussed hair. Had they really spent the night together once again? It seemed so natural, yet so strange that this man with whom she knew she only had a temporary relationship should have been here for her when she most needed someone. She could not have asked for a more loyal and faithful companion at her side, she reflected with a sigh. But now that the funeral was over she had to force herself to pick up the threads of her life.

Slowly Araminta sat up and drew away the covers, aware that her body felt warm and loved and wishing the sensation could go on for ever. Then suddenly she felt the familiar nausea growing steadily in her stomach.

'Oh, no, not again,' she begged, stumbling to the bathroom.

'What's the matter?' Victor followed her, concerned.

'I don't know what's wrong with me. I just feel so sick all the time—especially in the morning,' she wailed, holding the basin for support.

'I'll get Manuel to make you some tea,' Victor said, his brows creased with worry. 'Are you sure you'll be all right by yourself?'

'Fine,' she nodded, thankful to see him go.

After several moments the sensation subsided and she was able to lean back and sit on the edge of the bath. It must all be due to the nervous strain of losing her mother and knowing that in less than a week she had to face television interviews and newspaper reporters, go through all the press junkets that Pearce was setting up for her which couldn't be delayed.

She would just have to pull herself together and get on with it, she realised, letting out a little sigh, wishing she could open a hole in the ground and let it swallow her up.

And Victor?

What about Victor? He'd been so attentive, so caring and kind, with the result that she knew the wrench when it came would be doubly hard to deal with. How could she pretend she didn't care for him when her whole being cried out for his love?

Dropping her head in her hands, Araminta gave way to a moment of self-pity. It was so hard to know she'd found the man of her dreams but that this very man didn't want her the way she wanted him, too cruel that fate should have seen fit to place him in her path only to have him disappear as soon as things got back to normal. For that, she realised, rising stiffly from the edge of the bath, was exactly what would happen. Victor was here for her now because he knew she needed him, needed a friend in her moment of sadness. But after that it would be over.

Suddenly Araminta looked at herself in the mirror. She seemed abnormally pale. Well, that wasn't surprising after all she'd lived through during the past days. Again she felt dizzy, and moved into the bedroom, where she sat down in the armchair by the window, wishing she could just stay put for a little longer, not have to rush anywhere or be on show for anyone.

At that moment the door opened and Victor came in, carrying a tray piled with tea and cups and toast.

'Here,' he said, depositing it on the ottoman next to the chair. 'This should make you feel better. Probably haven't had enough to eat. I should think that's what's wrong with you, *querida*.'

'Probably,' Araminta agreed. 'Victor, I think I should go back to Taverstock Hall today. The press will have gone by now, and I need to make so many arrangements before I go to London.'

'I don't like the idea of you being there on your own,'

he remarked, pouring a cup of tea and handing it to her. 'You should have someone there with you.'

'I'll ask Olive to sleep over. I'm sure she'll agree.'

'All right,' he conceded reluctantly, wishing she could stay but knowing that of course she was right. 'I'll drive you over later on.'

'Thank you,' she answered gratefully, taking a small sip of tea. 'You've been so wonderful to me these past few days, Victor. I don't know how I would have got through it without you.'

'Not at all,' he responded gruffly.

'No, I mean it.' She reached over and touched his hand, noticing how he tensed as she did so. Was he already regretting his overtures of friendliness? she wondered, sudden pain hurtling through her. Could it be that he was afraid she would interpret his gesture as meaning more than he'd promised?

Quickly Araminta withdrew her hand, determined to leave as soon as possible. 'I'll get showered and dressed, and then if you don't mind we'll go,' she said, laying her cup regretfully back in the saucer.

Victor looked at her for a minute, his face hard and taut, and she wondered what she'd said to cause this reaction.

'Okay,' he said at last. 'I'll leave you to get ready.' Then he rose and left the room without so much as a backwards glance.

Half an hour later Araminta was downstairs, thanking Manuel for all his kindness. The Brazilian manservant had been extremely solicitous, attending to her every need, and she felt grateful to him.

Then Victor picked up her tote bag and she followed him down the steps to the Range Rover.

It took only a few minutes to drive to Taverstock Hall, and Araminta found herself wishing the journey was longer.

All at once they were back in that no-man's-land she'd lived through twice before, that dreadful blank nothingness, where feelings could no longer be expressed and only politeness remained. She felt hurt and stunted and— Oh, what did it matter what she felt? The sooner it was over the better.

When Victor drew up she jumped out quickly, holding her bag.

'Thanks for everything,' she said again as he came around the car. 'You've been a wonderful friend.' It seemed so inadequate to say this to a man whom she'd loved with more passion than she could have believed possible only hours earlier.

But so it was.

'Goodbye, Araminta. And please promise you won't disappear on me again?' His expression was dark, but it softened slightly at these words.

'No, I won't disappear,' she murmured. 'I'm renting a flat in London not far from you—in Wilton Crescent.'

'Good, then I shall expect to find you there.'

The authoritative tone was restored and she glanced at him, wondering what could be going on in his mind.

'Right. Well, I'll be seeing you, then,' she murmured awkwardly.

'I'll phone you tonight to make sure you're all right. I may have to pop up to London for a couple of days, but I'll be back by the weekend. If you need anything be sure to call Manuel. He'll take care of it for you.' He dropped a kiss on her brow and squeezed her arm.

Araminta watched as he climbed back into the car and drove slowly off down the drive, wondering if a heart could actually physically break. And knowing that if anybody's could it was hers.

CHAPTER FOURTEEN

FOR the next couple of days Araminta concentrated on dealing with all the practical matters pertaining to her mother's estate. She met with her lawyer, who read her the terms of the will. Everything had been left to her. Now she had to think what to do with Taverstock Hall. She loved the place dearly, for it reminded her of her childhood and her late father, and now of her mother as well. Well, there was no need to make any rushed decisions.

Olive came in and told her lunch was ready.

'Thanks, Olive, but I really don't think I—'

'Now, now, Miss Araminta, what's this nonsense about not eating?' she interrupted, placing her hands on her wide hips and shaking her permed grey head.

'I just feel so sick the whole time. Well, not the whole time, actually,' she said, tilting her head to one side. 'Just in the morning, really.'

'Is that so?' Olive peered at her, eyes narrowed, and drew her own conclusions. 'Have you seen the doctor?'

'No. I don't think I'm really ill—just a bit off-colour.'

'Have you thought that it might be something else?' Olive queried in her matter-of-fact manner.

'What do you mean?' Araminta looked up at her, eyes questioning.

'Well, now, Miss Araminta, I would have thought that a woman of your age would realise that it could be—you know—' Olive made an embarrassed gesture and Araminta stared at her, aghast, suddenly understanding the meaning of her words.

'Oh, my God,' she whispered. 'You mean I might be pregnant?'

'Well, there's no saying. These things do happen,' Olive muttered. And by the way Miss Araminta and the gentleman up at the Manor had been carrying on, close as Siamese twins, she wouldn't be in the least surprised.

'But that's awful.' Araminta gulped. 'I mean, not awful, it's wonderful as well, but, oh, Olive—' Suddenly she burst into a flood of tears, and Olive hurried over to the sofa.

Sitting next to Araminta, she put an arm around her and patted her shoulder. 'Now, now, don't get upset, dearie. If you are pregnant it'll do the baby no good. If I was you I'd pop down to the village and ask Dr Collins to do one of those newfangled pregnancy tests. My niece had one the other day. She knew at once. No waiting around for weeks, like in my day.'

'Do you think so?' Araminta asked doubtfully, scared of what the answer might be, an image of Victor flashing before her.

How could they have been so foolish as not to have taken any proper precautions?

What was she to do? In her heart of hearts, Araminta thought that she already knew the result of the test. Still, Olive was right. The best thing to do was make an appointment as soon as possible and find out the truth.

Next morning Araminta stepped out of Dr Collins's office into the blistering wind and shivered—not with cold but with emotion; she was expecting a baby.

Part of her was experiencing the thrill of knowing she was going to be a mother, the other, the part that knew she'd been thoroughly irresponsible, was in a tumult of confusion.

What would she tell Victor? she wondered as she walked

down the street towards her car, parked in the same spot where she'd first run into him. She stood there a moment and stared. It seemed like many months ago, yet it wasn't that long.

Long enough to get pregnant, she rationalised, clicking open the car door and climbing in, more careful with her movements, as though she might harm the tiny bit of life throbbing inside her.

As she drove Araminta thought of all the possibilities open to her. She'd barely buried her mother, yet here she was expecting a baby. What would her mother have said, had she known? Araminta quailed at the thought. Would she have expected her to have an abortion? The thought left her trembling, and she almost had an accident as she turned a corner too abruptly, causing another car to veer perilously to the left.

All at once Araminta knew that whatever happened she was keeping this baby. After all, she didn't need Victor. Lots of women had babies on their own nowadays. What was the problem? She was financially independent, could provide for the child perfectly well without any help. So why was she so unhappy?

Back at the hall Araminta told Olive the truth, but begged her to remain silent on the subject. And, although she was bursting with excitement, Olive promised to keep her employer's secret.

The problem she faced now, Araminta realised glumly, was whether or not she should tell the child's father.

She spent the rest of the afternoon churning the problem over in her mind. Perhaps she wouldn't tell him right away. Perhaps she'd wait. But then what if he found out? How would he react? Would he want to be a part of the child's life even though he didn't want any long-term commitment with her? It was all so difficult and confusing, and in the end Araminta decided the best thing to do was leave before he returned and give herself some more time to think about it.

'You're what?' Pearce exclaimed, staring at her across the table at Mark's Club, wondering if he'd heard right.

'I told you, I'm expecting a baby,' Araminta answered in a low voice. 'Now, don't make a scene for goodness' sake. It's not a big deal.'

'Not a big deal?' Pearce spluttered. 'Araminta, are you aware of what a publicity coup this will be? When is it going to be born? In time to coincide with the next volume, I hope?' he said severely.

'Pearce, I did not get pregnant to oblige you or satisfy my fans,' she said, laughing despite her agitation. 'And, please, this is a secret. I only told you because I thought you should be aware of what was going on.'

'And who, may I ask, is the lucky father?'

'I don't want to talk about it,' she said, clamming up.

'Don't want—? But, Araminta, this is crazy. You sit down here, cool as a cucumber, and tell me you're expecting, and then don't want to tell me who the father is. Though I'd take a guess at it,' he said, eyeing her shrewdly.

'Really?' Araminta tried to sound nonchalant, but her colour was up and she swallowed tightly. Surely Pearce hadn't guessed that Victor was the one?

'Haven't you told him yet?' Pearce asked, taking a sip of his Buck's Fizz.

'No. No, I haven't.'

'May I ask why not?' he enquired severely. 'Doesn't he have a right to know?'

'Yes. No. I don't know.' Araminta lifted her glass and took a long sip of champagne, then remembered that she shouldn't be drinking.

'Araminta, are you telling me that you are expecting Victor's child and he knows nothing about it?'

She stared down at her hands, clasped in her lap, and nodded glumly.

'Well,' Pearce exclaimed, digesting the information, 'I think that's something you'd better remedy at once, old girl. If there's one thing the man loathes, it's being lied to.'

'I'm not lying. He might not want to know. After all, he's a married man, and may not want the responsibility of a child.'

'Who told you he was married?'

'He did.'

'I see.' Pearce frowned, trying to make head or tail of the situation. The last time he'd seen Victor he'd been anxious to reach Araminta and only too glad to tell him that his divorce had come through. None of this made any sense.

'Pearce, promise you won't say anything about this to Victor, or anyone else for that matter. I told you in the strictest confidence.'

'I'm aware of that. Still, it's my duty to advise you, as your friend—and as a friend of Victor's, I might add—that I think the only decent thing to do is to tell him the truth.'

'I'll think about it,' she conceded, then quickly changed the subject before he could go on questioning her.

'Aren't you going to invite me round to see your new place?' Victor asked, switching the cellphone to his other ear as he walked down Sloane Street, content with his purchase at Chanel—a handbag that for some reason he'd decided would be perfect for Araminta. 'I'm at a loose end right now and I have something I want to give you. Plus, I'm only a five-minute walk away.' He glanced at the black and white carrier bag and smiled, hoping she'd like it.

'Okay. Come over, if you like.'

'Try not to sound too enthusiastic,' he rejoined, laughing.

'Sorry, I'm a bit distracted, what with one thing and another. But come. I'll be waiting.'

'See you in ten minutes, then.'

What was she to do? Araminta wondered, her heart beating nineteen to the dozen. She slipped her hand protectively over her tummy. She simply couldn't tell him about the baby, not right now. For what if he reacted badly? What if he got cross and she got upset and—? Better not to think about it at all, just receive him normally and not let it worry her. There would be plenty of occasions further down the line when she could tell him, when the moment was right.

The sound of the doorbell had her hurrying to the front door.

'Hello.'

'Hello. Come in,' she said, forcing a bright, welcoming smile onto her face, and hoping the thud of her pulse could not be heard.

'This is for you.' Victor handed her the Chanel carrier bag, then slipped off his black cashmere coat.

'For me?' Araminta took the package and stared at it. Why was he giving her a present?

'Open it and see if you like it,' he said as they walked through into the living room. 'Nice place,' he murmured admiringly, taking in the pale lemon walls, the cream sofas and tasteful antiques.

'You shouldn't have brought me a gift,' Araminta said uncomfortably as she undid the ribbon, opened the box and removed the beautiful cream *matelassé* leather handbag—the one she'd been looking at only yesterday and had thought of buying.

'This is unbelievable!' she exclaimed, forgetting her worries for a moment in her delight. 'I saw this bag yesterday and thought of getting it. How did you guess? Thank you so much.' She leaned over to kiss him on the cheek. But Victor slipped his palm lightly against the back of her neck and drew her lips to his.

'I've missed you, *minha linda*, missed you more than I thought possible.'

'Victor, don't—' But her words were muted by his lips skimming hers, his tongue playing relentlessly, and the feel of his body pressed hard against her. She knew she must stop at once, knew she must not let him render her senseless, must keep her wits about her.

But it was impossible not to surrender to the insistence of his hands, moving so knowledgeably up and down her body, not to yearn for more than just his hard chest pressed against her already aching nipples. What did this man do to her? Why was it she could already feel herself melting inside? Feel herself going liquid at his touch? Feel her limbs weakening as she inhaled the scent of his aftershave, that unique scent that was his and his alone?

With a sigh Araminta dropped the handbag on the sofa and gave herself up to his embrace, knowing that in doing so she was only stepping in deeper. But there was simply nothing else she could do, no way she could resist. For a moment she wished she could pull back, tell him the truth, share this wondrous yet terrifying experience with him. But something stopped her and she gave way to his kisses, pushed the problem to the back of her mind and sank with him onto the couch.

If this was all she was going to be allowed then she would take it now and store the memories for the difficult days up ahead, when he probably wouldn't be about and she would have to face the future with her baby alone.

Victor drew back, caressed her cheek and frowned. 'Is something the matter, *querida*? You seem distracted.'

'No, I—' She couldn't go on, couldn't look into his eyes, see that searching yet autocratic look and not tell him the truth. Instead she buried her head in his shoulder and muffled the tears that were always so close to the surface these days.

'What is the matter?' he whispered, bringing his arms about her and holding her close as he caressed her back. 'Please tell me what is wrong. Is it your mother you're grieving for? Is that what is causing all this unhappiness?'

Araminta hesitated. It would be so easy to lie. Then she remembered Pearce's words at lunch. Bracing herself she drew back and got up from the sofa while Victor watched her, his dark brows coming together in a thick line above the bridge of his patrician nose.

'What is it, Araminta? You look very worried and upset. Tell me,' he ordered.

She moved closer to the window, looked out a moment, then swallowed and turned to face him.

'Something's happened, Victor. I—' She felt desperate, looking at him with fearful eyes, watching as he rose from the sofa and seeing his face close.

'What is it?' he asked harshly, a sinking sensation gripping him.

He should have known it was too good to last. His mind ran back over what Pearce had told him. Of course—she'd found another man when she'd been away in the Caribbean! How could he have been such a fool? Isabella had always shown him what women were capable of. While he had been sitting waiting like an idiot in Eaton Place, Araminta had obviously been up to other things.

More fool him.

'Victor, I need to tell you this before things get any more complicated between us.'

'Don't bother,' he retorted forcefully, his face set in hard taut lines, his memory held fast by another, past and devastating betrayal. 'I can guess. Well, it was good while it lasted, Araminta. I knew, of course, that it was only a passing fling, which is why I didn't bother to become emotionally involved. So much easier this way, don't you think?' He laughed, a short, harsh laugh that left her in no doubt as to his feelings. 'Look, I'd better dash now,' he said, glancing at his watch. 'I'll see you around some time. No need to see me to the door.'

Araminta stayed glued to the spot while he turned on his heel and marched out into the hall. She wanted to run after him, plead with him, tell him to wait, that she needed to explain. What had he guessed? she wondered. Had he realised what she was about to tell him, that she was expecting his baby? Or had he understood something completely different? Why had he reacted so angrily?

Desperate, she sank into the nearest chair and dropped her head in her hands. This was it. It was over. Any hopes she'd had were dead. There was nothing for it but to face the future alone and make sure her baby was loved and provided for, even if it didn't have a father.

She sat up then, determined not to give way to her emotions. It wasn't good for the baby, and that was her uppermost priority now. She would not allow anyone or anything, least of all Victor and his selfish arrogance, to harm her child.

Araminta rose and stared for a moment at the bag lying on the sofa next to the box and the tissue paper. She would probably never use it now she realised with an anguished sigh, never look at it. For it marked a turning point in her life, a milestone that she would never forget for as long as she lived.

*   *   *

Victor left Wilton Crescent furious and walked the rest of the way to Eaton Place trying to understand why Araminta's feckless behaviour—which, of course, he'd expected all along—should have left him so entirely undone and upset.

Damn her.

Damn all women.

Why was he a sentimental fool? Why had he believed, during those days spent at the Manor after her mother's death, that things between them had developed into something deeper—something that, even though he had been loath to admit it, he craved?

And now, as always, came the reality check.

Well, so much the better. The last thing he needed was another ride on the emotional rollercoaster.

He let himself into the apartment and went immediately to the living room, where he poured himself a stiff whisky and stared into space, seeing her face before him and wishing he'd never laid eyes on it. He would sell the Manor, he decided abruptly. Get rid of the place and not be subjected to the possibility of running into her.

At that moment the ring of the phone brought him back to earth.

'Hello?' he answered tersely.

'Hello, old chap, it's me—Pearce.'

'Hi, what can I do for you?'

'You sound a bit down at the mouth, old chap. Everything okay?'

'Fine. What is it that you want?' Victor snapped.

'Well, actually, I was wondering if you'd like to have a bite of dinner somewhere. But of course if you're not in the mood we'll do it some other time.'

Victor hesitated. He didn't want anything right now. Then suddenly he changed his mind. What was the point of sitting here staring into space, making a bloody fool of himself? 'That's a good idea,' he replied. 'I'll meet you at Green's at eight.'

'Looking forward to it.'

Pearce hung up the phone and grimaced. Something was definitely wrong, and it didn't take a rocket scientist to tell him it had to do with Araminta. He let out a long breath. He was going to have to do something about those two. He simply couldn't allow things to deteriorate. After all his own future was at stake, he reasoned. Araminta might suddenly decide not to write any more books.

And then where would they all be?

CHAPTER FIFTEEN

'How about a bottle of Pouilly Fuissé,' Pearce murmured, glancing over the wine menu. 'You look as if you could do with a drink.'

'I most certainly could,' Victor agreed. He'd simmered down somewhat in the past few hours, but the indignation, humiliation and bitter anger still lingered.

Pearce ordered the wine and settled back in the booth, looking his friend over. Victor's dark features looked stormy, and he wondered if Araminta had summoned up her courage and this was the result.

'I had lunch with Araminta today,' he remarked, deciding to plunge in at the deep end.

'Did you, now?' The twist of the other man's mouth became cynical and he smiled, a harsh, unamused smile. 'Quite a little number, your friend Araminta.'

'*My* friend?'

'Well, isn't she?'

'Yes, I suppose she is.'

'Why didn't you tell me she had it off with some chap in Barbados?' Victor threw in suddenly, unable to suppress his anger. Damn Pearce. He was an accomplice, after all.

'Excuse me?' Pearce drew his brows together and sent his friend a haughty look. 'I have no idea what you're talking about.'

'Come on, Pearce, surely you have some loyalty to me, despite your commercial interest in Araminta,' Victor muttered bitterly.

'I'm afraid you're going to have to be a little more ex-

157

plicit,' Pearce replied coldly, nodding to the wine waiter, who was ready to pour. 'I have no idea what you're talking about.'

Victor waited impatiently while the sommelier poured the wine and Pearce tasted it and approved. Finally the ritual was over and he leaned across the table.

'She told me this afternoon—or rather tried to confess. But I didn't give her the chance,' he added, with a mirthless laugh.

'Let me get this straight,' Pearce said slowly. 'You saw Araminta this afternoon and she tried to tell you something?'

'Yes. It can only be that she had an affair with another man while she was away celebrating the New Year.'

'And what makes you so sure of that?'

'Well, what else could it be?' Victor exclaimed, taking a long sip of wine. 'What else could make a woman pull back, stand there fidgeting, clasping her hands, saying she has something to tell me and looking guilty as sin?' he enquired, with a sarcastic lift of his brow.

'Personally, I can think of a number of things,' Pearce replied dryly. 'Don't you think that perhaps you've been a bit hasty?'

'I don't see why,' Victor responded, suddenly less sure of himself. 'It was obvious.'

'Perhaps not,' Pearce answered, looking him straight in the eye.

'What makes you say that?' Victor pounced, attentive all at once.

'I'm afraid I'm not at liberty to say.'

'To hell with all this subterfuge. Just tell me.'

'I'm sorry, old chap, but I'm afraid it's not my place.'

'Look, don't start this cat and mouse business all over again,' Victor ground out. 'It's Araminta we're talking about here. I thought she was different. I was imbecile enough to believe that maybe—' He cut himself off, realising what he was admitting, and bit back the words that he didn't want to hear himself, let alone tell another.

'That you're in love with her?' Pearce asked softly.

'Of course I'm not in love with her, that's perfectly ridiculous. It's just that—'

'Why don't you admit it, Victor?' Pearce laid his glass down and looked his friend straight in the eye. 'My advice to you, old chap, is to go back to Araminta and ask her exactly what it was she wanted to tell you this afternoon. And don't go there looking like a bad-tempered bear or she'll kick you out, lock, stock and barrel, and you'll get no sympathy from me.'

'You know something—' Victor controlled his temper with difficulty. Then, throwing down his napkin, he rose. 'I'm not standing for this a moment longer. I'm going there to clear this whole thing up right now.'

'An excellent idea, old chap.' Pearce raised his glass and watched him leave with a smile. Those two really were made for each other, he concluded, taking another long sip of deliciously cold wine. He just hoped that now they might finally manage to sort themselves out.

With a sigh he resigned himself to a solitary dinner, content in the knowledge that he'd done all he could to right matters.

Victor's temper was not improved by the time he'd searched vainly for a parking place in Wilton Crescent. In the end he valet-parked the Bentley at the Berkeley Hotel and took the few steps over to Araminta's. What was the matter with her? If it wasn't another man, then why had she looked so guilty, so self-conscious?

Two minutes later he rang the doorbell and waited. She'd

damn well better be in, or he'd be left feeling even more frustrated than he already was. Tapping his fingers impatiently on the doorknob, he waited. Then the intercom hissed and with relief he heard her voice.

'Araminta, it's me—Victor. I need to talk to you.'

There was a moment's hesitation. 'I don't think there's anything left to say.'

'Look, please—I'm sorry I was so abrupt this afternoon. We need to talk.'

'I don't think so.'

'Araminta, I'm warning you, if you don't let me in I'll break down the door and cause a hell of a fuss out here. Is that clear?'

He really was impossible, Araminta reflected in silent outrage as she crossly pressed the release button for him to enter. Why should she be subjected to his tyrannical behaviour? Wasn't it enough that he'd walked out?

With a resigned sigh she went to the door, prepared to face the storm. Now that she'd made up her mind to assume her responsibilities she wasn't frightened any more, and knew exactly what she had to do. She would listen to what he had to say, then get rid of him once and for all and put an end to this whole wretched nonsense.

The knot in her throat tightened. She touched her belly protectively as she heard the elevator come to a stop on the landing. Then, swallowing, she pulled back her shoulders, glanced at herself in the mirror and, head high, went to open the door. Thank goodness she was wearing a soft white cashmere sweater and skirt and didn't look a frump.

She simply couldn't have borne facing him without the right armour.

She looked too beautiful for words! Victor swallowed, standing uncomfortably on the threshold.

'Come in,' Araminta said, turning and moving regally towards the drawing room, where a fire was lit and the room shimmered softly in the lamplight. Somehow she looked even lovelier than he'd remembered her, almost ethereal as she sat down next to the fire.

'I won't offer you a drink,' she said coldly, 'as I presume what you have to say won't take long.'

'Actually, if you don't mind, I could use one,' he said ruefully.

'Then be my guest.' She pointed to an antique lowboy on which a tray with decanters and tumblers stood. Victor moved towards it slowly, giving himself time as he poured himself a whisky.

'Can I get you anything?' he asked.

'No, thank you.'

It wasn't so easy now he was actually here to broach the subject, when she was seated so cool, calm and collected. Suddenly everything that earlier had seemed so clear and which he'd been so sure of didn't seem quite so etched in stone.

'Look, I came back because I think I was rather hasty this afternoon,' he said, raising his glass and taking a sip, eyeing her carefully over the rim of the tumbler, a sudden pang of desire shooting through him.

'I don't know why you bothered,' she murmured. 'You appeared very sure of your actions.'

'Did I?' he asked, eyes narrowing.

'Well, you made it abundantly clear what kind of opinion you hold of our relationship, so I really don't think there's very much else to be said.'

'Look, I'm sorry. I may have made a mistake. I'm afraid I've become rather cynical over the years. Things have happened in my life which make it hard for me to trust in others.'

'What a shame,' she said in a languid voice.

'Yes. Actually, it is. I see that myself now. Look, Araminta, when you began telling me something this afternoon, I thought you were trying to tell me you'd been with another man.'

'And why was that suddenly so important? After all, we have no commitment.'

'I know, but—'

'No,' she interrupted, getting up, her eyes suddenly blazing with anger. 'You are the one who said you couldn't commit. *Let's live the moment* were your very words. If I had gone off with somebody else it would have served you right.'

They were facing each other now, Araminta stormy-eyed, Victor watching her warily, enchanted by this flaring attack that told him all he needed to know.

She had not been unfaithful to him, her anger proved it.

'Look, *querida*, I'm sorry.' He moved towards her. 'Can't we forget this and start over?'

'Start over? No. I don't think so. The way you've behaved is appalling. I've had enough. I don't want to see you ever again.' Tears were swimming in her eyes as she spoke.

'But, Araminta, darling, you must understand. This is far more serious than I believed. I've just realised how much I feel for you and that—'

'Oh, have you?' she raged furiously. 'Well, it's too late, Victor Santander. You should have thought of this before. And you're married, so there's no future for us anyway.'

'If you'll let me explain—'

'What is there to explain?' she threw, hot tears pouring down her cheeks. 'Married is married, and there are no half measures about it. I got a letter from your wife,' she added bitterly, 'with pictures of both of you together. I've been a fool, and wrong to have let you anywhere near me after that.'

'What do you mean, a letter?' He frowned angrily. Isabella was up to her old tricks.

'Exactly that.'

'When?'

'After I got back from Barbados. Look, can't we just drop this whole thing? You go your way, I go mine? This whole discussion is pointless.'

'Araminta, please, give me a chance to explain,' Victor begged, moving forward and grabbing her arms. 'I'm not married to Isabella any longer. I got divorced when I was in Brazil, that's why the trip took me so long and why I didn't get in touch. I was tying up all the loose ends.'

Araminta stood perfectly still in his grip and stared at him. 'Divorced?' she whispered, unable to believe her ears.

'Yes, divorced.'

'Why didn't you tell me?' she bristled, a cold fury rising within her as full realisation heaped on her. He'd allowed her to go on thinking he was married, deluded her so that she wouldn't ask for anything, wouldn't expect any commitment from her. In other words he didn't trust her.

All at once she tore from his arms in pain and rushed to the window. 'Get out of my house,' she hissed, trembling, unable to control her intense hurt any longer. 'Get out of here and never come back. I think you're utterly despicable. And I never want to see you again. Ever.'

Then she turned and ran from the room, slamming the door behind her.

Victor stood staring at the door, assimilating all that had just transpired. She was deeply hurt, that much was obvious, and apparently all his suspicions had been unfounded. Then what was it that she'd been trying to tell him earlier?

Dragging his fingers through his thick black hair, Victor stared at the pattern of the oriental rug beneath his feet and tried to analyse the situation. What could have made her look so guilty, so confused and embarrassed?

For a moment he gazed at the door, inclined to follow her, insist that she tell him the truth, whatever it was. But he hesitated. She'd been through so much lately, what with her mother's death, the excitement of the book, and not least what he himself had put her through. He felt ashamed of his own precipitous conclusions. It just went to prove how cynical and hard-bitten he'd become, how the events of the past few years had marked him.

All at once he looked up and his eyes fell upon a picture of Araminta in a silver photo frame. She was seated cross-legged, staring out at the sea, in a typical pose of hers. His mouth softened, his eyes lingered, and he realised for the first time just how much this woman had come to mean to him, how much she'd changed him. Should he go in there and seek her out? Or give it a little time to let the dust settle?

Reluctantly he decided on the latter course. She was too upset right now. It would serve no purpose to harangue her. Better to allow her to rest and try again in the morning once they'd both calmed down and had time to think. He didn't take seriously her intimation of never wanting to see him again; that was an empty threat, he reasoned. But in the back of his mind a niggling sensation told him it might just be true.

All at once he decided he wasn't going anywhere. He would stay here and sleep on the couch. That way she couldn't escape him even if she wanted to.

Araminta threw herself onto the bed and let go the flood of stifling tears. She could bear it no longer. Thank goodness she'd finally told him to leave and never come back. The deed was done and there was no going back on it. She wept bitter tears of pain, hunger, anguish, anger and remorse.

After a while the sobbing subsided and she pulled herself up into a sitting position and forced herself to think straight. She could not get into this emotional state. It might affect the baby. She could feel shooting pains in her abdomen and became afraid. Carefully she shifted her position, lay back against the pillows, breathing deeply, and drank some water from the Evian bottle next to her bed.

Little by little she regained her composure, but still her heart felt shattered to smithereens. The future seemed so bleak now, despite the baby and the pleasure she knew it would bring into her life. But it was *his* baby, *his* blood, and she was sure that it would be a little boy, and look just like Victor, with thick black hair and perfect features, reminding her at every turn of just how much she missed him.

Slowly she got up and forced herself to undress. She slipped on a pale pink silk spaghetti-strap negligée and, too tired to do more than clean her face and brush her teeth, collapsed into bed and turned off the light.

Maybe she'd be lucky and fall asleep, and forget this whole mess for a few glorious hours.

CHAPTER SIXTEEN

AT THREE a.m. Araminta woke up to rattling windows and slashing rain. She shivered and switched on the light. It must be a winter storm hitting London. She rubbed her eyes and, still shivering, reached for her dressing gown, remembering all at once that in her tempestuous state last night she'd forgotten to secure the front door.

Donning her slippers, she padded out of the bedroom and made her way down the passage into the hall to check the front door, frowning when she realised it had been locked. She turned and moved into the drawing room, where one lamp remained lit. Surely she hadn't had time to turn off all the lights?

The wind was stronger and the rain beating harder as she entered the room. She hated storms. Araminta felt suddenly fearful and alone, she and the tiny being alive inside her. Wrapping her arms around her, she moved further into the room. Then a movement from the couch made her gasp and stand frozen to the spot.

Somebody was in the flat, in this room. What was she to do? Terrified, Araminta knew she must protect her baby and herself from the invader.

Victor turned on the sofa, trying to find a comfortable position and failing to do so. Then he heard a noise and sat up. He looked towards the door and saw Araminta standing rigid as a statue in the doorway, her face white and terrified.

Leaping up, he moved across the room in two masterful strides.

'Why did you get up? Are you okay?' His brows creased in concern.

'Wh-what are you doing here?' she whispered, staring at him, limbs weak, as slowly she released the fear that had gripped her.

'Come over here and sit down.' Victor grabbed her arm and steadied her as, shaking, Araminta moved towards the couch.

'What are you doing here?' she asked again, bewildered yet desperately thankful that she wasn't alone, that there was no intruder, that although she'd told him to leave Victor had stayed.

'I didn't want to leave you alone,' he answered, lowering her to the cushions and wondering if she wasn't feeling well, for she had her right hand clamped over her stomach. 'Are you feeling all right?' he queried, standing over her, his face set in hard, worried lines. She looked so pale, so fragile. 'I'll get you a brandy.'

'No—please, I can't,' she murmured automatically.

'Rubbish, *querida*. Of course you can,' he replied briskly, 'it'll do you good.'

'No—no alcohol.'

'Araminta, don't be silly,' he said, touching her hair with his fingertips. 'Brandy will help revive you.'

'But I can't drink right now,' she murmured, leaning back and letting her head rest against the cushions, too tired to measure her words.

'Why not?' Victor asked peremptorily.

'Because I'm—'

Suddenly the full implication of what she was about to say hit her full in the gut and she sat up straight, face pale and hands shaking. 'Look, please, just leave me alone. I'll have a glass of water.'

'Araminta, I demand that you tell me immediately why

you can't drink alcohol,' Victor commanded, his voice low and determined, his eyes narrowed as he surveyed her pale cheeks, turning suddenly rosy.

'It's not important,' she muttered, trying to stave him off. She couldn't—mustn't tell him.

'Araminta, don't lie to me. I hate lies. Tell me the truth at once.' He stood over her, eyes boring relentlessly into hers, allowing for no escape.

What was she to do? For a moment Araminta thought of denying the truth, then a wave of anguish swept over her and she knew she couldn't. For better or worse, she was going to have to admit reality.

'Well?' His features were hard and demanding, his mouth a thin line of determined expectation.

'I—I'm expecting a baby,' she whispered, holding his eyes for a moment, then lowering them to her hands, clasped nervously in her lap, as she waited for the storm she was sure would break over her head.

Stunned, Victor stood for a long moment absorbing the words. She was pregnant, was going to have a baby. So he'd been right after all.

The treachery of it seemed so intense, so vile. He swallowed, trying desperately to master his anger, his boiling rage at the thought of her *carrying another man's child*.

How could she have done this to him?

Araminta looked up at him warily. 'I know that we should have taken precautions. It's just that I haven't had a relationship since Peter died, and as he couldn't have children—well, I'd got used to never worrying about contraceptives. I don't expect you to assume any responsibility,' she continued nervously. 'It's my baby. I'll deal with the consequences.' She raised her proud chin a fraction, determined to be brave. 'You'll not have to worry about anything,' she murmured, unable to keep the bitterness from her voice.

Victor stared at her, unbelieving, the realisation of what she was saying dawning on him at last. It was *his* baby she was carrying, *his* child. Not some other man's but the fruit of their—love. The word hit him like an inside curve ball. Never, in all his years as a grown man, had anything affected him as Araminta's last few words.

'Araminta,' he whispered hoarsely, needing to confirm the truth, 'are you telling me we're going to have a baby?'

'No,' she said, rising, feeling far more in control now that the truth was aired and she'd accepted reality for what it was. '*I'm* having a baby.'

'*Our* baby,' he insisted, shoving his hands into the pockets of his grey pants, caught in a myriad of emotions he could hardly define.

'Victor, there is no need to get dramatic about this. *I* assume the responsibility. I'm perfectly able to provide financially for the child. Neither of us will be a burden on you,' she said, her head high.

'A burden?' he repeated, mystified. What was she talking about?

'Yes. I will register the baby in my name, that way it will cause you no embarrassment.' She looked him straight in the eye and took several steps back, then turned and hid the mounting tears, staring out of the window at the slashing rain, barely aware now of the howling wind, her pain was so great.

Victor watched her, wanting to react and unable to. Then all at once the full implication of her words hit him. His face turned dark with fury and he crossed the room and gripped her shoulders mercilessly. 'How dare you?' he demanded, his eyes flashing arrows. 'How dare you say these things?'

'What things?' Araminta trembled at the sight of his anger. It was worse than she'd believed. 'Please,' she said, suddenly frightened, 'don't be angry. It makes me so nervous, and that's not good for the baby.'

Victor gazed down at his hands, gripping her shoulders, and immediately let go. 'I'm sorry,' he said stiffly. 'I had no intention of harming you. Araminta, when did this happen? How long have you known? Why didn't you tell me before?' All at once a thousand questions poured from his lips. 'Why didn't you tell me at once?'

'Because I knew it would be a problem for you and I didn't know how you'd react,' she murmured, trying to be sensible, to ignore the torture that knowing he didn't care had caused.

'A problem? What the hell are you talking about? What kind of a man do you think I am?' he threw.

'I—'

'You had no right to keep this from me, to deny me this knowledge. You should have told me immediately—shared this news with me. I—I can't believe it,' he said, shaking his head, his expression changing to one of bewildered delight. 'You're carrying my child. But are you all right? You should be resting.'

To Araminta's amazement he slipped his arms under her and lifted her into them. '*Minha linda*, my beautiful Araminta. Let me lay you down somewhere. You must not be upset by anything, must not go anywhere,' he said in a masterful tone, laying her tenderly onto the couch.

'But—' Araminta blinked as he dropped a gentle kiss on her forehead and wrapped the throw around her.

'You must keep warm, you and the baby.'

'You—you mean you're not upset?' she whispered, staring up at him, unbelieving.

'Upset? Of course I'm not upset. It will be a boy, of

course. My first son. Now, let me think. We must get married immediately.'

'But that's absurd, Victor,' she protested, struggling to a sitting position. 'I don't think you've thought this out properly. Please don't say things you don't mean.' The pain of hearing him fantasize left her with tears in her eyes. Perhaps to him this was all just a game, an amusing sideshow.

Victor looked down at her and gripped her hands in his. 'I do mean it. I am divorced now.'

'But you said when you left for Brazil that you had to see your wife. I don't understand any of this.'

'Yes. At that time I was separated from Isabella.' His face hardened. 'She was up to her tricks again, trying to stop me from divorcing her. But I was able to convince the judge and I got the decree. It's over. She will no more torment my life.'

'I see.' Araminta let out a tiny sigh, her relief and joy at his words tempered by common sense and what she knew she must say. 'But that doesn't necessarily mean that you want to get remarried so soon.'

'We are going to have a baby, Araminta. Of course we'll be married at once.'

'But this isn't the Middle Ages, Victor. People have babies without being married all the time.'

'Not in my book they don't,' he answered autocratically. 'We shall be married as soon as we can.'

'Might I point out,' she murmured, a little smile twitching the edges of her mouth, 'that you haven't asked me yet?'

'Haven't asked you? What do you mean?' He raised an astonished, uncomprehending brow.

'Exactly that. You haven't proposed.'

Victor stared down at her, flabbergasted. 'You mean you don't want to marry me?' he asked.

'I never said that. I just pointed out that I haven't been asked. Plus, I think I'd like a little time to think about it.'

'But this is ridiculous,' he exploded, letting go her hands and staring down at her in astonished outrage. 'Here I am, proposing to do the right thing by you, and you react in this absurd manner.'

'It's not absurd, merely realistic. I don't need any favours or to be dictated to,' she said haughtily, aware all at once that she was not going to be ordered about by him or any-one. 'I don't want to marry you just because I'm pregnant and you feel some old-fashioned need to prove you're an honourable gentleman. No, thanks.'

'Well!' Victor exploded, moving away, his mind in tur-moil. 'If that's how you feel then there is really very little left to say. I think you are being ridiculous, childish, irre-sponsible and, I might add, selfish. I shall leave you to come to your senses,' he said, in a tone of umbrage, anger and pride battling as he refused to admit that the carpet had been neatly pulled from under his feet.

'You can't go out in this weather,' Araminta exclaimed. 'It's pouring cats and dogs.'

'I wouldn't give a damn if there was a force ten hurricane blowing,' he retorted. 'I'm out of here.'

'Well, it's entirely up to you.' She shrugged, a tiny smile dimpling her cheeks at the sight of him so flustered just because he wasn't getting his own way.

'I shall call in tomorrow and make sure you're in good health,' he announced coldly, putting on his coat. 'I want you to go straight to bed. You should not be up and about. If nothing else I insist that you take proper care of my child.'

With that he turned on his heel and stalked out of the apartment, leaving Araminta on the sofa, sadly wondering if she'd been too hasty in her response. But she knew she was right. Unless it was the real thing, unless he truly loved her as much as she loved him, there would be no hope for a marriage based on obligation.

It was all or nothing.

This time, she knew, she couldn't deal with anything less.

CHAPTER SEVENTEEN

'AND that's not all,' Victor pointed out, full of righteous indignation. 'Can you believe that she refused to marry me?' he exploded, leaning over Pearce's desk.

'Well, this is quite a turn of events,' Pearce muttered thoughtfully, watching his friend rise and pace the floor like a caged tiger. 'How did you put it to her?'

'As soon as I knew the truth I told her we would be married at once, of course. It was the obvious step to take. What else was I expected to have said?' He threw up his arms in despair. 'It's clearly the right solution.'

'Hmm. But Araminta doesn't agree, you say?'

'No. She must be mad. Do you know what she said?' he added, whirling round and slamming his hands on the desk.

'No, but I'm sure you're about to tell me,' Pearce murmured patiently.

'She said—' Victor pronounced the words with cold fury '—that I hadn't asked her. I don't understand.'

'Well, had you?'

'Had I what?'

'Asked her?'

'I just told you,' he reiterated impatiently. 'I made it quite clear that we'd be married right away.'

'Victor, I was referring to the verb *ask*, as in *solicit the co-operation of the other party*. Did you *ask* her? Or did you just *tell* her?' Pearce twiddled his gold pen and waited.

'What does it matter? It's all the same thing.' Victor dismissed the question with an autocratic gesture.

'I don't think so.'

'You don't think what?' he asked, bewildered.

'That it's the same thing.'

'Why on earth not? The result is the same, isn't it?'

'Not really. From what I'm gathering, Araminta believes you merely want to marry her to do your duty by the child—give it a name and so on.'

'Well? Isn't that a good enough reason?'

'Not any more. Women want to be loved for themselves. Having a child out of wedlock is not a big deal these days. Araminta needs to know that you love her.'

Victor stopped dead in front of Pearce's desk and frowned. 'But that should be self-evident,' he said with a half-laugh, lifting his hands in a gesture of incomprehension.

'Apparently not,' Pearce murmured dryly. 'Perhaps you should start working on a practical demonstration. Now, if you'll excuse me, old chap, I've got a pile of work to get through before lunch.'

Four days had passed and not a word from Victor.

Perhaps he'd regretted his hasty offer of marriage, had thought about her words and decided that she was right. Well, if that was the case it was certainly better to get it straightened out now rather than later. The last thing she wanted was a short, unhappy marriage that could only end in pain for all three of them. For now it was not just she and Victor she had to think about, but the baby too.

Araminta sighed, smothered the dull pain that hovered permanently below the surface, knowing she'd have to get used to it, and went about her business. Today she was having lunch with Pearce, to finalise her schedule for the interviews that would be taking place the week after next, and she must start thinking about contacting a nanny agency. Apparently they got booked up very quickly, and nannies needed to be reserved months before the birth.

As she was getting ready to go out the doorbell rang. Araminta moved towards the door, stifling the ever-present tiny hope that perhaps it might be Victor and that— But, no. It was a courier service and her heart sank.

'Thank you.' She smiled at the delivery man and looked down at the letter. Probably something to do with her new book contract.

With a sigh, she went into the drawing room and was about to lay the large envelope down on her desk and leave it until later when she frowned. She really must learn to be more businesslike and attend to these things immediately. After all, it might be something urgent that needed a signature. She could discuss it with Pearce over lunch.

Slitting open the large cardboard cover, Araminta removed a handwritten envelope from inside. And all at once her heart leaped. It was Victor's writing. Fingers trembling, she opened it and unfolded the letter.

Dear Araminta,
After much reflection, I agree that this whole matter must be discussed carefully before any final decisions can be made. Therefore, I am inviting you to join me this weekend in the hope that we can pursue further discussion in an adult and sensible manner. My plane is at your disposal. If these arrangements are agreeable to you please contact Captain Ferguson at the following number. He awaits your instructions at your earliest convenience.
Victor

Araminta sank onto the desk chair and read the missive over twice, her heart heavy. So he had thought better of it after all, had realised that getting married for all the wrong reasons held no purpose. Bravely she swallowed. She might as well go and have it out with him. They would have to maintain a civilised relationship for the child's sake, so the sooner she got used to it the better. Today was Thursday, and she had nothing to do over the weekend anyway.

But there was no mention of where he wanted her to join him.

Typical, she reflected, letting out a sigh. Well, she'd find out soon enough. Perhaps it would be better to settle the future on neutral territory rather than in her house or in Sussex, where they'd lived through so many emotions.

Picking up the phone, Araminta rang the plane's captain and told him she'd be ready to leave at four o'clock the next day. It was only when she laid down the receiver that she realised she'd forgotten to ask where they were flying to.

She was being flown to Normandy.

Araminta sat in the luxurious white leather seat of the Gulfstream and swallowed. Why did he want her to come to the spot where, according to the time-frame, she was certain the baby had been conceived? It seemed too cruel when he had obviously changed his mind and wanted nothing but a civilised adult relationship. He would probably insist on maintaining the child—might want some visiting rights.

She sighed and sipped the mineral water the steward had brought her, and watched a freighter navigating the English Channel below. At least after they'd settled things the situation would be clear-cut. There would be no more hoping, no more illusions, no room for any regrets.

There had been moments over the past few days when she'd questioned herself, wondered if she should have been less radically opposed to his proposal of marriage. But then she'd remembered his reaction, his need to be implicitly obeyed without dispute. And of course the formal wording of the note inviting her for the weekend told its own tale.

He had only spoken out of pride and a sense of duty, nothing more. His words had been uttered on the spur of the moment and were nothing more than a desire to find a practical solution to what he considered to be a problem.

And that she could never have borne.

Several minutes later the plane began its descent, and soon they were landing in Deauville. Araminta picked up her overnight bag—she didn't intend to stay more than one night—and stepped out of the aircraft, surprised and not a little disappointed to see no sign of Victor. The Aston Martin and the same chauffeur who'd driven them in London were waiting instead. She masked her regret, reasoning that it was better this way, and, smiling, climbed into the back of the car.

It was only after half an hour's drive that she became aware that instead of entering the historic town of Falaise they were entering the gates of the lovely château where Victor had taken her to see the horses. She sat up, brows creased, as the car glided up the drive and they stopped in front of the exquisite building, lit up like a fairy castle in the wintry mist.

The car came to a halt and the chauffeur opened the door and took her bag. Next thing she knew the doors were being flung open and a housekeeper was ushering her inside. The place was beautiful, she realised, looking about her at the black and white marble hall, the Louis XVI table decked with a magnificent flower arrangement under a sparkling eighteenth-century chandelier.

Why had he brought her here instead of to Le Moulin? she wondered, following the housekeeper up the wide staircase. And where was Victor? There had been no sign of him since her arrival. Perhaps he was too busy and only planned to spend the minimum time necessary in her company.

The housekeeper, a grey-haired woman with a pleasant smile, opened a wide door off the carpeted corridor and Araminta stepped inside a little salon, off which was a bedroom suite. It was charmingly decorated—very French, in creams and gold, but not too gilded or ornate. She loved the striped brocade curtains that brightened the room, and the little fireplace where logs crackled and by which a small sofa with plumped cushions looked comfy and inviting. And on the antique tables were cut-crystal vases filled with fresh flowers, brightening the winter's night.

The bedroom too was delightful, and as Araminta stepped inside it she was surprised to see a huge package lying on the bed. Intrigued, she moved towards it and frowned. What did this signify? She picked up a white envelope with her name written on it in Victor's inimitable hand, and her heart raced despite her desire to stay utterly cool. She opened it and read.

I shall expect you downstairs at eight. Dinner is formal.
Victor

Well. Araminta let out an annoyed breath and threw the note on the night table. He certainly didn't mince his words. And how was she expected to know that he was having a formal dinner party on the night of her arrival? This was hardly an occasion to be having guests over. In fact very much the contrary. He could at least have warned her. Now what was she going to wear?

Just as her anger against Victor was steadily mounting Araminta glanced again at the huge box on the bed. Hesitating, she opened it. And, to her surprise, from inside a sea of tissue paper she removed a gorgeous black and silver designer evening dress. The soft rich fabric moulded the curves of her body as she placed it against her and looked at herself in the mirror, realising it would be perfect. Then, looking again in the box, she saw a pair of exquisite black satin and diamanté evening shoes, and a matching clutch purse.

Was there anything the man hadn't thought of? she wondered, staring at the things, wishing suddenly that she didn't need them and could fling them back in his face with a proud refusal to accept. But then what would she wear?

Araminta let out a long, frustrated sigh and sat down crossly on the bed. She really didn't have much choice. It was wear the outfit or go to dinner in sporty trousers and a jacket.

She glanced at her watch and realised that it was already seven o'clock. After laying the clothes carefully back on the bed, she entered the huge marble and mirrored bathroom. She turned on the taps of a gloriously voluminous tub, added some delicious smelling bath lotion and began to undress. As she did so she observed herself in the mirror, noticing for the first time how her body had become fuller, more feminine, how her breasts were slightly swollen and the curve of her hips more rounded.

Not that she'd put on any weight, she assured herself. It was just different. She smiled and bit her lip, thinking of the baby growing inside her still-flat belly. A rush of new emotion flowed through her.

Then with another tiny sigh, determined not to linger on a future that could not be, she pinned up her long golden hair and climbed into the bath.

An hour later Victor was anxiously pacing the floor of the *grand salon* downstairs. Occasionally he glanced at the ornate ormolu clock, centred on the mantelpiece under the vast gilt mirror, while keeping his eyes trained on the stairs as well.

On the chime of eight Araminta began her descent of the majestic staircase. She had donned the beautiful gown which fitted her perfectly and flowed to the ground. In her hand she held the small evening purse. She wore little make up, just a touch of lipgloss and a sweep of mascara. Her hair was brushed and gleaming, shimmering like silken strands under the crystal chandelier.

And Victor held his breath as he watched her, so elegant and lovely, descending the stairs, controlling an impulse to rush forward and take her in his arms. This was the mother of his child, he reflected, the woman he loved but who needed to be wooed. So instead he waited for her to reach the bottom step before moving forward to greet her.

As she stepped into the marble hall Araminta saw Victor, perfectly attired in black tie, coming forward to greet her, and she swallowed. He looked so incredibly handsome, so smooth, dark and sophisticated.

No wonder he'd changed his mind about her.

'Good evening,' he said formally, raising her hand to his lips. 'Welcome again to the Château d'Ambrumenil.'

Araminta shuddered involuntarily as his skin grazed hers and the all too familiar memories surfaced.

'Good evening,' she responded, hoping she sounded sufficiently calm, cool and collected.

'Come in. Can I offer you a soft drink?' he asked, showing her into the *salon*—a beautiful if somewhat formally decorated room, decked with Aubusson carpets, brocade and gilt furnishings and a number of Old Masters on the walls—and moving towards a silver ice bucket where a bottle of Cristal stood chilling.

'That would be very nice, thank you,' she replied with

barely a smile, searching the room for any other guests. Apparently she was the first to arrive.

Victor poured two drinks, then joined her near the fireplace. 'Please, sit down,' he said, handing her the soft drink and indicating one of the Louis XVI armchairs.

'Thank you,' Araminta murmured, and perched on the edge of the chair.

'I see the dress fits you to perfection,' he murmured, his eyes coursing over her, leaving her flushed despite her desire to stay completely unaffected by the sight of him, by the closeness wreaking havoc with her system.

'Yes. It was most kind of you to think of it. I had no idea you were planning a formal dinner party. How many guests are there?'

'Two.'

'Ah.'

Conversation did not seem to be getting very far, she reflected, taking a sip.

'Did you have a good flight?'

'Excellent, thank you.' This was awful, far worse than she'd anticipated. It was like talking to a perfect stranger.

'Dinner will be served in ten minutes.'

'Really? What about the other guests?' she asked.

'Araminta, I have already told you there are only two guests,' he murmured, his eyes turning darker, the lines of his face suddenly intense.

'Wh-what do you mean?' she said, suddenly nervous.

'That you and I are dining alone, my dear, *à deux.*'

'Oh, but surely—' She swallowed and took a quick gulp of her soft drink that nearly made her choke.

'I feel we have a lot to say to one another,' he continued, leaning against the mantelpiece, arm casually resting there.

'I don't. I think we said all we had to say the other night. In fact, I'm not quite sure why you asked me to come here,' she muttered, trying to stay calm although her heart was lurching and a thin film of perspiration beaded her upper lip.

'Aren't you?' His eyes bored into her now, belying his casual stance. He looked rather like a leopard, ready to pounce. 'I would have said rather that we hadn't even begun talking, *querida*.'

'Victor, if this is your idea of a joke I'm afraid I find it most unfunny,' Araminta said, in a voice that reminded her distinctly of how Lady Drusilla might have spoken.

'A joke? I hardly think so.' Posing the glass flute on the mantelpiece, he moved to her side and sat down in the chair next to her.

How she wished he'd keep his distance, that the scent of his musky aftershave wouldn't reach her quite so intensely, that she could keep that light-headed delicious tingle far removed from her body.

'Araminta, I think it's time you and I faced the truth,' he said, stretching out his arm and laying his hand on hers.

'I don't know what you mean,' she jabbered nervously. 'I made it very clear the other night that—'

'Let's forget the other night.'

'Oh, please, Victor,' she said, suddenly unable to stand this much longer. 'I can't bear it. Just leave me alone. Why did you ask me here?' she exclaimed, suddenly losing control as tears rose and she willed herself not to cry.

'Because of this,' he replied.

In a swift movement he was out of the chair and raising her into his arms. Before she could move he pulled her against him, snaked his hand into the mass of golden hair at her neck and drew her head back, his black shining eyes gazing down possessively into hers.

'Did you think for one moment that I would allow you to disappear from my life, *minha linda*? That I would contemplate leaving the woman I love to her own devices? Do you for one instant believe that I would allow another man to take you in his arms as I am taking you now?'

Araminta's pulse galloped. 'You love me?' she blurted out, surprise and doubt written in her eyes.

'Oh, my darling, my silly, ridiculous darling. Can't you tell, *querida*, how much I love you? I know it took me a while to understand, and a kick in the pants from Pearce to make me realise it, but of course I love you.'

'Well, that's hardly very complimentary,' she murmured, smiling, trying to stifle the rush of joy, surprise and relief overwhelming her.

'Complimentary or not, it's the truth, my love. That's why I brought you here.' He loosened his grip and slipped his arms around her waist, smiling down at her now, his eyes filled with a new intense expression she'd never seen before but which she recognised for what it was.

'Why exactly *did* you bring me here?' she whispered, unable to take her eyes from his face, unable to believe that this was really happening.

'Before I tell you, may I ask you a question?' he said in a gentler tone.

'All right,' she murmured, disappointed when he took a step backwards, leaving her standing in the middle of the Aubusson carpet wondering what he was going to do next.

'In that case, here goes. I'm not very good at this, I'm afraid. I've never done it before.' He smiled wryly at her, and before her unbelieving eyes fell on one knee. 'Will you, Araminta, my love, do me the honour of becoming my wife?' From his pocket Victor produced a sparkling diamond ring which he held up.

'I—' Araminta gasped, tears of joy and tenderness blinding her.

'All you need to say is yes,' Victor murmured, taking

her left hand and slipping the ring onto her engagement finger. 'Well?' he asked, his eyes laughing now as he looked up at her. 'I don't know how long I can carry on in this pose, *querida*, without feeling completely idiotic.'

Araminta laughed and cried all at once. 'Yes,' she whispered, biting her lip and staring unbelieving at the man she loved holding her hand.

'Good. That's settled, then,' he said, rising relieved from the floor. 'May I kiss the future *comtesse*?'

Before she could answer, or absorb this information, Victor enveloped her in his arms and his lips came down on hers. He held her close and pressed his hands into the small of her back, making her feel the intensity of his desire while his tongue played havoc with hers.

Oh, it was glorious, wonderful, unique to be back in his arms, where she knew she belonged. And all at once Araminta threw her arms about his neck and kissed him back hard, needing to feel every inch of him. She thrust her fingers into his glorious black hair and gloried in it, caught between desire and laughter, joy and delight.

Then Victor swooped her into his arms, and in several masterful strides they were climbing the stairs.

'What about dinner?' she whispered, kissing his ear.

'Damn dinner. It'll just have to wait.'

Next thing she knew they were in a large bedroom and she was being laid in the middle of a vast silk canopied bed. Eyes glued to one another, they undressed quickly, each too anxious to feel the other to concede to any niceties as a pile of clothes littered the floor and Victor joined her between the deliciously cool sheets.

'*Meu amor,*' he whispered, suddenly slowing the pace and allowing his fingers to trace from her throat down her ribcage until they reached her belly. Then with new tenderness he lowered his head and kissed her there. 'Our child,' he muttered between feather kisses. 'Our baby. Oh, Araminta, I'm so happy, so proud of it, of us, of all that awaits us, now and in the future.'

'Victor,' she murmured, heart full, arching as his fingers trailed slowly lower, reaching down between her thighs, gently parting her, caressing, needing to feel her soft, warm, liquid response.

Then, as she gasped out his name, he entered her, long and slow, with a tenderness so great that Araminta thought she would weep from sheer joy and delight.

And together they journeyed on a newly discovered ocean of emotion, rising and falling on the swell, reaching out and discovering new heights of passion and sensation to which neither had been privileged before.

After, when it was finally over, when at last he lay with his head on her breast and she cradled him there, feeling his spent body moulding hers, Araminta knew what true happiness was.

And that nothing could equal it. Ever.

Victor took Araminta's arm and walked her to the dining room.

'So why,' she finally asked, her curiosity piqued, 'did you want to bring me here specifically?'

'For the very good reason that I wanted you to see your future home, *querida*.'

'My future home? You mean you want to come and live here?'

'Yes.' Stopping as they reached the hall, he looked into her eyes and murmured, 'I do.'

'But I don't understand. Why did you buy Le Moulin?'

'It's a long story,' he said with a sigh. 'Basically, I didn't want to share this place with Isabella. It has too many child-hood memories, too many family connotations. I bought Le

Moulin to keep her happy, and away from what I subconsciously must have been preserving for this moment.'

'You mean she never came here?'

'Never. The only other woman who used to come here was my mother—the late *comtesse*.'

'*Comtesse?*'

'Yes. My mother was a French countess. When I inherited this château and these lands from her I also inherited the title. Up until now I have never used it, but that is something I plan to change.'

'Why?'

'Because I want you to become my *comtesse*.'

'Oh, Victor.' She laughed, glancing down at the beautiful engagement ring which fitted her perfectly. 'I still haven't thanked you properly for this lovely ring.'

'It was my mother's engagement ring,' he murmured, caressing her cheek. 'It is appropriate that you should have it.'

Araminta smiled at him and raised her lips to his.

'I shall endeavour to do it justice.'

'Of that I have no doubt,' he said with an arrogant laugh, sweeping her into his arms and bestowing a long kiss on her lips. 'But now, my dear, it's getting late. And we must eat, or tomorrow we shall be without a cook.'

Rolling her eyes lovingly and taking his arm, Araminta fell into step beside him, knowing there was little use arguing. For, she admitted finally, glancing tenderly at his proud profile, she loved him and would love him always.

Just the way he was.

THE ITALIAN
MATCH

KAY THORPE

CHAPTER ONE

STRANGE to think that this could have been her homeland, Gina reflected, viewing the lush Tuscany landscape spread before her as the car breasted the rise. Beautiful as it was, she felt no particular draw to the place.

Pulling into the roadside, she took a look at the map laid open across the passenger seat. If her calculations were correct, the collection of red-slate roofs and single-bell tower some mile or so distant had to be Vernici. Smaller than she had imagined, though big enough to offer some kind of accommodation for the short time she was likely to be spending in the vicinity. This close to her destination, she still had doubts as to the wisdom of what she was planning to do. Twenty-five years was a long time. It could be that the Carandentes no longer even resided in the area.

If that turned out to be the case, she would put the whole thing behind her once and for all, she vowed. If nothing else, she would have seen parts of Europe she had never seen before.

Surrounded by olive groves, the little town had an almost medieval air about it, its narrow streets radiating from a central piazza. The car that burst from one of the narrow streets at breakneck speed would have hit Gina's car head-on if she hadn't taken instant evading action. There was only one way to go, and that was straight through a flimsy barrier protecting some kind of road works, finishing up tilted at a crazy angle with her offside front wheel firmly lodged in the deep hole.

Held by the safety belt, she had suffered no more than a severe shaking up, but the shock alone was enough to keep her sitting there like a dummy for the few moments it took people attracted by the screeching of brakes to put in an appearance.

Her scanty Italian could make neither head nor tail of the voluble comment. All she could do was make helpless gestures. Eventually one man got the passenger door open and helped her clamber out of the vehicle, all the time attempting to make himself understood.

The only word Gina recognised was garage. *'Si, grazie, signor!'* she responded thankfully, trusting to luck that he would take her meaning and call someone out for her. That the car would be in no fit state to be driven when it was pulled out of the hole, she didn't doubt. She simply had to hope that repairs could be effected without too much trouble.

Her helpmate disappeared up a side street, leaving her to lean weakly against the nearest support and wait for succour. It was gone two, the heat scarcely diminished from its midday high; her sleeveless cotton blouse was sticking to her back. An elderly woman addressed her in tones of sympathy. Assuming that she was being asked if she was feeling all right. Gina conjured a smile and another *'Si, grazie. Inglese,'* she tagged on before any further questions could be put to her.

It might have been an idea to learn at least enough of the language to get by on before setting out on this quest of hers, she thought wryly, but it was a little late for if onlys. She was in Vernici, and quite likely going to be stuck here for however long it might take to get her car back on the road.

Straightening, she walked round the vehicle to view the uptilted front end, in no way reassured by what she saw.

The wheel had been crushed inwards by the impact, the whole wing and a corner of the bonnet badly crumpled. It was some small consolation that the car itself was Italian. If new parts were needed that surely had to help.

Hindered more than aided by the all-too-ready helping hands and eager advice, it took the two men who eventually arrived in a battered tow truck almost half an hour to drag the car free. It was, Gina saw with sinking heart, in an even worse state of disrepair than she had thought. The wheel was buckled, the wing a total write-off, the bonnet probably salvageable but unlikely to look pristine again without a lot of expert hammering and filling.

The happy-go-lucky manner employed by both mechanics gave little rise to confidence. One of them, who spoke some English, indicated that it would be necessary to send to Siena, or perhaps even to Florence for a new wheel and wing. When asked how long that might take, he spread his hands in a gesture only too easily recognisable. Perhaps a week, perhaps even longer. Who could tell? And then, of course, there would be the work. Perhaps another week. The possible cost? Once more the hands were spread. The cost would be what the cost would be, Gina gathered, by then in no fit state to press the issue any further.

Declining an offer to squeeze her into a seat between the two of them, she followed the truck on foot to a small backstreet garage, to see her only means of transport tucked away in a corner to await attention. The parts would be ordered at once, the younger man assured her. In the meantime, he could supply a good place for her to stay.

Faced with his overt appraisement of her body, Gina gave the suggestion scant consideration. For the first time she turned her mind to the car that had caused the accident. The driver had been female not male, and young, the car itself big and blue.

With faint hope, she described both car and occupant to her mechanic friend, to be rewarded with a grinning acknowledgement. 'Cotone,' he said. 'You go to San Cotone. Three kilometres,' he added helpfully, and drew a map in the dust. 'Very rich. You make them pay!'

Gina had every intention of trying. She was covered by insurance, of course, but claims for accidents abroad were notoriously difficult to get settled. The more she thought about it the angrier she became, her object in coming to Vernici in the first place temporarily pushed to the back of her mind. She was stuck out here in the back of beyond because of some spoiled teenager with nothing better to do than tear around the roads without regard for life or limb. Recklessness didn't even begin to cover it!

The question was how to reach the place. 'Taxi?' she queried. 'Bus?'

He shook his head. 'You take car.'

'How the devil can I—?' she began, breaking off abruptly when she saw where he was pointing. With almost as much rust as paint on the bodywork, and tyres that looked distinctly worn, the little Fiat's better days were obviously a long way in the past. Beggars, however, couldn't afford to be choosers. If that was the only vehicle available that was the one she would take.

'How much?' she asked.

The shrug was eloquent, the smile even more so. 'You pay later.'

In cash, not kind, she thought drily, reading him only too well. Her bags were locked in the boot of her own car. After a momentary hesitation she decided they would have to stay there for the present. She had to get this other matter settled while the anger still burned good and bright. The question of accommodation could wait.

Despite its appearance, the Fiat started without too much

trouble. Gina headed out along the route by which she had approached the town, to take the turning her adviser's drawing had indicated through the gently rolling landscape.

Olive groves gave way to immense vineyards tended by what appeared to be a regular army of workers. Only then did Gina make the connection with the label she had seen on Chianti wines back home. A rich family indeed, she thought, well able to pay for the damage to her car, for certain.

A pair of wide wrought-iron gates gave open access to a drive that curved through trees to reach a stone-built villa of stunning size and architecture. Gina drew to a stop on the gravelled circle fronting the place, refusing to allow the grandeur to deflect her from her aim. A member of this household had driven her off the road; the onus was on them to reimburse her.

Set into the stone wall beside imposing double doors, the bell was of the old-fashioned pull-type. It emitted a deep, repeated note, clearly audible from where she stood. The elderly man who answered the summons was dressed in dark trousers and matching waistcoat along with a sparkling white shirt. A member of staff rather than family, Gina judged. His appraisement was rapid, taking in her simple cotton skirt and blouse. The disdain increased as his glance went beyond her to the battered vehicle standing on the gravelled forecourt.

'I'm here to see the owner,' she stated before he could speak, wishing she had thought to get a name from her mechanic friend. '*Padrone*,' she tagged on, dredging the depths of her scanty vocabulary.

The man shook his head emphatically, loosed a single, terse sentence, and began to close the door again. Gina stopped the movement by placing her hands flat against the wood and shoving.

'*Padrone!*' she insisted.

From the look on the man's face, she wasn't getting through. Which left her with only one choice. She slipped past him before he could make any further move, heading for one of the doors leading off the wide, marble-floored hall with no clear idea in mind other than to block any immediate attempt to remove her from the premises.

There was a key in the far side lock. She slammed the heavy dark-wood door to and secured it, leaning her forehead against a panel to regain both her breath and her wits. That had been a really crazy thing to do, she admitted. A move hardly likely to impress the owner of the establishment, whoever he or she was.

A knock on the door was followed by what sounded like a question. Gina froze where she stood as another male voice answered, this time from behind her. She spun round, gaining a hazy impression of a large, book-lined room as her gaze came to rest on the man seated at a vast desk on the far side of it.

Slanting through the window behind him, the sun picked out highlights in the thick sweep of black hair. Dark eyes viewed her from beneath quizzically raised brows, the lack of anger or even annoyance on his leanly sculptured features something of a reassurance.

'*Buon pomeriggeo,*' he said.

'*Parla inglese?*' Gina asked hopefully.

'Of course,' he answered in fluent English. 'I apologise for my lack of perception. I was deceived by the blackness of your hair into believing you of the same blood as myself for a moment, but no Italian woman I ever met had so vividly blue a pair of eyes, so wonderfully fair a skin!'

A fairness that right now was more of a curse than an

asset, Gina could have told him, dismayed to feel warmth rising in her cheeks at the sheer extravagance of the observation. She was unaccustomed to such flowery language from a man. But then, how many Latins had she actually met before this?

'It should be me apologising for breaking in on you like this,' she said, taking a firm grip on herself, 'but it was the only way to get past the door guard.'

A smile touched the strongly carved mouth. 'As Guido speaks little English, whilst you obviously speak even less Italian, misunderstandings were certain to arise. Perhaps you might explain to me what it is that you are here for?'

Feeling like a stag at bay with her back braced against the door, Gina eased herself away, conscious of a sudden frisson down her spine as the man rose from his seat. No more than the early thirties, he had a lithe, athletic build beneath the cream silk shirt and deeper-toned trousers. Rolled shirt sleeves revealed muscular forearms, while the casually opened collar laid the strong brown column of his throat open to inspection.

'I need to see the head of the household,' she said, blanking out the involuntary response.

He inclined his head. 'I am Lucius Carandente.'

Shock robbed her of both speech and clarity of thought for a moment or two. She gazed at him with widened eyes. There had to be more than one Carandente family, she told herself confusedly. This couldn't possibly be them!

Yet why not? asked another part of her mind. She knew nothing of the family other than the name. Why assume it more likely that they be of proletarian rather than patrician stock?

The dark brows lifted again, a certain amused speculation in his gaze. 'You appear surprised.'

Gina pulled herself together. 'I was expecting someone

older,' she prevaricated, in no way ready to plumb any further depths as yet. 'The father, perhaps, of a girl who drives a blue tourer.'

Speculation gave way to sudden comprehension, all trace of amusement vanished. 'Donata,' he said flatly. 'My younger sister. What did she do?'

'She caused me to crash my car an hour or so ago. Down in Vernici. It's going to need new parts. The garage down there tells me they'll have to be ordered from Florence, and it's going to take a lot of time—to say nothing of the cost!'

'You carry no insurance?'

'Of course I carry insurance!' she returned with asperity, sensing an attempt to wriggle off the hook. 'Waiting for the go-ahead from my company would take even more time. In any case, it's your sister's insurance that should be responsible for the damage—always providing *she* carries some!'

She paused there, seeing his lips take on a slightly thinner line and aware of allowing her tongue to run away with her. 'I'm sorry,' she tagged on impulsively. 'That was very rude of me.'

'Yes, it was,' he agreed. 'Though perhaps not entirely unmerited. If you will kindly unlock the door behind you and allow Guido entrance, I will take the necessary steps.'

Gina obeyed with some faint reluctance, not at all certain that he wouldn't order Guido to toss her out on her ear. The manservant entered the room without haste, his glance going directly to his master as if she didn't even exist.

Lucius Carandente spoke in rapid Italian, despatching the older man with a final *'Subito!'*

'Please take a seat,' he told Gina, indicating the nearest of the deep club chairs.

He didn't sit down himself, but leaned against the desk edge as she complied, placing her at a distinct and probably intentional disadvantage. No matter, she thought resolutely; she could always stand up again if she felt the need.

'You have yet to give me your name,' he said.

'I'm sorry,' she proffered once more. 'I'm Gina Redman.'

'You are here on vacation?'

It was easier at the moment to say yes, Gina decided, not yet convinced that the name wasn't just a coincidence. Other than the obvious characteristics, this man bore no great resemblance to the photograph in her handbag.

'I'm touring,' she acknowledged. 'I've driven all the way through France and Switzerland without a single mishap. If your sister hadn't been going so fast...'

Lucius held up a hand. 'It would be better that we wait until she is available to speak for herself, I think. She arrived home, I know, so it should not be long before she joins us. Until then,' he added in the same courteous tones, 'we will talk of other matters. The colour of your hair does not suggest the English rose. Is it possible, perhaps, that you have mixed parentage?'

Short of telling him to mind his own business, Gina was left with no choice but to answer. 'My father was Italian.'

'Was?'

'He died before I was born.' She forestalled the next question, hoping he would leave it at that until she had time to consider just how she was going to find out if he was indeed one of the Carandentes she had come so far to find. 'I was adopted by my English stepfather.'

'I see.'

To her relief he refrained from asking the name discarded for Redman. He probably assumed that her mother had never held title to it to start with.

The opening of the door heralded the entry of a girl whose appearance was totally at odds with her surroundings. Multilayered and finger-raked into a rough tumble about her tempestuous young face, her hair looked more like a bird's nest than the crowning glory it must once have been. She was clad in black leather, the trousers skin-tight about rounded hips, the jacket outlining a well-endowed figure.

It was apparent at once that she recognised Gina, though she gave no sign of discomfiture. She addressed her brother in Italian, switching to English with no more effort than he had displayed himself when told to do so—and with even greater fluency.

'The blame wasn't mine,' she declared flatly, without glancing in Gina's direction. 'There's no damage to *my* car.'

'Only because I managed to avoid what would have been a head-on crash!' Gina asserted before Lucius could respond. 'You were going too fast to stop. You didn't even attempt to stop! Even to see if I was all right!' She was sitting bolt upright in the chair, not about to let the girl get away with her denials. 'Leaving the scene of an accident is against the law where I come from—especially where there are possible injuries to either party.'

'If you'd been injured you wouldn't be sitting here,' Donata returned.

Gina kept a tight rein on her temper. 'That's not the point. I'm going to be stuck in Vernici until my car can be repaired—with a hefty bill at the end of it. At the very least, I need your insurance details to pass on to mine.'

'But what you really want is for Lucius to give you money now!' flashed the younger girl.

Her brother said something short and sharp in Italian, increasing the mutinous set of her jaw. When she spoke again it was with sullen intonation. 'I'm sorry.'

Lucius made no attempt to stop her from leaving the room. His mouth tautened as the door slammed in her wake.

'I add my apologies for the way Donata spoke to you,' he said. 'I also apologise for her appearance. She returned last week from her school in Switzerland...' He broke off, shaking his head as if in acknowledgement that whatever he had been about to say was irrelevant to the present matter. 'I believe it best that I take responsibility for the financial affairs,' he said instead. 'You have accommodation already arranged?'

Gina shook her head, the wind taken completely out of her sails.

'So where is your luggage?'

'I left it locked in the boot of the car,' she said. 'My car, not the one I came here in. I hired that from the garage.'

'It will be returned, and your luggage brought here. If you give me your car keys I will make the necessary arrangements.'

'Here?' Gina looked at him in some confusion. 'I don't—'

'You will naturally stay at Cotone until your car is repaired,' he stated. 'That will be done in Siena.'

'I can't let you...' she began again, voice petering out as he lifted a staying hand.

'You must allow me to make what reparation I can for my sister's lack of care. It would be most discourteous of you to reject my hospitality.'

'Then I must of course accept,' she said after a moment. 'Thank you, *signor*.'

His smile sent a further quiver down her spine. 'You will please call me Lucius. And I may address you by your first name?'

'Of course,' she said, bemused by the totally unexpected turn of events. 'You're very kind.'

The dark eyes roved the face upturned to him, coming to rest on the curve of her mouth. 'I find it difficult to be otherwise with a beautiful woman. A weakness, I know.'

Gina gave a laugh, doing her best to ignore the curling stomach muscles. 'I doubt you'd allow anyone, male *or* female, to get the better of you!'

'I said difficult, not impossible,' came the smooth return.

His gaze shifted from her as the door opened again to admit a young maidservant. He must, Gina surmised, have summoned her via some hidden bell press.

'Crispina will show you to your room,' he said, having spoken to the girl. 'Your bags will be brought to you. Until then, you would be advised to rest. An ordeal such as the one you experienced can produce delayed shock.'

Gina didn't doubt it; she felt in the grip of it right now. She got to her feet, vitally aware of his eyes following her as she crossed to the door. Crispina answered her greeting smile with a somewhat tentative one of her own. She shook her head when Gina asked if she spoke English, which left the pair of them with very little to say as they climbed the grand staircase to the upper storey.

The bedroom to which she was shown was every bit as grand as the rest of the house, with glass doors opening onto a balcony that overlooked the magnificent view. The spacious *en suite* bathroom had fittings Gina was pretty sure were solid gold, the walls lined in mirror glass. She eyed her multireflection in wry acknowledgement of a less than pristine appearance. Clambering from a car halfway down a hole in the ground had left its mark in more ways then the one.

Back in the bedroom, she extracted the long envelope from her bag, and sat down on the bed edge to study the photograph afresh. Arms about each other, the young couple portrayed looked so blissfully happy, the girl's fair skin and pale gold hair a total contrast to her partner's Latin looks—both of them scarcely out of their teen years.

Gina had come across the photograph while browsing in the attic one rainy afternoon when she was fifteen. The accompanying marriage licence had tilted her world on its axis, the explanations reluctantly furnished by her mother when confronted with the evidence even more so.

Her mother and Giovanni Carandente had met as students at Oxford and had fallen madly in love. Knowing neither family would approve the match, they had married in secret, planning on taking their degrees before telling them. Her pregnancy had changed everything. Giovanni had set out to face his family with the news in person, only to meet his death in a road accident on the way to the airport. Two months later, with her parents still unaware of the truth, Beth had married her former boyfriend, John Redman, the two of them allowing everyone to believe that the baby was his.

Sitting here now, Gina went over the scene in her mind once again, recalling the anguish. Although she bore no facial resemblance, John Redman's colouring had always lent credence to hers. She would never in a thousand years have suspected the truth.

Asked why she hadn't attempted to contact the Carandentes herself, her mother had made a wry gesture. She knew nothing about them, she admitted, except that they lived in the town of Vernici in Tuscany. They had been the ones informed of Giovanni's death not her. She had found out only on reading about the accident in the following day's newspaper.

'It was a terrible time,' she acknowledged. 'I hardly knew which way to turn. If it hadn't been for your father—'

'But he isn't my father, is he?' Gina said hollowly.

'In every other way he is. He gave you his name—provided us both with a home and a good life. He's a good man. The very best.' Beth's voice was tender. 'I love him dearly.'

'But not the way you loved Giovanni?'

Beth shook her head, her smile wry again. 'No two loves are the same, darling. What Giovanni and I had was wonderful, but whether it would have lasted—well, who can tell?' She hesitated before continuing. 'I know it's a lot to ask, but can we keep it just between ourselves? John regards you as his own child. He'd be terribly upset if he knew that you knew you weren't.'

Loving him the way she did herself, she'd had no inclination to tell him what she knew, either then or since, Gina reflected, but the knowledge couldn't be wiped out. For years she had toyed with the idea of some day coming out here and searching for her forebears, only an idea was all it had been until now. She had three more weeks before she started the new job she hoped would rekindle the interest and ambition so lacking this last year or so. Once into that, her free time would be severely restricted.

It was coming up to six o'clock, she saw, glancing at her watch. She'd been sitting here for more than half an hour thinking about it all. The question of whether these Carandentes were of the same family line as her father still remained to be answered. The most direct way was to ask outright, of course, but she was somehow reluctant to do that.

A knock on the door signalled the arrival of her bags. Dinner, she was advised by Guido in fragmentary English, would be served at nine-thirty in the salon. The master requested that she join the family for prior refreshment on the terrace at nine.

Gina thanked the man, receiving a bare nod by way of return. It was obvious that her presence was not looked on with favour. As an old family retainer, he would naturally take Donata Carandente's side in the matter of who was to blame for the accident, she supposed. It was possible that the rest of the staff would take the same attitude— although Crispina had shown no sign of it.

Whether through the delayed shock Lucius had spoken of, or simply the effects of a long day behind the wheel, the weariness overtaking her was not to be denied. It was doubtful if she'd sleep, but a couple of hours just resting would revive her for the evening to come. She would hate to nod off over the dinner table.

She took off her outer clothing before lying down on the silk bedspread, stretching out luxuriously beneath the spinning fan. So much nicer than functional air-conditioning, she thought, watching the moving blades. The soft, whirring sound was soporific in itself.

Lucius had said Donata was his younger sister. Were there other siblings? For him to be *padrone*, his father must be dead too, but perhaps there was still a mother alive. If these people really did turn out to be her father's kith and kin, then she and Lucius could be cousins. She found the idea oddly displeasing.

Daylight had faded to a dim glimmer when she awoke. It was a relief to see there was still half an hour to go before she was expected to join the family on the terrace.

The sleep had refreshed her, the shower did an even

better job, but no amount of revitalisation could make what was to come any easier. At some point this evening she had to bring up her father's name and learn the truth. For peace of mind alone she needed to know her origins.

Having planned on staying at good hotels throughout her journey, she had packed clothes to suit most circumstances. Cut on the bias in deep blue silk jersey, the dress she picked out to wear to dinner skimmed her figure to finish on the knee. Teamed with a pair of high-heeled sandals, it should fit the bill, Gina reckoned.

A stroke or two of mascara along her lashes, a dash of lipstick, and she was ready to go. There hadn't been time to put her hair up into the French pleat she would have preferred, but it would have to do. Thick and glossy, it fell in soft waves to her shoulders—the bane of her life when it came to drying after washing, but she could never bring herself to have it cut short.

Night was fast encroaching when she reached the wide, stone-balustered terrace, the lamps already lit. Of the five people gathered there, three were female, the family resemblance pronounced.

Lucius came forward to greet her as she hesitated on the threshold of the room through which she had emerged, the look in his eyes as he scanned her shapely length tensing muscle and sinew. He was making no secret of the fact that he found her as much of a draw as she had to admit she found him. A man who might well be her cousin, she reminded herself forcibly. A first cousin, even.

The prospect of a family relationship was hardly enhanced by Donata's open hostility. Her sister, Ottavia, was around twenty-seven or eight and married to a man some few years older named Marcello Brizzi. Their response to the introduction was courteous enough on the surface, but it was apparent that they too regarded her presence as an intrusion.

It was left to the matriarch of the family to show any warmth in her welcome. Skin almost as smooth as Gina's own, the still luxuriant hair untouched by grey, she scarcely looked old enough to have a son Lucius's age.

'My son tells me you are half Italian yourself,' she said. 'I believe you never knew your father?'

Seated in one of the comfortable lounging chairs, the gin and tonic she had asked for to hand, Gina shook her head. 'He died before I was born.'

Signora Carandente expressed her sympathy in a long, drawn sigh. 'Such a terrible thing!' She was silent for a moment, contemplating the girl before her. 'You have older siblings, perhaps?'

Gina shook her head again, eliciting another sigh.

'For a man to die without a son to carry on his name is a sad matter indeed! Should anything happen to Lucius before he produces a son, our own lineage will be finished too. You would think, would you not, that he would recognise such a responsibility?'

'I am not about to die,' he declared calmly.

'Who can tell?' his mother returned. 'You must marry soon. You have a duty. And who better than Livia Marucchi!'

His shrug made light of the moment, but Gina sensed an underlying displeasure that such matters should be discussed in the presence of a stranger. She'd found the episode discomfiting enough herself. From what little she had seen of him, she judged him a man who would make his own decision about whom and when he should marry anyway. His choices, she was sure, would in no way be limited to one woman.

'What was your father's name?' asked Ottavia, jerking

her out of her thoughts and into sudden flaring panic. She wasn't ready! Not yet!

'Barsini,' she said, plucking the name out of some distant memory without pause for consideration. 'Alexander Barsini.'

She regretted the impulse the moment the words left her lips, but it was too late to retract.

'Barsini,' Ottavia repeated. 'Which part of Italy did he come from?'

Having begun it, she was left with no option but to continue, Gina acknowledged ruefully. 'Naples,' she said off the top of her head.

'He has family still living?'

This time Gina opted for at least a partial truth. 'I don't know. I came to Italy to try and find out.'

Ottavia's brows lifted in a manner reminiscent of her brother, though minus any humour. 'Your mother failed to maintain contact?'

Gina returned her gaze with a steadiness she was far from feeling. 'My mother never met his family. They knew nothing of the marriage.'

'I think that enough,' Lucius cut in before his sister could continue the catechism. 'Let the matter rest.'

Ottavia looked as if she found the command unpalatable, but she made no demur. Gina doubted, however, that her curiosity would remain contained. Catching Donata's eye, she tried a smile, receiving a glare in return. There would be no softening of attitude there for certain. She was well and truly in the doghouse!

Dinner proved less of a banquet than anticipated, with no more than four courses. Gina drank sparingly of the free-flowing wines. She loved the reds, but they didn't always love her. The last thing she needed was to waken with a hangover in the morning.

Lucius insisted that all conversation was conducted in English for her sake, which made her feel even more of an outsider. Marcello, she learned, was the estate comptroller, Ottavia a lady of leisure. The latter confined her questions this time to Gina's present background, expressing astonishment on hearing she was a qualified accountant.

'Such an unusual job for a woman!' she exclaimed. 'Do you not think so, Lucius?'

'An admirable achievement for anyone,' he returned, directing a smile that set every nerve in Gina's body tingling. 'Especially at so young an age.'

'I'm twenty-five,' she felt moved to respond. 'Not that much younger than yourself, I imagine.'

The smile came again, accompanied by an unmistakable glint in the dark eyes. 'Eight years is no obstacle, I agree.'

Obstacle to what, Gina didn't need to ask. Neither, she was sure, did anyone else. That his interest in her was purely physical she didn't need telling either. It could hardly be anything more.

Her cool regard served only to increase the glint. Opposition, it appeared, was an enticement in itself. More than ever she regretted the situation she had landed herself with. If she wanted to know the truth, not only was she faced with the prospect of explaining a lie she had no logical reason to have told in the first place, but the possibility of mortifying Lucius with the news that he had been making advances to a relative.

'And what does your stepfather do for a living?' Ottavia persisted, claiming her attention once more.

'He's in textiles,' she acknowledged.

'On his own account?'

'His own business, yes.' A highly successful one, Gina could have added, but saw no reason to go into greater detail—especially when said success was dependent on factors she found rather worrying at times.

Ottavia seemed content to leave it at that for the moment, but Gina sensed that the digging was by no means done. Plain nosiness, she assured herself. There was no way the woman could suspect the truth.

Midnight brought no sign of an end to the evening. Hardly able to keep her eyes open, Gina finally gave in.

'I hope it won't be taken amiss if I go to bed,' she said. 'I was on the road at seven this morning, and didn't have all that good a night's sleep before it.'

'But of course!' Signora Carandente responded. 'You must feel free to do whatever you wish while you are our guest. Perhaps you would prefer to have breakfast served in your room?'

'Not at all,' Gina assured her. 'I'll be fine.' She added impulsively, 'Your hospitality is second to none, *signora*.'

'Contessa,' corrected Ottavia with some sharpness of tone.

'You may call me Cornelia,' her mother told Gina graciously.

Still grappling with the implications, Gina inclined her head. 'Thank you.'

She took her leave with a general 'Goodnight,' avoiding any clash of glances with Lucius himself. If his mother was a Contessa, his father obviously had to have been a Count, which meant the title must have been handed down. It made the likelihood of her father having any connection seem even more remote. What would a son of such a family have been doing attending an English university as an ordinary student?

On the other hand, it was surely unlikely that either now or in the past another, entirely unconnected, Carandente family resided in Vernici.

She was going around in circles, Gina acknowledged. The only way to be sure was to do what she should have done several hours ago and tell the whole story. Concealing the name had been an idiotic gesture all round. Tomorrow, she promised herself, she would come clean. It was hardly as if she was after feathering her nest in any fashion. All she wanted was to know who her father had really been.

CHAPTER TWO

DESPITE her tiredness, Gina was wide awake at six. The early morning sunlight beckoned her out onto the balcony to view the beautifully landscaped gardens stretching to all sides. The vistas beyond were shrouded in early morning haze.

There was no one about that she could see from here. On impulse, she returned to the bedroom to don a pair of light cotton trousers and a shirt. Half an hour or so's exploration would still leave her plenty of time to get ready for the day proper.

She could hear the muted sound of voices coming from somewhere towards the rear of the premises as she descended to the lower floor, but no one appeared to question her purpose. Not that any member of staff would do that in any case, Gina supposed. As a guest of the house she was, as Cornelia had assured her, entitled to do as she wished.

All the same she reduced the chances of running into anyone by using the front entrance. The Fiat was gone, the driveway clear of vehicles of any kind. There would be garages around the back somewhere, she assumed.

She headed left, away from the house, dropping down stone steps between white marble pillars to terraces overhung with luxuriant plant life and strewn with classical statues. Gina revelled in the beauty of it all against the clean, clear blue of the sky.

On one level lay a pond laced with water lilies of every hue, the carved stone bench at its edge positioned to take full advantage of the harmonious view across the valley. She slowed her steps on sight of the man already seated there.

'I didn't realise anyone else was up and about yet,' she said a little awkwardly. 'I thought I'd take a look around before breakfast.'

'I saw you from my window,' Lucius admitted. 'It seemed probable that you would eventually reach this spot.' His regard this morning was fathomless. 'So, how do you find our home?'

'It's truly beautiful,' she acknowledged. 'A dream of a place! Why didn't you tell me you were a Count?' she tagged on.

He gave a brief shrug. 'I have no use for status symbols.'

'Ottavia doesn't appear to share the aversion.'

'My sister clings to an order long gone.' He patted the seat at his side. 'Come sit with me.'

'I have to get back,' she said hurriedly. 'It must be getting on for breakfast time.'

'Food will be served whenever and wherever required,' he advised. A hint of amusement in his eyes now, he added, 'You are afraid of me, perhaps?'

'Of course not!' she denied.

'Then, of what I make you feel?' he continued imperturbably.

Pretending not to know what he was talking about would be a waste of time and breath, Gina knew. 'You take a great deal too much for granted,' she retorted.

The amusement grew. 'That is your English half speaking. Your Barsini blood responds to mine.'

The time to tell him the truth was now, but the words wouldn't form themselves.

'Grateful as I am to you for what you're doing with my

car, I'm not about to become your playmate for the week,' she said coolly instead.

'Playmates are for children,' he returned, not in the least rebuffed. 'We are neither of us that.'

'But we *are* strangers,' she replied with deliberation. 'You don't really know anything about me.'

'Then, tell me,' he invited.

The moment was there again, but Gina still couldn't bring herself to take advantage of it.

'I should be getting back,' she repeated.

'Then, I will come with you,' he said.

He got to his feet, lean and lithe as a panther in the black trousers and shirt. Gina steeled herself as he moved to where she stood, but he made no attempt to touch her, falling into step at her side as she turned back the way she had come. Catching the faint scent of aftershave, she was supremely conscious of the fact that she had yet to shower, yet to put a brush to her hair.

'Are you always up this early of a morning?' she asked.

'I rise when I awaken,' he said easily. 'No later than six, sometimes as much as an hour before that.'

'Even when you don't get to bed until the early hours?'

'A matter of custom. If I tire in the day I may take siesta. It depends on my commitments.'

'I imagine those are extensive.'

'Not too much so.'

Doing her best to keep the conversational ball rolling, she said, 'You speak excellent English.'

'But somewhat structured compared with the way you speak, yes?'

Gina cast a glance at the chiselled profile, responding to the curve of his lips. 'My old English teacher would approve every word. It's usually tourists who introduce bad habits.'

'Few tourists find Vernici,' he said. 'It is off the regular routes.'

'I know. I had some difficulty finding it myself.'

It was Lucius's turn to slant a glance, expression curious. 'Why were you looking for Vernici at all if your father came from Naples.'

Do it now! an inner voice urged her, even as she mentally cursed the slip-up. 'Latterly,' she heard herself saying regardless. 'But he was apparently born in Vernici, so I thought it worth taking a look there too.'

'I see.' From his tone, it was obvious that he was wondering why she hadn't mentioned that fact last night. 'The name is unfamiliar to me,' he went on after a moment, 'but the older townsfolk will surely recall the family. I will have enquiries made.'

She was getting deeper and deeper into the mire, thought Gina unhappily. What the devil was wrong with her that she kept on fabricating things?

They had reached the front of the house. Lucius preceded her up the steps to open a door for her to pass through, too close by far for comfort as he followed her in. Soles wet from their passage across the grass, her sandals had no purchase on the terrazzo. Lucius shot out an arm as she skidded, hauling her up against him, his hand warm at her waist.

'You must take more care,' he said, making no immediate attempt to let her go again.

'I will,' Gina assured him. 'I'm fine now, thanks.'

His laugh was low, the brief pressure of his lips at her nape where the curtain of hair had parted stirring her blood in a manner she deplored.

'I'd prefer you didn't do that,' she got out.

He laughed again, but this time released her. Gina made herself meet the dark eyes. 'I realise you probably won't be used to it, but I'm telling you again that I'm not…available.'

'Do you not think that you might be the one now taking too much for granted?' Lucius returned with mock gravity.

'Am I?' she challenged, and saw the glint return.

'No. I would be only half a man if I could look at you and not want you in the instant, *cara*.' He gave her no time to reply—if she could have come up with a reply at all. 'I will begin enquiries about the Barsini family this very morning. I would hope to have news of them before the day is over.'

A forlorn hope, Gina reflected ruefully. The longer this charade of hers continued, the harder it became to revoke.

'There's something I—' she began, breaking off as Guido heaved into view.

'Something you…?' Lucius prompted.

She shook her head, courage lost. 'Forget it.'

Leaving him standing there, she ran lightly up the stairs to head for her room. The situation was becoming increasingly difficult. If it weren't for her lack of transport, she would be tempted to abandon the whole idea and return home. She was vitally attracted to a man who might just be a close blood relation, a man who was making no effort to conceal *his* objective. Even if there should prove to be no connection, she wasn't into the kind of casual, ships that pass in the night, relationship that was all Lucius would have in mind.

Despite last night's refusal, breakfast was brought to her at eight o'clock. Gina ate it out on the balcony, enjoying both the view and the warmth. The sky was so blue, the quality of light a joy in itself. It was possible that her father had viewed the same scene—perhaps even from this very room. Could she really bear, Gina asked herself, not to know for certain?

She went downstairs again with no notion of how she was going to spend the day. Wandering out to the terrace, she found Ottavia stretched out on a lounger beneath an opened umbrella. She was wearing a gold-lamé bikini that barely covered her voluptuous curves, her eyes shielded by designer sunglasses. Her toenails, Gina noted, were painted the same shade of scarlet as her fingernails and lips, the whole effect more reminiscent of the film world, she thought, than Italian aristocracy.

'*Buon giorno,*' she proffered tentatively.

Ottavia pulled down the sunglasses a fraction to run a disparaging eye over the cotton dress Gina had elected to wear. 'You are quite recovered from your weariness, I trust?' she enquired, without bothering to respond to the greeting.

'Quite, thank you,' Gina confirmed. She felt it necessary to add, 'The breakfast was very good, but I really don't expect to be waited on while I'm here.'

'As you are here at my brother's invitation, you are entitled to be treated as any other guest,' came the smooth reply. 'You realise, of course, how fortunate you are to have gained his support in this affair.' She didn't wait for any answer. 'A word of warning, however. Lucius may pay you some attentions because he is a man and you are attractive to look at, but it means nothing.'

'In other words, don't run away with the idea that he might be about to offer marriage,' Gina returned. 'I'll certainly bear it in mind.'

The irony left no visible impression. 'Good,' was the only comment.

Her presence wasn't exactly welcome, Gina gathered, as the glasses were replaced and the head returned to the supporting cushion. She was tempted to stay anyway, just for the hell of it, but there was little to be gained from keeping company with someone who so obviously didn't want her there.

She had only covered a small part of the immediate grounds earlier. Now would be the right time to take a turn round the other side of the house before the heat became too great for comfort. With several days to fill, and no-where else to go, she was probably going to be spending a lot of time out of doors. Which in this climate would be no great hardship, she had to admit.

She was crossing the drive when a low-slung sports car came roaring round the bend. Gina leapt instinctively for safety, missed her footing and went down on one knee in the gravel, steeling herself for the impact she was sure was to come. The car screeched to a halt with its front bumper bare inches from her. Spouting Italian at a rate of knots, the driver leapt out without bothering to turn off the engine, a look of concern on his handsome face as he came to lift her to her feet.

'*Inglese,*' Gina said for what seemed like the millionth time in response to what she took to be a spate of solicitous enquiry. '*Non capisco.*'

'English!' he exclaimed on a note of surprise.

'That's right.' Gina gave a wry grimace as she eased her knee. 'Does everybody round here drive like bats out of hell?'

His brows drew together in puzzlement. 'Bats?'

'It's just a saying,' she explained, regretting the use of it. 'It means fast, that's all.'

The frown cleared. 'Ah, fast!' Concern leapt once more in his eyes as he caught sight of the trickle of blood running down her leg. 'You are hurt! Why did you not tell me you were hurt?'

'I hadn't realised it was grazed,' Gina admitted, lifting the edge of her skirt to view the not inconsiderable damage. 'I thought I'd just knocked it.'

'It must be cleaned and dressed,' he declared. 'Before it becomes infected.'

'It will be,' she assured him. 'Just as soon as I get back to the house. I'm a guest there,' she added, in case he was in any doubt. 'Gina Redman.'

'A friend of the family?' He sounded intrigued.

'Not exactly. There was an accident. My car was badly damaged. Lu—Signor Carandente very generously invited me to stay until it's repaired.'

His lips curved. 'But of course. Lucius is the most generous of men. I am Cesare Traetta. You must allow me to drive you to the villa.'

'It's hardly any distance,' Gina protested. 'I might get blood on the upholstery.'

'If so it will be cleaned.' He went to open the passenger door. 'Please to get in.'

Gina wiped away the trickle of blood with her handkerchief before doing so. The soft leather seat cocooned her, its contours designed to hold the body in position. Definitely needed, she thought, as Cesare set the car into motion again with a force that caused the rear wheels to spin. She judged him around Lucius's age, which made him Donata's senior by fifteen years, yet the two of them appeared to be on a par when it came to road sense.

They rounded the final bend to come to a further screeching stop outside the house. Switching off the engine, Cesare got swiftly from the car to help Gina from the seat she was struggling to vacate without having her skirt ride up any further than it already had.

'I think I can manage, thanks,' she said drily when he

made to assist her up the steps. 'A damp flannel, and I'll be as good as new!'

'You are bleeding!' exclaimed Lucius from the doorway, startling her because she hadn't seen him arrive. 'What happened to you?'

'I slipped and fell on the drive.' Gina saw no reason to go into greater detail. 'Signor Traetta was kind enough to give me a lift.'

'Cesare,' urged the man at her back. 'You must call me Cesare.'

She gave him a brief smile. 'Cesare, then.' To Lucius she said, 'I'll go and clean myself up.'

'The necessary materials will be brought to you.' he said. 'We must be sure no foreign substances remain in the wound.'

'Of course.' Gina was fast tiring of the fuss. 'I can cope.'

'I am sure of it.' His tone was dry. 'Your self-sufficiency does you credit. You will, however, wait for assistance in this matter.'

He took her agreement for granted, indicating that she precede him into the house. Gina battened down her instincts and meekly obeyed. 'I'm sure you know best,' she murmured in passing, tongue tucked firmly in cheek.

The dress was not only dirty but torn at the hem, she found on reaching her room. Not beyond repair, she supposed, examining the rip, though she was no expert needlewoman. At any rate, she had plenty of other things to change into, so it could wait until she got home.

Despite instructions, she ran hot water in the bathroom basin and began cleaning off the worst of the mess. The graze was quite extensive, with tiny pieces of gravel embedded in the shredded flesh. Concentrating on extracting them, she was taken unawares when Lucius entered the room bearing a first-aid box.

'You were to wait until I brought this!' he exclaimed.

Seated on a padded stool, her foot raised on the bath edge to enable her to see what she was doing, Gina resisted the urge to pull down the skirt she had raised to mid thigh.

'I hardly expected you to bring it up yourself,' she said lamely.

Dark brows rose. 'You think such a task beneath me?'

'Well, no, not exactly. I just took it…' She left the sentence unfinished, holding out her hand for the box. 'It's very good of you, anyway.'

Lucius made no attempt to hand it over. Placing it on the long marble surface into which the double basins were set, he seized soap from the dish and washed his hands. Gina watched in silence, reminded that she should have done the same before attempting to touch the graze at all.

His presence in the confines of the bathroom—spacious though it was—made her nervous. She found it difficult to control the quivering in her limbs when he took a pair of tweezers from the box and sat down on the bath edge to start work on the gravel.

The hand he slid about the back of her calf to hold her leg still was warm and firm against her skin, his fingers long and supple, the nails smoothly trimmed; she could imagine the way they would feel on her body—the sensual caresses. Her nipples were peaking at the very notion.

Stop it! she told herself harshly, ashamed of the sheer carnality of her thoughts. It might be a long-established fact that women were as capable as men of enjoying sex without love, but she had never followed the trend. From her mid teens she had determined not to settle for anything less than the real thing: the kind of love her mother had known for Giovanni Carandente. The possibility that

Lucius could be her father's nephew was enough on its own to prohibit any notion she might have of relaxing her ideals.

'I am sorry if I hurt you,' Lucius apologised as her leg jumped beneath his hands. 'There are only a few more small pieces to come, and then we are finished but for the antiseptic.'

'No problem,' she assured him. 'You're being very gentle. It's quite a mess, isn't it? I didn't realise how deep some of the bits had gone.'

'Thankfully, there should be no lasting scars,' he said without looking up from his task. 'It would be a pity to mar such a lovely leg.'

'Don't you ever stop?' she asked with a sharpness she hadn't intended.

This time he did look up, expression quizzical. 'You find my admiration irksome?'

Gina drew a steadying breath. 'I find it a little too…practised, that's all.'

'Ah, I see. You think I express the same sentiments to all women.' The dancing light was in his eyes again. 'Not so.'

He was hardly going to admit it, Gina told herself as he turned his attention once more to her knee. Not that it made any difference.

The antiseptic stung like crazy, but Lucius made no concessions. He finished the dressing with an expertly applied bandage.

'You may remove the dressing tomorrow to allow the healing tissue to form,' he said, relinquishing his hold on her at last.

Gina got to her feet to try a somewhat stiff-legged step, pulling a face at her reflection in the mirrored wall. 'I haven't had a bandaged knee since I was eight!'

'Long skirts, or the trousers women everywhere appear to have adopted, will cover your embarrassment.'

The dry tone drew her eyes to the olive-skinned face reflected in the mirror. 'You disapprove of the trend?' she asked lightly.

'I prefer a woman to dress as a woman,' he confirmed. 'As most men would say if asked.'

'Donata wears them,' Gina felt bound to point out, stung a little by the implied criticism. 'With that attitude, I'm surprised you allow it—to say nothing of the rest!'

'I said preference not outright rule,' came the steady response. 'Assuming that by the "rest" you refer to the state of my sister's hair, no amount of castigation can hasten the regrowth.'

Gina turned impulsively to face him, ashamed of the dig. 'I spoke out of turn. You said yesterday that she'd recently returned from school?'

The smile was brief and lacking in humour. 'She was despatched from her school for behaviour no reputable establishment could tolerate.'

'Not just for a haircut, surely!'

'A minor transgression compared with breaking out of the school in order to attend a nightclub in the nearby town. Not for the first time it appears. This time she was caught by the police when they raided the place in search of drugs.'

Gina gazed at him in dismay. 'You're not saying Donata was actually taking them?'

'She assures me not.'

'You do believe her?'

Lucius lifted his shoulders, mouth wry. 'I hardly know what to believe. I bitterly regret allowing her to persuade me into sending her to Switzerland at all. Her education was complete enough without this "finishing" she was so anxious to acquire.'

'She can't have been the only one to kick over the traces,' Gina ventured.

'If by that you mean was she alone on the night in question, the answer is no. There were two others caught with her. One American girl, one English. They too were despatched to their respective homes.'

'I see.' Silly as it seemed, Gina felt like apologising for the part the English girl had played. 'I don't suppose it helps much.'

'No,' Lucius agreed. 'I am still left with the problem of a sister turned insurgent. While she resides here at Cotone I can demand that she obeys certain rules of conduct, but there are limits to the penalties I can impose should she choose to defy me.'

'I can appreciate that,' Gina said carefully. 'It isn't as if she's a child any more.'

'She is eighteen years of age,' he advised on a harder note. 'By now she should be looking towards marriage and children of her own!'

'Marriage isn't the be all and end all of every woman's ambition.' Gina felt moved to protest, turning a deaf ear to the faint, dissenting voice at the back of her mind.

The dark eyes regarded her with a certain scepticism in their depths. 'You intend to stay single all your life?'

'I didn't say that. It depends whether I meet a man I want to marry.'

'And whom, of course, also wishes to marry you.'

'Well, obviously.' The mockery, mild though it was, stirred her to like response. 'Two hearts entwined for all eternity! Worth waiting for, wouldn't you say?'

'The heart has only a part to play,' he said. 'The body

and mind also have need of sustenance. The woman I myself marry must be capable of satisfying every part of me.'

'Typical male arrogance!' She exploded, driven beyond endurance by the sheer complacency of the statement. 'It would serve you right if...' She broke off, seeing the sparkle of laughter dawn and realising she'd been deliberately goaded. 'Serve you right if you were left high and dry!' she finished ruefully. 'Not that it's likely, I admit.'

The sparkle grew. 'You acknowledge me a man difficult for any woman to resist?'

'I acknowledge you a man with a lot more than just looks going for him, Count Carandente,' she said with delicate emphasis.

If she had been aiming to fetch him down a peg or two, she failed dismally. His shrug made light of the dig. 'Despite Ottavia's claim, the woman I marry will not carry the title of Contessa because she will be no more entitled to do so in reality than anyone in the last few hundred years. As I told you this morning, it is simply a status symbol. One for which I have little use myself.

'Which leaves me,' he went on with a wicked gleam, 'with just the looks you spoke of going for me. The looks that warm both your English and your Italian blood to a point where the differences no longer have bearing. Or would you still try to deny what lies between us, *cara*?'

The pithy response that trembled on her lips as he moved purposefully towards her was rejected as more likely to inflame than defuse the situation. What was she doing indulging in the kind of repartee scheduled to bring this very situation about to start with? she asked herself.

'Whatever you have in mind, you can forget it!' she said with what certainty she could muster, resisting any urge to try fighting him off physically as he drew her to him. 'I already told you, I'm not playing!'

'Words! Just words!' He put a forefinger beneath her chin to lift it, bending his head to touch his lips to hers with a delicacy that robbed her of any will to resist.

She was conscious of nothing but sensation as he kissed her: the pounding of her blood in her ears, the warmth spreading from the very centre of her body, the growing weakness in her lower limbs urging her to give way to the need rising so suddenly and fiercely in her. He drew her closer, moulding her to the contours of his masculine shape—making her aware of his own arousal in a manner that inflamed her even further. The words he murmured against her lips transcended all language barriers.

This man might be a close relative, came the desperate reminder, pulling her up as nothing else could have done right then.

'That's enough,' she got out, jerking away from him. 'In fact, it's more than enough!'

Anticipating at the very least a show of frustrated anger at her withdrawal from what must have appeared a near foregone conclusion, she was taken totally aback when Lucius simply laughed and shook his head.

'I think not, for either of us, but there is no haste. You will find Cesare and myself on the terrace should you care to join us for refreshment. He will be anxious to know that you suffered no long-lasting injury.'

He gathered the items he had taken from the first-aid box, and departed, leaving Gina standing there feeling all kinds of an idiot. Aroused he might have been, but he was obviously more than capable of controlling it. He certainly wouldn't demean himself by insisting on satisfaction, however encouraged to believe it forthcoming.

Telling him the truth now, and discovering that there was indeed a close blood relationship, could only prove embarrassing for them both. Probably the best thing she could do was forget the whole affair and head for home as soon as her car was repaired.

And spend the rest of her life wondering, came the thought. She was Giovanni Carandente's daughter. Having finally started on the quest, she had to see it through to the end, no matter what. There must be some way of finding out if this really was his place of origin that didn't involve giving herself away.

Her inclination was to spend the rest of the morning right here in her room, but that was no way for a guest to behave. With the bandage in mind, she donned a long, sarong-type skirt along with a silky vest, and slid her feet into a pair of thonged sandals. Not exactly haute couture, but it served the purpose.

Hair loose about her shoulders, face free of make-up apart from a dash of lipstick, she hid behind a pair of tortoiseshell sunglasses on going out to the terrace. Not just Lucius and Cesare to face, she saw, but Ottavia and Donata into the bargain, the former now fully and beautifully dressed.

Wearing a pair of deck trousers and a T-shirt, her hair raked through with a careless hand, Donata looked hardly less of the teenage rebel than she had in the leather outfit yesterday. She viewed Gina's arrival with a marked lack of enthusiasm.

Not so, Cesare, who leapt to see her seated with a solicitude that went down like a lead balloon with both sisters.

'Your leg must be supported,' he urged, raising the chair's built-in foot rest for her. 'You are in much pain?'

'None at all,' Gina assured him, submitting to his ministrations only because it was marginally less awkward than asking him to desist.

'I ordered fresh orange juice for you,' said Lucius as

one of the younger male staff members came from the house bearing a loaded tray. 'It can, of course, be replaced by something stronger if you prefer.'

'Thanks, but this is just what I need,' Gina assured him as the tall, ice-cool glass was set before her. She seized on it gratefully, sending a good quarter of the contents down her throat in one gulp.

'Iced drinks should be sipped so that the stomach suffers no sudden shock,' commented Donata with a certain malice. 'Isn't that so, Lucius?'

'Advisable, perhaps,' he agreed easily. 'If you are finding the heat overpowering we can move to a cooler part of the terrace,' he said to Gina herself.

The only heat she found overpowering was the kind he generated, came the fleeting thought. 'I find it no problem at all,' she assured him. 'I always did enjoy the sun.'

'What little you see of it in England.'

'Oh, we have our good days,' she returned lightly. 'Sometimes several together. You've visited my country?'

'Never for any length of time.'

'Tomorrow is the Palio,' Cesare put in with an air of being left too long on the sidelines. 'I have grandstand seats long-reserved should anyone care to share them.'

'*Si!*' declared Donata before anyone else could speak. '*Vorrei andare!*'

Lucius said something in the same language, wiping the sudden animation from her face. Pushing back her chair, she got jerkily to her feet and stalked off, mutiny in every line of her body.

'What exactly is the Palio?' asked Gina in the following pause, feeling a need for someone to say something.

It was Cesare who answered. 'A horse race run twice a year between Siena's *contrade*. Riders must circuit the

Piazza del Campo three times without the benefit of saddles.'

'A bareback race!' Gina did her best to sound enthused.

'A little more than just that,' said Lucius. 'The city's seventeen districts compete for a silk banner in honour of the Virgin. A tradition begun many centuries ago. The race itself lasts no more than a minute or two, but the pageantry is day long. You might enjoy it.'

'You were only there the one time yourself that I recall,' said Cesare. 'Why do we not all of us attend together?'

'It has become a tourist spectacle,' declared Ottavia disdainfully. 'I have no desire to be part of it. Nor, I am sure, will Marcello.'

'Then, perhaps the three of us,' he suggested, undeterred. 'Gina cannot be allowed to miss such an event.'

If Lucius refused too, it would be down to the two of them next, Gina surmised, not at all sure she would want to spend a whole day in Cesare's company. Equal though he appeared to be in age to her host, he lacked the maturity that was an intrinsic part of Lucius's appeal.

'The three of us, then,' Lucius agreed, to her relief. 'Providing that I drive us there. I would prefer that we arrive without mishap.'

Cesare laughed, not in the least put out. 'You have so little faith in me, *amico*, but I accept your offer.'

It had been an ultimatum not an offer, but Lucius obviously wasn't about to start splitting hairs. Gina found herself wishing it was just going to be the two of *them* taking the trip. Safer this way though, she acknowledged ruefully. With Cesare around to act as chaperon, there would be no repeat of this morning's assault on her senses. Whichever way things might turn out, she was in no position to risk that kind of involvement.

CHAPTER THREE

CESARE took his departure shortly afterwards, accompanied by Lucius who wished to discuss some obviously private matter with him. Left alone with Ottavia, Gina made an effort to open a conversation, but soon gave up when her overtures failed to draw more than the briefest of replies.

'I think I'll go and find that cooler spot Lucius mentioned,' she said at length, getting to her feet. 'It's too hot to even think straight out here.'

The older woman made no reply at all to that; Gina hadn't really expected one. She could understand Donata's attitude regarding her presence in the house, but what axe did Ottavia have to grind?

There had been neither sight nor mention of Cornelia so far this morning. Either she was a late riser, or had gone out, Gina surmised. It still needed half an hour or so to noon. Lunch, she imagined, wouldn't be served much before one-thirty or even two. Not that she was hungry yet, but there was a lot of day still to get through.

The coolest place at this hour was going to be indoors. She went in via the glass doors to the *salotto*, welcoming the immediate flow of cooler air from the overhead fans. Reaching the hall, she stood for a moment wondering in which direction to head. Of the rooms that opened off it, she had so far only seen the one she had just come through and the library where she had first run into Lucius.

Feeling a bit of an intruder still, she opened a door under the right wing of the staircase, looking in on a small room

that appeared at first glance to be something of a deposi-
tory for unwanted items of furniture, with little in the way
of style about it.

About to close the door again, she paused as her eye
caught a reflection in the mirror almost directly opposite.
Eyes closed, Donata was seated in a high-backed chair that
concealed her from casual observation. From the look of
her, she had been crying.

It was likely that her company would be far from welcome, Gina reckoned, but she found herself stepping quietly into the room and easing the door to again regardless.
What she was going to say or do she had no clear idea.

The floor in here was laid in parquetry, the design
largely obscured by the heavy pieces of furniture. Donata
opened her eyes at the sound of footsteps, coming jerkily
to her feet as she registered the identity of the intruder.

'Leave me alone!' she urged. 'You have no right to be
here!'

Still not at all certain just what it was she hoped to
achieve, Gina halted a short distance away. 'I know I
haven't' she said, 'but, as I am, supposing we bury the
hatchet?'

Distracted by the unfamiliar phrase, Donata drew her
brows together. 'Bury the hatchet?'

'It means we forget about the accident and start again.
I'd rather be your friend than your enemy.'

A variety of expressions chased across the younger
girl's face as she gazed in silence for a moment or two.
When she did finally speak, the belligerence seemed almost forced. 'Why should *you* wish to be my friend?'

Why indeed? Gina asked herself, answering the question
in the same breath: because in all probability they shared
the same genes—or some of them, at any rate.

'I suppose I just don't like being disliked by anyone,'

she said on a semi-jocular note. 'Not that I'm having much success where your sister's concerned either.'

'Ottavia has little concern for anyone but herself,' declared Donata with unconcealed animosity. 'What *she* would most like is to be in Lucius's place.'

Gina could imagine. As *padrone*, Lucius would have total control of all Carandente affairs. Playing second fiddle wouldn't come easy to a woman of Ottavia's temperament. She wondered fleetingly what had prompted her to marry a man who appeared to be little more than an employee of the estate. It could hardly have been for lack of any other choice.

'You must miss your father,' she said softly, changing tack. 'How long is it since you lost him?'

The question took Donata by surprise; her response was automatic. '*Padre* died six years ago.'

'He can't have been all that old.'

'He was forty-eight.'

Which meant there had been just seven years between him and Giovanni Carandente, Gina calculated. Not that the knowledge brought her any closer to either proving or disproving a family connection.

'A big responsibility for your brother to take on so young,' she said. 'Especially as the last in line. It must put a lot of pressure on him.'

Donata eyed her suspiciously. 'Why should it matter to you?'

'It doesn't,' Gina hastened to assure her. 'I was just musing, that's all. It was very rude of me to make any comment at all on your family affairs.' She made a wry gesture. 'I'd better go. I shouldn't have intruded on you in the first place.'

'Then, why did you?'

'I could see you were upset.' Gina hedged. 'I couldn't just leave you like that.'

'You thought your offer of friendship all the comfort needed?'

Gina paid no heed to a sarcasm that had little real bite to it. 'Not all, but perhaps a little.' She hesitated before taking the plunge, aware of treading on delicate ground. 'Lucius told me what happened to you. It must have been a dreadful experience.'

The sympathy had an unexpected effect. Donata's face suddenly crumpled. 'He believes I took drugs!'

'I'm sure he doesn't.' Gina resisted the urge to go and put her arms about the girl. 'You just happened to be caught in the wrong place at the wrong time. It's only been a few days. He'll get over being angry about it.'

'No, he won't.' The tears were threatening to spill again, all trace of insurgency vanished. 'He can't bear even to look at me! No one can!'

And therein, thought Gina in swift understanding, lay the true source of misery. She kept her tone calm and level. 'Because of your hair, you mean?'

'Yes. It was like yours before I allowed Meryl to take scissors to it. She told me it would look so much smarter cut short.'

'Meryl is a hairdresser?'

'No, she was my friend.'

Some friend! Gina reflected. 'A very jealous one, I'd say,' she observed. 'It's going to take time to grow back,' she went on, seeing no point in pretending otherwise, 'but it could be made to look much better than it does.'

Faint hope dawned in the girl's eyes. 'You could do this?'

It wasn't exactly what Gina had had in mind, but she could scarcely make a worse job of it, she decided. 'I can try,' she said. 'You should really have a properly qualified stylist take a look at it.'

'Now is the most important,' declared Donata with growing eagerness. 'If I look less like the scarecrow Lucius called me, he might allow me to accompany you to the Palio tomorrow. He likes you very much, I can tell. He would listen if you asked him.'

Gina very much doubted it, but she couldn't find it in herself to refuse the request out of hand. 'I can but try,' she said again.

'Thank you.' The smile was radiant. 'And I'm truly sorry about your car. It *was* all my fault. I was driving recklessly.'

'Don't worry about it.' Gina could hardly credit the change in the girl. 'I'm sure it will come back as good as new. Anyway, we'd better get to it if we're to be through before lunch.

'Luncheon is at two o'clock,' Donata confirmed. 'Almost two hours away yet.'

Almost two hours to effect a make-over that would persuade Lucius to relent; Gina only hoped she was up to it.

It took every minute, and some judicious snipping, to achieve anything of a success. By the time she'd finished blow-drying the thick dark mass, she was beginning to regret ever having got involved.

She drew a breath of cautious relief on viewing the finished product. With the layers given some shape and lift, and shorter fronds framing the face, it was no salon creation, but it was certainly a vast improvement. Donata seemed pleased enough with it, at any rate.

At Gina's suggestion, she exchanged the deck trousers for a cream linen skirt, the T-shirt for a pale green blouse. She was, she declared extravagantly, happy to accept any advice from someone she now regarded as the only true friend she had ever known.

Something of an achievement in less than twenty-four hours, Gina supposed. She hoped Lucius wouldn't see it as presumption on her part.

Lunch was served on a side terrace beneath a projecting canopy. Ottavia viewed her sister's transformation with limited interest. Better than no effort at all, she said, though hardly a cause for celebration.

It was left to Lucius to express a more complimentary opinion. All the same, Gina had the feeling that he didn't really like the idea of her pitching in on a family affair. In which case, he should have kept his mouth shut about the whole thing, she told herself stoutly.

With Donata urging her in every way without actually saying anything, Gina collared him straight after the meal before she could lose courage.

'About tomorrow,' she began.

'You no longer wish to see the Palio?' Lucius asked.

'Yes, of course I do.' She paused, sidetracking for the moment. 'Although I'd hate to feel I was dragging you away from more important matters. I'm grateful for what you're already doing. I certainly don't expect you to provide entertainment too.'

'I have no other commitment,' he assured her. 'Unless you would prefer to spend the day with Cesare alone?'

'Oh, no!'

The denial was quick—too quick—drawing a smile to his lips. 'Then, where is the problem?'

'Donata hopes to come with us.'

'Commendable though your efforts to improve her appearance are,' he said on a suddenly curious note, 'I find myself asking why you would go to such lengths for someone who has given you nothing but aggravation?'

'I can't help feeling some sympathy for her,' Gina admitted truthfully. 'She's young for her age, and impressionable. I'd say this friend of hers—Meryl—has a lot to answer for. She was the one who persuaded her to have a hair cut. She was probably the one who instigated the break-out in the first place. Some people get a lot of pleasure out of leading others astray.'

'You appear to speak with some authority,' he said.

'I went through a bad phase myself in my teen years through mixing with the wrong kind of people—' she forbore from mentioning that she had been just fourteen at the time '—so I do have some insight into what's been driving Donata since she came home.' Gina had the bit too firmly between her teeth to consider letting go now. 'She's simply living up to the image she believes everyone has of her. What she needs is a little compassion. Did you never get yourself into unfortunate situations when you were a boy?'

'Nothing of any great note.' There was no telling what Lucius was thinking or feeling. 'You consider me lacking in humanity, then?'

Gina eyed him uncertainly, aware of having rather overstepped the mark as a mere guest in the house. 'I think you're probably finding it a difficult situation to deal with all round,' she said at length, feeling it a bit late to start apologising. 'Your mother, or Ottavia, would surely be better equipped.'

'Not all women are necessarily attuned to others,' came the dry return. 'You are certainly the most outspoken I have met.'

'I never did know when to mind my own business,' she

admitted, going for a lighter note. 'Forget I spoke, will you?'

The strong mouth slanted. 'I would find that difficult indeed. You may tell Donata you succeeded in convincing me of my harshness in refusing her request to attend the Palio.'

'Thank you.' Gina was taken aback by the sudden capitulation. 'I'm sure she'll really appreciate it.'

'I doubt that Cesare will share the feeling.'

'Oh?' She searched the olive features. 'Why not?'

Lucius lifted expressive shoulders. 'Donata has had what I believe is termed a crush on him since she was sixteen. She counted, I think, on this year in Switzerland turning her into the kind of woman he would want for a wife.'

'Cesare knows how she feels?'

'Of course. He used to find it amusing, but not so much now.'

'You should have said.'

'And have you accuse me of putting Cesare's feelings before those of my own sister?' he responded with irony. 'No, he must find it in himself to bear with the situation. Unless, of course, you can make use of this rapport the two of you appear to have formed to persuade her of her foolishness in pursuing a man so many years her senior.'

'I really did jump in with both feet, didn't I?' Gina said wryly. 'I don't imagine anything I could say would change the way she feels.'

'It can do no harm to try.'

Gina regarded him in some doubt. 'You seriously want me to talk to her?'

'It can do no harm,' Lucius repeated. 'She has somehow to be convinced that Cesare will never see her in the way she wants him to see her.'

'She'd have to accept it if he married someone else,' she said. 'Is that likely to be happening in the near future?'

'Not that I am aware of.'

'I suppose, like you, he's looking for an ideal.' Gina kept her tone light. 'I saw a film not so long ago where women were turned into robots programmed to satisfy a man's every desire.'

Amusement sparkled in the dark eyes. 'An on-off switch might have its uses at times, but my needs would be far from satisfied by programmed compliance.'

They were still seated at table. Gina resisted the urge to snatch her hands away as he reached across to take them in his.

'So smooth and lovely!' he murmured.

'I thought we were discussing your sister,' she said, willing herself to reveal no hint of the turbulence his very touch aroused in her. 'I'm no agony aunt, but I'll give it a go.'

Lucius raised a brow. 'Agony aunt?'

'They give advice to people who write in with problems. I imagine magazines over here have them too.' Gina could no longer contain her quivering reaction to the gentle circling of his fingertip in the centre of her palm. 'Don't!' she said huskily.

Lucius complied at once, sitting back in his seat to regard her with a quizzical expression. 'What is it that you fear about me, *cara*? That I may pass on some dread disease?'

'It hadn't even occurred to me.' She could say that in all honesty. She made herself look him in the eye. 'I just don't like being taken for granted, that's all.'

'I take nothing for granted, if by that you mean you believe me convinced of my ability to conquer,' he responded equably. 'I make no secret of the fact that I find you desirable because I see no point in pretending other-wise, but there is little pleasure to be gained from a fore-gone conclusion. Would you deny your own desires?' he continued when she made no reply. 'Are you telling me that your response to my touch is a figment of my imag-ination?'

Gina lifted her shoulders, fighting to stay on top of her warring emotions. 'I find you physically attractive, yes. That doesn't necessarily mean I want to jump into the nearest bed with you.'

'It doesn't mean that you *have* to jump into bed with me,' Lucius amended. 'Could it be that you fear being thought a woman of easy virtue if you give way to your urges?'

'Isn't that the way a lot of men still secretly feel about women who do?' she challenged.

'I can speak only for myself. I find nothing wrong with a woman indulging her needs.'

'Even the one you eventually marry?'

'Ah!' The exclamation was soft. 'That would be a dif-ferent matter.'

'That's sheer hypocrisy!' Gina accused.

'Perhaps,' he returned. 'I make no claim to faultlessness. The mother of my children will have known no other man but me.'

He meant it, she realised. Every word! 'If you're plan-ning on a family, you're leaving it rather late to get started, aren't you?' she said with a tartness that fired a sudden spark in his eyes.

'I doubt that my ability to father a child is much im-paired. As to the woman I do take to wife, she will obvi-ously be young enough to bear as many babies as it takes to produce a son who will carry on the name of Carandente.'

'It's all so damned clinical!' Gina could scarcely contain her repugnance. 'I pity whoever you do marry. I really do!'

This time he showed no visible reaction. 'There are many who will envy her the life she will lead. Many who would all too willingly take her place.'

'Fine.' Gina pushed back her chair to get to her feet, the scorn in her voice reflected in her eyes. 'Gives you plenty of choice, then. I'm going to take siesta, if that's all right?'

'But of course,' Lucius said smoothly, having risen to his feet with her. 'Perhaps we may talk again later when you are rested. There are matters we should have clear between us.'

Gina gave a brief nod, unable to trust her voice. She had gone beyond the boundaries again, and this time a little too far for comfort. Lucius might not show it, but she could sense the anger in him at her unequivocal condemnation. Distasteful as she found his attitude, it was hardly her place to revile him for it. He would no doubt be pointing that out to her.

She made it to her room without running into Donata. Kicking off her sandals, she lay down on the bed, welcoming the airflow from above. This was only her second day at the villa, and already she had managed to alienate her host. She couldn't possibly stay on here now. She must find accommodation in town until repairs to her car were completed. No Palio trip for certain.

She hadn't expected to sleep, but she did, waking to the sound of a tentative knock on the door an hour or so later.

'Am I disturbing you?' asked Donata, hovering on the threshold.

The obvious answer was yes, but Gina hadn't the heart to say it. 'I was about to get up anyway,' she said instead, suiting her actions to her words. She pulled a wry face. 'I'm getting into bad habits sleeping in the middle of the day!'

'*Madre* always takes siesta,' rejoined the younger girl. 'She considers it essential for her well-being.'

'A matter of what you're used to, I suppose. Is your mother not at home today?' Gina added casually.

'She went to visit with friends in Umbria. She won't be at home for three more days.' The pause was brief, the anxiety spilling over. 'You asked Lucius about my accompanying you to the Palio?'

Gina hesitated, wondering how best to say what she had to say. 'I did,' she responded. 'But—'

'He said no!' Donata's face set into lines recognisable from the day before, her eyes glittering with resentment. 'I hate him!'

'As a matter of fact, he said yes. You didn't give me chance to finish. It will be just the three of you. I shan't be coming.'

Her fury dying as swiftly as it had arisen, Donata looked flatteringly disappointed. 'But why?'

'Because I've decided to move to Vernici first thing in the morning.'

Disappointment gave way to perplexity. 'But your car won't be ready for several more days at least.'

'I know. I just feel it too much of an imposition to stay here all that time. The car can be delivered straight to the garage in Vernici.'

'Lucius won't allow you to go,' Donata declared with confidence. 'He'll insist that you stay.'

Lucius, Gina reflected drily, would probably be happy to see the back of her. She'd blotted her copybook with a vengeance.

*   *   *

Dinner was an uncomfortable meal. Lucius treated her with no less courtesy than before, though there was precious little humour in the gaze he rested on her from time to time.

Donata waited until halfway through the meal before announcing Gina's intention of leaving the villa in the morning.

'She feels she is imposing,' she said. 'But she must stay, must she not, Lucius?'

'There can be no question of it,' he returned levelly. 'Vernici has no suitable hotel.'

'My standards aren't that high,' Gina interposed.

'Mine,' he declared, 'are very high. You will please not insult me by refusing to accept my hospitality.'

Gina met his eyes, flushing a little. 'I didn't mean to insult you.'

'Then, the matter is settled.'

Ottavia kept her own counsel, although Gina suspected that she for one would have been more than ready to see her depart. Short of simply walking out on the household, she really had little choice. Lucius might not be feeling too friendly towards her after her diatribe earlier, but his breeding prevailed. Like it or not, she was here for the duration.

Anticipating some eventual move on his part to take her aside for the clarification he had spoken of, she was on tenterhooks for the rest of evening. By the time they retired for the night she had come to the conclusion that he'd decided to let silence speak for itself. One thing did appear clear: there would be no further flirtation on his part. A relief, she told herself.

Morning brought a fresh dilemma. With no way of knowing whether the Palio trip was still on, she was uncertain of how to dress. Her now unbandaged but scabby knee ruled out any short skirts for certain. She settled in the end on the bottom half of a white linen-mix trouser suit, to which she could easily add the jacket if necessary, along with a sleeveless blue top for coolness.

She was just about ready to venture downstairs when Crispina arrived with breakfast. The note she brought with her was short and to the point. Cesare would be here at nine. There was no indication as to whether Lucius would be accompanying the party, but Gina believed it unlikely. Having breakfast sent to her room was probably his way of expressing his lack of desire to see her at all. She considered developing a sudden headache and crying off herself, but that was too much like crawling into a hole.

Convinced by the time she did go down at five minutes to the hour that Lucius would not be around, she was torn between conflicting emotions on finding him waiting with Donata and Cesare in the hall. Like the latter, he was wearing a lightweight suit in a neutral colour, both jacket and shirt collar left open. Two equally devastating males, Gina acknowledged, yet it was only the one who could make her heart beat faster.

Cesare greeted her with an admiration that was more than a little overdone in her estimation.

'*Bella!*' he exclaimed. '*Sfarzosa!* Your injury?' he added solicitously in English. 'It gives you no pain this morning?'

'None at all,' she assured him. 'It looked a lot worse than it actually was.'

'I thank the heavens that I caused you no greater hurt!'

Gina looked away from him to give Donata a smile, unsurprised to receive a somewhat strained response. Having the man of one's dreams show interest of any kind in another woman was bad enough; having him lay it on as thickly as he'd just done was too much altogether. Donata was, Gina suspected, already beginning to regret last night's eagerness to have her remain.

'Shall we go?' said Lucius crisply.

The car awaiting them out front was an opulent saloon that looked as if it had just been fetched from the show-room.

'Gina must sit up front with Lucius,' declared Donata, and made sure of it by sliding into a rear seat herself.

Looking resigned, Cesare saw Gina into the car while Lucius went round to get behind the wheel, then took his seat at Donata's side.

Gina did her best to relax as Lucius put the vehicle into motion, but it was impossible while the atmosphere be-tween them remained so cool. If she was going to be here for several more days, then steps had to be taken to restore at least a measure of harmony. And it was up to her to make the move.

CHAPTER FOUR

DOMINATED by the sparkling white fantasy of its cathedral, Siena was a maze of narrow streets lined with Gothic mansions. Reaching the Campo to see the throng crushed into the centre where viewing was free of charge, Gina could only be thankful for the shade and relative comfort of their grandstand seats.

She took advantage of the first opportunity that arose to speak with Lucius out of earshot of the other two.

'I owe you an apology for what I said to you yesterday,' she tendered frankly. 'I was out of order.'

Expression enigmatic, he inclined his head. 'You are entitled to an opinion.'

'But not to express it in such a manner.' She made a rueful gesture. 'I really am sorry.'

A reassuring glimmer of humour lit the dark eyes. 'The humility is appreciated. So we are friends again, yes?'

Gina smiled back a little tentatively, wondering how he would react to the news that they possibly shared the same blood-line. 'Friends,' she agreed.

As promised, the day was full of spectacular pageantry, with costumed processions, flag-hurling and drumming. Gina enjoyed that far more than the race itself. A hectic, three-lap circuit with few holds barred, it left several horses and riders with injuries.

There would be another race in August, Lucius advised, with practice races and qualifying heats held between. By then this whole episode would be just a memory, Gina reflected dispiritedly.

Retracing their steps to the place where they had left the car proved no easy task in the milling throngs. Having paused for a moment to watch a puppet show in the belief that the others were at her back, she was surprised and a little perturbed to find herself apparently abandoned when she turned. She pushed on through the crowd in the direction she thought they had been taking, expecting to come on the three of them waiting for her to catch up at any moment.

It was a relief to see Cesare's face through the sea of heads, although he appeared to be approaching from a different direction altogether.

'I came back to find you,' he said on reaching her side. 'Lucius and Donata are waiting up ahead. To where did you vanish?'

'I stopped to look at a sideshow,' Gina admitted. 'I thought you'd all done the same. I was just about to start panicking,' she added with a laugh.

'There is no need now that I am with you,' Cesare assured her. He took her arm. 'We must go this way.'

Totally disorientated, Gina stuck to his side as he forged a passage through the crowds. Hard as she looked, she could catch no glimpse of either of the Carandentes.

'We must be going in the wrong direction!' she exclaimed after several fruitless minutes had elapsed. 'We'll never find them now!'

'We will all of us meet back at the car in due course,' Cesare consoled. 'At the moment you look very much in need of refreshment. A cool drink would be welcome, yes?'

Gina hesitated, torn between the urge to keep on searching, and the thirst she couldn't deny. It was so hot here in the midst of the surging throng, the humidity oppressive. Thirst won the battle. As Cesare had said, they would all meet at the car in due course. Meanwhile, a few minutes respite over a drink was surely going to make little difference.

They were lucky enough to slide into seats just vacated on the terrace of a nearby bar. Gina asked for a lager as the drink most likely to settle the dust in her throat, closing her eyes in near ecstasy as the icy cold liquid slid down.

'That,' she declared, setting her empty glass on the table, 'was pure nectar!'

'You would like another?' asked Cesare.

She shook her head. 'One's quite enough thanks. I'd hate to turn up at the car tipsy.' She eyed his own glass, which was still half full. 'How long do you think it will take us to get to where we left it?'

'It will depend,' he said, 'on whether I can accurately recall the exact street. Did you take note of the name yourself, by any chance?'

Gina shook her head again, this time in some alarm. 'It never occurred to me.'

'Nor to me. My mind was on other matters.' He made a wry gesture. 'I find it difficult to know how to deal with Donata's feelings for me. She is little more than a child!'

Gina hesitated before responding to the unspoken plea. 'In your estimation, perhaps, because you've probably known her all her life, but not in hers.'

'But I am almost twice her age!'

'Some girls go for older men. Especially those who've lacked a father figure, I've read.'

Cesare looked anything but flattered. 'Lucius has been a father to her these past six years since Paulo died.'

'Lucius is her brother. It's a totally different thing.'

'I have given her no cause to think of *me* in such a role!'

'It's only a suggestion,' Gina assured him. 'You don't exactly fit the image, I have to admit.'

A smile lit the handsome features. 'I would hope not indeed!' He viewed her with frank appreciation, gaze travelling from her face down the firm line of her throat to linger for a second or two on the thrust of her breasts. 'Lucius tells me you are half Italian yourself, with a father *you* never knew at all. Shall you continue to search for his family when your car is ready to drive again?'

'It depends how much time I have left,' she said. 'I'm due to start a new job in a couple of weeks.'

'You should stay here in Italy,' he returned caressingly. 'You belong in the sunlight, *cara*.'

Odd, thought Gina, how the same endearment could have such little impact when used by another man. Not that Lucius employed the word in any really meaningful sense either. It was just a term of address that came all too easily to male lips in this part of the world.

'I belong where I'm accustomed to being,' she said on a light note. 'I can't even speak the language.'

'The language of love is universal. We could speak it together, you and I.'

'We could, but we won't.' Gina was taking him no more seriously than his sparkling eyes indicated. 'Are you going to finish your drink?'

He gave a mock sigh. 'You will never know what you miss!'

'What I don't know can't be missed.' She let a moment or two pass while he took another pull at his glass before saying casually, 'How long *have* you known the Carandentes?'

'Since they first came to Tuscany seventeen years ago,' he acknowledged.

Gina felt her heart give a sudden lurch. 'So who owned San Cotone before they arrived?'

'Cotone has been in the family for many generations. As a distant cousin, Paulo was not in the direct line of inheritance, but he was the only one left to carry on the name.'

'What happened to the rest of them?'

'The son who should have been the next in line was killed some years before his father passed on. There was no other issue.' Cesare gave her a quizzical look. 'Lucius is the person to ask about the family history if it interests you.'

Grappling with the implications of what she'd just been told, Gina raised a smile and a shrug. 'Just plain old curiosity. I think it's time we went in search of the car, don't you?'

With the crowds still thick, and lacking a definite location, it took them more than half an hour to find the vehicle, and only then because Gina happened to recognise an ornate building on the corner of the street where they had parked. Donata was already seated inside the car, which was within shade; Lucius greeted the pair of them in mingled relief and annoyance.

'We,' he declared, 'have been waiting here for almost an hour! I was on the verge of calling for assistance in finding the two of you!'

'My fault,' claimed Cesare. 'I forgot to take note of the location. But for Gina's better senses, we could have wandered the streets for ever!'

'Sheer luck,' Gina disclaimed. 'It was my fault we got separated in the first place. I'd have been in real trouble without Cesare. I wouldn't even know how to say "I'm lost" in Italian!'

'A few basic phrases should be simple enough for even

the English to learn,' came the unsympathetic retort. Lucius opened the rear door, indicating that she should get into the car. 'We had best be on our way before the roads from the city become blocked with traffic, as will begin to happen very shortly.'

As was starting to happen already, if the route she and Cesare had just traversed was any example, Gina reflected. She weathered a glowering look from Donata as she slid into the seat at her side. The younger girl had nothing at all to worry about so far as she was concerned, but this was hardly the time or the place to tell her so. It was up to Cesare to put her straight with regard to his feelings— or lack of them. And the sooner the better.

There had been little opportunity up to now to go over the information Cesare had supplied. With Donata in no mood for conversation, she was able to put her mind to it at last. The coincidences were too many for there to be any mistake. The son who had been killed must have been her father. If Paulo Carandente hadn't been in the direct line of inheritance, then the blood connection between her and Lucius was too remote to be of any account.

So what now? she asked herself, thrusting that latter thought aside. If she told the truth she would not only be faced with the problem of explaining the fabrications, which would be difficult enough, but all the questions, the probing—the possible assumption that she was after financial gain. All she'd ever really wanted was to know where her father had come from. Why cause unnecessary disruption?

Cesare took off in his own car almost immediately on reaching the villa, leaving Donata to make what she would of his excuses for not staying longer. Now wasn't the time to try talking to her either, Gina reckoned, as the girl headed indoors without so much as a glance in her direction. Whatever rapport they had developed yesterday was right out of the window at present.

'I think she believes I'm interested in Cesare myself,' she remarked to Lucius as they followed her inside.

'And are you?' he asked.

Gina glanced his way uncertainly. 'Is that meant to be a joke?'

His mouth slanted. 'Why should I joke about such matters? Cesare has many admirers.'

'I don't doubt it,' she said. 'But I'm not one of them. Not in the way you mean, at any rate.'

Suit jacket slung casually over a shoulder, Lucius paused in the hall to view her with a certain cynicism. 'How many ways are there?'

'More than one, for certain,' she returned, not altogether sure where this was going. 'I like Cesare as a person, and he is very good-looking, but he doesn't attract me as a man.'

'But *I* do?'

Gina kept a tight rein on her impulses, lifting her shoulders in a brief shrug. 'In some respects.'

This time his smile was genuine. 'I would be interested to hear what you find disfavourable in me. Apart from the matters we discussed yesterday, that is.'

'Your arrogance, for one thing,' she said with purpose.

'You prefer a man who is unsure of himself?'

'Of himself, no. Of me, yes.'

'You believe me incapable of knowing what you are thinking, what you are feeling?' His voice had softened, his eyes acquiring an expression that set every nerve aquiver. He brought up a hand to trace the tip of a finger down the side of her face and across her lips. 'You feel the same desire I feel for you, *mi tesoro*. The desire we must both of us satisfy before too long.'

'I'm going to get a shower,' she said with what composure she could rally. 'I'd suggest you take a very cold one.'

His laughter followed her as she turned away to mount the stairs. Gina fought to stop herself from looking down on reaching the gallery, though her senses told her he was still standing there. Staying celibate was easy enough when there was no real temptation to do otherwise, but the whole idea of saving herself for Mr Right held little sway right now, she had to admit.

If the day had been long, the evening seemed to stretch to infinity. Donata was subdued, picking at her food with little interest. Nothing anyone could say was going to help, Gina judged. The girl had to come to terms with the unlikelihood of Cesare returning her feelings.

Used to eating no later than seven-thirty at home, unless being taken out to dinner, she found it difficult to accustom herself to a mealtime that not only started when she would normally be long finished, but could last into the small hours if the diners were of a mind. As always, wine flowed freely, with the house Chianti readily available.

'Would it be possible for me to see the vineyards?' she asked over coffee. 'I've never visited one before.'

'By all means,' Lucius said easily. 'I will show you them myself tomorrow.'

Gina met his eyes, unable to penetrate the dark depths. 'Thank you.'

'You will find it all very boring,' Ottavia advised. 'To see one grape is to see them all!'

'Gina will make her own assessment,' her brother responded. 'Perhaps you might like to take a walk around the gardens before we retire for the night?' he added on the same easy note.

Was there just the slightest emphasis on the 'we', Gina wondered, or was she reading too much into too little? She knew a sudden reckless surge. There was only one way to find out.

'I would, yes,' she said.

Lucius got to his feet, the coffee left in his cup ignored. 'Then, we will go now, while the mood is on us.'

Gina rose from the table to join him, keeping her expression under strict control as she sensed Ottavia's gaze. '*Buona sera,*' she murmured.

'*Sera* is evening, *notte* is night,' came the tart reply. 'Enjoy your stroll. The night air will, I am sure, aid restful sleep.'

Gina refused to let the suspected innuendo affect her. So what if Ottavia did have a notion of what was in her mind? Why should she care *what* the woman thought of her? Once she left here she would never see her again.

Lucius neither, came the thought, bringing a momentary despondency before her spirit reasserted itself. Forget next week. Concentrate on now.

The night was warm, the skies cloudless, the stars so much bigger and brighter than they ever appeared back home. Lucius made no immediate attempt to touch her in any fashion, strolling at her side much as he had done the previous morning, hands thrust into trouser pockets.

'There is a difference about you tonight,' he remarked shrewdly after a moment or two. 'Would I be wrong in thinking you ready to acknowledge what lies between us?'

'I decided it was time to start being honest with myself, yes,' she said, fighting the urge to run for safety while she still had the chance.

'You admit that you want me in the same way that I want you.' It was a statement not a question. 'What was it that made this decision for you?'

Gina gave a light shrug. 'I just saw no point in further pretence. After all, we're both adults.'

'True.' There was just the faintest trace of irony in his tone. 'So we waste no more time.'

Blood hammering in her ears as he drew her to him, nerves jumping all over the place, Gina met his lips, every last doubt vanishing at the first spine-tingling contact. The arms he slid about her were already possessive, drawing her close, making her feel his strength, his heat. She clung to him, lips opening to the silky pressure of his tongue, tasting him the way he was tasting her. There was no room for anything else in her mind but what was happening this very minute. She wanted what he wanted. *Everything* he wanted.

'Not here,' he murmured roughly. 'Come.'

They made it to her room without running into anyone, although by that time Gina was past caring.

Aroused though he was, Lucius refused to hurry, kissing her into a state where she hardly knew whether she was standing on her head or her heels before removing a single garment.

Nude, he was magnificent: a bronze statue come to full and vibrant life. Her skin looked almost translucent in contrast. She trembled to the feel of his hands as he slowly traced a passage down over her slender curves, breath catching in her throat when he slid a gentle finger between her thighs to penetrate her most intimate depths. She moved instinctively in rhythm with the motion, the tumult gathering until she could no longer contain it, overcome by wave after wave of overwhelming sensation.

Only then did he lower her onto the bed, supporting

himself on his forearms as he nuzzled her breasts. Gina opened her thighs to accommodate the burgeoning pressure, thrilling to the sheer weight of him, the size of him—moving her body in urgent seeking of even closer encounter.

It took her a moment to realise what was happening when he lifted himself away for a brief period. She hadn't even thought about protection until now, she realised. She forgot about it again almost instantly as he lowered himself back to her. The feeling as he slid inside her was indescribable. Flesh to flesh, spirit to spirit, came the hazy thought before everything merged into one great spinning Catherine wheel.

He was still there when she awoke at first light. For a moment or two she just lay studying his face, committing every wonderful, masculine line to memory. He had taken her to a place no amount of imagination could have painted for her, with little of the half anticipated pain to mar the moment of merging. Not that it wouldn't have been worth any amount of pain.

No regrets, she told herself firmly. And no backsliding on the decision previously made either. There was nothing to be gained from the truth.

She became suddenly aware that Lucius was awake, his eyes fired by the same memories as he looked back at her. His smile was a caress in itself.

'You,' he said softly, 'are a beautiful, warm and passionate woman, *cara mia*!'

'It must be the Italian in me,' she murmured, and saw the embers flare into vibrant life again.

The first time had been wonderful enough, but this surpassed it. If there had been any restraint left in her at all, she shed it in those tumultuous minutes, wrapping slender limbs about him as he came into her once more; loving his power, his passion, his very dominance.

They lay together in drowned repletion for some time afterwards. Gina was the first to stir, albeit with reluctance.

'I have to visit the bathroom,' she whispered.

Lucius kissed the tip of her nose before releasing her. 'I must leave you,' he said with obvious reluctance. 'The sun is already well-risen.'

He sat up as she slid from the bed, watching in some amusement as she pulled on a cotton wrap. 'A little late, I think, for such modesty. You have no secrets from me now.'

She had one, she thought wryly. 'Call it a foible,' she said. 'I'm not used to flaunting myself.'

'There is no shame in showing so beautiful a body. But the choice, of course, is your own.' He threw back the covers and rose to his feet, totally at ease with his own nudity. 'We will go to the winery immediately after break-fast,' he said, reaching for the clothing he had discarded in such haste a few hours ago.

Gina tore her eyes away from him with an effort, and headed for the bathroom. So far as Lucius knew, she had done nothing with him that she hadn't done with other men before him. All this talk about a man being able to tell when it was the first time for a woman was obviously rubbish. True, he'd made sure she was thoroughly aroused—which perhaps many men neglected to do.

The euphoria of a few minutes ago had diminished. While she couldn't bring herself to regret giving herself to him, he had probably set a precedent it was going to be difficult to match. It was also possible that having achieved his aim with so little effort, he would have no interest in pursuing it any further himself.

Expecting him to be gone when she returned to the bedroom to look out something to wear, she was surprised to find him standing fully dressed by the bed. The expression on his face unnerved her.

'Why did you make yourself out to be what you are not?' he asked softly.

For a fleeting moment she thought he was talking about the lie she had told, but he would hardly have waited until now to face her with it if he'd somehow learned the truth. Which left only one thing he could possibly mean.

There was no point in prevarication, but she found herself doing it anyway. 'What are you talking about?'

He stretched a finger to indicate a point on the bed. 'That.'

Gina moved forward reluctantly to view the exposed sheet, biting her lip on seeing the smear of blood. It hadn't occurred to her to even consider the possibility of such evidence appearing. Further denial was obviously useless. Lucius was fully aware of what the stain signified.

'Does it really matter?' she got out. 'I had to lose it sometime.'

'But why now, and to me?'

Gina tried a smile, a hint of irony. 'I hardly need to tell you what you're already well aware of.'

'You found me impossible to resist.'

'That's right.'

Lucius studied her hardily. 'If you waited this long, it can only be because you intended saving yourself for the man you marry.'

'I waited this long,' she said, 'because I never met anyone else who made me want it enough.'

'Or who could perhaps offer you sufficient return?'

Gina pushed a distracted hand through her hair, leaving it standing out in a dark cloud from her head. 'You can't possibly think—'

'I think it possible that our conversation the other afternoon may have led you to believe I would consider an offer of marriage obligatory in the circumstances.'

'That's ridiculous!' She could still scarcely credit the suggestion. 'I'm not looking for marriage with anyone!'

'You would refuse me, then?'

'You can count on it!' She was too furious to care what she said, or how she said it. 'You may consider yourself the catch of the century, but I'd be looking for a great deal more in a husband than *anything* you could offer! If you—'

'I take your word,' he interrupted drily. 'Although I would dispute the *anything*.'

Gina caught herself up, eyeing him in sudden confusion. 'If this is your idea of a joke, it certainly isn't mine!'

'No joke,' he assured her. 'Just a means of discovering the truth.' He paused, his expression difficult to read. 'If you had no thought of entering into a relationship before we met, I assume that you use no form of protection?'

'Does it matter?' she said again. 'You did.'

'A habit to be cultivated in this day and age. But supposing I had neglected to do so. You would have been running the very real risk of becoming pregnant.'

'I assumed you'd be careful,' she lied.

His lips twisted. 'A dangerous assumption indeed.' He seemed about to say something else, then apparently changed his mind. 'We will talk again later,' he declared.

He left her standing there, closing the outer door quietly behind him. 'A means of discovering the truth,' he'd said, but he didn't know the half of it, thought Gina hollowly. She hesitated to think what his reaction might be if he made *that* discovery.

With Ottavia watching for any sign that her suspicions had foundation, breakfast was an ordeal. Not that Lucius appeared to be aware of the interest his sister was taking in the pair of them. Men being men, he probably wouldn't be in the least bit fazed by it anyway, Gina reflected with a cynical edge.

Donata hadn't put in an appearance at all this morning. As no one had commented on her absence, she could only assume that it wasn't an unusual occurrence. She resolved to have a word with the girl at the first opportunity. It might not do any good, but at least she would have tried.

At dinner last night her mind had been on other matters; thinking about it now, she realised that if her father hadn't been killed, none of these people seated at table would have been here, while she herself might well have been. While she regretted never having known her natural father, it was the only thing she did regret. She'd certainly suffered no deprivation.

Contrary to Ottavia's prediction, the visit to the vineyards proved anything but boring. Lucius took her through the whole process from the harvesting of the grapes to the finished product in its distinctively shaped, dark blue bottle. Marcello left him to it.

Gina found the man a difficult character to fathom all round: part of the family, yet aloof from it too. She had tried once or twice to draw him into conversation, but his responses had been so monosyllabic she had given up.

She hadn't called home for several days, she recalled guiltily in the car returning to the villa. While her parents were accustomed to her living her own life in her own flat, they did like to stay in regular contact. So far as they knew, she was touring in Europe with no set itinerary. They would be starting to worry about her by now.

She had already decided that there was no question of

telling her mother about finding the Carandentes. Why rake up a past that for her was over and done with long ago? All she need say was that she'd had an accident with the car and was waiting for repairs to be completed.

Right now, the car was the least of her problems. She stole a glance at the man at her side, wishing she could tell what was really going on behind the impassive profile. There had been little indication of intimacy between them during the past few hours; she suspected he'd come to the conclusion that the affair was best left to die a natural death. He was probably right, but it still left an aching sense of loss.

'You still have to tell me why you pretended to be a woman of experience,' he said unexpectedly, as if sensing something of her thoughts.

'I pretended nothing,' Gina denied, gathering herself. 'You simply took it for granted.'

'You had the opportunity to correct me.'

'It would have made a difference?'

'It would have caused me hesitation, yes. Virginity is a precious commodity, not to be taken lightly. I have robbed your future husband of the gift.'

'I may not get married at all,' Gina replied with careful control. 'If I do, few Englishmen would expect an un-touched bride—especially one my age, or more—so you needn't feel guilty about it.'

Lucius was silent for a moment or two. When he spoke again it was in neutral tones. 'So there is no reason why we should not continue to enjoy what we feel for each other?'

Every reason, came the thought, if she was to avoid even deeper involvement. 'None at all,' she heard herself saying regardless. 'You do realise that Ottavia already suspects what's going on?' she added, blotting out the consequences. 'She was watching us like a hawk at breakfast.'

'It concerns you?' he asked.

'I thought it might concern you.'

The sculptured face took on a certain austerity. 'I am not accountable to anyone but myself for my actions. If Ottavia utters one word out of place to you, you will tell me at once.'

If this morning was anything to go by, words were unnecessary, Gina could have told him. Something she was going to have to put up with because it was beyond her to forgo any further contact while she was here.

They had reached the villa. Lucius drew the car to a stop, putting out a hand to detain her when she made an automatic move to open the door.

'There are matters we must discuss,' he said with serious expression. 'First and foremost—'

He broke off as Ottavia emerged from the villa, her face like a thundercloud. She descended the steps to the open-topped car, thrusting the long white envelope she was carrying at Gina, her eyes glittering with anger.

'What kind of trickery is this?' she demanded.

CHAPTER FIVE

GINA found her voice with an effort. 'You had no right to search my things!'

'What is it?' Lucius sounded bewildered. 'Ottavia?'

His sister lapsed into rapid Italian, from which Gina was able only to recognise the words Giovanni and *conjugali*. She didn't dare look at Lucius, sensing his growing confusion.

'I think this would be best discussed indoors,' he said at length, cutting through Ottavia's continuing tirade. He slid from his seat to come round and open Gina's door as she sat in frozen silence, eyes penetrating her defences. 'Come.'

She got out of the car and accompanied him up the steps into the villa, Ottavia following on behind. Lucius made for the library where they had first met, ushering both women through ahead of him, and closing the door.

'First,' he said in English, 'I will see for myself what is contained in the envelope.'

Ottavia handed it over, the look she gave Gina as she did so like a knife stab. 'A fake, of course,' she stated.

'I'm afraid it isn't,' Gina felt moved to retort. 'It's only too real.'

Lucius quelled her with a glance. Extracting the contents of the envelope, he studied first the photograph and then the licence, the muscles about his mouth tautening ominously as he read. Gina was unsurprised by the icy quality of his regard when he finally looked up.

'Who are you?' he demanded.

'Giovanni was my father,' she admitted.

'You told us your father was named Barsini,' Ottavia chimed in. 'Alexander Barsini!'

Gina lifted her shoulders in a helpless little shrug. 'I lied.'

'Why?' Lucius's voice was clipped, his whole demeanour the antithesis of the man she had known to date.

'It just seemed...easier, at the time.'

'Easier?'

'I wasn't sure you were the same Carandentes I was looking for.'

'You could have asked.'

She searched for the words to explain. 'I didn't feel able. I thought you might think I was looking for handouts. Money,' she translated, seeing his brows draw together afresh. 'All I wanted was to know who my father really was.'

'This is all lies!' Ottavia burst out. 'There was never any marriage!'

'Yes, there was!' Gina flashed. 'They fell in love at university. They didn't tell anyone about the wedding because they knew it wouldn't meet with approval—from either side. Giovanni was on his way home to tell his family when he was killed. My mother knew nothing of his background, except that he came from Vernici.'

Ottavia made a repudiative gesture. 'All lies!'

'Why would she make no effort to seek out his family herself?' asked Lucius.

Gina shrugged again. 'Perhaps because she was afraid of some claim being made to the baby she was carrying.'

'The child being yourself.'

'Yes.' She put up a somewhat shaky hand to her hair. 'This, and my mother's word, is the only real proof I have, of course.'

'You were conceived before the marriage took place.'

Her cheeks burned at the assumptive tone of the question. 'No, damn you!'

Lucius held up a staying hand. 'Anger alters nothing. If this licence is valid, you are a Carandente by right, regardless of the circumstances under which the marriage took place.'

'No!' Ottavia looked and sounded outraged. 'There can be no question of it!'

'You don't have to concern yourself,' Gina told her shortly. 'I want nothing from you.'

Lucius made an abrupt movement. 'Your requirements have no bearing on the matter. If you are Giovanni's child, you have more right to be here than we ourselves.'

'No!' Ottavia cried again.

Gina ignored her, her whole attention on Lucius. 'I'm not interested in rights. I told you, all I wanted was to know something about my father.'

The pause was lengthy, the eyes resting on her face, shorn of all expression. 'We will talk again when I have considered what is to be done,' he said.

Further protestations would be a waste of time and effort, Gina judged. For the moment, at any rate. Short of renouncing all claim to San Cotone in her favour, which was hardly likely, there was little enough he could do.

Ottavia burst into furious Italian again, answered by her brother in equally vehement tones. Gina left them to it. Clear of the room, she stood for an indecisive moment or two wondering what to do. With no transport available, she couldn't even ditch the whole problem and head for home. She had to stay and front it out: to somehow convince Lucius that she had no ulterior motives.

With memories of the night before hanging in the air, her bedroom proved no retreat. She had rinsed out the blood stain in the bathroom before going down to breakfast, with the intention of replacing the sheet on the bed when it was dry. It was gone now, the bed remade with fresh linen. Probably a daily happening, Gina thought wryly, wondering what conclusion the person given the task might have reached. One thing was certain: there would be no more nights like the last.

It still needed more than an hour to lunch. Not that food held any great appeal. She didn't give a damn about Ottavia, but she dreaded seeing Lucius again. And Donata. How was she likely to react? It was such a mess, and all her own fault. If only she'd left things alone!

Barely half an hour had passed when Lucius came to find her. He looked, Gina thought, as if weighty decisions had been made.

'We have much to discuss,' he stated.

'There's nothing *to* discuss,' she responded staunchly. 'I'm here under false pretences, and I'm sorry, but the way I feel is genuine enough. So far as I'm concerned, San Cotone is all yours. I want no part of it.'

Lucius eyed her with open scepticism. 'So why did you sleep with me last night?'

'Because I wanted to,' she said. 'Because you made me want to.'

'I was unaware of our relationship then. You were not.'

'We're hardly close relations.' Gina protested weakly. 'From what Cesare told me, we're no more than distant cousins.'

Lucius curled a lip. 'So you drew Cesare into your web too.'

'It wasn't like that. I wasn't sure I even had the right Carandente family until I spoke with him.'

'Which was when exactly?'

'Yesterday, when we were separated in Siena.'

'After which, you decided the time was right to surrender your virginity to me.'

'No!' Gina could see where this was leading. 'Not the way you mean. I felt…attraction towards you the moment we met, but I couldn't let myself give way to it until I was sure we weren't closely related. If Ottavia hadn't taken it on herself to search my room for some reason, you'd none of you ever been any the wiser.'

'You planned to leave the moment your car was ready for use again?'

'Yes.'

'Having spent several irresistible nights in my arms between times.' The scepticism had increased to searing proportions.

Gina passed the tip of her tongue over dry lips, trying to keep a level head. 'Having been there once, I daresay I might have succumbed to temptation again, but I'd still have gone when the time came. If I'd intended otherwise, why keep the photograph and licence concealed? I could hardly count on Ottavia coming across them.'

'How can I be sure of that? How can I be sure of anything where you are concerned?' Face set, eyes like black coals, Lucius wasn't giving an inch. 'Whatever your intentions, you leave me little choice. The obligation now is twofold.'

Gina gazed at him uncertainly. 'Obligation?'

'We must marry.'

Shock held her rigid for a several seconds, her mind blanked of all rational thought. 'That's quite ridiculous!' she managed at length.

'Other than relinquishing title to everything my family has known these past seventeen years, it is the only way I have of restoring honour.'

Gina searched her mind for the words needed to counteract the preposterous proposal, finding nothing of sufficient note. 'You said twofold?' she queried, playing for time to come up with *some*thing.

'A matter of honour once more.'

Blue eyes widened anew as his meaning went home. 'Because of last night? But it was my own choice.'

'It makes no difference. It is *my* duty to make reparation.' He was speaking now with a clipped quietness more telling than any amount of ranting and raving. 'Arrangements will be made immediately.'

'They most certainly will not!' Her voice had gathered strength, spurred by an anger that overwhelmed all other emotions. 'I've absolutely no desire to marry you! To marry anyone, if it comes to that!'

There was no hint of relief in his eyes at the pronouncement; if anything it served to firm their purpose even further. 'You would deny me the means of righting the wrong done to you?'

'You've done no wrong,' Gina insisted. 'This is the twenty-first century, for heaven's sake, not the Middle Ages!'

For all the impression she made she may as well have saved her breath. Lucius was already turning away. 'Arrangements will be made,' he repeated.

This was getting more and more incredible by the minute, thought Gina dazedly as he departed. Four days ago she had arrived in Vernici with just the one thought in mind. Never in a thousand years could she have imagined finding herself in a situation like this. She had a mental image of Ottavia's face when Lucius informed her of his intentions, and knew a sudden insane desire to laugh. Hysteria, she told herself, taking a firmer grip. Hardly surprising in the circumstances.

It wasn't going to happen, of course. She could hardly be forced into a marriage she didn't want. Lucius couldn't possibly want it himself. Not in any way that mattered.

She was still standing there in a daze when the door was flung open without ceremony. Ottavia looked ready to kill.

'You think yourself so clever!' she snapped. 'But I am not so easy to deceive! *You* are no Carandente!'

Much as she might wish at the moment that she had never come near the place, Gina took exception to the accusation. 'If I'm not,' she said with control, 'how would you explain the photograph and marriage licence?'

'You had them forged in the hope of making claim to San Cotone for yourself! It is a simple matter to join two photographs together!'

'And how would I have got hold of a photograph of Giovanni to do that?'

'It is quite possible that your mother and he were at the university at the same time. Possible too that they had a relationship, of which you were the result.' The last comment was on a contemptuous note that brought Gina's blood to near boiling point. 'But no Carandente would marry beneath their class!'

'Including yourself?' The words were out before Gina could stop them—immediately regretted.

Ottavia's olive skin had visibly paled. When she answered it was with venom. 'Marcello's ancestry is no less than my own. How dare you suggest otherwise!'

'How dare *you* come bursting in here accusing me of deception?' Gina retorted, abandoning the apology trembling on her lips. 'Like it or not, the marriage took place. If you don't believe the licence is real, you can have it checked quite easily. Not,' she added with deliberation, 'that your brother appears to doubt it.'

'Lucius is a fool!'

Gina raised a meaningful eyebrow. 'You're prepared to tell him that?'

The older woman looked as if she'd bitten into a bitter lemon. *'Vacca!'* she spat out.

Whatever the word meant, it was far from complimentary, Gina gathered from the tone. She checked the inclination to reply in kind, forcing a conciliatory note instead. 'There's no point in this. Ottavia. I no more want to be here than you want me to be.'

'Then, why come at all?'

Gina sat down on the bed, her legs too shaky to support her any longer. 'I already told you downstairs. I just wanted to trace my father's background. I had no idea of all this. Neither, I'm sure, did my mother.'

'You believe an English university within reach of the lower classes here?'

She had a point, Gina had to admit. The cost alone would have been prohibitive. 'I didn't consider that angle,' she confessed.

Ottavia still looked far from convinced. 'If it was so important to you to know Giovanni's background, then why have you waited so long?'

'I was fifteen before I knew anything at all about it. With school, university and then work, there hasn't been time to think about it before this. I'm between jobs at present, so I decided to take advantage of the break.' Gina spread her hands in a gesture meant to convey her own confusion. 'I never anticipated anything like this happening.'

'Including spending the night with a man you had known only a few days?'

Biting her lip, Gina said hollowly, 'He told you that?'

'That and more.' The antagonism was muted though by no means extinguished. 'My brother is a man to whom family honour is of great importance. To restore it he would make whatever sacrifice he considered necessary. You, he tells me, were a virgin before he unbeknowingly took you. In his view he would have no choice but to offer marriage, even without this other matter.'

'An offer I already turned down on both counts,' Gina stated, hating the thought of Ottavia being privy to the intimate detail, hating Lucius for making free with it. 'If you want to put a stop to it all, you can help me get away.'

Ottavia regarded her narrowly for a lengthy moment or two. When she did finally answer, it was on a rather more amenable note. 'Your own car has yet to be returned. If I drove you to Vernici you would still be without transport.'

'Then, drive me to Siena. If you can discover where my car is being repaired, there's a chance it might be ready.'

'And if it is not?'

'I'll deal with that if and when,' Gina answered with a confidence she was far from feeling. 'Just get me there.'

'If I did, it would have to be at night,' Ottavia said after a brief consideration. 'If we left after everyone is asleep, I could be back in my own bed before morning—able to deny any knowledge of your departure.'

'What about Marcello?' Gina asked.

'Marcello would say whatever was required.' Ottavia's voice had softened just a fraction. 'I believe I may have done you an injustice.'

As apologies went, it left something to be desired, but it was, Gina guessed, all she was going to get. She couldn't really blame the woman for feeling the way she did. She was hardly going to welcome the news that Giovanni Carandente had not after all died without issue.

'Think nothing of it,' she said.

If Ottavia noted any trace of satire, she gave no indication of it. 'That leaves us with the rest of today to get through. We must act naturally, the two of us, so that Lucius has no suspicion.'

Gina gave a brief, wry smile. 'Like enemies, you mean.'

There was no trace of regret in the other eyes. 'It should not be difficult.'

For her, perhaps not, Gina reflected. For herself, it was going to be the most difficult day she had ever spent. She still found it hard to believe it wasn't all some stupid dream she was going to waken from any minute. Except that dreams tended to have little consistency.

'You have fifteen minutes to prepare for lunch,' the other woman advised, glancing at her watch. 'I would suggest a change of clothing. The trousers you have on are stained. Tonight, we will meet at the garage compound. Two o'clock.'

She departed at that, leaving Gina to get stiffly to her feet to view herself in the cheval mirror. Her trousers were indeed stained, although the mark was small enough to go unnoticed by all but the most critical eyes. She exchanged them for a long skirt nevertheless. The grazes on her knee were healing fast but still needed covering. The memory of Lucius pressing his lips to the injury last night brought a painful tightness to her chest. He would take some forgetting for certain.

She turned her mind to the planned escape, forced to acknowledge the flaws. If, as was likely, her car wasn't ready, she could hardly abandon it and fly home, which meant she would have to sit it out in Siena hoping that Lucius would see fit to let the whole affair drop. In either case, she would probably have the repair bill to pay herself, with all the subsequent problems entailed in claiming on insurance, although that was a relatively minor detail in comparison.

*   *   *

It was three women to the one man at lunch, Marcello not in evidence. She found Donata already in possession of developments. Any ill-feeling over Cesare apparently forgotten for now, the girl seemed to view the whole situation in a totally different light from her sister.

'So you're actually a cousin!' she exclaimed. 'And soon to be a sister too!'

Blue eyes met impassive black ones across the width of the table. 'I'd doubt it,' Gina said levelly.

Donata looked from one to the other in sudden confusion. 'But Lucius told me—'

'It takes two to tango.' The flippancy was deliberative. 'I already said I wasn't interested.'

'Your lack of interest is duly noted,' he responded drily.

Donata looked even more confused. 'I don't understand. Did you not come to claim the inheritance that should have been yours?'

'No.'

'Then…why?'

'Curiosity.' Gina was tired of repeating the same thing over and over. 'It killed the cat.' She took pity on Donata's obvious incomprehension. 'Finding out who my father was seemed important once. I realise now it would have been better to let things alone.'

Lucius made an abrupt gesture. 'Too late for regrets. What must be must be.'

Catching Ottavia's eye, Gina refrained from comment. It was easier for now to let him believe her resigned to the prospect. By this time tomorrow she would be long gone. He might not be willing to acknowledge it, but he could only be relieved to find the onus removed.

She had little appetite for food, beautifully prepared and served though it was. Try as she might, she couldn't close out the memories evoked by every movement of the masculine hands. Last night those same hands had roved her whole body—had discovered her every intimate secret. It was going to be a long time before she could bring herself to make love with any other man.

He left them the moment the meal was over. To do what, he didn't say. Ottavia vanished too. Reluctant to be on her own with her thoughts, Gina was happy to settle for Donata's company on the terrace, even if it did involve answering more questions.

'It will be good to have a sister I can talk with,' declared the girl when her curiosity regarding Gina's life up to now was at last satisfied.

'Even one you believe was making up to Cesare only yesterday?' Gina asked steadily.

'I had reason then to be jealous,' she said. 'Now that you're to be married to Lucius, I have no more.'

Gina hesitated before making the attempt. 'I appreciate how you feel about Cesare, but he's almost twice your age.'

'Older men have so much more to offer than younger ones,' came the unconcerned reply. 'Cesare is not only the most handsome man I know, but the richest too. If I marry him I will be a marchioness.'

'Does everyone in this country have a title?' Gina queried only half in jest.

Donata took the question quite seriously. 'In our society there are few with no claim at all. Lucius is an exception in declining to use his own entitlement. You realise he won't allow you to take title yourself?'

'I wouldn't want to.' Gina could say that with truth.

'*Madre* is going to have such a surprise when she returns!' Donata declared. 'You'll be expected to produce a son to carry on the family name as soon as possible.'

One member of this family she wouldn't have to lie to,

thought Gina thankfully. 'Who is this Livia Marucchi she spoke of the other night?' she asked, surprising herself because she hadn't realised she even remembered the name.

'No one of any importance,' Donata assured her. 'Not now.'

'But Lucius has considered her as a prospective wife?'

'She would be suitable.'

Gina kept her tone casual. 'Is she attractive?'

'She is beautiful, but I have never seen Lucius look at her in the same way that he looks at you. I overheard him telling *Madre* once that he needed more than suitability in a wife. I know now that he meant he wanted someone who could also stir his blood.'

She'd done that all right, thought Gina ruefully. But it was still no basis for marriage.

The day wore on. Lucius was still absent when she went to change for the evening. Emerging from the bathroom some twenty minutes later to find him seated on one of the elegant chairs was a total shock. Motionless in the doorway, only too well aware of the emotions just the mere sight of that patrician face and lean, lithe body aroused, she took refuge in belligerence.

'What the devil do you think you're doing just walking in here?'

He studied her in turn before answering, eyes travelling her slender, shapely length in the short towelling robe all the way up from her bare toes to her flushed cheeks and sparking eyes, his expression unrevealing. 'The arrangements are made,' he said without apology.

'Like hell they are!' Hands clenched, Gina fought the small, treacherous part of her that leapt at the thought. 'There's no way I'm going to marry you!'

'You would betray your father by turning your back on the inheritance that should have been his before you?'

'That's utter rot!' she exclaimed.

'It is a fact,' he stated, still without raising his voice. 'Your mother and stepfather will, of course, be welcome to visit you.'

Gina felt hysteria welling up again. 'Will you get it through your head that it isn't going to happen,' she said through gritted teeth. 'So far as I'm concerned, your honour can go take a running jump!'

'It would be difficult, I think, for an abstract to perform such a feat.'

She made an abrupt gesture. 'There's nothing in the least bit funny about this!'

'I agree,' he said. 'It is a very serious matter.'

The pause was lengthy, the growing purposefulness in his regard increasing Gina's pulse rate by the second. Her heart leapt into her throat when he rose from the chair.

'It seems there is only one way to convince you,' he affirmed.

Gina's first thought as he moved towards her was to step back into the bathroom and close the door in his face. But there was no key, she recalled, no means of locking it at all, in fact.

'Whatever you have in mind, you can forget it!' she flung at him.

He paid no heed. Pulling her into his arms, he quietened her protests with his mouth, his hands sliding the length of her back to draw her up close against him.

Gina felt no sense of violation in the embrace; his hold on her was light enough to allow her to pull away from him again if she wanted to. Only, while her mind was saying one thing, her body was saying quite another, pressing instinctively closer to his heat and hardness. There was no doubting his desire for her—no denying her own for him. Conquering the urge to give way to it called for a strength of mind beyond her to summon right now. Did the whys and wherefores really matter? asked the fading voice of reason.

He lifted her without effort and carried her across to the bed. Gina made one last effort to drag herself out of it as he parted the towelling robe, but the feel of his lips at her breast was too much for her. Her legs parted on their own accord to his gently insistent urging, body arching as he found the tiny bud. All thought of resistance had flown. She wanted, needed, had to have the whole of him again!

The sensation when they came together was even more incredible than before: warm, vibrant velvet wrapped around a steel core. It was only on feeling the final hot rush of his release that she realised why he felt so different, and by then it was too late. Far, far too late!

'You did that purposely,' she whispered when he finally rolled away from her to sit up and adjust his clothing.

'True,' he agreed. 'I saw no other course.'

Gina sat up herself, pulling the robe jerkily around her. 'There's no certainty of pregnancy!'

'The chance alone should be enough,' he said.

She gazed at him in confounded silence for a moment or two, unable to come to terms with the sheer ruthlessness of his action. He met her gaze without a flicker of remorse.

'There are compensations for the loss of freedom for each of us.'

'If you mean, what we just did, I wouldn't let you near me again for a fortune!' she retorted.

A spark momentarily lit the dark eyes. 'I think you might be persuaded.'

He gave her no time to form a reply. Feeling totally at a loss, Gina made no move for several minutes after he'd left the room. Conception wasn't guaranteed, but it was a very real possibility. It would be another couple of weeks before she knew for certain.

One thing *was* certain, she told herself forcefully: whatever the outcome, there could be no marriage. She had planned to leave tonight, and leave she would. If she had to hang around in Siena waiting for her car to be ready, then so be it. Any attempt on Lucius's part to fetch her back would be dealt with by the police.

The question of what she would do if she did turn out to be pregnant she pushed to the back of her mind. There was nothing to be gained from dwelling on things that might not happen.

The others were already gathered in the *salotto* when she eventually geared herself into going down. Lucius poured the gin and lime she asked for and brought it across to where she sat, lifting a sardonic eyebrow in response to the black look she gave him. Little more than half an hour ago they had been together in the most intimate sense. It was hard, Gina thought hollowly, to equate the man who had held her then with the one who faced her now. They were two different people.

She refrained from drawing away when he took a seat at her side, although every instinct in her prompted the action. She could feel his body heat, smell his masculine scent. Casting around for some distraction, she caught Ottavia's meaningful glance, assuming it meant that tonight's venture was still very much on. Lucius would be bound to suspect his sister of having a hand in it, but that was her problem. She had enough to worry about on her own account.

If Donata sensed any untoward atmosphere, she showed no sign of it. Gina was sorry to deceive her—especially after what she had said earlier about having a sister she could talk with. She would need someone to turn to for solace when Cesare finally plucked up the guts to tell her where she stood with him, and she almost certainly wasn't going to get it from Ottavia.

As anticipated, it proved to be one of the longest, most fraught evenings Gina had ever spent. She stood it as long as she reasonably could before pleading tiredness. It was only on taking her leave that the possibility of Lucius planning a further visit to her room tonight occurred to her, although there was nothing in his attitude to suggest that he might have it in mind. Something else to be dealt with if and when, she thought wearily.

She felt safe enough, when no approach had been made by one-thirty, to get dressed again, having packed her suit-case earlier. Silence reigned when she left the bedroom. The suitcase was heavy. She regretted not ditching at least some of its contents; clothes could always be replaced. It was too late now, anyway. She would just have to manage. Once at the car there would be no problem.

There were lights still lit on the stairs and down in the hall, but no tell-tale strips beneath the doors. Glad of the flat pumps she had chosen as the most practical wear, Gina descended as quietly as she could.

Her elbow felt as though it was being pulled out of joint by the time she reached the hall. She set the suitcase down for a moment in order to ease the muscle. All this could have been hers, came the thought as she viewed the superb decor. This, and more. If only...

She stopped herself right there, unwilling to acknowledge the particular if only that had crossed her mind.

Traversing the whole of the ground floor to reach the rear of the house took longer than she had allowed for,

escaping via the bolted doors even longer. It was well gone
two when she finally reached the compound, to find
Ottavia waiting in a fever of impatience.

'I was beginning to think you had changed your mind,'
she snapped. She flung open the door of the car she had
already brought from the garage. 'We must go at once!'

Gina slung her suitcase in the back, then got into the
front passenger seat. It was too late now to change her
mind, even if she wanted to. And she didn't want to. Quite
definitely she didn't. There was nothing here for her.

The morning light did nothing to enhance the room's bare
white walls and sparse furnishings. Rising without reluctance from the bed that had afforded her little sleep, Gina
consoled herself with the thought that it was at least clean.

Best that she stay somewhere Lucius would never think
of looking for her, Ottavia had said on dropping her at the
door of the small backstreet hotel. The name and location
of the company handling the car repairs had completed her
contribution.

Gina hoped to be heading north before the day was
done, but until she could be sure she had to keep the room
on. Breakfast could wait. First and foremost she had to
check on the car.

Last night's desk clerk had shown a lively curiosity at
her late arrival. It was a relief to find him replaced by a
woman who called a taxi for her without showing any
interest whatsoever.

Ottavia had written the details down, enabling her to
simply show the paper to the driver with the minimum of
verbal exchange. The repair shop was no backstreet business. Not that Gina would have expected it. She was relieved to find the receptionist in the impressive front office
bilingual.

'My car is here for repair,' she advised. 'I'd like to know if it's ready yet, please.'

Armed with the registration number, the man brought up the details on computer screen, a frown creasing his brow as he studied them.

'There must be a mistake. This vehicle is to be returned to the Villa San Cotone when repairs are completed.'

'I'm staying there,' Gina said quickly. 'I thought I'd just check on it while I was in town.'

The frown gave way to apology as he once more scanned the screen. 'I'm afraid the work is not yet complete. A difficulty in obtaining a part.'

'How much longer might it take?' she asked, doing her best to mask the disappointment.

'If the part arrives today, the car will be ready tomorrow.'

If the part arrived today. Gina conquered the urge to demand some better assurance, doubting if it would do any good to get stroppy. Considering what she'd said about taking the chance while she was in town, it might look a little odd if she called in again tomorrow, but it was all she could do.

She spent the whole day exploring parts of the city not already seen, returning to the hotel to spend another night tossing and turning. By morning she was almost ready to abandon the car altogether rather than spend any more time hanging around.

She couldn't, of course. Cars didn't grow on trees. If it still wasn't ready, the best she could do was find somewhere a little more upmarket to stay until it was.

The hotel had neither lift nor porter to help with the transportation of luggage, but it was at least a little easier carrying her suitcase down three flights of stairs than it had been lugging it up. This was the very last time, she vowed, that she travelled with anything but a capsule wardrobe. Her arm sockets were never going to be the same again.

She reached the shabby lobby at last, with a sigh of relief. The same sullen woman who had been on duty yesterday watched without batting an eyelid as she dragged the case across to the desk.

'I'd like to check out please,' she said.

'*Non capisco,*' declared the receptionist without expression.

Gina gazed at her in rapidly mounting impatience. It had to be obvious to anyone but a total moron that she would hardly be touting a heavy bag all the way down here for any other purpose but to leave.

'*Terminare,*' she tried, reminding herself that she was the foreigner here. '*Quanto costa?*'

'*Adesso!*' ordered a crisp voice.

The woman went without haste to leaf through one of the card files on the desk, leaving Gina to turn and face the man at her back.

'How did you find me?' It was all she could think of to say.

Lucius regarded her dispassionately. 'Ottavia was persuaded to tell me where you were.'

'A few minutes more and I wouldn't have been.'

'So it appears. Fortunate then that I arrived when I did.'

He reached past her to take the slip from the woman behind the desk and give it a cursory glance. Gina made a small sound of protest as he took a billfold from an inner pocket of his jacket and extracted a clutch of notes, but he ignored her, tossing them down on the desk and bending to swing the suitcase up without effort.

'I have a car outside,' he said.

Gina had little choice but to go with him—for the moment, at any rate. The open-topped Lancia had already created a jam in the narrow, one-way street. Lucius turned a deaf ear to the irate shouts from those unable to proceed, slinging the suitcase in the boot and making sure Gina was secure in her seat before going round to get behind the wheel.

'I'm not coming back to San Cotone with you,' she stated as he put the vehicle into motion.

'How do you intend stopping me from taking you there?' he asked.

A good question, she acknowledged wryly. Jumping from a moving car was not to be recommended.

'You don't really want this,' she appealed. 'You can't possibly want it!'

'Do not,' he returned, 'tell me what I do or do not want. I make my own decisions.'

'A very bad one in this case.'

'The only one open to me.'

'But not to me.' Gina was doing her best to stay on top of her emotions. 'As I already told you, I want nothing from you.'

Expression unyielding, he said, 'You may have no choice in the matter.'

He meant the possibility of her being pregnant, Gina surmised. 'A chance I'm prepared to take,' she claimed with a great deal more certainty than she actually felt.

Lucius concentrated on extracting the car from a three-lane confluence before answering, 'You consider it no more than a chance?'

'No slur on your virility, but yes.'

The taunt made no visible impression. 'And if that chance became reality?'

She swallowed on the sudden lump in her throat. 'I'd deal with it.'

'In what manner?' His tone had sharpened.

She took his meaning immediately, with no need to consider her reply. 'It certainly wouldn't be abortion!'

'So you would bring up the child alone.'

'I wouldn't be alone. I'd have—' She broke off abruptly, shaking her head. 'There's no point in thinking about something that might not even happen! That definitely *wouldn't* be happening if you hadn't...done what you did!'

'As you yourself were unprotected the first time, it may still have happened,' came the brusque reply. 'There is no such thing as a hundred per cent guarantee.'

There was a pause while he negotiated a busy junction. When he spoke again it was on a moderated note. 'I make no excuses for my actions. It was wrong of me. I have no right to stop you from leaving, if that is what you wish, but you must promise me one thing.'

Gina swallowed again on the same lump. 'What?'

'That if there is to be a child, you will allow me to take responsibility for the welfare.' He winged a swift glance when she failed to reply right away, mouth tautening anew. 'On this I *must* insist.'

'All right.' It was the only reply she could make in the circumstances. Eyes fixed on the traffic ahead, she added tonelessly, 'So where now?'

'We go to pick up your car,' he said. 'The readiness was confirmed to me late yesterday afternoon. You can be on your way home before noon.'

Gina felt her chest constrict. 'You intended that all along?' she got out.

'Only if you made it quite clear to me that you have no interest in becoming my wife, whatever the incentive.' His tone was as flat as hers. 'My conscience must, it seems, remain unappeased.'

'You don't have anything to feel guilty about,' she reiterated. 'If I'd left well alone, you'd never have known about me.'

'But you did come, and I do know. And I must learn to live with the knowledge that San Cotone is mine only by default.'

Gina had no reply to that. None, at any rate, that would help him come to terms with the situation. She should be feeling relieved that he'd seen sense regarding the marriage idea, but all she did feel was despondency.

Washed and gleaming, the Fiat looked fresh from the showroom. Lucius hoisted Gina's suitcase into the boot, and locked it, handing over the keys without further delay.

'You have your route planned?' he asked.

'I'll just reverse the one I took coming down.' She hesitated, searching the incisive features, reluctant now that the moment was here to make the final move. 'I'm really sorry for putting you in this position.'

The dark eyes concealed whatever thoughts were going on behind them. 'I am the one who should apologise for attempting to force you into a union that would benefit only myself. Just remember your promise.'

She murmured some assurance, unwilling to acknowledge the possibility that she might be called upon to keep her word. With no more reason to linger, she got into the car and started the engine, taking a moment to fasten her seat belt before releasing the handbrake. The last glimpse she had of Lucius was through the driving mirror as she turned out onto the road: an image that was to stay with her throughout the long journey home.

CHAPTER SIX

COMING three days after starting her new job, the evidence that she wasn't pregnant should have proved a source of relief not despondency. Gina contemplated putting Lucius's mind at rest on that front at least, but shrank from making contact again.

The one visit she had paid home since her return from the European trip had been difficult. Her parents had naturally wanted to hear all about it. If she had turned out to be pregnant they would have had to know the truth, of course, but with that particular pressure removed there was no need for them to know anything.

She left it till the end of the month before making another trip, travelling up on the Friday evening in order to have a lengthier stay. Her mother's greeting was unusually subdued.

'I suppose you have to know sometime,' she said. 'Hayes and Harlow have cancelled their contract.' She made a wry gesture. 'Turning over the whole production line to one company was a big mistake.'

With Redman's not the only one to make it, Gina reflected. Not that knowing it was any solace. She had entertained doubts herself over the contract set up five years ago, but hadn't felt qualified at the time to express them. Now her worst fears had been realised.

'What's the outlook?' she asked, already knowing the answer.

'Bankruptcy, if substantial new orders aren't forthcoming inside the next month or so,' Beth confirmed. 'John borrowed to the limit again to renew the machinery last year. The bank will foreclose if he can't prove his viability. We could lose the house too.'

Gina let out her breath on a faint sigh. It was worse even than she had imagined. 'Where's Dad now?'

'In the study, trying to make the figures add up differently. He's spent the whole week looking for new business. Without very much success, I'm afraid.'

Not really to be wondered at after five years, Gina thought. Even if orders could be gleaned it wouldn't help the immediate problems. What was needed was an injection of capital to keep things going until the company was in profit again—fortune allowing.

Only how? She could probably manage to scrape ten thousand or so together, but it was going to take a great deal more than that.

'Is it all right if I go in to him?' she asked, shying away from the thought that sneaked into mind.

'He'll welcome the interruption,' her mother assured her. 'He's very depressed, although he tries hard not to show it.'

Gina didn't wonder. It would be very hard to be anything else but depressed over a situation like this one.

She left her mother in the sitting room, and went through to the front of the house where the study was. Compared to San Cotone, a four-bed detached set in a bare acre was no big deal, but she had spent an idyllic childhood here, and still regarded it as home.

San Cotone. She closed her mind to the images—and to the suggestion still hovering. There had to be some other way!

Her tap on the door elicited no response. She opened it to find her father seated at his paper-strewn desk under the window with his head in his hands and a look of defeat about his bowed shoulders.

'Hallo, sweetheart!' he said, making a visible effort to lift his mood along with his head. 'When did you get in?'

'About twenty minutes ago,' Gina confirmed. 'You didn't hear the car?'

'I didn't notice. How are things with you?'

'Fine.' She went on impulse to slide her arms about his neck and press a kiss to the bald spot developing at his crown. 'Mom told me about H. and H. I'm so sorry.'

'My own fault for putting my faith in long-term assurances,' he said. 'I'm just sorry that your mother has to suffer the consequences too. It will break her heart to lose the house. She's put so much into it over the years.'

'Will it really come to that?' Gina asked.

'Unless a miracle happens, very probably. I've managed to secure a couple of one-off orders, but it takes time to build up a reliable customer list again, and time is in pretty short supply. I'll have to start laying people off, which means I'm not going to be in a position to accept substantial work if and when it becomes available.' He broke off, shaking his head in self-recrimination. 'I shouldn't be burdening you with it all!'

'Who else but family?' She paused, unable this time to turn a deaf ear to the inner voice. 'I might be able to provide some time.'

Her father gave a faint smile. 'It's a nice offer, darling, only the amount I'd need to have any chance at all of sticking it out would be more than you could possibly hope to raise.'

'I'm not talking about raising a loan,' she said. 'It would be more of an investment.'

His brow puckered. 'Just who do you think would be

prepared to invest in a company that's so close to going to the wall?'

'Someone I recently met might.' Gina straightened purposefully. 'I'll need to make a phone call. In private, if you don't mind.'

John Redman made no protest as she left the room. She went upstairs to use the extension in the master bedroom. It would be around ten-thirty Italian time, which would probably mean dragging Lucius away from the dinner table, but it had to be now, before she had time to think too deeply about it.

It took the international operator several minutes to make the connection. Guido answered, his voice instantly recognisable.

'It's Signorina Redman,' Gina said slowly and clearly. 'I want to speak with Signor Carandente. *Urgente*,' she tagged on.

Whatever the man's thoughts, he made no protest. Gina drew an unsteady breath when the familiar, sensual voice came on the line bare moments later.

'Gina? Where are you?'

'At my parents' home.' She hurried on before he could comment. 'I'm in need of help.'

There was a pause before he answered. 'Of what kind?'

'Money.' She made the statement deliberately bald. 'What else?'

'What else indeed?' His tone had hardened. 'For what reason do you need money?'

'Not what you're thinking,' she denied. 'My father's business is under threat of bankruptcy. Given a little time he can bring it round—' she hoped that was true '—but he doesn't have the capital available to see him through. I thought you might care to make an investment on the strength of our...relationship.'

The pause this time was even lengthier. 'And the sum in question?' he said at last.

'I'm not sure,' she confessed, having focused only on the actual request up to now. 'You'd have to speak to my father about that.'

'He knows you are making this call?'

'No. As a matter of fact, he doesn't even know you exist yet. Neither does my mother. I only found out about this whole mess half an hour or so ago. If you're going to say no,' she burst out, 'just say it!'

'My answer will very much depend on the return offered,' he said. 'I think it a subject best discussed in person. I can be with you by tomorrow afternoon. That will give you a whole night and morning to explain to your parents who exactly I am.'

So what had she expected? Gina asked herself hollowly: that he'd simply write out a cheque and post it to her? The last thing she wanted was to see him again, but she didn't have a great deal of choice if she was to secure the rescue package her father so desperately needed.

'I suppose,' she said, 'I'd better tell you where to come.'

'No need,' came the smooth return. 'I had both you and your family traced.'

'How?' she asked blankly.

'The information you gave me when you were here was sufficient. I had no trust in your promise.' He paused briefly. 'You must know by now.'

'I'm not pregnant,' she said.

The silence was weighty. 'Until tomorrow, then,' he said at length.

Gina replaced the receiver, wondering whether it was relief or disappointment she had sensed in his voice. His failure would probably weigh heaviest with him, she decided with irony. Men took such pride in their virility.

She had the task now of explaining things to her parents. Of the two of them, it was going to come as the greatest shock to her father, who wasn't even aware that she knew about Giovanni Carandente.

It seemed best to put her mother in the picture first. She found her in the kitchen, making coffee. Beth listened in stunned silence to the carefully edited story.

'I never realised quite how deeply you felt about it all,' she confessed ruefully. 'I knew Giovanni came from a good background, but he never said very much about his home life.' She paused, her brow puckering as she went over the detail in her mind again. 'What I can't understand is what interest this Lucius could possibly have in John's business problems.'

'He feels he owes me for what should by rights be mine.' That much Gina could say with truth.

'Which very likely would have been yours if I'd had the courage to go and find his family myself.'

'And robbed us both of the life we've had here with Dad. I wouldn't exchange that for *any* fortune!'

'Bless you,' Beth responded gratefully. She shook her head. 'It's still hard to take in. Lucius Carandente sounds a very upright and principled man.'

Gina wondered if she would say the same of the man who had made purposely unprotected love to her.

'He'll be relieved to unload some of the burden,' she said. 'I'm only sorry that Dad has to know where the money's coming from.'

Beth sighed. 'I shouldn't have asked you to keep it from him that you knew about Giovanni in the first place. He'll be reluctant to accept help from such a source, but he can hardly afford to turn it down.' She made a decisive movement. 'I'll tell him the story myself if you don't mind.'

Gina didn't mind at all. It had been difficult enough

telling it the once. The bits she had left out weighed heavily on her mind, but at least she didn't have pregnancy to add to the score.

Lucius arrived as promised the following afternoon, in a car hired from the airport. Opening the door to him, Gina composed her features into what she hoped was an inscrutable expression, the tightness in her chest increasing painfully on sight of the arresting face. He was wearing a superbly tailored suit in mid blue, with a darker toned shirt and tie, the whole effect stunning.

'Good journey?' she asked huskily.

'As to be expected,' he said. He dropped the suitcase he was carrying on the floor next to the umbrella stand, studying her narrowly. 'You look drained. Were you telling me the truth last night?'

'Yes,' she confirmed. 'My parents are waiting to meet you in the drawing room, but perhaps you'd like to go up to your room first?'

The expression that flickered across the dark eyes was come and gone too swiftly for analysis. He shook his head. 'I see no reason to delay matters.'

Gina had expected no less. He wouldn't want to be here any longer than absolutely necessary. She paused with her hand on the doorknob to say levelly, 'You realise, of course, that there'll be little chance of capital repayment? The best Dad could offer is a partnership.'

The lean features acquired a sudden austerity. 'There will be no question of either. Whatever sum I invest, it can only be a small part of your entitlement.'

Both Beth and John Redman came to their feet as they entered the room, the former advancing with a somewhat strained smile.

'It's so good of you to come all this way, Signor Carandente.'

'The very least I could do,' he assured her. He took the hand she offered in greeting and raised it briefly to his lips, his own smile as he lowered it again totally at ease. 'Please call me Lucius.'

From her expression, her mother was as bowled over by him as she herself had been on first acquaintance, Gina thought. Shades of Giovanni, perhaps.

John Redman had also come forward, his reticence apparent from the tension in his jaw line. 'It's been shock on shock this last couple of days,' he said. 'I hope you'll forgive me if I seem a bit dazed by it all.'

'I understand your feelings,' Lucius assured him, shaking hands. 'I felt the same sense of shock on first discovering the truth. Gina tells me you have business problems. Perhaps we might discuss them together.'

Meaning in private, Gina assumed. She opened her mouth to dispute the idea, closing it again on catching her mother's eye. She was right, of course. This was between the two men now.

'Have you had lunch?' she asked.

'On the flight,' Lucius confirmed. 'But I would welcome a coffee while your father and I talk.'

'I'll bring it through,' she said. 'Dad?'

'I'll have the same, please.' He was obviously finding it difficult to adjust to the younger man's direct approach. 'If you'd like to come to the study, I can show you the books.'

Lucius inclined his head. 'That would be a good start.'

Gina looked at him sharply, but there was nothing in his expression to suggest sarcasm. He wouldn't stoop that low, anyway, she assured herself. He was here to right what he considered a wrong in any way that he could.

She gave her mother a faint smile as the two men left the room. 'And that, as they say, is that! Or it will be by the time he's finished. I'll go make the coffee.'

They were already well into it when she took the tray through some ten minutes later. Neither man paid her more than a passing attention, leaving her feeling distinctly miffed. She, after all, was the catalyst in all this.

It was well over an hour before they emerged from the study. Her father, Gina thought, looked considerably better than he had earlier, if not altogether his usual self.

'Everything okay?' she asked.

Lucius answered for them both. 'It will be. If you would show me where I am to sleep, I would like to change into something a little more casual.'

'Of course,' she said.

She made an attempt to pick up his suitcase from the hall, to find it taken firmly from her hand. 'I will do my own carrying,' he declared. 'Just lead the way.'

Gina did so, vibrantly conscious of his presence at her back as they mounted the stairs. So far he had shown no inclination to touch her in any fashion at all. Hopefully, he would continue to observe the same rule.

She was lying through her teeth, and she knew it. She *ached* for him to touch her! Had done since the moment she'd laid eyes on him again. And not just touch either. She wanted him the way she had always wanted him.

The guest bedroom was next door to the one still regarded as hers. 'No *en suite* bathroom, I'm afraid,' she said with forced lightness, pausing in the doorway as Lucius moved forward to swing his suitcase up onto the blanket chest at the foot of the double bed. 'It's right opposite though, and there is a shower, if you want one.'

'I am sure I shall be very comfortable.' He looked back

to where she stood, raising an ironic eyebrow. 'You fear my actions?'

Not so much his as her own, she could have told him. 'Not in the least,' she denied. 'I just want to say how much I appreciate what you're doing. If there had been any other way...'

'You would have taken it.' The pause was brief, his expression resolute. 'There is a condition attached.'

Gina gazed at him in slowly dawning realisation, heart beginning an irregular tattoo against her ribcage. 'You're saying you'll only advance the money to my father if I agree to marry you?'

There was no element of apology in his regard. 'Exactly that. It is the only course I have left to me.'

'You're putting me in an impossible position!' she protested thickly.

'You would prefer to see your father made insolvent?' He gave her no time to answer, jaw firming afresh. 'Nothing you can say or do will change my mind this time. I will know no peace until your rights are restored.'

He meant it, she knew. Throat constricting, Gina closed the door on him, leaning against the jamb for a moment to try and calm herself down. None of this would be happening, she thought wretchedly, if she'd left well alone to start with!

Except that there'd be no rescue package for Redman's at all if she had, of course. If nothing else, she could be thankful for that.

She found her mother in the kitchen preparing a special dinner in celebration.

'We have a lot to be thankful for,' Beth acknowledged. 'Although John is still having trouble coming to terms. Talk to him, will you?'

No amount of talking could alter the fact that he was

having to rely on a member of her real father's family for aid, Gina reflected, but she kept the thought to herself. There was a whole lot she was keeping to herself. For as long as she could, at any rate.

The guest room door was closed when she went up for a shower and change of clothing, with no sound of movement from within. She wondered if Lucius had seen fit to inform his family of his renewed intentions. Their reactions if he had were fairly predictable. While Donata might be willing to accept it, Ottavia certainly wouldn't. Neither could his mother be expected to look on the union with any favour.

The whole thing was impossible, she thought desperately. One way or another, Lucius had to be made to see sense!

In her own room, she undressed and put on a cotton wrap, laying out clean underwear and a blue silk tunic in readiness for her return. There was still no sound from Lucius when she got to the bathroom. She flicked the catch on the door handle before sliding out of the wrap and starting the water running in the cabinet.

Soothed by the warm flow, she lingered longer than usual. The shock when Lucius opened the cabinet door and stepped inside with her rendered her speechless for several vital seconds.

He wasted no breath on words himself, turning off the water and sliding a hand beneath the dripping black mass of her hair to draw her to him. Her protest died beneath the pressure of his lips, her response instantaneous and uncontrollable. She tremored at the feel of him, nipples peaking as they rubbed against his chest hair, thighs parting to the lordly demand—no thought in mind other than the breathtaking sensation when he lifted her to receive him.

She stood with eyes closed when he finally set her down again, trying to regain control of herself.

'The door was locked,' she got out. 'How—?'

'The door was not locked,' Lucius denied softly. 'Although it is now. I came to take a shower myself, not realising you were already here.'

'You could have left again.'

'I could,' he agreed. 'But the flesh was weak. As was your own.'

She opened her eyes to view the water-beaded face, her body reacting even now to his closeness. 'Don't do it,' she pleaded. 'Don't force me into marrying you!'

'I have no choice,' he said. 'There is no other way.'

He stepped from the cubicle, unself-conscious in his nudity as he seized a towel and held it up for her, expression relentless. 'You have had your shower. I still need mine.'

Gina took the towel from him and wrapped it about herself before stepping from the cubicle. He took her place, closing the door between them before turning on the water flow again, body clearly outlined through the glass.

The short silk robe tossed carelessly on the floor was mute testimony to his claim, but she didn't believe for a moment that what had just happened between them was any spur-of-the-moment idea. His failure to impregnate her struck right at the heart of his manhood. Other matters apart, he would know no rest until he proved himself.

He was still showering when she left the bathroom, having made certain that neither of her parents were in the vicinity first. If she couldn't convince Lucius to abandon his stance they were in for another shock anyway, but she would hate them to know just how far things had already gone.

Beth had prepared a meal fit for a king, though Gina scarcely tasted any of it. Dressed casually now in trousers and light cotton sweater, Lucius appeared completely at ease with himself. When he made the announcement over coffee it took her every ounce of self-control she possessed to conceal her reactions.

John Redman was the first to recover his power of speech. 'Isn't this a little sudden?' he said with admirable restraint. 'You barely know one another!'

'It is not without precedent,' Lucius answered smoothly. 'History often repeats itself.'

The intimation was lost on neither one of the older couple. Seeing the expression that flickered across her mother's face, Gina could have choked at the cause of it.

'Why didn't you tell us about this yesterday?' asked her father. 'You gave no indication.'

'It hardly seemed the right time,' she prevaricated. 'You had too much on your mind already.'

'Matters which will be taken care of tomorrow,' said Lucius.

There was discomfiture in the older man's response. 'Grateful as I am for what you're doing, I can't pretend to be happy about it.'

'Your daughter is *my* only concern,' Lucius returned. 'San Cotone is where she belongs.'

'Just how soon are you planning on making the wedding?' asked Beth with constraint. 'It isn't something that can be arranged overnight.'

'We would prefer an informal ceremony,' Lucius answered, once again before Gina could speak—had she had a reply ready anyway. 'And as soon as is possible.'

'What about your family? They'll surely want to attend?'

This time Gina got in first. 'I'd doubt it. We don't have their approval.'

'That applies only to my elder sister,' Lucius advised calmly. 'My mother and younger sister are very much in approval. My mother unfortunately broke a bone in her foot, so she would find it difficult to travel. And Donata would be reluctant to come alone.'

Like hell she would! Gina thought. What he meant was she wouldn't be offered the chance.

'I'm sorry to hear about your mother's accident,' she said, not believing a word of it. 'How did it happen?'

'She fell getting out of the car on her return from Umbria,' he answered without batting an eyelid. 'She has it in a plaster cast.'

'Poor Cornelia!' Gina laid on the sympathy with a ladle. 'She must hate being incapacitated!'

There was a growing spark in the dark eyes, but his tone remained easy. 'Very much so.' He glanced over to the window where the evening sun slanted through. 'Perhaps we might take a walk in the garden while the light lasts?'

'Yes, do,' Beth urged, obviously desperate for breathing space. 'It's at its best right now.'

Hardly to be compared with what he was used to, Gina reflected, but that wasn't the point of the exercise.

It was pleasantly warm outside, the flower beds aglow with colour, the lawns immaculate as always.

'This all your stepfather's work?' Lucius asked.

'His and my mother's,' Gina confirmed. 'I never think of him as my stepfather,' she added. 'He gave me his name.'

'Soon to be exchanged for the one to which you were always entitled.'

She slanted a glance at the hard-edged profile outlined

against the setting sun, unable to deny the stirring deep inside her at the thought of being married to this man. A bare month ago she hadn't even known of his existence.

'There's still time to change your mind,' she said.

He turned his head to look at her, expression difficult to decipher. 'I already told you, I have no intention of changing my mind. Tomorrow, after your father's affairs are dealt with, we make the arrangements.'

'Is it really necessary to do it in such a hurry?'

'In the possible circumstances, yes.' Lucius shook his head as she started to speak. 'Whether or not, it makes no difference.'

'It does to me.' Gina made every effort to keep her tone level. 'I have a job for one thing. I can't just walk out on it.'

The shrug was eloquent. 'The matter will be taken care of.'

'There's a limit to the things money can buy!' she flashed, losing what tenuous control she still possessed. 'There are women, I'm sure, who would think a loveless marriage was no big deal in such circumstances, but I'm not one of them!'

Something flickered deep down in the dark eyes. 'We are hardly indifferent towards each other.'

'I'm not talking about sex! You could get that anywhere. We both could.'

This time there was no mistaking the expression in his eyes. 'There will be no other man in your life,' he stated brusquely. 'I will make sure of that!'

Gina lifted her chin. 'And no other woman in yours?'

'Of course.'

She didn't believe him for a moment. He might desire her now but, with nothing else to sustain it, the appetite would wither. The same, she imagined, for herself—eventually.

'It's impossible!' she burst out desperately. 'Please, Lucius, don't carry this through!'

'I have no choice,' he repeated. 'We neither of us have a choice. As to sex not being enough...' his lips slanted with slow sensuality '...then we must make it so.'

'Not here,' Gina whispered as he drew her to him. 'It isn't even dark yet!'

He stilled her protests with a kiss so passionate it blotted out everything but the feel of it. He slid his hands into the thickness of her hair to caress the tender skin behind her ears with his fingertips, starting a burn that spread rapidly throughout her body. Gina moved instinctively closer to him, the need to be closer still overwhelming in its force. The desolation when he put her suddenly and firmly away from him was almost too much to bear.

'Is love really so vital to you?' he asked softly. 'Can you not be content with what I make you feel?'

Contentment was the last thing she felt at the moment, she could have told him, fighting to contain the emotions coursing through her. He had her hog-tied in every direction.

'It seems I have to be,' she got out.

'There will be other compensations,' he said.

He meant motherhood, Gina surmised. She felt a sudden, spreading warmth at the thought. Marriage and children might not be every woman's ultimate aim in life, but it held infinitely more appeal for her than the career she had been pursuing so half-heartedly these last years, she had to admit.

'I suppose I owe it to Giovanni,' she murmured, giving way to the growing urge, and saw the unreadable expression flicker once more in his eyes.

'I also.' For a brief moment as he studied her he seemed about to say something else, then he made an abrupt move-ment. 'It grows cool. We should return to the house.'

By English standards it was a balmy evening, but the temperature was a whole lot lower than it would be in Tuscany right now, Gina knew. She would be a liar if she tried to pretend that the idea of living in such surroundings had no bearing. If only...

She cut the thought off before it could come to fruition.

It was a fraught evening all round, although the older cou-ple did their best to put a good face on things. Most of all, Gina regretted the deception being practised on them, but knew her father would rather the business went down than allow her to marry Lucius against her will. Which it wasn't anyway. Not any more.

All the same, it took everything she had to restrain her-self when Lucius suggested they visit the register office to make the necessary arrangements first thing on Monday.

'I have business in Rome on the seventh,' he said. 'We can continue from there to wherever you would like to spend the following days.'

Gina eyed him uncertainly. 'You mean a honeymoon?'

'Of course.' His smile was devoid of mockery. 'All newlyweds have need of a little time alone together.'

'The seventh is little more than a week away,' Beth pointed out. 'Isn't that rushing things a bit too much?'

Lucius turned the smile her way. 'Had it not been for Gina's insistence on returning to England to break the news to you in person, the wedding would have taken place three weeks ago—with your attendance, of course. Now that I am here myself, there seems no further reason to delay.'

'There's your job,' John Redman appealed to Gina. 'You can't just up and leave!'

'If some financial adjustment has to be made, it will be done,' Lucius answered before she could respond.

'But what about your career?' the older man insisted. 'The work you put in to get where you are? Are you going to throw all that away?'

Gina conjured a smile of her own. 'A career isn't everything, Dad.'

He made a resigned gesture. 'If that's the way you see it, there's nothing more to say.'

'Just so long as you're happy,' said Beth.

'I am.' Gina could only hope she sounded confident of it. She caught Lucius's eye, wishing she could tell what was really going on in that arrogant dark head of his. 'We both are.'

'Very much so,' he agreed. 'Your daughter will want for nothing, I assure you. I will take the greatest care of her always. As soon as you have your business affairs under control, you must come and visit with us.'

The thought must have crossed Beth's mind that, had Giovanni not been killed, San Cotone could well have been her own home, but her response gave no hint of it. 'We'll look forward to that.'

She stirred herself, looking at Gina with obvious intent. 'Come and help me with coffee.'

'If all this was arranged while you were over there, why didn't you tell us as soon as you got back?' she asked when the two of them were alone together.

Gina made a wry face. 'It was difficult to find a way. Especially when I hadn't even told you I was planning to look the Carandentes up in the first place. I was going to come clean about the whole thing this weekend anyway. It just worked out a little differently.'

'It's all happened so fast!' her mother exclaimed. 'You can't have known Lucius more than a few days!'

'How long did it take you to know how you felt about Giovanni?' Gina asked softly.

It was Beth's turn to pull a wry face. 'Point taken. I was head over heels on first sight of him. He was very much like Lucius,' she added reminiscently. 'Not all that much in looks, perhaps, but definitely in manner. He knew exactly what he wanted, and wouldn't take no for an answer.' She gave a little laugh, her colour rising. 'As you might have gathered. At least you're not...' She broke off, eyes asking the unvoiced question.

Gina shook her head. After this afternoon, she couldn't be wholly sure, but that was something to be thought about later.

'But you do love him? I mean, you're not marrying him for...other reasons?'

'Money, you mean?' Gina shook her head again, able to say that much with total truth. 'I don't feel any sense of being done down that way. There's no certainty that San Cotone would ever have been mine even if Giovanni had lived.'

'But you told me yesterday that Lucius considered himself under obligation to you.'

'That's the kind of man he is.' Gina kept her tone light. 'Nothing to do with the way we feel about each other. One look was enough for us both, just the way you said.'

'As *he* said, history repeats itself.' Her mother's eyes were misty. 'I'm sure you'll have a wonderful life together!'

Gina made the appropriate response, hoping she was right. Love could grow between two people, she supposed. Of a kind, at any rate. If she wasn't pregnant already, it was odds on that she would be before too long. Lucius needed a son if the Carandente name was to survive. Children could cement a shaky marriage.

Contrary to her expectations, Lucius made no attempt to invade her room that night. Considering what had happened in the shower earlier, it was a bit late for courteous gestures on the grounds of this being her parents' home, leaving her to conclude that his desire for her was far from irresistible. It was a long time before sleep overcame the hunger churning her own insides.

CHAPTER SEVEN

EVENTS moved quickly over the following week. With Redman's safeguarded, and the wedding booked for the sixth, it left just five days in which to settle personal affairs. The company Gina worked for proved surprisingly amenable to her leaving at a moment's notice—causing her to suspect that Lucius had already made an approach behind her back. Certainly, his offer of six months' rent on the flat in lieu of notice settled any protests her landlord might have made.

Apart from her clothes and a few bits and pieces, there was nothing she wanted. Definitely nothing she needed, considering where she was going to be living. She still found it difficult to take in that her whole life could change so radically in the space of a few weeks.

The one London friend she considered close enough to be put in the picture viewed the whole situation from a purely romantic aspect. A fairy tale come true, was her summing up.

'Drop-dead gorgeous, *and* superrich!' she commented when Lucius left the two of them alone for few minutes in the restaurant where they'd met for lunch. 'What more could anyone want!'

Some deeper emotion than duty alone, perhaps, thought Gina wryly. They had made love at the flat last night— she felt her stomach muscles contract at the very memory of it—but she was no closer to knowing the man within.

* * *

'I'm leaving my whole life behind,' she said in the car on the way back north that afternoon. 'Family, friends, career…'

'You can visit family and friends whenever you wish to,' Lucius answered steadily. 'Or have them visit you. If you fear becoming bored with no job of work to attend, you might like to join Marcello in the winery offices on occasion.'

Gina stole a glance at the clean-cut profile, suspecting satire. 'Oh, I'm sure he'd go for that!'

'It would not be his place to refuse.'

She hesitated before voicing the thought. 'It seems odd that your sister's husband should work for the company at all. Especially when she told me he shares the same kind of ancestry as the Carandentes.'

'His forebears held title, yes,' Lucius agreed. 'Unfortunately, he made some extremely bad investments after he and Ottavia were married, and lost what was left of the family fortune—including their home. He became comptroller as a means of salvaging his pride on being forced to take up residence at San Cotone.'

'I see.' Gina felt a pang of sympathy for the man. 'Well, I daresay I'll find plenty to occupy me without forcing myself on him. It's going to be bad enough as it is.'

'Ottavia will not be making life difficult for you,' Lucius stated authoritatively.

Maybe not while he was around, came the thought. She shrugged it off. There were far more important things to think about.

The wedding day was hot and sunny, the ceremony brief. Gina wore a cream dress a few shades lighter than Lucius's suit, her wide-brimmed coral hat a last-minute impulse buy she was only too glad to abandon on changing into something a little more practical for the journey to Rome.

Their flight to Heathrow was at a quarter to four, with a connection at five-thirty. They took their leave of her parents at the house. Whatever reservations John Redman might still harbour deep down, he had given the two of them his wholehearted support this past week. Gina turned her face resolutely forward as the car pulled away. She was a Carandente in name now, with a whole new life to live. There was no going back.

The domestic flight was uneventful, the connection on time, landing in Rome just before nine. The hotel where they were to spend the next two nights before travelling south to Capri was set in a square off the Via Claudia, its interior decor a symphony in gilt and crystal and silk-screened walls. Their suite was sheer luxury.

No more so than San Cotone, Gina reflected, taking it in. Something she was going to have to get used to—though hopefully never become complacent about.

'Tired?' asked Lucius softly as she turned from the window with its superb views over the illuminated city.

If she had been, the look in the dark eyes would have roused her. Make the most of it while it lasted, she told herself.

He undressed her slowly, sensually, somehow managing to rid himself of his own clothing at the same time. The smooth olive skin felt wonderful, the muscle rippling beneath as she traced a passage down the length of his body with her fingertips to claim the vibrant manhood. His mouth was a flame searing her breast, the curl of his tongue about her tingling nipple a pleasure close to pain.

He turned back the silk covers on the wide bed before lowering her to it, his lips creating mayhem in their intimate seeking. Gina writhed beneath him in an onslaught of sensation. She could live without love, came her last, fading thought as he slid inside her, but she couldn't live without this. Not ever!

Lucius was gone from the bed when she awoke to morning light. He came through from the sitting room already fully dressed in a formal dark blue suit, bending to press a brief kiss to her lips as she raised herself.

'I have to go,' he said. 'I cannot say for certain how long I will be gone. You only have to ring room service for anything you require. Full English breakfast, if you like,' he added with a smile. 'The staff all speak your language.'

Gina stilled the urge to ask him not to go. Business obviously took precedence this morning. 'What do I do with myself while you're out?' she said instead.

'Whatever you wish,' he rejoined. 'The Colosseum is close by, although I would recommend that you take a taxi if you decide to go there. A woman walking the street alone is apt to attract the kind of attention best not experienced.'

'You mean I might get my bottom pinched?' she said flippantly.

'That could be the least of it.' He didn't look particularly amused. 'Promise me you will take no foolish risks.'

'I won't,' she assured him. 'I'll probably stay around the hotel anyway.'

'It might be best,' he agreed. 'Tonight we will eat at one of Rome's finest restaurants.'

'Can't wait,' Gina murmured, her mind more on the sustenance that would hopefully come later. 'See you later, then.'

She watched him cross the room, appraising the broad-shouldered, narrow-hipped physique. All man, and all hers: in bed if not out of it. This marriage might be missing an ingredient, but what they had was enough to carry it through—for now, at least. It had to be enough.

Breakfast was brought to the suite by a young and handsome waiter who made it clear that he was open to any suggestion the 'lovely *signorina*' might have in mind. More amused than annoyed, Gina despatched him with a few well-chosen words—a joke she doubted Lucius would appreciate. Some things were best not shared.

By mid morning she had had enough of being on her own. She should have plumped for at least a couple of days in Rome when Lucius had asked where she would like to spend the honeymoon, she thought ruefully. By the time he returned it would probably be too late to see anything, and tomorrow they would be motoring south. Providing she stuck to the main thoroughfares, she could hardly come to much harm.

She put on a pair of beige linen trousers and a short-sleeved white blouse as the least likely outfit to attract undue attention. The air outside was hot and humid, the Via Claudia thronged with traffic. As Lucius had said, the Colosseum was close enough to walk to.

As he had also said, a woman on her own tended to draw attention of a less than welcome nature. Gina studiously ignored the whistles and ribald invitations—as she assumed the latter were from the leers accompanying them—niftily sidestepping two grinning youths who attempted to bar her way. A bit like running the gauntlet, she admitted, glad to reach the Colosseum entrance at last.

Despite the crowds, she was overcome by the timeless spell of the place. Looking down from the terraces on the crumbling arena, it was all too easy to imagine an age long gone, when the exposed cells would be filled with wild animals and slaves to be sacrificed for the entertainment of the masses. A cruel age, Gina reflected, thankful not to have lived in those times herself.

She took a taxi from there to St Peter's Square, marvelling along with countless others at the wonders of the Sistine Chapel, then another to see the Trevi Fountain. Hunger finally drew her attention to the time. She was dismayed to see it was already almost three o'clock. Lucius probably wouldn't have returned yet, she assured herself, heading back to the hotel.

She was wrong. Lucius had not only returned, but had been there for the last two hours. He was furious with her. So much so that she was drawn to retaliate with equal ferocity.

'I'm not some chattel to be told what to do and when to do it!' she stormed. 'You left me to twiddle my thumbs with no idea of when you might be back, so you've no room to complain!'

Eyes like black coals, Lucius drew in a harsh breath. 'I will not be spoken to in that manner!' he said in a clipped tone. 'If I have nothing else, I will have your respect!'

About to lash out with further invective, Gina took a hold on herself. Little more than twenty-four hours married and already at loggerheads, she thought dispiritedly. What price the future if this was all it took?

'I apologise,' she said, although it cost her to do it. 'I owe you a great deal, I know.'

'You think I look for gratitude?' he demanded. 'The debt is mine.'

'You think *my* only interest is financial compensation?' she rejoined. 'So far as I'm concerned, the investment you've made in Redman's wipes the slate clean.'

'The investment we both made,' he said. 'Everything I have is now yours too.'

Gina searched the chiselled features in dawning comprehension, mind reeling. 'Was that the business you had to take care of this morning?' she asked faintly.

The dark head inclined. 'My lawyers had the matter already in hand but there was still a great deal to be gone through. As of this day we are partners in every sense.'

Gina sank into the nearest chair, legs suddenly too weak to support her. A fairy tale Isabel had called it, but this went far beyond that.

'There was no need,' she got out. 'I never wanted—'

'It was necessary.' His tone was level, his gaze steady. 'Should anything happen to me, San Cotone will be yours alone, as it would have been had Giovanni lived.'

Alarm leapt in her eyes. 'What do you mean, should anything happen to you? There's nothing wrong with you, is there?'

A smile touched the firm mouth. 'It would pain you to lose me?'

The very thought was a stab in the heart. 'Of course it would!' she said thickly. 'Lucius, what—?'

'So far as I am aware, my health is excellent,' he assured her. 'I spoke only of contingencies. All I ask is that you would care for my family in the event.'

'It goes without saying.' Gina didn't even want to think about such an event. 'I'm sorry about taking off the way I did without even leaving you a note,' she added impulsively. 'It was totally inconsiderate.'

'I will put the blame on your independent English half,' he returned on a lighter note. 'You had no problems?'

She made an effort to match his mood. 'Nothing I couldn't handle. I saw the Colosseum and St Peter's. Oh, and the Trevi Fountain too.'

'You made a wish?'

'No,' she admitted. 'The crowds were too thick to get near enough to toss a coin.'

'Then we must return this evening. Those who visit the Fountain must complete the ritual, or bad luck may befall them. For now, however…' he paused, the smile this time sending her pulse rate soaring '…you wish to continue with your sightseeing?'

Food took second place in the hunger stakes, Gina acknowledged. Would there ever come a time when she failed to want this? she wondered as he took his cue from the shake of her head to draw her into his arms. Right now it seemed impossible.

Capri was as beautiful as Gina had anticipated, although the summer crowds proved something of a drawback. She readily agreed to Lucius's suggestion after a couple of days that they move on, not really caring where they were providing it was together.

The little village in the mainland mountains where they'd spent several precious days and nights was a memory to be treasured. Totally lacking in all but the most basic facilities, though clean as a whistle, the one hotel had boasted just two rooms. Gina had loved every moment of their time there.

Knowing it all had to come to an end eventually made it no easier to accept when the time came. San Cotone might be her home now, but it didn't feel like it. She hated the thought of facing Ottavia's enmity again—and wasn't yet convinced that Cornelia's feelings were any different. Donata was the only one she looked forward to seeing.

They took the train from Naples. Gina grew more despondent with the passing of each mile. She summoned a smile on catching Lucius's eye, reluctant to have him guess her feelings.

'I suppose you already made arrangements for us to be met?'

'Of course,' he confirmed. 'Pietro is to bring a car.'

'Pietro?'

'*Madre's* chauffeur. Tonight we sleep in the suite your grandmother and grandfather would have occupied in their time. The suite your mother and Giovanni would have shared in their turn had he ever completed his journey home.'

'You can't really know what would have happened if he had,' Gina returned. 'His father might not have been prepared to recognise the marriage.'

Lucius gave a brief shrug. 'It would have been up to Giovanni to make him recognise it, but there is little use, I agree, in speculation. It is our place now to extend the Carandente line.'

Towards which end they'd already made serious efforts, Gina reflected, with a familiar stirring in the pit of her stomach at the very thought. She was back to waiting a couple of weeks again before she could be sure, but some inner sense told her it was already an established fact. In nine months she would hold Lucius's child in her arms. Boy or girl didn't matter to her, but it would to him.

The car was already waiting at the station. Pietro greeted the two of them with deference. Gina sat through the journey in growing dread of the ordeal to come. Six short weeks, that was all it had taken to bring her to this point. It hardly seemed possible.

Lit by the evening sun, San Cotone was even more beautiful than she remembered. Stepping from the car, she stood for a moment just gazing at it, unable still to believe it was all hers.

'Welcome home,' said Lucius softly at her back.

Cornelia's appearance in the open doorway cut off any reply Gina might have made. Aided by a walking stick, the older woman limped to the top of the stone steps, her smile a reassurance in itself.

'I have waited so long for this!' she exclaimed. 'Come, *nuora*, let me embrace you!'

Gina went willingly, moved beyond words by the warmth of the greeting. Donata came rushing out to join them, flinging her arms about Gina's neck to hug her with unbridled enthusiasm.

'I'm so happy to have you return to us!' she exclaimed. 'I've had no one to talk with these past weeks!'

Gina made the appropriate responses, wishing she could hope for the same attitude from Ottavia. The latter's absence from the welcome party underlined the unlikelihood.

Donata led the way indoors chattering nineteen to the dozen, Cornelia and Lucius following on. Gina heard her mother-in-law say something in Italian, recognising one word with a sudden dampening of the spirits raised. Livia was the name of the woman Cornelia had proclaimed the ideal wife for her son. Was it possible that the welcome just extended had been no more than a front after all?

Her spirits sank even lower on reaching the salon to see the two people awaiting them. Perhaps a year or so older than herself, Livia Marucchi was one of the most beautiful women she had ever clapped eyes on, her smoothly swathed, blue-black hair drawn back from the perfect oval of her face. There was no warmth in the smile that touched her lips as she looked from Gina to the man at her back.

'I offer my congratulations,' she said in heavily accented English.

There was no telling anything from Lucius's voice when he thanked her. Gina refrained from glancing his way as he moved to her side to perform the unnecessary introduction, summoning a smile of her own. 'Nice to meet you,' she lied.

The curl of Livia's lip was slight enough to go unnoted by most. 'And you also,' she said.

Silent so far, Ottavia came forward to take Gina by the shoulders and place a kiss to both cheeks, the glitter in her eyes the only indication of her true feelings. 'So we are sisters now!'

If Lucius had any inkling of his sister's frame of mind he wasn't allowing it to affect him. 'You will excuse us if we leave you so soon,' he said evenly. 'We are both in need of a shower and change of clothing after our journey.'

Gina accompanied him from the room feeling anything but happy. She longed to be back in the village they had left that morning.

'I didn't ask if the things I had sent from home had arrived,' she said as they mounted the stairs.

'This is your home now,' Lucius responded a little curtly. 'You must begin thinking of it as such.'

She gave him a swift glance, noting the set of his jaw. There was a difference in him since their arrival: a change of mood attributable to Livia Marucchi, if she was any judge at all. Donata had given the impression that her brother had had no intention of marrying the woman, but what would she have really known of his plans?

The suite they were to occupy was on the far side of the villa from the room that had been hers before. Her mind on other matters, Gina viewed the spacious, beautifully furnished rooms with scant interest. Her things had indeed arrived, she saw on opening one of the vast wardrobes in the dressing area. It was going to take a great deal more clothing than she possessed in total to fill even one of them.

There were two bathrooms, each superbly equipped. Lucius was already in the shower, the closed door a barrier she wouldn't have thought twice about breaching only yesterday. It was ridiculous feeling this way on the strength of one short meeting, she told herself hardily. If Lucius had wanted to marry Livia he would have done it before she ever came on the scene. She had to put the whole thing from mind.

He was fully dressed when she emerged from the other bathroom some fifteen minutes later.

'Useful when time presses, perhaps,' he said drily when she commented on the advantages of the arrangement. 'Did you not wish to join me?'

'I wasn't sure you'd want me to,' Gina admitted, drawing a line between the dark brows.

'You consider the home no place for such behaviour?'

'Of course not.' She tried to make light of the situation. 'I suppose I just feel a bit inhibited with all the family here.'

'It is most unlikely that any of them would intrude on our privacy.'

'I'm sure. It's not—' She broke off, spreading her hands with a wry little smile. 'Getting used to being here on a permanent basis at all is going to take time. It was never part of the plan.' She hesitated before putting the question. 'Do they know…everything?'

The shrug was brief. 'I keep no secrets.'

'How did they take it?'

'My mother is already well-provided for, and Donata will no doubt marry well in time.'

His tone discouraged further enquiry, but Gina refused to leave it there. 'And Ottavia?'

'She and Marcello would be reliant on your charity for a time should the need arise.'

'Is that fair?' Gina protested. 'Surely provision can be made!'

'That decision is no longer mine alone,' Lucius returned. 'As I told you, everything I have is now yours too. If I die before you, it will all be yours.'

A sudden little shudder ran through her. To never see him again, never feel his arms about her again...

'If I have a say in things, then I'd like Ottavia and Marcello to be provided for now,' she declared. 'Enough for them to make a new life for themselves without having to rely on family charity.'

'You think Marcello so lacking in pride that he would accept such a gift?' Lucius asked on a note of anger. 'You believe *me* so devoid in humanity that I offered him no other choice than to become comptroller? He chose to draw a salary. One sufficient—if properly invested—to enable him to achieve independence again in the not-too-distant future by his own efforts.'

Gina bit her lip. 'I'm sorry. I should have known better.'

'We have a great deal to learn about each other.' The anger had gone from his voice, replaced by a flatness of tone that was even less desirable. 'It will, as you said, take time.'

Uncertain of his response, Gina quelled the impulse to reach out to him as he turned away. He was right, of course, she thought depressedly. Outside of bed, they were still almost total strangers.

CHAPTER EIGHT

IT WAS a relief not to see Livia when they went down to join the family on the terrace at nine. Gina wouldn't have put it past Ottavia to insist that the woman stayed to dinner. Knowing what she knew, she could understand something of her sister-in-law's feelings. To be ousted from inheritance by someone she hadn't even known existed a couple of months ago took some getting over. It was improbable that they could ever become friends.

If Donata felt done down in any way herself, she gave no sign of it. Her hair had grown considerably in the last month, although it was going to take a year or more for it to achieve any real length.

'I've grown used to it,' she acknowledged cheerfully when Gina commented on the difference. 'I may even keep it short. It's so much cooler in summer!'

'You will never find a husband looking the way you do,' declared Ottavia. 'A woman's hair is her crowning glory! Providing, of course, that she puts both the time and the effort into keeping it so.'

A dig at her, Gina gathered, catching the sly, sideways glance. One she could ignore in the knowledge that her own hair was in no way neglected. For a moment she found herself wishing she was blonde like her mother, just to be different, but the feeling soon passed. She was a Carandente in looks as well as name.

'With a face and figure like Donata's, I'd doubt any man is going to bemoan the lack of a little hair length,' she said with purpose. 'Where I come from, she'd cause riots in the streets!'

'When can I go?' asked Donata promptly, eyes sparkling.

'I think it can be safely said that you caused enough mayhem already in your life,' commented her brother with a sternness belied by the twitching of his lips. 'I shall have a great deal of sympathy for the man who is foolish enough to make you his wife. He will never know a moment's peace of mind again.'

'Cesare has sadly neglected us these past weeks,' observed Ottavia with a malice Gina could have hit her for. 'Perhaps he found himself more pressing interests.'

The sparkle died from Donata's eyes, though she kept her head high. 'I no longer have feelings for Cesare,' she declared, 'so your spitefulness goes unrewarded.'

So put that in your pipe and smoke it! thought Gina, delighted with if not entirely convinced by the response. Ottavia's sisterly empathies left a whole lot to be desired. She looked distinctly put out by her failure to gain a rise.

She answered in rapid Italian, the tone alone enough to convey the meaning of the words spilling from her lips. Lucius put a stop to it with a tersely spoken sentence in the same language. Master of the household in every sense, Gina reflected as Ottavia lapsed into silence.

She felt sympathy for Marcello who was obviously discomfited by the episode. Hopefully for him, it wouldn't be too long before he gained that independence. Not that having Ottavia for a wife could be any picnic. It was surprising that she'd stuck by him at all.

Of them all, Cornelia seemed the least affected by the altercation. Gina doubted if anything ever really upset her. With Lucius married, and likely to produce a grandson to secure the future, she could live out her life however it suited her. In many ways she could be envied.

Tired from the journey, Gina found herself nodding off over coffee, but hesitated to take her departure before Lucius was ready to retire for the night. By the time he did make a move she was almost dead on her feet.

For the very first time she was unable to summon a response when he turned to her in bed, try as she might to keep her mind focused.

'I'm just so tired,' she murmured apologetically. 'If I could just have an hour or two's sleep.'

'There is no compulsion,' Lucius answered drily. 'We have a lifetime ahead. The rest will benefit us both.'

Weary as she was, Gina couldn't deny the pang as he settled himself for sleep. The least he could do was put an arm about her—make her feel wanted for more than just conscience and sex alone. Was he thinking about Livia Marucchi? she wondered dully. Did he wish it was she who shared his bed?

It was just coming light when she awoke. Less than three-and-a-half hours' sleep, she calculated, stretching a cautious arm to turn the bedside clock, yet she felt fully revitalised.

Lying on his back, Lucius was still in the land of nod, his breathing deep and even. He had thrown back the covering sheet in the night, revealing the full length of his body. In the past week, Gina had grown accustomed to sleeping in the nude herself, delighting in the freedom from restraint. Looking at him now, outlined against the pale grey of the window, she felt the familiar stirring in the centre of her body, the quickening of her pulses.

It took everything she had to stop herself from reaching out to waken him with a caress usually guaranteed to create instant arousal. She had refused him last night; why should she expect him to respond to her this morning?

She turned away from him, gazing sightlessly at the far wall. One thing she had learned these last weeks was that real love didn't have to come as a blinding flash, but could grow from a far greater depth through knowledge of a person. Lucius was a man infinitely worthy of love, a man any woman would find it difficult not to love. She might rebel at times against his masculine dominance, yet that in itself was an intrinsic part of his attraction.

What she didn't, and might never have, was his love in return. Not the kind she wanted from him anyway.

Getting through those first days of residence at the villa proved far from easy. There were times when Gina would have given almost anything to turn back the clock. She'd been happy enough in ignorance of all this. Sooner or later she would have met a man she could feel enough for to marry and have children by. A man whose lovemaking would have laboured under no comparison because there would have been none to make.

Where the latter was concerned, she certainly had no cause for complaint. Lucius kept her fully indulged. It was so simple for a man, she often reflected in the darkness when she lay listening to his even breathing and envying him the ability to sleep: the deeper emotions held so much less significance. She was the one who longed to hear the words themselves. Only it wasn't the way he felt about her, and he was no hypocrite.

Suspicion hardened into certainty as the days passed. The thought of the life growing inside her gave rise to a whole new set of emotions. The first of at least three, she decided, having yearned all her life for a brother or sister.

For Lucius's sake, she hoped this one was a boy; so far as she was concerned, good health would be enough.

It was only through Donata that she discovered Lucius had a birthday coming up. Ottavia, she was sure, would have allowed her to continue in ignorance until the day itself, while Cornelia would have probably taken it for granted that she already knew. She resolved to save the news of her pregnancy until then as an extra special present to be given in private, in the meantime racking her brain for some idea on the public front.

In the end she settled on a modernistic Tuscany landscape by an artist she had heard Lucius mention in approving terms, signing the considerable cheque with a sense of burning the final bridge behind her. She not only bore the Carandente blood and name, but was now a fully fledged member of the money-no-object brigade.

Lucius received the painting with gratifying expressions of pleasure. It would, he declared, take pride of place in the study. Gina hugged the knowledge of the present still to come to herself as she watched him open gifts from the rest of the family. Cornelia had arranged a luncheon party in celebration of the event, though not with her son's approval. He would, Gina gathered, prefer to spend the day like any other.

'I grew out of birthday parties long ago,' he said when she commented on his lack of enthusiasm. '*Madre*, unfortunately, refuses to accept it. If this occasion follows the pattern of previous years, there will be champagne in which to toast my continuing health and prosperity.'

'I'll drink to that,' Gina rejoined. 'The health part anyway.'

Lucius raised a quizzical eyebrow. 'You have no interest in prosperity?'

'Money isn't everything.'

'You told me that once before,' he said. 'But you have to admit that it has its uses. Without it, San Cotone would not exist.'

They were in the study, where he had insisted on coming to hang the painting himself. Looking at him as he leaned against the desk edge to admire the landscape, Gina was reminded of the very first time she had set eyes on him. The attraction that had flared in her that day bore no comparison with what she felt for him now.

'I have something to tell you,' she said softly, unable to wait any longer. 'You're going to be a father.'

He came slowly upright from the desk, the dark eyes meeting hers holding an expression that lifted her spirits even further.

'You are certain?' he asked.

'As much as I can be without confirmation from other sources.'

Lucius came over to where she stood, taking her in his arms to deliver a heart-stirring kiss. '*Madre* will be delighted.'

'Providing it's a boy.'

Dark brows lifted quizzically. 'You believe she would look on a girl with disfavour?'

'I believe she might regard *me* with disfavour for producing one.'

Lucius smiled and shook his head. 'The gender is decided by the particular sperm that first reaches the egg, so if anyone is to be held responsible it would be the father. She will, I assure you, receive whatever we produce with open arms.'

Blue eyes bored into his, doing their utmost to penetrate the impenetrable. 'You don't care about carrying on the Carandente name?'

'Naturally I care. The three hundred years of our ancestry makes it imperative that I make every effort to extend it. But if I fail...' he lifted his shoulders '...then, I fail. The world will carry on without us.'

'We don't have to stop at the one in any case,' said Gina impulsively. 'Children need companionship.'

Lucius reached out a hand to smooth the hair back from her face in a gesture so tender it moved her immeasurably. 'You felt the lack of siblings yourself?'

'Yes,' she admitted.

'Your parents had no desire for a family?'

'I think it was more a case of it simply not happening for them.' Gina lightened her voice, bearing down on the urge to declare her love for him there and then. 'The Carandente virility isn't given to every man.'

'I knew failure myself not long ago,' Lucius reminded her. 'Your stepfather is no exception.'

He drew her to him, his kiss this time stimulating a passionate response. Gina knew real regret when he released her again, wishing now that she had waited to tell him about the baby until later when they were unlikely to be interrupted by anyone.

If Lucius suffered the same degree of frustration, his smile as he touched her lips with a fingertip was steady enough.

'With all respect to your instincts, I think it best that we keep the news to ourselves until we have the confirmation you spoke of. I'll make an arrangement for you to see a physician.'

It made sense, Gina supposed. 'That's the first contraction I ever heard you use,' she remarked brightly.

He laughed. 'My English improves by leaps and bounds, as you would say! Soon I'll be speaking it like a native!'

'Not with that accent,' she teased. 'You sound like an

Italian film star all the girls in school used to be crazy about.'

Amusement curved the strong mouth. 'Including yourself?'

'Oh, definitely! He was a real hunk! A bit old, I suppose, thinking about it. He must have been all of thirty-four or five.'

The amusement deepened. 'Tonight,' he promised, 'I will show you what an old man of thirty-four is capable of!'

Gina pulled a face at him, wishing it was tonight already. 'I tremble at the thought!'

'Our guests will soon begin arriving,' declared Cornelia from the open doorway. 'Do you not think it time to prepare for their reception?'

'Of course,' Gina said hurriedly. 'I hadn't realised it was that late.' She hesitated, mindful of the decision already made, yet yearning to tell her mother-in-law the news she knew for certain to be a fact not a fancy. 'Is it to be a very dressy affair?' was all she could think of to say instead.

'No more than you care to make it,' said Lucius. 'Go on ahead. I'll follow in a moment or two.'

Gina would rather he accompanied her now, but with Cornelia there, hardly felt able to make the request. She left the two of them, and headed upstairs, still not at all sure what she should wear for this luncheon party. The buffet was to be served on the terrace, which suggested a certain informality. The white linen tunic she had bought last week and not yet worn should be suitable.

She was already changed when Lucius came up. He closeted himself immediately in his bathroom. As he had made no comment on her choice of dress, Gina could only assume it was suitable to the occasion. Considering the price of it, it darn well should be, she thought, viewing her slender curves in the cheval mirror.

With her legs tanned golden brown, she had deemed the wearing of stockings unnecessary. The kitten-heeled sandals were designed for comfort as well as style; if she was going to be on her feet for two or three hours, the former was essential. Her only jewellery was the single strand of cultured pearls given her by her parents on her eighteenth birthday, along with the filigree silver watch Lucius had bought her in Rome.

Plus her engagement ring, of course. She held up her hand so that the stone caught the light from the window, wishing now that she hadn't allowed Lucius to talk her out of the simple hoop she would have chosen for herself. The solitaire could hardly be called ostentatious, she had to admit, but it was still too much of a statement of worth for her tastes.

She was still standing there watching the colours dance when Lucius emerged from the bathroom. He was nude but for the black silk boxer shorts he had taken in with him, his skin gleaming with health and vitality.

'I thought you would have gone down by now,' he commented.

'It's your birthday not mine,' Gina returned lightly. 'You're the one people will want to see.'

'On the contrary, *you* will be the main attraction. Some will be attending only in order to meet the woman of my choice.'

Except that he'd had no choice, Gina reflected. Not in his estimation, at any rate.

'We call it vetting in my country,' she said, trying for a jocular note.

Pulling on a cream silk shirt, Lucius gave her a slightly sharpened glance. '*This* is your country now.'

'It's where I live,' she responded. 'I still hold a British passport.'

'Born of an Italian father, you will have little difficulty obtaining full citizenship.'

'Always providing I want to become an Italian citizen.'

Lucius stopped buttoning buttons to gaze at her in some exasperation. 'With an Italian father and husband, why would you wish otherwise?'

Up until that moment, Gina had to confess, she had given the matter little if any consideration. Now, she found herself struggling for words to convey what she felt.

'My mother is English. I was brought up to English ways. I can't turn my back on twenty-five years of my life.'

'You think I would ask it of you?'

'Isn't that just what you are doing?' she said. 'I don't *feel* Italian. Not in any sense. Why should it be taken for granted that I'll be prepared to become one?'

'If for no other reason, to honour your father's memory. Had he lived, you would have known no other life.'

'There's no certainty of that even if he had lived.'

Lucius shook his head emphatically. 'With a child on the way the marriage would have been accepted.' He held up a staying hand as she opened her mouth to dispute the statement. 'You have no basis for disagreement. I knew my cousin. You did not.'

Gina had to give best on that score. What she couldn't do was let the rest pass. 'I'm staying British,' she stated flatly.

The dark eyes acquired a sudden steely core. 'You must do as you wish, of course, but our children will take their father's nationality as is customary.'

He turned away to finish his dressing. Gina looked on silently as he donned one of the pale-shaded suits that sat his lithe frame so well, wishing now that she'd tackled the subject in a less confrontational manner. Not that she'd any intention of changing her mind. Her own feelings apart, it would be like a kick in the face for her mother.

When it came to their children, she didn't have much of a leg to stand on. They would learn to speak English as a matter of course, but it would be Italy they regarded as their homeland. She had to accept that.

'It seems like it might be a dressier occasion than I thought,' she commented as Lucius finished fastening gold cuff-links. 'Should I choose something else?'

He ran a cursory glance over her, expression unrevealing. 'I see no reason for it. Your taste, as always, is impeccable. We must go.'

People were already beginning to arrive when they got downstairs. Over the course of the next half hour, Gina was kissed on both cheeks so many times she lost count. Speculation was rife among both male and female alike. She wondered just how much was known of her background.

Thankful to see someone she already knew, she greeted Cesare with pleasure.

'Why have you left it this long to come over?' she asked, drawing him aside. 'We've been back almost two weeks!'

'I was out of the country myself until yesterday,' he acknowledged. 'I was given the news only last night.'

'It must have been quite a shock for you,' Gina said softly.

His smile was a reassurance in itself. 'Lucius had already acquainted me with the fact of your birthright—and with his intention to right the wrong done to you. Giovanni can now rest easy in his grave.' He studied her for a moment. 'You are happy, yes?'

'Of course,' she said. 'Who wouldn't be happy to have all this?'

Cesare looked a little uncertain. 'But you have some regard for Lucius too, I trust?'

'Of course,' she said again, wishing she could tell him—tell anyone—just how much. 'I couldn't have married a man I didn't have any feeling for at all. And what about you?' she went on, eager to change the subject. 'Did you find the girl of your dreams yet?'

The wicked sparkle she remembered leapt in his eyes. 'The girl of my dreams has been taken from me by another, so I must look afresh.'

'You could do worse than Donata,' Gina murmured.

'I could indeed,' he agreed surprisingly. 'I thought about her much these past weeks.' He cast a glance around. 'She is here today?'

'Somewhere, yes.' Gina tried not to let her hopes for her younger sister-in-law rise too high. 'Look for a scarlet dress. Not that she's likely to stand out at a glance,' she added on a humorous note. 'I seem to be the only bird around with dull plumage!'

Cesare made a slow and lingering scrutiny of her arresting face with its wide-spaced, vivid eyes and full-lipped rosy mouth, the glossy cascade of black hair. 'Your plumage,' he declared, 'could never be anything but dazzling! Lucius is a fortunate man.'

But did he know it? she thought, spirits taking an abrupt dive as her gaze went beyond Cesare to the couple seemingly engrossed in conversation a short distance away. Livia Marucchi looked divine in a form-fitting dress the colour of ripe apricots, her feet clad in a mere whisper of light tan leather. From the way Lucius was looking into the eyes fixed on his, no one else existed.

She should have known, of course, that the woman

would be invited. As a long-standing friend of Ottavia's—to say nothing of Lucius himself—she would hardly have been left out. The question uppermost in her mind right now was just how close that latter relationship had been.

'Was there anything between Lucius and Livia before I came on the scene?' she heard herself asking.

Cesare looked disconcerted. 'That is a question only Lucius can answer.'

'I know.' Gina already regretted the unstudied enquiry. 'I'm sorry, Cesare. I shouldn't have asked.'

'Livia is not a woman I would have chosen to relate with myself, if that is of any help,' he proffered after a moment.

Meaning what? she itched to know. It was unlikely that she left him physically unstirred: it would be against nature for any hot-blooded Italian male to look at a woman of Livia Marucchi's undoubted beauty and feel no effect in his loins. It was obvious however that he'd said all he was going to say on the subject.

When she looked again, both Lucius and Livia had disappeared. To where, and for what, she didn't care to consider.

Donata came weaving through the throng, the scarlet dress emphasising every line of her supple young body. The flower in her hair was scarlet too, perfectly matched by the colour of her lips. Flamboyant, perhaps, Gina thought fondly, but it suited her.

She greeted Cesare in Italian, her manner easy. He responded in the same vein. An act on both parts, Gina judged, watching the two of them as they chatted. Her Italian was still too limited to understand more than a few words, especially at the pace in which they were speaking, but the nuances came through loud and clear.

It was Donata who called a halt, apologising in English for her discourtesy.

'I'm hardly going to improve my grasp if everyone speaks English all the time for my benefit,' Gina reassured her. 'I hope to be bilingual by this time next year.'

This time next year she would be a mother too, came the thought. Whether she would be any closer to knowing the man she had married was something else.

She had been aware for some time of a man on the periphery of her vision who appeared to be watching her. Murmuring something about circulating, she moved on, donning a social smile as the man stepped smoothly into her path. She couldn't recall having seen him prior to this moment.

'Mario Lanciani,' he supplied. 'I have waited so long to speak with you alone.'

'About what?' Gina asked.

The good-looking if somewhat dissipated features creased in a smile. 'To speak is perhaps the wrong word. I wish only to tell you that your beauty outshines that of every other woman here today!'

As a line, Gina reflected, she'd heard better. She kept a straight face with an effort. 'You're very flattering, Signor Lanciani.'

'Mario,' he said. 'You must call me Mario if we are going to be friends.'

The straight face was even harder to maintain this time. '*Are* we going to be friends?'

'But of course,' he said. 'You feel what I feel myself. I see it in your eyes.'

It was reprehensible to play him along, but Gina found the temptation too much to resist. He was so utterly confident of his charms. She infused a note of regret in her voice. 'Some things we must fight against.'

Outside of lovemaking, she had never seen a man smoulder before, but she was seeing it now, feigned though she took the emotion to be. 'Why must we?' he demanded softly.

Enough was enough, Gina told herself: in fact, more than enough in this case. 'I have a husband,' she said, letting him down more gently than he merited.

The shrug was dismissive. 'He has liaisons outside of the marital bed, so why should you not?'

She should treat the suggestion with contempt, Gina knew, but her better judgement had gone for a walk. 'With whom?' She jerked the words out.

'Why, Livia Marucchi, of course.' He made it sound as if she shouldn't have needed to ask. 'It is no secret. Doubtless there are others too. Lucius is the kind of man for whom one woman could never be enough.'

Gina bit back the instinctive retort. It was no more than she had thought herself on more than one occasion. 'I think you'd better leave,' she managed with a fair degree of control.

'A pity.' He sighed. 'I believed you a woman of the world.'

She turned on her heel and left him there, not trusting her tongue to stay cleaved to the roof of her mouth for much longer. They had been under surveillance by people in the vicinity, she realised, catching a glance or two in passing. She donned a smile. However bad she might feel inside, she was dammed if anyone else was going to know about it.

CHAPTER NINE

As Lucius had predicted, Cornelia called for a toast to be drunk. What Gina had not anticipated was her own inclusion in the pledge, although she should have realised that the party served a dual purpose in celebrating both birthday and marriage. She set herself to show no resistance when Lucius drew her to him to kiss her first on each cheek, and then on the lips, to smile into his eyes despite her conviction that hers wasn't the only mouth he'd kissed in the last hour.

'Long life and happiness,' she echoed in English, careful to iron out any hint of sarcasm from her tone.

Not quite careful enough though, if the sudden narrowing of the dark eyes was anything to go by. Lucius was all too capable of seeing through the dissimulation.

He kept her by his side for the following half hour or so, an arm about her waist, his hand resting lightly on her hip-bone. There was no sign of Livia. Not that it made any difference, Gina admitted. The woman was here in spirit if not in actual presence.

It was almost five o'clock before the last guest drifted away. With several hours to fill until dinner, and reluctant to spend them alone with Lucius, Gina took herself off into the gardens. The weather had turned sultry, with a heavy build-up of cloud gradually blotting out the blue. They were probably in for a storm, the first she'd have known in this neck of the woods.

Despite the lower heels, her sandals weren't all that

comfortable when it came to extended walking. She took them off in the end and continued in bare feet, sticking to the grass as much as possible and enjoying the feel of it between her toes. She still found it difficult to realise that all this splendour was her home. She doubted she would ever learn to take it for granted, the way her children would in time to come.

Children? Right now, she could conjure little enthusiasm for the one already on the way. There was still a possibility that she was wrong anyway.

Unlikely, she was bound to admit. She'd always been regular as clockwork. In nine months, minus a week or two, she would be giving birth to a son or daughter who would never go short of anything money could provide.

She had wandered out of the formal gardens and into one of the old olive groves edging them, she realised, coming down to earth again. The sudden, startling lightning flash was followed by a clap of thunder right overhead, deafening her for a moment or two as it rolled around the heavens.

Gina sought shelter under a tree as the rain came pelting down with the force of a sledgehammer, but the protection was minimal. There was a tumbledown hut some short distance away. Too wet already to care over-much, she made her way across to it, sinking to a seat on the rough bench running around three sides to view the unremitting downpour through the doorless doorway with unthrilled eyes. It was obviously going to be some time before she could make her way back to the villa, and no one would know where she was. The thought that Lucius might be concerned was somewhat satisfying.

She could hardly believe it when the next flash of lightning revealed the figure dashing through the trees towards the hut. The thunder this time was a little further away, but still loud enough to drown out the words spilling from Lucius's lips as he gained shelter. He was furious, that much she could tell, furious and soaked, his suit a sodden ruin.

'How did you find me?' was all she could think of to say for the moment.

'You were seen heading in this direction,' he snapped. 'What possessed you to come so far with a storm about to break?'

'I didn't notice the cloud coming up until the sun disappeared,' she prevaricated. 'Anyway, you didn't need to come looking for me. I'm a big girl. Storms don't scare me.'

The anger suffusing his face in no way diminished. '*I* will scare you if you ever do this to me again!' he threatened. 'You could have been struck by the lightning and killed—along with the child you are carrying!'

'Which would concern you most?' The question was out before she could stop it, wiping his face clear of all expression as he gazed at her.

'You think me capable of such a choice?' he said at length.

Gina would have given a great deal to turn back the clock just a few minutes. She would rather face his anger, she reflected wryly, than this total blanking out of emotion.

'No,' she said. 'Of course not. I was being…' She broke off, spreading her hands in a helpless little gesture. 'I'm not sure what I was being. Can we forget it?'

'You must have had reason to ask such a question,' Lucius persisted. 'Why should such a thought even cross your mind?'

'I *wasn't* thinking. It was a stupid thing to say at all.'

He studied her a moment longer, then abruptly inclined his head. 'Very well, it's forgotten.'

It wasn't, and wouldn't be, she was certain, but at least she was off the hook for now. She sought a safer topic. 'Is it going to be a long storm, do you think?'

'Long enough for alarm to be raised when we fail to make our appearance,' he said.

'You mean *you* neglected to tell anyone where you were going too?'

The sarcasm lit fresh sparks in the dark eyes. 'My tolerance is stretched very fine,' he warned.

'It must be my hormones,' she claimed, seeking refuge in humour. 'Indulge me, will you?'

His smile was brief. 'It appears I must.'

He slid off his jacket, hanging it on a jutting edge of the rough stone wall. The rain had penetrated through to the shirt beneath in huge damp patches. He took that off too.

'You should remove your outer clothing,' he advised, viewing her saturated dress. 'Better by far than sitting in it until the rain ceases.' He was unzipping his trousers as he spoke, sliding the clinging material down his legs and kicking off his shoes in order to remove the garment and hang it to join the other items. 'We're fortunate here in retaining the warmth when it storms.'

Gina put her tongue to lips gone suddenly dry as she contemplated the superb physique. The black silk shorts he favoured did little to conceal the swell of his manhood. Despite all Mario had said, she wanted him so badly it was like a fire lit inside her, spreading rapidly into every part of her.

He knew it too. It was there in his eyes as he looked at her—in the slow, sensual widening of his lips. He came over to where she sat and drew her unprotestingly to her feet, turning her about to slide the long back-zip of her dress and ease it from her shoulders. Despite the heat, she shivered to his touch, limbs quivering, insides turning to molten lava as he unclipped the flimsy lace bra and slid both hands beneath to cup the firm curves.

'Bella!' he murmured.

The dress fell unheeded to the dry earth floor. Gina leaned against him, eyes closed, relishing the feel of the warm bare flesh at her back, the possessiveness in his touch. It didn't have to be true, she told herself. None of it was true!

He lowered his head to kiss the side of her neck, his lips leaving a trail of fire as they moved slowly upwards. The sensation when he ran the tip of his tongue over the rim of her ear to nuzzle the sensitive lobe was indescribable. Shuddering, she twisted in his arms to press her lips into the coating of hair on his chest, tasting the faint, salty tang of a dampness that had nothing to do with the rain.

The silk shorts were no obstacle. Gina followed them down the muscular length of his legs to remove them completely. It was Lucius's turn to shudder, his whole body tensing to the exquisite embrace. He stood it for no more than a few seconds before drawing her upright again to kiss her with a passion that fired her to even greater heights, murmuring guttural, indistinguishable words against her lips.

There was no softness in the earth floor, but she was past caring about such creature comforts. She lifted her head to look down the length of her body as he poised himself above her, thrilling to the size of him, the leashed power. He entered her slowly, purposefully, watching her face contort as he began the movement she craved. Gina wrapped her legs about the hard, masculine hips as the world came crashing in on them.

It took the sight of her dirt-streaked arms cradling the dark head against her breast to bring her back to reality again. The floor had been dry, her skin and hair hadn't; she must, she thought, look as if she'd taken a mud bath!

'I'm a mess!' she exclaimed. 'How on earth am I going to get cleaned up?'

Lucius lifted himself up to survey her, lips twitching. 'A little less impeccable than before, I agree.'

'Not just me!' she pointed out, eyes seeking the white dress crumpled where it had fallen. 'How can I put that back on?'

'One problem at a time.' He pressed himself to his feet, reaching a hand to pull her to hers. 'The rain is still heavy enough.'

They were outside in it before Gina could find breath to protest. Not that she could come up with a better idea, she acknowledged as the water sluiced over her. She gave in to it, laughing as she raked her hands through her hair to cleanse it of the clinging earth, the streaks running down her body.

Lucius had picked up comparatively little himself. Standing there, body glistening, he exemplified physical perfection: a Michelangelo masterpiece come to vibrant life. She wanted him again, right there and then. Sheer gluttony, she admonished herself.

His damp shirt was little help in drying themselves, although they did the best they could. Gina grimaced as she donned the scraps of underwear and pulled on the badly soiled and crumpled dress.

'I don't suppose there's a secret passage we can get back indoors by?'

Lucius laughed and shook his head. 'Unfortunately no.'

'It's all right for you,' she complained. 'You took care to keep *your* things out of the dirt. What's going to be thought when I turn up like this!'

'That you had a fall,' he said without undue concern.

'It would be probable enough in such a torrent. It will cease shortly now that the storm centre has passed over us. We may even see blue skies again before nightfall.'

The rain was certainly lessening. Gina glanced at her watch, surprised in the circumstances to find it still going—even more surprised to find that barely an hour had passed since her departure from the villa.

'Are they likely to send search parties out for us?' she asked.

'After several more hours perhaps. As we are already so wet, there seems little point in lingering further. You should put on your shoes,' he added. 'They will afford some protection for your feet.'

The state they were in, Gina doubted it, but she complied anyway. Worms liked the wet, and she hated the thought of stepping on one.

Even with the rain letting up, it was hard going through the long grass. Gina was relieved to reach the narrow path she had been following when the storm had begun. Lucius supported her with a hand under her elbow until they were back in the cultivated grounds where the way was smoother.

They entered the villa by a side door. Thinking they'd got away with it when they reached the main staircase without running into anyone, Gina froze with her foot on the first step as the *salotto* door opened.

It had to be Ottavia, of course. And she wasn't alone. Livia looked equally dumbfounded on sight of them.

'We were caught in the storm,' said Lucius before either woman could speak. 'You will excuse us if we go straight away to find dry clothing.'

He urged Gina on up the stairs with a hand in the small of her back, a direction she wasn't loath to take. If it had been Ottavia on her own it wouldn't have mattered as much, but to appear in this state before the woman she still believed was something more to Lucius than a mere friend of the family—even if not to the extent Mario had intimated—was unbearably humiliating.

They reached their suite without a further word passing between them. Lucius strode directly across to his bathroom, leaving Gina to strip off the ruined dress and step under her own shower.

She washed her hair first, rinsing it thoroughly before soaping her body. The euphoria she had felt back there in the hut had vanished completely. She'd given him nothing he wouldn't have experienced before, and no doubt with a great deal more expertise. She was a pure beginner when it came to sexual stimulation, while he knew every move in the book. If not already seeking other outlets, how long would it be before he became bored enough to do it?

Wearing a bathrobe much like her own, he was lounging on the bed when she finally emerged.

'I was beginning to think you had fallen asleep,' he remarked. 'What could have taken so long when the dirt was all but removed already?'

'I felt like a good long soak, that's all,' she said.

'Then, you should have run a bath.' He allowed his gaze to drift the length of her body and back again, his slow smile starting the all too familiar strumming on her heart strings. 'Come here to me,' he invited softly.

Something in her refused to give way to the urge. 'I need to dry my hair,' she said. 'It takes hours!'

'Something of an exaggeration, I think.' His tone was dry. 'Perhaps I can help speed the process.'

He got up from the bed and walked over to the dressing table to take her dryer from its drawer. Plugging it into the nearby socket, he switched it on and picked up a brush, turning to look at her with lifted brows.

'The sooner we begin, the sooner we finish.'

Short of telling him to get lost, Gina was left with little choice but to let him have his way. She took a seat on the padded stool, watching through the mirror as he lifted the first thick strands and got to work.

It felt good, she had to admit. He showed a rare dexterity in his use of both brush and dryer.

'It isn't the first time you've done this, is it?' she felt moved to ask.

'The first time in practice,' he acknowledged. 'I used to watch my mother dry her hair when I was a boy. It always fascinated me to see the difference emerge.'

'You might have been a hairdresser in a previous life,' she said lightly. 'Did you ever try regressing?'

'A waste of both time and energy,' he returned. 'We have the one life to make the best of.'

The one life into which to pack as much as possible was what he meant, Gina surmised, unable to keep the doubts at bay any longer. Why should a wife curtail that aim?

'Might you have married Livia Marucchi?' she heard herself asking without conscious intention, and saw the face in the mirror acquire an indecipherable expression.

'At no time,' he said.

'Why not?' she insisted. 'She's surely everything any man could want?'

'In the purely physical sense, perhaps. I had other requirements in a wife.'

Gina swallowed on the hard lump in her throat. There was no point in feeling hurt by the admission that he found the woman physically desirable when she'd already suggested as much.

'You mean she wasn't a virgin,' she said flatly. 'Didn't she know how you felt about that?'

'I never discussed it with her.'

'But you have slept with her?'

The reply was a moment or two coming, his expression still giving little away. 'Nothing that happened before you came into my life has any relevance,' he said at length. 'It's the future that matters not the past.'

Gina said softly, 'You see us growing old together?'

'The fates providing. Marriage, in my mind, is for life.'

How about marital fidelity? she yearned to ask, but doubted that she would get an honest reply.

'Mine too,' she returned, and saw a smile widen the firm mouth.

'It had better be.'

Her hair was dry enough by now to be brushed into order. Lucius switched off the dryer and unplugged it, rolling the flex around the handle before putting it back in the drawer he'd taken it from.

'We have an hour to spare before we need dress for dinner,' he observed, watching her smooth the shining tresses.

'So read a book,' she suggested, stifling her involuntary response. 'Improve your mind.'

The smile came again. 'You think my mind in need of improvement?'

'I think it's possible to have too much of a good thing,' she said with purpose, needing to get at him in some way. '"Surfeiting, the appetite may sicken, and so die."'

His shrug made light of the intimation. 'Your Shakespeare was a man of many words.'

Regret came swift and sharp as he turned away. If she wanted him to go looking elsewhere for sex, she was going the right way about it. It was hardly as if she found his appetite for lovemaking any hardship. She was usually of the same mind.

*   *   *

Livia, it turned out, was not only staying on to dinner, but had been invited to spend the night—by whom, it wasn't clear. Gina found herself analysing every word and glance that passed between Lucius and the other woman. Ridiculous, she knew, but she couldn't help herself.

It was Ottavia who brought the conversation round to the luncheon party.

'I saw you talking with Mario Lanciani,' she said to Gina. 'You should be cautious in your dealings with a man of his kind.'

'What kind is that?' Gina asked.

'Why was he here at all?' Lucius demanded of his mother before his sister could answer.

Cornelia shook her head in obvious bafflement. 'He was not invited.'

Lucius turned his attention to Gina, his expression no encouragement. 'What was it you spoke of with him?'

'We just passed the time of day,' she claimed, not about to admit the truth.

Livia gave a laugh. 'Then, he is indeed changed!'

'You know him so well?' Gina challenged.

'His reputation is known to everyone,' came the smooth reply. 'Many women find him captivating.'

Looking at her, Gina wondered if anyone else saw the malice glistening in her eyes. She had a sudden notion that Mario Lanciani's gatecrashing this afternoon had been orchestrated for him; he certainly hadn't put up much of a struggle to retain her company once the message had been delivered, and she'd seen nothing of him afterwards. What Livia might hope to gain by it, she wasn't sure. It might be satisfaction enough to her just to plant the seeds of doubt.

'I'm not all that easily impressed,' she answered with equal smoothness.

Seemingly about to make some further comment, Lucius apparently thought better of it. Conversation moved on—as did the clock. Stifling a yawn, Gina wondered if she would ever become accustomed to the order of things. Apart from when she'd been out somewhere for the evening back home, she'd been used to going to bed around eleven at the latest.

Back home. It wasn't the first time she had felt the longing to be there. For all its grandeur, San Cotone could never mean as much to her as the house where she had been born and done her growing up. She missed so much about her life previous to the one she was leading now.

There had been times when she had felt just being with Lucius at all was enough, but it wasn't. She needed to be loved the way she loved him. She stole a glance at him as he listened to something his mother was saying, remembering the way he had looked that afternoon in the hut—the things he had done to her. If lovemaking was an art, then he was master of it, but it was no substitute for the real thing.

She caught Marcello's eye as she looked away again, surprised for a moment by the empathy she saw there. She had had so little to do with him up to now. He tended to keep himself very much to himself—in public, at any rate. They had something in common by virtue of the fact that both of them were newcomers to the Carandente clan, but his position, reliant on what he probably considered little better than charity, was a great deal harder than hers to bear.

She gave him a tentative smile, rewarded by a glimmer in return. From now on, she resolved, she would make an effort to get to know him a bit better.

For the first time since their marriage, Lucius contented himself with no more than a kiss on retiring. Quid pro quo

for her refusal earlier? Gina wondered hollowly as he settled himself for sleep.

Unlikely, she was bound to acknowledge. Lucius wasn't
a man to play that kind of game. Which left a lack of
desire as the only explanation—with Livia very much to
the forefront as the possible reason for it.

She slept eventually, coming half awake again some
time later to stretch out an instinctive arm to the warm,
male body at her side. Except that there was no body, and
hadn't been for some considerable time if the coolness of
the sheets was anything to go by.

Rolling onto her back again, Gina lay like a log, trying
not to think the worst. No matter how great the temptation,
Lucius would surely hesitate to give way to it in such a
manner. Yet he wasn't in either of the bathrooms because
no light showed beneath the doors, so where the devil *had*
he gone?

An age seemed to pass before the bedroom door was
softly opened. Gina stifled the urge to demand to know
where he'd been, controlling her breathing to appear asleep
as he slid into the bed. The silence was heavy, then she
heard a long, drawn sigh. If he'd touched her in any way
at that moment she would have been physically sick.

Awake half the night, she was late surfacing from a sleep
that had held a quality of emotional if not physical exhaustion. It was no surprise to find Lucius already gone.
As he'd told her that very first morning, he was an invet-
erate early riser.

She'd know nothing of this if she'd been content to
leave the past alone to start with, she thought wretchedly
as she got herself ready to go down and face the woman
she was pretty sure had seen a great deal more of her

husband than she had herself last night. Running a wife *and* mistress might be common practice for a man out here for all she knew, but in the same house was surely beyond the pale!

Breakfast was long over by the time she reached the terrace, the family dispersed. Gina drank the fresh coffee Crispina brought out to her, and nibbled a croissant without appetite. She felt listless, movement of any kind an effort. It took the sight of Lucius approaching from the lower gardens with Livia by his side to rouse her from her lethargy.

'Buon giorno!' greeted the other woman as they mounted the terrace steps. The derisive gleam in her eyes belied the solicitation in her voice as she added in English, 'You must have been very weary last night to sleep for so long!'

Gina took care to keep her own voice level. 'I suppose I must. I take it you've been up and about for hours!'

Livia laughed and lifted her shoulders. 'Perhaps two, no more. Even so, I found Lucius was before me.'

'Two early birds!' This time Gina couldn't quite eradicate the sarcasm, drawing a narrowed glance from Lucius. 'A big help when it comes to worm-gathering.'

It was Livia's turn to frown. 'Worm?'

Lucius answered in Italian, turning the frown to a comprehensive nod.

'So true,' she said.

Gina would have loved to know just what translation he'd given. One thing she did know: *he* was fully aware of her meaning.

'The coffee's fresh if you fancy some more,' she said.

Lucius shook his head. 'I have things I must do.'

'I will join you,' declared Livia. She turned an intimate

smile on her host. 'Perhaps you would ask Crispina to bring me out a cup?'

There was a bell connected to the table by which to summon the staff, but he didn't point it out. 'Of course,' he said.

He gave Gina a penetrating look in passing. She returned it unblinkingly. Let him wonder just how much she guessed of his night-time activities.

Livia took a seat, her whole manner proprietary. 'You must find our world very different from your own,' she remarked.

'Not all that much,' Gina responded. 'We have women like you where I come from too.'

The well-shaped brows lifted in sardonic enquiry. 'Women like me?'

'Who can't leave any man alone.'

Livia looked amused. 'It takes two of the same mind. Lucius and I have been…friends for many moons.'

'But he married *me*.'

'He was bound by a code no *Inglese* could ever understand,' came the unmoved reply.

She was half Italian, Gina could have pointed out. She didn't because it was a futile exercise.

Crispina's arrival with fresh crockery afforded her breathing space. It was unlikely that the girl would understand a word, but she waited until she had departed before voicing the declaration already formed in her mind.

'This will be your last visit to San Cotone, so make the most of what's left of it.'

All trace of derision suddenly flown, Livia looked ready to explode. 'Who are you,' she demanded, 'to tell me that?'

'Owner of everything you see, for one thing.' Gina regretted the retort the moment the words were out of her mouth, but there was no going back on them now. 'That gives me the right to say who is and who isn't welcome,' she added, thinking she may as well go the whole hog. 'So I'd be grateful if you'd pack your bag and leave as soon as possible.'

'If you think that Lucius will allow you to do this, you have little knowledge of him.' Livia spat the words at her. 'When I tell him what you have said to me—'

'You can tell him whatever you like,' Gina cut in, losing what little tolerance she had left. 'He's my husband, not my controller! If you—'

She broke off as a sudden wave of nausea gripped her by the throat. She fought to keep her face from reflecting what was going on inside her—glad of the lack of comprehension in Livia's expression.

'I'll leave you to finish your coffee,' she said, getting carefully to her feet.

Another wave of nausea made further speech impossible. She headed indoors, only just making it to a lavatory. If confirmation was needed, she thought weakly when it was over, then this had to be it. Right now, it was the last thing she wanted to think about.

Emerging from the room with the intention of going upstairs, she was dismayed to run into Cornelia. Her mother-in-law took one look at her wan face and jumped to an immediate and delighted conclusion.

'Why have you not said you were with child?' she exclaimed.

Gina attempted a smile. 'We thought we'd wait until it was official.'

'I would say there is little doubt of it. I too suffered the malaise. It only lasts the first weeks. After that, all is well.'

With the baby perhaps, Gina thought hollowly.

'You must take care not to overexert yourself,' her

mother-in-law advised. 'And you must see a physician at once!'

'Lucius is going to arrange it,' Gina assured her, anxious to escape any further catechism. 'I think I'll go and lie down for a few minutes until it passes.'

'Yes, do that,' Cornelia urged. 'I am so very happy! A grandchild at last!'

'It may not be a boy,' Gina felt bound to point out, and received an expansive gesture.

'If not this time, then the next.'

Gina gave a weak smile, and made her escape. It was difficult enough dealing with the here and now.

Just how difficult was brought home to her some fifteen minutes later when Lucius came to find her. The words he was about to utter faded on his lips when he saw her lying on the bed, replaced by concerned ones.

'You are feeling ill?'

'No more than is normal, according to your mother,' she said.

'You told her?'

Sitting up now, Gina shook her head, wishing she hadn't, as nausea stirred once more. 'I didn't need to tell her. She guessed. Apparently she went through the same thing during the first few weeks. She's delighted, by the way.'

'I would hope so,' he returned. 'We are to see the gynae-cologist tomorrow at eleven.'

'We?' Gina queried softly.

'You think I would allow you to go alone?' Lucius paused, expression clouding again. 'I spoke with Livia a few moments ago. She tells me you have forbidden her to visit San Cotone.'

'True.' Gina saw no point in beating about the bush.

'I'm exercising my right as mistress of the house...' she gave the term subtle emphasis '...to choose who is and isn't welcome.'

'As Ottavia's closest and dearest friend, Livia has always been welcome here.'

'As Ottavia's friend, I've no objection to her.'

A spark sprang to life deep down in the dark eyes, though his tone remained level. 'What is it you are saying?'

Gina knew a sudden flicker of doubt, but she gave it no time to grow. 'I'm saying that whatever the custom in this country, I don't have to go along with it. I gave up a whole way of life to salve your conscience, but turning a blind eye while you console yourself with old friends wasn't part of the bargain!'

The silence that followed was weighty. All expression had been wiped from Lucius's face. When he did speak it was with control. 'You believe that is what I am doing?'

'Well, isn't it?' She shot the words at him. 'Where else did you go last night if it wasn't to...her?'

'Where indeed?' The dark eyes were shuttered, the lines of his face etched in sharp relief. 'Denials would obviously be a waste of time and breath. Of course, there will be nothing to stop me from seeing Livia away from here.'

He was turning as he spoke, with the obvious intention of leaving the room. Gina's chest hurt from the pressure building within. So now she knew for sure. For what good it had done her.

'Don't you dare ever touch me again!' She flung the words after him. 'Not in any way! Do you hear me?'

The broad shoulders stiffened, but he made no answer. Gina sank back into the pillows as the door closed in his wake, misery swamping her. This time yesterday she had been so happy. Why had she had to go and spoil it all?

Because there was no way she could live with suspicion locked away inside her, came the answer. What she had to decide now was where she went from here. Home, was her immediate inclination. Her parents would welcome her with open arms.

Except that it wasn't only herself she had to consider. The child she was carrying had rights too.

The knock on the door some time later jerked her out of it. She sat up and swung her legs to the floor before inviting the knocker to enter. Cornelia regarded her in some concern.

'If you are still suffering the nausea I will have the doctor sent for,' she said.

'I'm not,' Gina assured her. 'Not any more. I must have fallen asleep.' She got to her feet, summoning a smile. 'I'll be right down.'

'There is no hurry,' her mother-in-law returned. 'Lucius said you were to be left alone, but what would a man know about such matters? He should have stayed with you to soothe your brow.' The last she said with a twinkle. 'Why should we have to bear all the crosses?'

'All part and parcel of being a woman, I suppose,' Gina answered in like vein. She made a show of examining the skirt she was wearing. 'This is all creased. I'd better change.'

'Then, I will leave you to do so,' said Cornelia. 'You will find me on the terrace should you wish for company. You knew Lucius had gone to Siena, of course?'

'Of course,' Gina echoed, doubting if it was true. He would be with Livia.

Knowing Lucius's opinion of the garment, she more often than not refrained from wearing trousers of any kind. Today, she donned a pair of loose silky ones in place of the skirt. No more kowtowing to his likes and dislikes. From now on she pleased herself.

A furious Ottavia cornered her on her way downstairs.

'I grew tired of waiting for you to appear!' she declared. 'How dare you tell Livia she cannot come here again!'

'How dare *you* tell *me* what I should or shouldn't do?' Gina countered, losing what self-possession she had managed to gather in face of this fresh attack. 'I'll make whatever decision I choose to make. If you object, you can always find somewhere else to live!'

The fury died as swiftly as it had arisen before the look on her sister-in-law's face. She knew instant shame that she could have stooped so low. 'I didn't mean that,' she said gruffly. 'I really didn't!'

'Why would you say it unless it was in your mind?' Ottavia retorted. 'I have known from the beginning that you resented both my own and Marcello's presence. No doubt you would prefer that my mother was also gone!'

'Not true.' Gina searched her mind for some way of undoing the harm she had done—finding nothing of any great help. 'The only one whose presence I resent is Livia Marucchi,' she appealed. 'You can surely understand that?'

Ottavia curled a lip. 'I understand your jealousy of her beauty, but banning her from San Cotone will not make Lucius more attentive towards you. My brother did what he considered his duty in marrying you. Why should he sacrifice everything?'

'He had the opportunity to marry Livia before ever I came along,' Gina responded, trying to keep a level head. 'Why didn't he take it, I wonder?'

'Because Livia herself was not yet ready to make the commitment.'

'I don't believe that.'

The shrug was expressive. 'You must believe what comforts you. I shall, of course, be telling Lucius of your wish for Marcello and myself to find other accommodation.'

Hopeless trying any further appeal, Gina accepted despondently as the older woman turned away. It would normally be against her nature to say what she had, but what about this whole situation was normal? She was married to and carrying the child of a man who not only didn't love her, but was at present very probably in the arms of the woman he had wanted to marry.

She avoided contact with any other member of the family by returning to the bedroom. The nausea had passed, for what difference it made to her mood. Lying on the bed, she went over the happenings of the last weeks. There had been good times—wonderful times, in fact—but how real had they been? How often when making love to her had Lucius imagined she was Livia? How often had he compared her responses with those of the other woman?

How did she go on living this life knowing what she knew?

CHAPTER TEN

She must have dozed off at some point, waking with a start to find Donata standing by the bedside.

'I was concerned when you made no answer to my knock,' said the girl. 'Are you still feeling ill?'

Gina raised herself up, forcing a smile. 'Not any more, thanks.' She glanced at the bedside clock, dismayed to find it approaching twelve-thirty. 'I can't believe it!' she exclaimed. 'Where did the time go?'

'You need whatever rest your body tells you you need now,' declared Donata with some authority. '*Madre* says she slept a great deal when she was with child.'

Gina's head jerked round. 'She told you!'

'But of course.' Donata looked momentarily nonplussed. 'Was she not meant to?'

'No. I mean, it hasn't been properly confirmed yet.'

'But you know yourself?'

'Well...yes.' Gina summoned another smile, a lighter note. 'I suppose I'm being overcautious.'

Dark eyes sparkled. 'It's so exciting! Lucius must be joyful!' She sobered to add sternly, 'He should have stayed with you while you were feeling ill.'

'I'm best dealing with it on my own.' Gina kept her tone easy.

'Do you wish me to leave you?' queried her sister-in-law with obvious reluctance.

'Not at all,' Gina assured her. 'You can find me something uncreased to wear to lunch while I take a quick shower to freshen up, if you like, then we'll go down together.'

Her multireflection in the bathroom was no confidence booster. She looked thoroughly washed out, her hair limp and lifeless. It was far too early yet, of course, to detect any change in her slender shape, but it was going to come. Whether she would still be here at San Cotone when the child came into the world was another matter.

Donata had picked out a sleeveless tunic in muted greens, along with a pair of low-heeled sandals.

'High heels are no longer suitable,' she advised. 'You must take no risks with your balance.' She eyed Gina's figure in the brief lace bra and panties. 'You'll need maternal clothing for when you begin to gain weight.'

'Maternity,' Gina corrected, unable to stay sombre in the face of such knowledgeable pronouncements. 'Maternal means mother.'

'Which is what you're to be.' Donata sounded as if the distinction was too slight to be of any great importance. 'And *I* am to be an aunt! Practice,' she added, 'for when I have children of my own.'

'You plan on Cesare becoming the father?' Gina asked, sliding the tunic over her head.

'Of course.' There was certainty in both voice and expression. 'He knows it too, even if the words themselves are still to be spoken between us.'

Recalling what he'd said yesterday, Gina felt it quite possible. She only hoped Donata wouldn't suffer the same disillusionment she was suffering in time to come.

Not looking forward to seeing Ottavia again, she was relieved, if only temporarily, to find Cornelia seated alone on the terrace.

'You look far from your usual self,' remarked the latter

candidly, viewing her. 'Would you not prefer to have a tray brought to you?'

'I'm fine now,' Gina assured her. 'Really I am. I was just a bit tired, that's all.'

'You perhaps have need of an iron supplement.'

'If I do, I'm sure it will all be sorted out tomorrow when I see the gynaecologist.' Gina sought a change of subject. 'The air feels heavy again. Do you think we're in for another storm?'

'There is a likelihood at this time of the year.' Cornelia sounded amused. 'It must be your English blood that makes you so concerned with the weather.'

Gina laughed. 'It's so rarely the same from one day to another back home!'

The older woman looked at her oddly. 'You still think of England as your home?'

She was saved from answering by Ottavia's emergence from the villa, closely followed by Lucius. There was little to be gleaned from his expression, but Gina had no doubt at all that he'd been fully apprised of her transgressions.

'Business concluded?' she heard herself asking.

'Whatever is left will be dealt with another time,' he returned without particular inflection. 'How are you feeling now?'

She stretched her lips in a smile she hoped didn't look as stiff as it felt. 'I'll live.'

Ottavia looked from one to the other in some obvious perplexity. It was left to her mother to put her in the picture.

'Did Lucius not tell you yet? You are to be a *zietta*!'

The expression in Ottavia's eyes was hardly one of pleasure at the news. 'You must forgive me,' she said with satire to Gina, 'for my failure to appreciate your condition earlier. My attention was on other matters.'

'I already told you I didn't mean what I said,' Gina responded on as steady a note as she could manage. 'I apologise for it.'

'Once said, such things cannot be easily forgotten,' came the brittle reply.

'But they can be put aside,' said Lucius crisply. 'Gina has apologised. Let that be an end to it.'

Ottavia lifted her shoulders in a gesture meant to express a reluctant acquiescence. Bursting though they obviously were with curiosity, neither Cornelia nor Donata voiced a question. Meeting her husband's hard eyes, Gina did her best to keep the desolation she felt from showing in hers. No way was he ever going to know her true feelings.

Reluctant to face the questions she was sure Donata for one would be asking, she escaped into the gardens after lunch. There was to be no escape from Lucius however. He found her down by the lily pond where they had met that first morning.

'There are matters we have to have clear between us,' he said.

Gina kept her gaze fixed on the dragonfly flitting from lily pad to lily pad. 'They're clear enough already. Unlike with Ottavia, I meant what I told *you* this morning. I don't want you anywhere near me again!'

'You expect me to accept such an edict?'

He had halted to the side and a little behind the stone seat where she was sitting, right on the periphery of her vision. Her heart was hammering so loudly he must have been able to hear it, but her voice was rock steady. 'You don't have a choice.'

'As your husband, I have certain rights!'

Her head jerked round, eyes blazing into his. 'Like hell

you do! I'm not your property to be used as and when you see fit!'

Dark eyes glittered back at her, the thrust of his hands into trouser pockets indicative of a barely controlled anger. 'I recall no complaints.'

'*I've* no basis for comparison,' she retorted. 'Yet.'

The glitter became a flame, searing her where she sat. He reached her in a couple of steps, jerking her upright. 'There will be no other man in your life!' he said in a clipped voice. 'Should you ever…'

A muscle in his jaw line contracted as his teeth came together. He released her abruptly, striding away without a backward glance. Gina sank back to her seat. She couldn't continue with this, she thought bleakly.

There was no sign of Lucius when she eventually forced herself to return to the villa. Neither was Ottavia nor her mother in evidence. Which left only Donata.

'I saw Lucius follow you to the gardens, and again when he returned,' the girl declared. 'He was angrier than I have seen him since I was sent home from school!'

'We had a disagreement,' Gina acknowledged.

It was apparent that her sister-in-law wanted to ask about what, but she refrained. 'Unlike Ottavia's, his anger doesn't last long,' she advised. 'He will have forgotten it when he returns.'

Not in this instance, reflected Gina hollowly.

Hot and sultry, the afternoon crept to a close. It needed another storm to bring relief. Lucius, it turned out, had gone to the vineyard. He returned with Marcello at six, seemingly bearing out Donata's prediction. Surface only, Gina judged, wondering if she was the only one to see the fiery flicker in the dark eyes whenever he glanced her way.

Taking it for granted that Ottavia would have filled him in on the day's happenings, she sought a few minutes with Marcello before going to change for dinner.

'I was in a bad mood this morning and let my tongue run away with me,' she said frankly. 'I'd hate for you to think I didn't want you here.'

His smile was wry. 'It would be understandable.'

'It's not the way I really feel,' Gina insisted. About you, at any rate, she tagged on mentally. 'San Cotone is as much your home as it is mine.'

'That can never be,' he returned. 'I am deeply indebted to Lucius for providing a roof over my head, but the time must come when I seek a home of my own again.'

The problem being that Ottavia was unlikely to settle for what she would regard as an impoverished standard of living, Gina reflected, feeling genuine sympathy for the man.

'Please try to excuse my wife if she appears resentful of you,' he went on. 'The realisation of who you were was a devastation to her.'

If Ottavia hadn't searched her things that day, in all likelihood there would have been no realisation, Gina could have told him.

'I suppose I can appreciate her feelings,' she said instead. 'Especially considering…'

'Considering my position,' Marcello finished for her as she let the words trail away. 'You must wonder that we are together still.'

'It's crossed my mind,' she admitted.

'As with most who have little knowledge of her. Her loyalty to me is steadfast. Never once has she berated me for my mistakes. To Ottavia, the marriage vows are sacred.'

Providing she wasn't called on to suffer the 'poorer' element, came the sneaking thought.

'You must love her a great deal,' she murmured.

'A very great deal,' he confirmed. 'She is everything to me.'

Gina had never envied anyone in her life before, but she felt a pang right now. One thing she could be certain of, Lucius was never going to say the same of her.

He was already in the shower when she went up. Reluctant to be drawn into any further altercations, she lingered as long as possible under the water herself, hoping he would have gone by the time she emerged. Finding her hope granted when she did eventually regain the bedroom brought only a temporary relief, of course. She had to be alone with him again at some point; while they still shared a bed, she could hardly avoid it. Just let him try exercising the rights he had claimed this afternoon, she thought fiercely, and the whole house would know about it!

It was a long evening, made even longer by Ottavia's unabated hostility. Apart from not having a great deal to say, Lucius gave no indication that anything was amiss. Gina put on a show herself, but was aware of Cornelia's thoughtful regard from time to time.

Donata was too wrapped up in her own affairs to sense any discord. 'Tomorrow,' she announced at dinner, 'Cesare is to take me to Firenze to meet with his grandmother. She will disapprove of me, of course, but I will win her over.'

Gina didn't doubt it. Shorn of the rebel outlook she had first displayed, her sister-in-law was capable of winning anyone over. She had certainly succeeded with Cesare, for all his protestations.

By midnight she had had enough. Cornelia nodded sagely when she announced her intention of going to bed.

'You must learn to take siesta,' she said. 'Rest is good for you.'

'I'll be with you shortly,' said Lucius. His tone was devoid of any undercurrents, but to Gina it still sounded like a threat.

She prepared for bed swiftly, sliding between the cool silk sheets to lie wide awake and tense. Only when the outer door finally opened did she close her eyes, turning her face into the pillow and deepening her breathing.

Every sound, every movement Lucius made over the following minutes seemed magnified. When he got into the bed, she could barely restrain the tremoring in her limbs.

'We must talk,' he said.

Gina gave up on the pretence. 'There's nothing left to say. If it weren't for the baby, I'd be out of here by now!'

He drew in a harsh breath. 'This has gone far enough! What proof do you have of your accusations?'

'Proof?' She rolled onto her back to direct a blazing gaze. 'You admitted it!'

Supported on an elbow, Lucius regarded her with held-in anger. 'I admitted nothing!'

'You didn't deny it.'

'You would have believed me if I had?'

She hesitated, searching his taut, olive-skinned features for some assurance—finding none because the dark eyes gave so little away. 'If you weren't with Livia last night,' she said at length, 'then where were you?'

His expression underwent an indefinable alteration. 'I was walking the gardens.'

'For two hours or more?'

'If that was how long I was gone, then yes.'

'You really expect me to believe *that*!'

The moments stretched interminably as he studied her, the muscles around his mouth showing white beneath his skin from the pressure applied. When he spoke at last it was with iron control. 'If you doubt it still, then you were right. There *is* nothing left to say.'

Gina lay like a stone as he switched out the bedside light and settled himself for sleep, his turned back a barrier. Even if she disregarded what Mario Lanciani had told her yesterday, Ottavia had made the situation clear enough this morning, she defended herself. What else could she believe?

Scarcely needed, the confirmation that she was indeed pregnant brought little immediate cheer. Driving back from Siena with a silent Lucius at the wheel, Gina contemplated a future devoid of even physical closeness, much less love.

She stole a glance at the finely carved profile outlined against a sky still heavy with cloud, wondering what was really going on inside the proud dark head. Even if she could extract a promise from him not to see Livia again, could she trust him to keep it?

'I have business in Rome tomorrow,' he said shortly. 'I must leave this afternoon.'

Gina made no answer, her despondency reaching new depths. Lucius tautened his jaw.

'I hope to find you in a more receptive frame of mind on my return.'

'Receptive to what?' she asked. 'More lies?'

This time it was Lucius who made no answer, knuckles paling as he gripped the wheel. Gina felt suddenly sick. As he had said last night, what actual proof did she have of his involvement with Livia Marucchi? The word of a man she'd never met before yesterday? Of a woman who hated her? Not so much the actual word in the latter case even. Ottavia had only insinuated.

'I'm sorry,' she said thickly. 'I think I might be on the way to paranoia!'

Lucius was a moment or two responding, his profile still austere. 'Are you saying you believe what I tell you after all?'

She made a wry gesture, turning a deaf ear to the misgivings still hovering at the back of her mind. 'Yes.'

He said no more on the subject, but the atmosphere remained heavy. Gina put her head back against the seat rest and closed her eyes. She felt so utterly dispirited.

Lucius left for Rome immediately after lunch. Gina saw him off, aware when he kissed her goodbye of constraint in his embrace. Telling him she believed him innocent of any double-dealing was only half the battle she had with herself, she acknowledged wearily. To do the job properly, she had to reinstate Livia's visiting privileges. That was going to be one of the hardest things she had ever done.

At Cornelia's urging, she retired to the bedroom for siesta, but found little rest. It was no use putting off the evil moment until tomorrow, she decided in the end. If it was going to be done at all, it had to be now.

There was only one Marucchi listed in the telephone book. She dialled the number, struggling against the urge to abandon the whole idea. The call was answered by a man whose manner indicated a member of the family rather than a servant. Gina asked in Italian to speak with Signorina Marucchi, but was forced to request a translation of the fast-spoken response.

She sat for several moments fighting a new inner battle after replacing the receiver—without success. It was too much of a coincidence that Livia should be away from home for a few days at the very same time as Lucius. If Rome was his destination, then it was hers too without doubt.

Like an automaton, she got up and made for the dressing room, selecting a lightweight skirt and jacket from the wardrobe and putting them on, then sliding her feet into a pair of shoes. With no suitcase to hand, she could take little with her, but she was going regardless. Home to England where she belonged. Back to those whose love she could count on.

Her face looked pale in the mirror, her eyes bruised. She closed her mind to everything other than the here and now, considering her options for getting away. Keys for all the cars in the garages were looked after by the man who tended the vehicles. All she had to do was request one. From Florence, she could fly home.

She made it to the garages without running into anyone at all, to find the off-shot room, where the keys were kept, unattended. Gina unhooked a set from the numbered pegs at random, only realising she had chosen the Ferarri when she reached the appropriate stall. She'd driven it only the once, and then with Lucius along, but she didn't hesitate. It would get her where she wanted to go.

Converted from stables, the garaging block had an individual door for every car. It slid open on oiled runners. There was plenty of fuel she saw on switching on the ignition. More than enough to get her to Florence.

The engine started at the first pull. Gina bit her lip at the powerful sound, expecting it to bring immediate attention. Not that it was anyone's business but her own if she chose to take the vehicle out.

A couple of the groundsmen were the only people to see her leave. She reached the Vernici road without mishap, turning north away from the town to head for the highway that would take her to Florence. It seemed more like years than mere months since she had traversed these same roads on the way here, she thought bleakly. If only she'd never bothered!

The rain started when she had gone barely five kilometres, so heavy the windscreen wipers could barely cope. She should stop and wait it out, Gina knew, but that would give her too much time to think about what she was doing. She didn't want to think about anything other than getting away.

The truck looming suddenly through the murk was right on the crown of the road. A sense of *déjà vu* swept over her as she took instinctive avoiding action. There was a timeless moment when the car skidded out of control as the tyres failed to grip, then a huge bang, and darkness.

She drifted up from the depths to the sound of voices, faint and far away at first, but becoming stronger. They were speaking in Italian, of course, and far too rapidly for her to follow. *'Non capisco,'* she murmured before drifting off again.

Her first clear recollection found her lying on her back with a white ceiling filling her line of vision. Her neck felt stiff. She lifted a nerveless hand to touch the collar encircling it, the pieces coming together slowly. Apart from the headache throbbing at her temples, there was no pain.

'You must lie still until they can be sure there is no further damage,' said Lucius from somewhere off to the side.

The anguish that swept her was like a sword thrust. 'The baby.' she whispered. 'I lost the baby?'

'No.' Lucius came into view, the strain evident in both face and voice. 'You still have the child. The seat belt saved you from being thrown around the car when it rolled.'

'Is it a write-off?' she murmured. 'The car, I mean.'

'You think I care about the car?' he demanded with force. 'Why were you driving at all in such weather?'

Gina gazed at the ceiling, in no fit state for the confrontation that would eventually have to come. 'It wasn't raining when I set off.'

'That is not—' Lucius broke off abruptly. When he spoke again it was on a more level note. 'You were drifting in and out of consciousness for several hours. That means you have concussion at the very least. The doctor will examine you now you're fully awake.'

He moved away, his place taken by an older man in a white coat. Gina submitted to his ministrations, responding to the questions translated for her by Lucius. Her relief at the removal of the neck collar, indicating that there was no spinal injury, was tempered by the headache still pounding at her temples. She sat up gingerly when asked, wincing a little as pressure came to bear on bruises she hadn't felt until then, but thankful to have no greater injuries to cope with.

The two men spoke together for a few moments, then the doctor left.

'You're to stay here at least for tonight to make sure there are no delayed repercussions,' Lucius declared. 'Sleep is the best medicine for you. A nurse will be in shortly to make you comfortable.'

'Where *is* here?' Gina asked, more because she felt it expected of her than through any great desire to know.

'The Emanuele Clinic. The accident happened less than a kilometre away.'

'You were on your way to Rome,' she said.

'I naturally turned back on receiving the news.' Tone

steady, eyes impenetrable, he added, '*Madre* was distraught. She was unaware of your departure from the villa at all. Where were you going?'

This was neither the time nor the place for confrontation, Gina acknowledged wearily. 'I just felt like a drive,' she said. 'I'm sorry to have given your mother concern.'

Fire flashed in the dark depths. 'You think her the only one to be concerned? If you could but—' He broke off once again, shaking his head as if in repudiation of what he'd been about to say, face set. 'Tomorrow will be time enough. You have need of sleep.'

Gina reached out an involuntary hand to grasp the bare, bronzed forearm as he began turning away, unable to hold out any longer against the emotions choking her.

'Don't go,' she said huskily. 'I need you, *mi amore*!'

His jaw contracted, the muscles in the arm she held taut beneath the skin. 'Do not use that term without true meaning!'

'I don't.' Gina was past caring about giving herself away. Her voice gathered strength along with her spirit. 'I know you don't feel as deeply for me as I feel for you, but you'd better start learning because I'm not letting go! I'll give any woman who fancies her chances with you a battle royal!'

It was a moment or two before Lucius responded, the expression dawning in his eyes as he gazed at her increasing her already galloping pulse rate to ungovernable proportions.

'From where,' he said at last, 'did you gather the impression that I had no depth of feeling for you?'

Gina lifted her shoulders uncertainly. 'You've never used the word love.'

The faintest of smiles touched his mouth. 'Would words of love have persuaded you to marry me?'

'It would have helped.'

'I doubt it. You were drawn to me physically, but no more than that.'

Gina searched the handsome face. 'You're saying the marriage wasn't *just* a matter of conscience on your part?'

His smile widened a little. 'I fell in love with the girl who gave herself so unreservedly to me that night. The girl I had every intention of making my wife, both before and after I discovered her true identity. Reprehensible of me though it was to take advantage of your father's financial problems, I saw no other means of persuading you.'

He took one of her hands in his, raising it to his lips. 'My love for you knows no limits, *mi tesoro*. You must believe me when I tell you that Livia Marucchi has never, nor ever could, hold a place in my heart. I was angry when you banned her from visiting San Cotone again, yes, but only because you accepted my guilt without question. I walked in the gardens two nights ago in an agony of mind, believing you would never come to love me the way I yearned for you to love me. To have you accuse me of spending those hours with Livia—'

'I was too eaten up with jealousy to see straight,' Gina cut in wryly. 'She's so beautiful!'

'Her beauty bears no comparison with yours!' Lucius declared. 'To look into her eyes is to look into soulless depths! A man may use a woman of her kind for release, but few could countenance any closer relationship.'

'Might you not find a need for that kind of release in future?' Gina murmured, and saw the dark eyes flare again.

'You still think me so devoid of integrity?'

'Love doesn't automatically instil total trust,' she defended. 'You've been used to a full and free sex life. Is one woman going to be enough for you?'

Lucius let go of her hand to place both of his about her

throat, lifting her face to meet his descending mouth. The tenderness in his kiss was more convincing than any words.

'*This* one woman, yes,' he avowed when he lifted his head again. 'You satisfy every craving in me—and always will.'

He released her with reluctance. 'Enough for now. You must rest. I'll return in the morning to—'

'No!' Gina ignored the ache in her head as she shook it emphatically. 'I'm coming home with you now!'

'The doctor said—' he began.

'I don't care what the doctor said! You can keep an eye on me yourself. If you try leaving me here I'll walk out and thumb a lift!' she threatened as he hesitated. 'I mean it, Lucius!'

'I knew you were going to be a trouble to me the first moment I saw you,' he remarked with humour. 'What I failed to foresee was the extent of it. If I removed your clothing from the wardrobe you would have no choice but to stay.'

'Don't count on it. I'd wrap myself in a sheet if necessary!'

Laughter creased the sculptured face. 'A risk I am not prepared to take! Do you feel capable of dressing yourself while I go and speak with the doctor?'

'Perfectly,' she assured him. 'I'll be ready and waiting.'

He kissed her again, long and passionately, before departing, leaving her with a brimming heart. She could deal with anything and anyone knowing he loved her—including Ottavia. San Cotone was her home, as it had been her father's before her. She finally felt she belonged.

EPILOGUE

EXTENDED along the length of the terrace to seat the laughing, chattering throng, the table groaned beneath the weight of dishes still nowhere near empty. Crystal and silver glinted in the sunlight, while myriad scents spilled from the massed blooms festooning the stone balustrades.

Gina turned her gaze from the distant views she never tired of to the infinitely dearer one closer to hand, tears of pure happiness prickling her lids as she surveyed each familiar face. It was wonderful to have everyone together like this: an occasion to be cherished in memory for all time. And all down to her mother-in-law, who had moved heaven and earth to make it happen.

Catching the latter's eye, she mouthed her gratitude, finishing off with a blown kiss, and receiving one in return. This meant so much more to her than any formal celebration, as Cornelia had known it would.

Secure in the knowledge of their own status in her affections, her parents watched the exchange without rancour. They were regular visitors to San Cotone, and would be welcomed as permanent residents if and when they finally chose. As Lucius himself often said, there was room enough and to spare.

Even more so these days, came the thought, bringing a momentary downswing in spirits, just as swiftly conquered. She had flown the coop herself at an earlier age than either Vittorio or Giovanni. Anyway, Doria was still within easy reach, and soon to give birth to a brother or sister for Pietro and Portia. They helped make up for the lack of day-to-day contact with the other grandchildren.

Sitting here now, it still scarcely seemed possible that so much time had passed. The silver in Lucius's hair served only to enhance the sculptured bone structure, the fine cotton T-shirt he was wearing outlining a body still as lean and lithe as when they had first met. Husband and lover without equal, Gina thought mistily, senses stirring as always to the sheer impact of those looks. There would never come a time when she failed to want him, never come a time when her love for him burned any less intense.

Her whole life here in Tuscany had been a joy. Not once had she known regret for the career she had given up to become a wife and mother. She and Ottavia had long ago reached an understanding—helped by Marcello's regaining of independence—and were now the best of friends. The two remained childless themselves, but took great delight in all their nieces and nephews. Donata and Cesare were the proud parents of no less than five children, all of whom were here today too, along with their respective families, making a grand total of thirty-eight. What might be called a typical Italian family gathering.

Lucius was getting to his feet, clinking a spoon against his glass to draw attention.

'I wish to propose a toast of my own,' he said. He looked down at the lovely, unlined face at his side, dark eyes filled with an emotion that brought a lump to Gina's throat. 'To my beautiful, incomparable wife, for twenty-five wonderful years! And for all those yet to come!'

LET'S TALK
Romance

For exclusive extracts, competitions
and special offers, find us online:

facebook.com/millsandboon

@MillsandBoon

@MillsandBoonUK

Get in touch on 01413 063232